DragonSkin II
RESTORATION

Sam Woodgarth

DragonSkin II
RESTORATION

Sam Woodgarth
Pagan Cat Publishing
PO Box 507
Trinity Beach, Cairns
Queensland, 4879

sam@pagancatpublishing.com

ISBN PAPERBACK: 978-0-6457168-3-2
ISBN EBOOK: 978-0-6457168-2-5
Cover design by GetCovers
Formatting by https://www.rwharrisonbooks.com/

ACKNOWLEDGMENTS

To Les Mitchell, my husband and rock of sanity in a turbulent
sea of crazy.
Without your support, I couldn't do what I do.
Thank you.

To Lovely Liz, Fabulous Fiona, and Marvellous Michele,
my spectacular support team.

I began this journey believing writing was a solitary endeavour,
but I have been blessed with friends and author colleagues who
have generously helped and supported me every step of the way.
The writing community is truly incredible.

Most importantly, my readers. You are the reason I write and
your feedback makes the sometimes precarious journey
worthwhile.
Thank you.

Sam Woodgarth

Each and every one of you.

CHAPTER ONE

Brummagen, the magician, chanted forbidden words in an arcane language, while ghostly fingers of green vapour writhed towards the ancient constellations painted on the flaking ceiling. Sparks flew from the foul brew roiling in the cauldron, then fizzled out, leaving the chamber in unholy darkness. When yet another spell spluttered into failure, Brummagen's chanting changed course, becoming a curse on all creation.

Xanderamm the hog huddled in the corner of the uppermost tower room, trying to occupy the smallest, least significant space possible. Half a decade in the care of this madman had trained the once haughty king to maintain a strict silence if he wanted to avoid unthinkable consequences. Brummagen constantly threatened to turn him into bacon. No magik or esoteric knowledge required, only a sharp knife. Xanderamm shuddered and closed his porcine eyes.

Brummagen lit the oil lamps and peered shortsightedly at the parchment in which he'd invested much hope and extravagant coin. One problem of speaking lost languages was no one alive truly knew how they ought to sound. A single mispronounced syllable could render a spell useless, or change the meaning completely, with disastrous consequences. Ancient arcanum was a risky business and for neither the faint of heart nor the meagre of means.

Most of the magician's glittering jewels and ill-gotten treasures were long traded for books and parchments which offered perfidious promises of power and influence. Vendors in the marketplace recognised Brummagen and sought him out when they had interesting or rare texts to trade. Their wealth grew in direct proportion to his increasing weariness and proximity to poverty.

The magician rolled up the antiquated parchment and stowed it on a shelf amidst a myriad of other failed spells. He cast himself onto the worn couch and eyed Xanderamm. "A mere woman shouldn't have that kind of power," Brummagen muttered. "The Consort should have kept her under control. She ought to know her place."

Xanderamm kept his eyes shut. During the first months after his transformation from King to hog, he'd squealed his indignation loudly and frequently, to no avail. He'd wept tears of frustration and humiliation.

Then he learned to listen.

The marketplace became his school. Buyers and sellers chattered freely before a madman and his pet pig. Unsubstantiated rumours from the Kingdom of Xanndene about the King's transformation gave way to definitive news of his death. None of the gossips expressed regret or grief over the King's disappearance and alleged demise. Xanderamm learned he was unloved by his subjects. He also learned his subjects respected and worshipped AnnieRah, Protector of the Realm. He'd shook his head, but couldn't deny reality. Now, he ignored Brummagen's ranting about AnnieRah, the Reborn Goddess, but the winged creature slithering about the rafters, unseen by anyone, swallowed the diatribe whole, ready to regurgitate for its master's pleasure.

The creature delivered its message and received a scrap of rancid flesh as a reward, which it gulped before the Master could change his mind.

"Are you certain Brummagen is ready?" The Master asked.

The creature nodded. "He and his pathetic pig are thin with hunger and disappointment. The foolishly vain Brummagen spent almost all he possessed on spurious spells. He no longer believes he can reverse the spell, and return Xanderamm to a man, but he burns to punish the woman whom he blames for his misfortune. A passion for vengeance motivates him."

The Master steepled skeletal fingers beneath his chin, pondering the implications of his creature's news. Brummagen possessed mediocre skills, but the Master had steadily fed him flawed magik over his years in exile to reduce his hauteur. The Master required humility from all his servants, and Brummagen's grooming period neared completion. A public degradation for the bumbling Brummagen. Not because it was necessary, but because The Master enjoyed seeing his victims writhe. His eyes glowed red with glee, deep within his hood, and he flicked a dismissive wave.

"You may go, Sneeth. Do whatever diabolical acts bring you pleasure," he hissed.

Sneeth simpered with satisfaction and slithered out of sight. The Master must be extraordinarily pleased to address him by name.

Brummagen rummaged through his collection of failed spells, searching for something saleable. A piece of exquisite but useless calligraphy a collector would purchase as art. He unrolled a scroll and held it to the light. The words danced across the page like dragonflies skimming over a lake on a sunlit evening. Sighing, he furled the fallacious spell and tucked the scroll inside his sleeve. He and Xanderamm needed to eat, and Brummagen was running out of funds and ideas. He slipped the harness on the hog and carefully negotiated the steep stairs. If he took his time haggling, the pig could snaffle scraps from the marketplace gutters.

Xanderamm didn't need reminding. He whiffled through the discarded crusts and peels, searching for the freshest flakes and juiciest morsels, while Brummagen sought a friendly face amongst the hard-eyed booksellers. The magician settled on the vendor from whom he'd bought the scroll and stepped through the entrance wearing his most sincere smile.

"Victor Brummagen!" The bookseller threw his arms into the air. "I didn't expect to see you around these parts, not after the salacious rumours I heard."

Brummagen stopped in his tracks. No one ever used his first name. How did the bookseller learn it? What rumours? Brummagen frowned, then readjusted his smile as he drew the scroll from his sleeve.

"I came to sell this—"

The bookseller stepped around the counter, flapping his hands and squawking. "Get out, your kind isn't welcome. You've got some gall, showing your face here. Out, go on, get out." The bookseller shoved Brummagen onto the pavement. "And take your pilfering pig with you!"

Brummagen flinched as the market stall holders took aim, and flung rotting fruit and gnawed bones at him. A well-placed boot sent him sprawling into the gutter, much to the market-traders' merriment. Scrabbling to his knees, he seized Xander-amm's leash, and pulled the bewildered hog close as a shield.

"It's true," called a rough voice. "See how the pervert's cuddling the pig!"

Eyes wide with fear, Brummagen hauled himself to his feet and set off at a limping trot, dragging Xanderamm beside him. The traders jeered his escape but did naught to impede his progress. The magician took refuge in a narrow alley to recover his breath, desperate to make sense of the experience.

"You dropped this, Sir." A startlingly beautiful girl proffered his now stained and torn scroll.

Brummagen didn't recognise her, and he was certain he'd remember such a beauty if he'd seen her before. An attractive woman hadn't voluntarily addressed him since he'd fled Kingston in disgrace. Xanderamm coughed, a warning the bewitched Brummagen ignored.

"Sir?" The girl waggled the scroll. "A fine gentleman like you should take more care. There's them as'ud take advantage."

Xanderamm nudged Brummagen behind the knee, urging him to leave the company of this enchanting woman, but Brummagen pushed him away.

"You're not from this district," Brummagen said. "I'd recognise you if you were local."

"No, Sir. I'm looking for work and lodgings." Humble and demure, her demeanour charmed Brummagen.

"I can't offer work," he said, "but I have a spare room."

The girl looked at her feet before meeting his gaze. "I can't pay rent until I find work, Sir. The nights are still warm, I'll shelter just fine under those stalls." She jerked her head in the market's direction. "If I'm lucky, I can forage like your pig."

"Nonsense. A pretty girl like you wouldn't be safe. You can stay with me, and in return you can perform light housework or cooking. How does that sound?"

"You're very trusting, Sir."

"You returned my valuable scroll, young lady. I think you've proven your honesty."

"Thank you, Sir." A pretty flush pinked the girl's smooth cheeks. "I'm Jenny."

Xanderamm snorted, certain the girl used a plethora of names, and equally positive she wasn't what she appeared.

Brummagen and Xanderamm listened to Jenny pottering around the ground floor of the tower. Brummagen's self-evident lust made Xanderamm huddle in his corner with his eyes shut. The girl possessed an indefinable something, a quality which made him nervous. The contretemps with the bookseller, followed by Jenny's appearance, was too convenient to be true.

Moonlight slid over Brummagen's pale face, the cool illumination making him appear a corpse on his catafalque bed. Xanderamm listened to the magician's breathing, neither hog nor man able to succumb to sleep. They waited in silent anticipation, Brummagen hoping for a sign, an invitation; Xanderamm secretly praying for dawn to break early.

The crash startled them both. Their eyes snapped open, but their bodies remained statue still, the better to listen.

Whispers.

Muffled giggles.

Shuffling feet, more than one pair.

A creak and a slammed door.

Brummagen swung his feet to the floor and jammed them into threadbare slippers. "Stay here," he said, already knowing the words to be as ineffective as his last spell. "I'll not tolerate sexual shenanigans from some strumpet under my own roof."

Xanderamm snorted at Brummagen's curious combination

of jealousy and hypocrisy. The pig waited at the door as the magician wrapped himself in a worn dressing-gown and a thick layer of self-righteous indignation. Holding up the hem of his gown with one hand and an oil lamp in the other, Brummagen navigated the steep winding stairs by leaning his right shoulder against the wall.

The door to the girl's quarters was firmly shut. Silence flowed over the listening pair, washing cold around their bare ankles.

Brummagen harrumphed and rapped on the door. "What's going on in there?"

An unnatural stillness threatened to swallow them. Brummagen banged on the door to combat the graveyard quiet. The door groaned open, revealing a blackness unrelieved by moonbeams. Jenny had hung curtains on the high-set windows, ensuring her privacy.

Xanderamm hesitated on the threshold. The stench of foul magik made him reel, but Brummagen, the professed magician, seemed oblivious as he stepped into Jenny's lair.

"Stone me!" Brummagen raised his lamp when he cracked his skin against a tumbled chair. He stifled a scream as Jenny's naked feet appeared at eye level. Her sheer cotton shift lent a modicum of modesty to her mortal remains as she swung lazily from a rope tied to the rafters. Oddly, her skin held a faint glow of green phosphorescence. She opened her eyes and smiled.

"You took your time getting here. Too late to rescue me."

"You're dead." Brummagen stumbled backwards, arms flailing to maintain his balance.

"Careful with that lamp," Jenny said. "You don't want to set this place afire."

Xanderamm nudged Brummagen and gently snorted, but Brummagen merely gaped aghast at the communicative corpse.

"As I see it," Jenny said, "you have three choices. You can

7

retreat to your upper room and pretend you know naught about this. When the townsfolk discover my rotting remains, they'll blame you. They already think you're poking the pig, so raping and killing a helpless girl wouldn't be too much of a stretch."

Brummagen trembled and shook his head. "But none of that is true."

"Truth is irrelevant. What matters is what folk believe. Your second option is to smuggle me out of the town and bury me. Of course, if you get caught..." Jenny shrugged. "You'll discover what it feels like to hang."

Xanderamm nudged Brummagen again, pushing him towards the door.

"The pig understands," Jenny said. "Your final and most sensible option is to flee. As far and as fast as you can, before the townsfolk discover your heinous crime."

"But I have nowhere to go."

"You're going into the service of The Most High Lord Draqshet."

"I serve no man," Brummagen said, floundering to reclaim his authority.

Jenny swung merrily from her noose, clutching her sides. "Whoever claimed The Master was a man?"

CHAPTER TWO

Jenny listened to the footsteps, pig and man, heading towards the city walls. "Cut me down, Sneeth."

The creature whipped out a razor-sharp claw and sliced through the rope with a single pass. Jenny collapsed in a heap on the unforgiving floor.

"No matter how many times I die, I never get used to it." She shuddered as she gained her feet and reached for her dress. Her phosphorescence dimmed and died. She finger-combed her hair and adjusted her clothing. "We've got them on the move. Come on, we must ensure they escape."

Xanderamm trotted ahead, his porcine senses more acute than Brummagen's, who staggered after him, shocked and dishevelled. When Brummagen had failed to salvage his books and scrolls of spells, Xanderamm heaved a sigh of relief. Either the magician finally recognised their inefficacy, or he was too stunned by events to choose. He'd filled his pockets with the remaining coin and wrapped a bundle of spare clothing before allowing Xanderamm to nudge him downstairs and past Jenny's chambers.

The full moon cast shadows of infinite darkness, and Xanderamm kept to the blackness as much as possible. Brummagen bumped into him when he paused. Clanking armour suggested soldiers on their rounds of the city walls. Low, gruff voices accompanied the harsh metallic clatter. Feet shuffling, not marching. Xanderamm edged backwards, away from the guards. They'd have to find another route.

Jenny stepped out of the shadows, brimming with health and beauty. She winked at Xanderamm and nodded at Brummagen.

"I'll distract these buffoons. Take the next alley. It leads to a narrow gate. You'll find it unlocked. Head north. I'll find you." Without so much as a backward glance, she flitted towards the guards, her laughter brightening the night as she greeted the bored soldiers.

Xanderamm chuffed down the alley and found the gate unlocked, as Jenny promised. He raised his snout and snuffled the air, finding naught unnatural nor unexpected. He jerked his head, indicating they should go in the opposite direction to Jenny's instructions, but Brummagen grabbed his harness and hauled him northwards. Xanderamm hesitated, but a pig alone was a walking ham. Much as it galled him to rely on the inept magician, he needed his continued protection. He nudged Brummagen off the highway and onto the grassy verge to muffle their footfalls. No point advertising their departure. Who knew what listening creatures inhabited the night?

The road unspooled before them, and Brummagen walked with an extra spring in his step, apparently energised by his proximity to real magik, and blind to the potential dangers.

"That girl overcame death," Brummagen said. "I'm sure she

has the knowledge to reanimate the Army of Dolls. Who knows, maybe she can reverse the spell keeping you in this form. How'd you like to be a man again, eh?"

Xanderamm shook his head. Was Brummagen deliberately ignoring what Jenny said about entering the service of The Most High Lord Draqshet? No doubt a personage of power, yet not a man. And what the stone was Jenny? Dead or alive? Or a cunning illusionist? Xanderamm doubted her mortality, with the same depth of suspicion he doubted Brummagen's sanity.

Jenny sashayed towards the guards. "This must be my lucky night. Two strong and handsome men to protect me."

The soldiers stood straighter, knowing smiles splitting their faces.

"You must be lost, out and unaccompanied past midnight." The younger man stepped forward.

"Allow us to escort you home, Milady," the older guard said.

Neither guard noticed the creature slither down the wall behind them and stand tall on spindly legs.

Jenny planted her fists on her hips. "I'm not sure I'm ready to go home yet, gentlemen. Mayhap I'd like some fun. What say you?"

The guards exchanged glances, then the creature struck, punching through the back of their armoured chests and ripping free their hearts. Jenny skipped backwards to avoid the splatter.

"When I said I planned to steal their hearts, this isn't exactly what I had in mind, Sneeth." She caught the still beating organ Sneeth tossed to her, and swallowed it whole, her jaws dislocating to accommodate the throbbing meat. She dropped one of Brummagen's famously futile parchments between the surprised-looking corpses. "That ought to be evidence enough."

Jenny and Sneeth slunk down the alley and out the unlocked gate. They sniffed the air, then Jenny fell to her knees, nosing through the grass. She nodded her satisfaction and sat back on her haunches.

"We'll find a place to sleep. The sun will be up soon. We can catch up with our new friends at our convenience."

The creature slumped, but refrained from arguing.

"Are you still hungry? Very well, go hunting, but follow the southern route. Leave a false trail for the outraged townsfolk to follow." Jenny smiled indulgently.

Sneeth slithered away, delighted to be granted a few hours of freedom from the fearsome Jenny.

Dawn burst over the rim of the world, an overripe fruit spilling light and a flirtatious promise of warmth. Already sweaty from the unexpected exertion, Brummagen moved like he wanted to outdistance his lengthy shadow. The settlement beckoned with the painted allure of a tawdry tavern wench, and Brummagen scurried forward with no thought spared for security.

Xanderamm raised his head as high as his porcine physiology allowed. Like most border towns, the architecture sported an amalgamation of styles. The walls nodded to an Enotsian influence, but being built around an oasis was purely D'Nasian. The eclectic mix of buildings promised cultural variety and an easy tolerance; a market to trade not only goods, but those who listened carefully could freely collect news and ideas.

Searching for a ride north, Brummagen headed straight for the area where traders stored their goods and stabled their beasts. Xanderamm's bowels churned when a flamboyant caravaneer offered Brummagen safe passage in exchange for his pig. He shuddered with relief when Brummagen regretfully declined the offer. The magician concluded a deal with the leader of a smaller and less well-defended caravan. Brummagen negotiated the copying of magikal and sacred texts as payment. Speed was more important than accuracy, Jarod, the caravaneer, informed him, because only the desperate or addle-pated ever bought such artefacts. Brummagen's eyes narrowed as he nodded sage agreement.

Jarod cleared a space in a half-filled wagon while Brummagen bought supplies for the five-day journey, diminishing further his dwindling supply of coin. The jewels on his fingers winked slyly, a reminder of past wealth and influence. He sucked his finger and pulled off the smallest ring, then hesitated. He looked at Xanderamm, who stared back, unblinking. Sell now in a backwater, or later in the great city of Kingston, where he hoped to achieve a higher price? Carry a bag of easily filched coin on a potentially dangerous journey, or keep the wealth close and portable? The pig nudged his leg, and he returned the jewel to his finger, certain he could strike a better bargain in a larger town.

Brummagen's berth was a straw-stuffed mattress between amphoras of olives and figs, and skins of wine. Jarod raised an eyebrow when Brummagen insisted on a ramp for the pig. The caravaneer didn't care who the shabby scribe shared a bed with, and if that was the stranger's preference, his daughters would be safe from unwelcome attention.

Jenny clawed her way out of the shallow sandy grave in which she'd rested. She shook soil from her hair and clothes, and reassumed the appearance of a gorgeous young girl. Sneeth lurked nearby, casually picking flecks of flesh from between his teeth and under his claws. Following Jenny's instructions to lay a false trail, he'd restricted his feeding to small prey, mainly chickens and cats, animals a deranged man could kill barehanded. Much as he'd salivated at the sight of drowsing horses and cattle, he'd restrained himself.

"Shall we ride the wild winds or trudge the roads?" Jenny phrased her question in such a way that the desired answer was clear.

Sneeth spread his leathery wings and shook out stray detritus from his feast, as Jenny rose effortlessly into the sky, her hair and skirts billowing in the balmy breeze. Her ability to fly without wings disconcerted him, an unease he struggled to hide on every mission. Jenny delighted in flaunting her gift, like a concubine flashing a new jewel, emphasising her status as favourite.

The creature shot past Jenny, his wings buffeting the air as he climbed. Jenny might well be The Most High Lord Draqshet's current favourite, but that was a position regularly refilled with fresh flesh. Sneeth took solace in his status as the Master's longest serving servant.

The pair rode the winds northwards, heading towards a shabby settlement recently grown around an oasis. The desert night descended quickly, cloaking their progress from idle view.

CHAPTER THREE

Roic groaned in his slumber, muscles twitching under furled wings. He slid open one eye to observe the starstrewn skies, his claws involuntarily grasping for something out of reach. The dragon flared his nostrils, inhaling scents from afar. He lumbered to his feet and stretched his wings, then refurled them tightly against his golden flanks.

A prickling sense of unease prompted him to extend his senses, but he found no evidence to support his growing dread. Roic huffed a smokey snort of annoyance and resettled himself into a comfortable sleeping position. Then he twitched and snorted until dawn splashed the mountain tops with lemon-sharp light.

Roic sighed with satisfaction as the sunlight caressed his gleaming scales, and he stretched to absorb as much energy as possible, dismissing his unease as foolish nonsense.

Theo watched Annie nursing her tea as she stared out over Salvation Valley. She'd tossed and turned all night, muttering unintelligible phrases. This morning she was listless and wan.

"What ails you, my love?" He wrapped his arm around her waist.

She laid her head on his shoulder, but remained silent. *I feel like a rabbit being watched by a snake. I know I am under surveillance, but have no sense of by whom or where they hide.* She shivered in the chilly morning air and sipped her cooling tea.

"What can I do to make you feel better?"

Annie shrugged. "Things are not as they ought, but I can't identify the source." She looked up at her husband and smiled. "This will sound foolish, but I can't describe it more truly. Imagine a missed stitch, no, a loose thread in a tapestry. I can't quite see it, but I know it's there, and someone is tugging a single thread of silk. They're trying to discover how much force is required to unravel the entire fabric."

"Can you identify which part of the tapestry? Is it a person or a place? Annie the Weaver, if you say the fabric has a fault, I believe you. For what it's worth, I too feel discomfort, but I cannot find a reason. If it's only a single stitch or loose thread, we can fix it before it becomes a gaping hole."

"We should talk to Roic." *The father I never had.* "Mayhap he has heard news, or sensed something amiss."

In his mountaintop eyrie, the dragon sprawled full length to absorb the sunlight, neck and wings extended to their utmost.

You also felt the dis-ease, Lady Annie. I foolishly hoped I was mistaken.

"Can you identify the problem? I fear this is the fruit of one of my earlier mistakes."

Roic shook his head, sending cascades of rainbows across the glade. *Whatever this threat is, it is ancient. As old as creation itself. This is not of your doing, but it may be your undoing. There lurks an intelligence out there, malevolent, cold...* Roic shuddered. *I am being fanciful. Forgive me, Lady Annie, Lord Theo. I misspoke.*

Theo rubbed his hands together. "Could be the power of suggestion, but I believe both of you." He spun slowly, listening with his eyes closed. "There." He waved an arm to the south. "The patterns are disturbed in the D'Nasian lands. An entity, but one I do not recognise, stirs... a subtle shift... had you not sounded the alarm, I would not have recognised aught amiss."

Gather what news you can from your usual sources. The threat is not immediate, there is no reason to panic. I will be gone, mayhap four days, hopefully less. When I return, we can admonish ourselves for being alarmists. Roic spread his wings and launched himself into the vastness of the sky.

Roic flew southward without cease. He battered the night air with his wings, feeding his rare fury of anyone daring to disturb the peace of his beloved friends. He slashed down, imagining he was disembowelling an unseen enemy, scattering their entrails over the mountain tops. He thundered his displeasure across spaces empty of people, where no one could bear tales of impossible creatures.

The southern air was redolent of figs and olives, of sweat and rich red wine. Roic savoured the scents, tracking the greening of the desert after AnnieRah and Theo had worked their magic. Oases and rivers crisscrossed the once barren and glassy land, and the inhabitants thrived.

The sliver of wrongness was nearby, out of sight, beyond

taste or touch, a smear of evil on the horizon. The dragon roared his frustration. How could he engage and defeat an adversary who deliberately remained defiantly undetectable?

Refusing to hide from the enemy, Roic settled on a prominent ridge of sand, daring the diabolical to venture into his presence.

Hot sand writhed and hissed as the winds caressed dunes into new and inventive shapes. Spiders and lizards skittered across the restless surfaces, their feet cymbals to the pounding bass drum of the beating sun. Noise swirled through the silence, drowning taste and sight.

Roic relaxed, his great bulk spread wide, absorbing the sun's power. Every beetle footstep registered as the dragon formed a mental map of the surrounding hills. Naught, larger than an industrious scarab, moved in the baking landscape.

The wrongness hovered on the periphery, folded in shadows, watching and waiting, patient as granite. Roic sensed a presence, but did not deign to raise his head in acknowledgment.

The Most High Lord Draqshet listened to the flamboyant patterns created by the sand and wind as they negotiated their way around the magnificent beast lying at leisure in the desert. Sunlight reflected fiercely from the dragon's metallic scales, producing incinerator temperatures, which even the desert denizens couldn't tolerate. The sheer bulk of the somnolent dragon impressed the Master, but a flying lizard could not intimidate him, no matter how massive.

Envy of the beast's casual courage flooded the Master's being, but he convinced himself the dragon would not be so brave once he learned the Master's implacable power. He would teach this creature to cringe in his presence, and to be grateful for each moment he allowed it to live.

Roic's snores vibrated the ground and created miniature sand avalanches. When they stopped, the desert held its breath, before releasing it in a broiling gust. The snakes and lizards continued their business, and the wind and sand sang songs of indescribable yearning.

The dragon stretched languidly before sliding open his jewel eyes. Disappointed not to see his adversary, Roic shivered the sand from between his scales, presenting as tame an image as he could to the evil he knew lurked out of range.

He lumbered, deliberately ungainly, and launched himself into the cloudless sky, making a show of graceless flapping. He inhaled, drawing the desert spiciness over the root of his tongue, searching in vain for that which ought to be there, but was conspicuously missing.

The wrongness was frighteningly adept at keeping itself secret. An evil with purpose and intelligence posed a genuine threat to all Roic held dear.

Roic flaunted his presence day and night, to no avail. Coldly jealous eyes scanned him, but he tasted naught, heard naught, saw naught. The wind carried no whispers of crimes committed, other than those common to men.

Only on his flight home did he scent the faint odour of fake magik, the senseless spells sold by the devious to the desperate. None of Roic The Magnificent's business.

Pacer, the Alpha of her pack, pricked her ears, straining to listen. The singer was far away, and the song was unfamiliar. A tale of a man stinking of ambition and delusions, travelling through D'Nasa accompanied by a pig; a man who peddled parchments, promised miracles, yet himself wallowed in penury. A comic song for the cubs, doubtless a lesson demonstrating the otherness of men and their discordant values. The song faded, whipped away by the wind, before the singer revealed the name of the fatuous fraudster. Pacer shrugged. A fool had no business being famous.

~

Annie crouched next to her loom, a frown creased her brow as her fingers caressed the delicate silks of the weft. She pressed her nose close to the textile, squinting at every line of thread. Show yourself, give me something to work with, damn you.

Netta stood across the room, her back to the window. "There's no point," she said, looking with her gift of far-sight once more. "Your tapestry is perfection, utterly flawless. But if you found a missed stitch, what would it mean? The threat isn't coming from your work, is it?"

Annie rose to her feet and rolled her shoulders. "I could fix a mistake there," she said, jerking her chin at the loom. "If I find something I can fix, I'm in control. But I've no idea what threatens us, nor from where it comes. Netta? I'm scared, I don't know what to do. How can I protect you all when I don't know what I'm facing?"

Netta crossed the room and embraced her friend. "I'm scared because you're scared, but you're not alone. We've faced dangers before and won. You and Theo, me and André, Vert, Roic, maybe Pacer and her pack. We're strong and smart, and we're here for one another."

"Thank you." Annie hugged Netta before pushing her away. "Fear of the unknown is the worst, so we need a plan to discover as much as possible about our mystery foe. Work out their weaknesses."

"Ladies, I hoped to find you here." Theo grinned from the doorway. "Roic returns. Shall we meet him in the meadow?"

Annie hauled Netta to Theo's side. "As fast-as-thought, my love."

Netta crossed her arms over her belly and squeezed shut her eyes.

Theo wrapped an arm around each woman's waist, holding them securely. "We'll be there before you can say heads-or-tails." He whisked them to the meeting place with miraculous speed. "See? We're here. And still in one piece."

Netta stumbled away, shaking herself. "I'm not denying the convenience, but I'll never learn to like it."

A shadow passed as Roic circled the meadow and negotiated his descent. As always, he came in fast and cracked the air with his wings to brake, creating a tornado of grass and dirt. Squinting against the swirling debris, Annie and Netta pelted to greet the dragon.

André and Vert jogged from the brewery, where they were preparing casks of beer for sale to the townsfolk. They slowed to a walk when they saw Roic's demeanour.

I failed, Roic said, once the group settled. *Much as it pains me to say, I found naught useful. There was a presence, we were mutually aware, but I failed to discern more.*

"Mayhap, we have this all wrong," André said. "You've identified a shift in the patterns, a movement of unknown origin in the D'Nasian lands. Why are we automatically assuming a threat?"

Roic snorted. *I flopped around that desert for three days. I felt it studying me, assessing and judging me. There was ample opportu-*

nity to introduce itself, but whatever it was, it remained deliberately disguised. An entity seeking friendship does not shroud themselves in this manner.

"But it offered no aggression, either," Netta said. "Is it possible it was too intimidated to introduce itself?"

I couldn't sense any emotion. Roic twitched his tail. *The creature isn't mortal, of that I am certain. The best I can describe the creature is a lack. Everything is missing. Even its presence felt like standing next to a giant hole. A gaping void where there ought to be a solid. It has less substance than a shadow.*

"You suggested this entity is as old as creation. There must be myths. Mayhap the priestesses would hold such knowledge?" Annie looked around the group.

"The wolves may keep those stories," Netta said, "or be able to communicate with ancestors who know."

"The oldest forests may remember stories," Vert said, "but getting them to communicate may take more time than we have. And they're notoriously difficult to reach."

"Theo could take you there," Netta said.

"I can get you there immediately, if you think it's worth trying. Are the trees awake enough to understand, or care?"

"Most of them are sleeping, or preparing to sleep. They are pulling away from the matters of man, though. Many have already ceased to care, but there is a copse I think worth talking to." Vert looked at Theo. "Give me time to put together a few belongings?"

Theo nodded. "I will detour on the way back and talk to Pacer."

⁓

Vert opened one eye, then the other. He shook his head. "I think I will never become used to this method of transportation. Nevertheless, thank you, my friend."

Theo nodded. "Call out when you're ready to come home. Good luck."

Vert watched Theo blink out of sight, then turned towards the copse he hoped would still have sentience enough to converse. The individual trees were thousands of years old, but well-known gossips and respected curators of knowledge. The Woodsman hummed wordlessly as he ploughed deeper into the forest, alerting the inhabitants to his presence.

Theo bowed to Pacer. "Mistress, I am indeed delighted to see you are well."

Greetings, Most High Lord Theo. I am pleased to see you, but your visage suggests this is not a social visit.

"You are correct, I am come seeking knowledge from the beginning of the world. Mistress Netta suggested you, or one of your ancestors, may have stories you might be willing to share."

My people cover the known world and have been here since the earliest creation. We have stories from everywhere and everyone. My Lord, you must be more specific. A name, mayhap? An event?

"That is our problem. Roic, Annie, and I, we all sense a discord, a change in the very fabric of the world... but we can't identify whence it comes. Roic visited the D'Nasian deserts... he felt a presence... or the absence of a presence... but could neither taste nor smell the source. We deduced an ancient entity is risen and moving. That it deliberately hides... and has the power to remain unidentified... fills us with foreboding."

Pacer cocked her head. *A lack of presence, My Lord? The enigma you describe sounds hauntingly familiar. This story is not in my repertoire, My Lord, but I'm sure I heard tell of such strangeness when I was a pup.* Pacer huffed. *But tales for pups are often foolish. I heard a song only yestereve about a man selling spurious spells to sad souls. The most ridiculous verse claimed he was travelling the desert with a pig. Can you imagine such a thing?*

"Mistress, I can. Did you perchance hear the name of the unlikely hero?"

The wind snatched the song before the singer revealed the name. Does it matter?

"Truly, I am unsure... Annie transformed King Xanderamm into a pig five years ago. Xanderamm and his Vizier disappeared from the city... amidst rumours Vizier Brummagen dabbled in the occult. There could be a connection between the disturbances we feel and this song. Can you contact the singer? If not to sing the song, to at least confirm the names."

Go home, be with Annie. Our songs carry best in the still of the night. I will discover the name of the desert traveller, and I will seek those who may share the memory of your mystery entity. The second will take longer, but I will get word to you through Rolf. I assume he and Bill Barry are still at Salvation Valley?

Theo smiled. "They are both well-grown, My Lady, and I'm not sure you'd recognise either. They are still with us, but I suspect not for much longer. Rolf is now a handsome and confident wolf, and Bill Barry has been courting a young lady from town all these years. He will be of age to ask for her hand when the snows come this year."

Take some advice from an old wolf. Celebrate whatever and whenever you can. Be prepared to defend yourself, but don't seek trouble.

CHAPTER FOUR

"What are you doing?" Jenny tapped Brummagen on the shoulder as he hunched over the array of parchments and tiny pots of coloured inks set out on a low table. For four tedious nights, she had watched from the shadows as he slaved over his ludicrous task, while the campfire cast a red glow across his sallow cheeks and glittered in his sunken eyes.

"How did you find me?"

Jenny raised her head and flared her delicate nostrils. "You leave a distinctive track. You and the pig. What do you call a pig in the desert? Grits and bacon." Her sharp teeth gleamed in the firelight. "Sorry, I forgot. I'm not supposed to talk about the King as potential food."

Brummagen flinched.

Jenny picked up a parchment and held it to the light. "This is excellent penmanship, but you know these won't work?" She turned to stare at him. "Real magik is something you earn, not buy and sell like a pair of slippers."

"Why are you taking an interest in me? What do you

want?" Brummagen's fingers trembled as he wiped clean his quills and brushes.

"You were once a man of power, fat on the fear of your enemies. Look at you now, a scrawny scribe scribbling spells for paltry pennies. Do you not dream of regaining your rightful place in the realm of men? I know you lust to have that redheaded Goddess in chains, your foot on her proud neck. I can help you. All you have to do is trust me." Jenny leaned forward. "I can make all your fantasies come true."

"Why would you do that? Why me?" Brummagen avoided her eyes.

"Haven't you ever helped someone without having an ulterior reason? For sheer altruism?"

"No. Never."

Jenny laughed. "Nor I. But my reasons are not your concern." She touched his threadbare sleeve with a fingertip and, for a heartbeat, the gown glowed with gold threads and semi-precious jewels. "Concentrate on your own concerns, Sir. There is naught you can imagine which I cannot provide, if you please me."

Brummagen looked up, but the girl had already returned to the shadows. Xanderamm snorted softly from within the wagon. Whatever this infernal girl offered, she would claim an exorbitant non-negotiable fee.

The magician dipped his quill, ready to complete his task, but when he reached for his parchments, he found each one already finished to an impossibly high standard. Gorgeous calligraphy flowed across the pages and jewel-coloured images of fantastical flora and fauna danced around the edges, each piece an astounding work of art. Brummagen dropped the pages in consternation.

"A token of my goodwill." The disembodied voice of Jenny

breathed into his ear, and ghostly fingers trailed across the back of his neck, making him shiver in the cool night air.

The following morning, Jarod, the caravaneer, inspected Brummagen's painted parchments. He cast a suspicious glance at the nervous magician. "I recognise the parchments as those I gave you, second class, for mere piece-work copies. But the workmanship, the artistry..." Jarod frowned at Brummagen. "This work is too intricate for you to create overnight. My business involves knowing every calligrapher and artist, but I do not recognise this work. I do not believe any mortal hand produced such extravagant work."

Brummagen pursed his mouth and shrugged. "Does it matter? You received better than you bargained for. You ought to be pleased."

"I heard conversations during the night," Jarod said, "but you crouched alone by your fire. Are you consorting with devils?"

"If I kept company with the demonic, do you think I would dress like this?" Brummagen held up the skirts of his worn gown.

"I will pay you a fair price for these parchments. They are exquisite and will fetch a goodly amount of coin. I have no desire to be indebted to a magician skilled in the dark arts." Clutching his unexpected treasures to his chest, Jarod backed away.

"At least we won't return to Kingston penniless," Brummagen said to Xanderamm.

The pig grunted. How could his ex-vizier be so deliberately foolish? They would enter the town with a purse pregnant with coin, but they would owe obligation to a dangerous demoness and her terrifying companion.

Xanderamm scrambled up the ramp and into the creaking wagon as soon as Jenny arrived. He shoved his snout between the wine skins and closed his eyes, feigning sleep. Slivers of self-satisfied laughter slid into his retreat, and his stomach churned. The soft chink of silver sounded loud in the night, as Brummagen showed Jenny the purse Jarod had tossed to him. Brummagen neglected to mention the caravan owner's hasty warning to stay in his own wagon for the rest of the journey.

"You are afeared of Jenny, are you not?" A sibilant voice hissed in his ear.

Xanderamm held his breath, hoping the nightmare creature would go away. Amphorae clanked and leathery wings rustled as the unwelcome visitor made himself comfortable.

"Allow me to introduce myself. I am Sneeth, trusted servant of The Most High Lord Draqshet. You, I know to be the once King Xanderamm, now a hapless hog. You and Brummagen are indeed fortunate to enter The Dark Lord's service. He will raise you above all men."

A rancid odour swirled around the interior of the wagon, and Xanderamm's eyes streamed.

"Tears of joy?" Sneeth asked. "I confess I do not understand the Master's purpose. Neither you nor Brummagen seem interesting, in and of yourselves. But I am a humble servant and my orders are to befriend you and provide you with all imaginable comfort."

Xanderamm risked opening one eye for a mere heartbeat. The winged creature wore a steely expression. Sinew and corded muscles rippled beneath coal-black leathery skin stretched across a fleshless skeleton. The monster appeared to have stepped out of an inferno.

The hog buried his face deeper between the wine skins. Asking the creature to leave would be futile, it was operating under orders. However, Xanderamm was under no obligation to respond to its overtures.

Sneeth tapped his talons on a ceramic amphora, and Xanderamm felt his innards liquify. The creature drew a single razor-sharp claw from between the pig's ears to his tail. "The Most High Lord Draqshet would prefer to raise you in mortal majesty over this world." Sneeth flicked the quivering pig's tail. "But Brummagen will perform equally well. Mayhap, he is the better candidate. More malleable. He appears unfettered by your burden of tiresome morality. In which case, keeping you alive is pointless. A word of advice, my friend: being too scrupulous may serve only to hamstring your decisions."

Xanderamm held his breath, waiting for the fatal blow, hoping Sneeth would be mercifully quick. The hog gasped when he ran out of air. He opened his eyes to find himself alone. The creature disappeared into the night as silently as he arrived, leaving questions and a stench of disquiet in his wake.

The hog heaved himself to his feet and listened. The desert silence was a balm to his battered soul. He trundled down the ramp and trotted over to Brummagen, still huddled around the fire, fondling his silver and humming to himself. Xanderamm threw himself to the ground, rolling and twisting in the gritty sand to erase the memory of that terrible talon tickling his hide.

"Sneeth made you a happy hog, I see. How could you not be merry, knowing you are destined to rule the world with me by your side?" Brummagen rubbed his hands gleefully.

Xanderamm regained his feet and shook off the dirt. He stared in amazement at his old vizier before turning and trudging up the ramp. The creature had been unequivocally clear: cooperate or die. Rejecting Draqshet's offer was not an option. Xanderamm imagined Sneeth not to be a dainty diner, and that night, he dreamed of the creature buried face first in his entrails while he screamed for mercy. He awoke exhausted and fearful.

Pacer sang to her neighbours, who responded with enthusiasm. The alpha wolf shook her head when she learned the song was not a comical story for pups. Hearing confirmation of the names Theo spoke disconcerted her, making more likely the reality that an unknown ancient threat had arisen.

She called to her neighbouring packs, asking if they knew of old myths or rumours of a monster which lived in the liminal spaces between life and death, light and dark, or matter and space. Legends and old-wives' tales trickled in, confirming and contradicting tangled threads of an ancient narrative.

In Pacer's opinion, gods, wolves, and people should each keep to their kind and mind their own business. But when a dragon introduced her to a woman destined to become The Mother of All, the excitement inexorably had drawn her in. She remained proud of the part she had played in saving the known world, but she sighed mournfully as she realised her part was unfinished, and the gods and mortal men required her services once more.

Rolf laid a heavy paw on Bill Barry's knee and gently whined. Wolf and boy stared intently at each other, the boy's eyes grew wide and his breathing accelerated as they spoke directly, mind-to-mind. The giant draft horses shifted in their stalls, the urgency of the situation communicated to them.

"Come on," Bill Barry ruffled Rolf's ears. "The Lady Annie will want to know."

Bill Barry and Rolf raced across the grass-seed heavy meadow, towards the track leading to Annie and Theo's house, but she was waiting for him at the edge of the forest.

"Milady." Bill Barry leant his hands on his knees to collect his breath. "Mistress Pacer has been mind-talking to Rolf. She confirms the silly song is about King Xanderamm and his vizier." Bill Barry straightened. "Rolf says Mistress Pacer sounds agitated. She's been investigating ancient mythology and is on her way here. She wants to speak with you in person, Milady. I don't mean to be forward, but how can I help?"

Annie smiled and shook her head. "I understand your coming-of-age day approaches, and that you have plans to offer for the young lady you've courted these five years."

Bill Barry blushed. "Yes, Milady. I'm confident she'll accept me."

"Then I'm certain you have much with which to occupy yourself. The best way you can help is to continue doing exactly what you planned." I'm the Mother of All. My job is to protect him, not the other way around.

Boy and wolf watched Annie stride up the mountain track to her home, her dragon-skin boots speeding her travels.

"Did you notice, Rolf? The Lady Annie didn't say there was naught to worry over. And if Mistress Pacer thinks this story business is worth making the journey, then there's summat much amiss."

Pacer and Swift lay flank to grey furred flank under a starry sky, breathing in unison.

I am loath to leave now, with Winter approaching, but I cannot discount the possibility Annie is in danger. Pacer leaned against Swift. *The ancestors have strange stories they want to share directly with Annie.*

Swift licked Pacer's silvered muzzle. *I am happy to accompany you. You do not need to travel alone. Our daughters would welcome the opportunity to practise their leadership techniques.*

Pacer thumped her tail. *I'm sure they will leap at the chance. Which is the reason I need you to remain. Someone needs to be here to soothe ruffled fur when the girls become over enthusiastic. I need to know, even if the world tears itself apart, our pack remains strong and secure.*

CHAPTER FIVE

A balmy breeze fluttered the flags atop the walls of
Kingston, welcoming visitors and traders. Brummagen scrambled from the wagon as soon as the
caravan halted, clutching his meagre bundle of belongings to his
chest, suddenly nervous that old friends would recognise him in
this reduced state. What friends, he chided himself. The hordes
who set out to find you when you disappeared? Nobody cared
then, and nobody cares now. But they will.

Jarod watched the peculiar old scribe and his porcine
companion hustle away into the heaving crowds. The caravaneer sighed with relief. The sooner he converted the parchments
into coin, the happier he would be. He ducked into his wagon
to collect the astounding artworks. Unable to resist one last
look, he unrolled them and sucked in a breath. The pages were
bare. No gorgeous calligraphy, no elegant illustrations of fabulous flora and fauna. Jarod ran his fingers over the empty spaces,
then raised the parchments to his nose. Not the faintest whiff of
ink or paint, not the slightest scratch, marred the surface of his
second-rate pages.

He turned to chase after Brummagen, but changed his mind. The damage to his reputation would be significant if people learned a charlatan had cheated him? He pursed his lips to stop himself outwardly cursing his foolishness. As a savvy trader, he ought to have recognised a scam.

Brummagen bustled along the street of booksellers, unnoticed and unrecognised, even with the pig by his side. Many of the faces were unfamiliar to him, as younger merchants replaced fathers and uncles, and enterprising individuals set up to compete with the establishment. Mothers and daughters ran independent businesses, doubtless encouraged by the flame-haired interloper.

The ex-vizier settled under a shady tree, galled yet relieved by his anonymity. He fingered the silver in his pocket, careful to keep it hidden from predators. Buyers and sellers haggled fiercely, parting with satisfied smiles. The ritual reassured Brummagen the city remained a source of wealth. Coin flowed from hand to hand, pocket to purse, and he needed to divert part of the stream into his coffers.

Although Jenny had vowed to raise him above all men, she hadn't divulged how she planned to achieve this miracle, nor when. Brummagen frowned. The silver in his purse would not last forever, which was precisely how long he intended to enjoy life, if he could convince Jenny to share her esoteric death defeating powers.

Brummagen tugged Xanderamm's halter and set out in search of cheap accommodation. He glimpsed Jenny threading her way through the throng. She turned and smiled seductively over her shoulder, beckoning him to follow. She led them to a highly respectable residential area; the lanes lined with prosperous properties and shady trees.

She stopped before the iron gates of a tall brick house. "I rented this property for your immediate use," she said. "I took the liberty of engaging a crew of servants. Tailors and jewellers will attend you tomorrow." She waved her hand. "I will take care of their accounts. Today, you will bathe and pamper yourselves. Chefs are already preparing a variety of dishes for your pleasure. Tomorrow, you will concentrate on becoming magnificent. It is imperative you look the part."

Xanderamm wept into his feather pillows. He'd dined on delicacies served on the finest porcelain platters and drank from crystal dishes. The silent servants fulfilled every whim, while keeping their eyes steadfastly averted. The staff treated him like a reigning king, and he trembled with fear as he felt the invisible bindings tighten around him.

Assuming he could escape from the confines of the house, the high walls around the gardens were beyond his ability to scale. The attentive servants enthralled the ex-vizier, but Xanderamm recognised them as ruthless prison guards, regardless of their sophisticated livery.

Sneeth made known his presence by tapping Xanderamm on the shoulder. "The Most High Lord Draqshet requires you to resume your original form before the tailors arrive tomorrow. He wants you dressed in the richest and most fashionable clothes. In a word, he wants you to appear regal."

Xanderamm regarded the creature, waiting for the corollary.

The creature laughed, like a knife being drawn over a whetstone. "You're cleverer than you look. The Most High Lord Draqshet grants you the form of a man, but still denies you the power of speech. For now, you will remain mute, unless you choose to humiliate yourself by snorting."

Xanderamm maintained a dignified silence, knowing the futility of resistance. Deep in the darkest recesses of his memory stirred a thought to which he clung. If he didn't agree to a demonic bargain, if they thrust it upon him, then they couldn't hold him accountable when the time came to render payment.

"Nod to indicate you understand," Sneeth said.

Xanderamm turned away. Nodding my understanding implies agreement. You won't catch me so easily.

Sneeth shrugged and opened his mouth, and out crawled words in a voice which wasn't his. The syllables slithered over Xanderamm's hide, commanding him to resume his rightful shape. The pig squealed in pain as his body transformed, limbs lengthening, face flattening, hips and shoulders remoulding.

"I'll leave you to rediscover yourself." Sneeth smiled, revealing gleaming fangs. "No doubt you'll want to walk about, relearn upright perambulation. The armed guards around the property's perimeter are there for your protection. Two wealthy strangers will attract attention, not all welcome. For your own safety, as a friend, I advise you to stay away from the walls and gates."

Once certain Sneeth had left, Xanderamm walked naked into the hallway. A waiting servant handed him a pair of loose trousers and a heavy dressing gown, all the while avoiding eye-contact. Xanderamm dressed himself, watching the servant from the corner of his eye. He decided the liveried man must be a demon in service to Draqshet. They did not offer slippers, no doubt one small and deliberate way to limit his mobility. He wriggled his toes, as pink and delicate as a newborn's, into the deep pile of the luxurious carpet. A sensation he hadn't realised he'd missed. Closely attended by his servant guards, Xanderamm explored the house. No expense had been spared decorating and furnishing the house, but with exquisite taste, resulting in a far more elegant home than his garish palace.

AnnieRah had meant to punish him when she transformed him into a pig, and indeed she had, but she'd also unwittingly offered him a learning opportunity. With no hope of undoing her curse, regardless of what the bumbling Brummagen tried, Xanderamm had found the time to reassess his lifestyle and his attitude towards his subjects. Fury and humiliation, coupled with a rampant desire for revenge, informed his thinking for months.

His ability to listen was unimpaired, and he listened as though his life depended on it. The changes Annie wrought increased the well-being and wealth of his erstwhile subjects, and they spoke of her with affection and respect, whereas they spoke disparagingly of him, if at all. His previous crass displays of riches and power made him cringe. He looked around, admiring everything he saw. The architect of this mysterious plot was evil, but Xanderamm had to admit his decorator had refined taste.

Smiling wryly, he walked into the kitchen where the staff stood stiffly in place. Unable to greet them verbally, he fluttered a hesitant wave. They remained statue still. Xanderamm paused mid-step. He nudged a vacant-eyed waiter who toppled over but retained his pose, a mannequin. Xanderamm examined each individual. None displayed life signs, not even breathing. He gestured for his guards to return the waiter to an upright position.

Discovering himself surrounded by creatures beyond his understanding, he plodded back to bed. Walking in the moonlit garden no longer held the same allure. He'd scope out the walls in daylight.

Xanderamm twisted and wriggled, unable to adjust his new shape to a comfortable sleeping position. Not that he dared to sleep, surrounded by inanimate creatures in thrall to Draqshet. He was certain they had the power to kill him whether he was sleeping or waking, but he preferred to meet his doom with his eyes open.

At first light, when he stood by the window staring at the shadow filled gardens, the guards brought him new clothes. He waved them out so he could dress in private. Why, he wondered, did the act of dressing feel more intimate than standing naked before them? They trailed him downstairs and into the dining area where a generous buffet awaited. He perched precariously on the edge of a chair, clearly remembering how to, but feeling uncomfortable. Walking on only two legs felt dangerously awkward; negotiating furniture seemed more trouble than it was worth. Nevertheless, he must persist. To be taken seriously, he must first gain acceptance as a respectable citizen, not an exiled and deeply unpopular monarch.

Brummagen made a beeline for breakfast. "Jenny said you'd be back. You look more youthful than I expected." He glanced at Xanderamm's empty plate. "Not hungry? You should eat, we have a busy day ahead."

Does the strangeness of the situation not affect you? Xanderamm watched the ex-vizier plough through plate after plate of food, gulping and swallowing like... like a pig. When did I get so fastidious? I was mooching scraps from the market floor mere days ago.

"Citizens may interpret your inability to speak as a weakness, so Jenny suggested we romanticise the muteness." Brummagen continued to shovel food into his mouth while he was talking, liberally spraying the table with partially masticated flecks. "We'll tell everyone you've taken a vow of silence and won't speak until you've fulfilled your mission. People will flock to your side because you're taking a stand. Genius."

Xanderamm shook his head, unhappy with the plan and disconcerted by the casual deceit and the assumption of his agreement.

"We need all the support as we can muster. A hero who

takes a vow of silence will enchant women in particular. The romance will mesmerise them. They'll convince their husbands and fathers because the men won't want to be less admirable than the fabulously wealthy and mysterious stranger."

A chattering stream of merchants, tailors, jewellers, hairdressers, and cosmetologists flowed through the house, whisking Brummagen and Xanderamm into a whirling eddy of indulgence. Whenever Xanderamm spied an escape route, a helpful hand guided him back for further torture.

Measured, pinned, swathed, styled, turned, pushed and pulled, buffed and polished; the preening and primping exhausted Xanderamm and the inane compliments sickened his soul. Dizzy with growing despair, he sank onto a silken couch, and closed his eyes against the colourful array of costumes which an infinite number of lackeys had declared divine and impossible to live without.

Dusk enveloped the property, a veil of modesty to disguise the culture of corruption within.

Jenny appeared out of the shadows and thrust the gilt-edged invitations at Brummagen, her eyes glittering with barely suppressed excitement. "These will get you into the Palace Ball, I have already paid your donations," she said.

"Donations?" Brummagen asked.

"Oh, yes," Jenny said. "The rich and influential get invited to these balls, but in practice, the selected attendees make substantial donations to the Palace, so in reality they purchase their tickets."

"What a clever idea." Brummagen's eyes lit. "A delightful way to raise revenue for the King's coffers."

"The Palace doesn't receive the coin," Jenny said. "AnnieRah has her pet, Captain Harry Field, collect the cash, which he subsequently disburses at his discretion."

"Captain Field must have accrued a fortune for himself," Brummagen said, silently reckoning the opportunities.

Jenny sneered. "Not a jot. The honourable captain keeps immaculate accounts open to any citizen with an urge to look. Field allocates funds to build roads and schools, even free hospitals. He approves payments for building improvement projects on farms. The fool runs a scheme where farmers or small businesses can apply for interest-free loans to buy machinery and equipment."

"How does he make a profit?" Brummagen twitched his new robes. "Is he building his own commercial empire?"

Jenny shook her head. "He doesn't. The dolt still draws the same meagre wage he's always drawn, not a copper more. He lives frugally, and from observation, he enjoys helping people." Jenny shuddered. "Unnatural."

"Will he recognise us when we turn up at the ball?"

"Five years is a long time, Brummagen. You and Xanderamm are both changed men. I doubt anyone who once knew you would recognise you, partly because nobody is looking for you. Nevertheless, I will lend you both glamours to deflect undue familiarity. You will leave a small package under the throne in the Audience Chamber. I confess, I am eager to see the infamous Doll Army."

"If you're going, why do you need us?" Brummagen asked, a sliver of mistrust sharp on his tongue.

"This is your best opportunity to meet the important citizens. I'll be there to provide a distraction, should things go awry. I have everything under control."

CHAPTER SIX

For three days and nights, Vert had tramped through the forest, his dragon-skin boots leaving no imprint in the rotting leaf-litter. The Woodsman hummed loudly, broadcasting his pedigree, his right to walk between the slumbering trees, and his desire for communion. He strained to hear a response, a rustle born from intelligence. He stopped and closed his eyes. There it was again, a whispered creak created not from any stray breeze or animal movement.

He glided closer, singing his song, and other voices joined him. Groaning, rasping, fluting voices only another forest-born could recognise. A shower of leaves blessed him and twigs bent towards him in affectionate greeting.

Had a mortal witnessed the meeting between Vert and the trees, they would have seen a scarecrow of a man shambling from tree to tree, whistling and muttering unintelligibly to himself, hugging and stroking their trunks. They would not have heard the exchanges of news, nor jokes shared. They would have been oblivious to the snippets of gossip eagerly traded.

When the ritual greetings were complete, Vert begged his favour.

He curled up, deep within the roots of the largest telltale tree, his knapsack bundled as a pillow. He listened to the slow heartbeat of the tree and breathed in unison. Leaves rained down, forming a blanket of recent memories. Vert drifted and slept, moving through scenes shared by the forest. He drifted deeper and deeper, farther and farther back, until time lost meaning. Empires rose and fell, tribes in colourful costumes came and went, as wars waged, and monarchs lost and won kingdoms.

The reel of time slowed and stopped, then stuttered to mortal speed. A redheaded woman moved over sun-drenched plains, fear etched in the lines around her eyes. A creeping darkness followed her, pushed back by the sun, but inexorably gaining on her. Vert twitched in his sleep and cried out in distress. He flailed to wakefulness, tears streaming down his thin cheeks.

"Elanrah?" He asked the trees. "Did she escape the darkness?"

The telltale trees maintained a heavy silence, having naught they considered useful to add.

CHAPTER SEVEN

The Palace hummed with directed activity, each well-trained individual intent on completing their assigned tasks in honour of AnnieRah, The Mother of All, and Goddess Reborn. Scents of floor polish and beeswax invaded every room, soon to be vanquished by enormous banks of floral displays. The guests would be drunk on the heady bouquet before they sipped the exotic wines.

Across town, Brummagen tucked the folded packet into his voluminous bejewelled and embroidered sleeves, and winked at Xanderamm. "One step closer to our rightful places, Your Majesty."

Xanderamm shrugged gracelessly into the austere evening coat held out by a guard servant. He refused to primp before the mirror, which servants guided him to, but submitted with eyes shut while they adjusted his clothes and tweaked his hair. When the assistants stepped away, he turned from the mirror before opening his eyes. His participation in this debacle would be minimal, and under duress.

Jenny appeared between them, crooking her arms through

their elbows. "We need to leave now, to arrive fashionably late, but without being rude to our hosts." She hustled them into the magnificent gilded carriage she had arranged as their evening's transportation, and sat with her back to the driver. "You should face forward, to your glorious future, gentlemen."

"Are you not interested in the future?" Brummagen asked.

Jenny giggled. "I don't need to see it. I wrote it."

Brummagen twittered and preened the entire journey, reminding Xanderamm how they had thoughtlessly stepped into the trap Jenny had presented. Brummagen was so delighted with the luxury of his birdcage he failed to realise he was a prisoner and blithely sang on demand.

When they descended from the carriage, Palace servants corralled the trio with a group of other privileged guests and took them on a tour, the highlights of which was the pretentiously vast Audience Chamber with its hundreds of living statues, the Doll Army. The guests oohed and aahed, clutching each other's arms in a semblance of horror, while not so secretly thrilling to the macabre spectacle. Protocols still forbade visitors climbing the dais to the throne, but in the fashionably excited melee Brummagen flipped the palm sized packet underneath the chair of state, where it lay in the dusty shadows.

Captain Harry Field made sure he spent the requisite moments with each guest, nodding and smiling at their obsequious comments, and complimenting their perfect costumes. A trio of strangers across the room intrigued him. The female flaunted her beauty and flirted with everyone, male and female. The shorter male stalked the ballroom with a proprietary air, managing to look down his nose even at the tallest guests. His finery declared his wealth for all to see, but his taste and intelligence were conspicuously absent. The younger man refused to raise his eyes and spoke to no one. Captain Field felt a tug of recognition, but his usually excellent memory couldn't place any of them. The girl locked eyes with him and offered a half-smile.

The Captain turned to dispose of his empty glass before making his way over to the strangers. When he looked again, they had disappeared. Harry scanned the room and peered into the open verandas. No sign of them among the overheated dancers trying to cool down in the night breeze. He pushed his way to the main entrance and stared down the long corridor. He frowned. Unless they had broken into an undignified gallop, he couldn't imagine how they had traversed the corridor so quickly. Why would the woman flirt, then flee?

Harry shrugged. Guests were free to leave whenever they chose, but leaving this early was a mild breach of etiquette. Mayhap foreigners had different customs, or one of them had become indisposed. The heat and music, combined with the heady scents of hothouse blossoms, often resulted in him developing a headache, and he wasn't sampling the wines and trays of delicacies the waiters plied.

The packet burst open with a soft pop.

Glittering black smoke flowed down the dais and over the floor of the chamber. Eddies whirled about the feet of the Dolls, then swarmed up the effigy-like figures, dark tendrils invading ears, noses, mouths, and eyes with malicious intelligence. A collective sigh rose from the Army as it sucked a collective breath, and its limbs softened. As one, the Army turned its unified gaze to the throne, waiting for a command.

Sneeth grinned, baring jagged teeth, and unfurled his wings. He rose and hovered above the disused seat of power. He flapped his way to the French doors, which opened onto the gardens. "Follow me," he hissed. "To freedom and vengeance."

The Doll Army turned in unison and marched across the lawns.

Sneeth guided the Army along the backstreets of the sleeping city and through an unlocked gate in the walls. The column of reanimated creatures snaked along the road, responding only to Sneeth's command. "March."

Sneeth fluttered behind them, erasing all signs of their passage. One who staggered on newly unwieldy limbs made a welcome snack. The other soldiers ignored Sneeth as he tore apart their companion.

They had received orders to march. They marched.

CHAPTER EIGHT

A white-faced man battered on Harry's door. Too distraught to speak, the Palace cleaner gestured for Harry to follow. Infected by the man's distress, Harry raced beside him. The trampled swathe of grass from the Audience Chamber French doors to the garden walls told a clear tale. Only an army of booted feet could commit that degree of damage. Holding his breath, Harry stepped into the chamber, his footsteps echoing in the recently vacated space. His heart beat an irregular tattoo.

Captain Harry thought back to the trio of strangers, and an icy stream of fear cascaded down his spine. He had no tangible evidence, but his gut told him they were involved, and beyond dangerous. Whoever, or whatever, could reverse a curse cast by AnnieRah, the Goddess Reborn, was no mere illusionist or festival entertainer.

He must warn Annie and Theo evil stalked their land and had thrown down an unmistakable challenge.

~

The marketplace throbbed with fearful energy. News the Doll Army had reanimated and was on the move eddied and whirled as the traders discovered and discarded facts, according to their biases. The first wave of gossip asserted the Doll Army had slaughtered the Palace inhabitants, usurped the city council, and would enact wholesale revenge on all citizens. The flotilla of Palace flunkies brought those facts into dispute, and the flood-waters of panic subsided, leaving shallow pools of opinion to be sloshed through and muddied by passing pedestrians.

Streams of speculation trickled into the market, swirling in treacherous currents around shifting islands of facts. Traders confidently declared the authorities had surreptitiously removed the Army in a plot to create fear and increase taxes to pay for protection. Others laughed at such foolishness; they knew it was a harmless apprentice prank and the Dolls would soon appear posed in public spaces. The wisest scandalmongers declared that the mourning families had grown tired of waiting for AnnieRah to grant either exile or retraining to the soldiers who had defied her authority, and had taken it upon themselves to repatriate the Doll Army.

These theories trickled into the Palace, crossing and recrossing, creating new and more outlandish rivers of rumour with each retelling. Soon, the royal residence was awash with misinformation, and tsunamis of untruths capsized any raft of reality intrepid enough to dare navigate the conflicting currents of news and scandal.

Captain Harry examined the lack of concrete evidence. Careless tracks of booted feet disappeared at an insignificant gate in the city wall. They didn't peter out; they didn't disperse in multiple directions, there were no misleading trails. There was naught. A complete absence. Gullible individuals might be persuaded the Dolls never existed or had crossed into a mysterious dimension. Harry shook himself. Codswallop. He would find a rational explanation.

Dexter the stablehand hummed to himself and the horses as he brushed their coats to a mirror shine. Harry hesitated on the threshold, unwilling to shatter the harmony.

"Come in, Captain Harry. You make the horses nervous when you hover," Dexter said, without looking up or changing the rhythm of his grooming.

Harry leaned his elbows on the stall gate. "I assume you've heard the rumours?"

"Aye, that I have. Never heard such tripe in me life. Tell me, Captain, what's truly going on?"

Harry blew out a breath. "Hard to say with any accuracy, Dex. The bare facts are the Doll Army has disappeared from the Audience Chamber, leaving only a track of boot prints which ends at a gate. No damage to other Palace property or personnel."

"You're worried," Dexter said, a statement not a question.

"Someone, or something, is challenging AnnieRah. An entity with the power to reverse her curse and reanimate the Doll Army. You don't need to be a genius to recognise trouble marches our way, lad."

"What would you have me do?"

"I can offer you no protection once you pass out of the city," Harry said. "I need you to take your fastest and strongest horse, ride without respite for Salvation Valley. Tell Lady Annie and Lord Theo what you know. Put yourself in their service."

Dexter tucked throwing-knives into his boots and a pair of daggers in his belt. He refused the sword Harry offered on the grounds he didn't know how to use the damned thing and would likely trip and kill himself. The destrier he rode suffered saddling by none but himself. Although not the fastest horse in the stables, he was strong and intimidating, with unusual endurance. He was also devoted to Dexter.

CHAPTER NINE

Harry stood atop the city walls as a steady stream of carts and wagons, laden with whatever constituted valuables for the individuals driving them, flowed out of the city. He couldn't forbid people leaving, but only within the city could he offer them protection; outside, they were on their own. He consoled himself that many showed enough sense to travel in small caravans. Almost all conspicuously bore arms, but he doubted they had the requisite skills or mindset to use them. He sighed with frustration as he turned away. Today, he had a self-imposed mission.

Across town, Brummagen and Xanderamm prowled their pretty prison.

"Isn't this delightful? A garden filled with cooling fountains and fragrant flowers." Brummagen said, not waiting for a response. "To find a patron who truly appreciates me is indeed a blessing. You must admit, it feels good to be back where we belong, among civilised people."

Xanderamm had naught to say. He studied the guards patrolling the perimeter and noted their workman-like weapons. No chased silver embellishments or fancy scrollwork. Unadorned, wickedly sharp blades, designed for one purpose.

"Good men, they are." Brummagen nodded proprietorially at the guards. "Jenny picked them herself. Men of wealth and influence can't be too careful." He patted his fattening paunch.

Xanderamm glanced at his ex-vizier. Wealth? We own precisely naught; we're living on the charity of an unknown benefactor whose motives are highly suspect. Influence? We're prisoners, paraded on our patron's whim. Who even knows we are here?

Doors slammed and booted feet echoed in corridors. Brummagen and Xanderamm stared into the dim interior of the house at the unexpected commotion. Captain Harry and his contingent of well-armed guards were granted reluctant entry by Jenny's mercenaries.

"This is a courtesy call." Harry addressed the man who appeared to be in charge. "I check on new residents, ensure they have what they need to settle in. Connect them with the appropriate people. My men will remain here with you."

Harry pushed past the perplexed servants, unsure who exactly was guarding whom, but having faith his own men could handle any difficulties. The sunlight momentarily blinded him after the carefully shaded room.

"Welcome, welcome." The fussily overdressed fellow surged forward to meet Harry and take him by the hand. "Come, enjoy some refreshments." The effusive man guided Harry to a bench strewn with silken cushions. He clapped his hands. "Refreshments for our honoured guest."

The other man nodded a greeting, but remained silent. The disdain for his companion, painted clearly on his face, made Harry wonder about the dynamics of the relationship.

"I am Captain Harry Field. My duties include welcoming all new residents. I saw you at the Palace Ball, but missed the opportunity to introduce myself. Are you planning to stay long?"

"I am Victor Strong, and this is my nephew, Rex."

Xanderamm slowly turned his head to look at Brummagen as copious lies spilled from his lips.

"Rex has taken a most sacred vow. He refuses to speak until he has put right a most egregious wrong." Brummagen shook his head. "Do not ask, for I am forbidden to discuss the matter. To answer your question, my nephew and I propose to make this city our permanent residence. Of course, we'll be looking for a house more befitting our status, but one doesn't want to attract the wrong sort of attention as a newcomer. We don't want to set ourselves up as a target for importunists. An unfortunate truism, my friend, but there are those who expect something for naught."

Xanderamm snorted, then covered his face with his sleeve.

"Excuse my nephew. He delights in the beauty of the flowers, but pays dearly for this innocent indulgence with debilitating hay-fever."

Xanderamm bowed and made his way into the house. Evading the guards who were busily eyeing Harry's men, he went straight to the library, where he tore a strip of parchment from a scroll and scribbled, *Please return*. He hovered by the entrance, waiting for Harry to take his leave.

When Harry left, Xanderamm stepped forward, smiling, to shake hands. He stared deep into Harry's eyes as he pressed the tiny packet of folded parchment into his palm.

"I am pleased to have made your acquaintance. I'm sure you'll be happy in Kingston. If you need advice or require introductions to our more eminent citizens, send word." Harry saluted.

Not until he was in his own office, with the door firmly closed, did he risk unfolding the secret message. He raised his eyebrows as he smoothed out the missive. Why would Rex, the hay-fever plagued nephew, need him to return? And why the furtive fumbling? Harry tucked the scrap into a drawer, then took it out and burned it over a candle stub. If the young man believed he needed to take measures to communicate secretly, then Harry wouldn't risk the message being found. He would find some pretext for another visit, something semi-official. The Strongs were hardly his social circle.

~

"Captain Harry has accepted you into Kingston. How magnanimous of him." Jenny curled her lip. "We need to capitalise on our success. You must get yourselves known and admired. Widows and orphans should do it. Everyone's a sucker for whiny widows and helpless orphans."

Brummagen looked blankly at her. "You want me to collect widows and orphans? And do what with them? Re-home them?"

"Don't be foolish. You organise a charity ball for Widows and Orphans, charge an exorbitant ticket price, and make an enormous display of donating the proceeds to the needy."

"How does that benefit me?"

Jenny rolled her eyes. "Let's say you collect ten bags of silver. You donate six bags and keep four for yourself. Or vice versa, even better. I'll provide receipts for costs incurred: musicians, refreshments, flowers, hire of the rooms, should anyone ask." She fluttered her fingers. "You'll emerge from the event the darlings of society and significantly richer. Even the miserable charity wins."

"I'm not sure how to—"

"Ask helpful Harry. This is exactly his thing. Helping those too inept to help themselves."

Brummagen frowned.

"Not you, the wailing widows and their puny whelps."

Harry leaned back in his office chair and turned over the creamy vellum, searching for clues. Usually, people who wanted to speak to him sent verbal messages. A guard from the Strong's residence waited wordlessly for a reply. Harry wondered if the mercenaries spoke the language. They usually had a smattering of words, picked up from their travels, but not always words and phrases useful in polite society. Mayhap the Strongs were not quite what they were striving so hard to appear. Harry wrote slowly and carefully, agreeing to meet that afternoon.

CHAPTER TEN

A liveried guard silently ushered Harry into the tastefully ornamental courtyard, where Victor Strange and his silent nephew awaited him. Before Harry could ask how he might assist, Victor launched his idea.

"I want to make a positive impact on this city. Your work is famous throughout the kingdom and my nephew and I wish to support your good works. Widows and Orphans are always with us and we wish to help relieve their distress."

"You desire to donate to the cause?" Captain Harry asked.

Victor shook his head. "No, no, no. I want you to organise a charity ball, which I shall host. I will donate the proceeds to the unfortunate."

Harry noticed the nephew shudder. Did he not approve of his uncle's good works? Or did he simply not wish to socialise whilst under his vow of silence?

The Captain took copious notes of Victor's demands and suggestions. The nephew picked up the discarded pen and doodled on a list of ideas deemed unworthy or not ambitious enough. Harry prepared himself to receive another secretive message, but the young man did not try to communicate.

"I will return tomorrow afternoon to confirm the arrangements." Harry stood to leave.

"Nonsense, a man of your importance doesn't run errands," Victor said. "Send a messenger. I wouldn't dream of monopolising your valuable time." He beamed a self-satisfied smile.

The nephew bit his lip and crumpled the inky page on which he'd been doodling.

Living in a draughty cave, while babysitting the mindless mannequins, bored Sneeth. The Doll Army provided no entertainment, and he dared not feed on more of them or The Dark Lord would punish him. Draqshet had kept his current pet, Jenny, for half a decade, far longer than Sneeth had expected, and his jealousy grew exponentially as his fragile self-esteem plummeted.

Jenny slunk into Sneeth's cavernous lair as the sun set.

"The Most High Lord Draqshet has a task for you," she said. "Bring this ridiculous Doll Army to the city walls the day after tomorrow. They have a special invitation to the Ball for Whiners and Whelps." Jenny viciously kicked the nearest Doll, but got no response. "The Dolls will dance with the city's finest. I do hope they are familiar with the latest steps."

Sneeth seethed at receiving orders from this favourite, but knew better than to dispute. Eventually, she would fall out of favour, like her predecessors. Then Draqshet would allow him to tear her to pieces, to devour her throbbing entrails while she screamed for mercy. Sneeth sneered in secret anticipation.

Jenny hid her revulsion of the creature. Soon, she reassured herself, Lord Draqshet would allow her to dispose of this snivelling shadow crawler. She would install more pleasing servants. Ones who recognised they owed their positions to her.

"Tomorrow at sundown. The Hanging Gate will be unlocked. You will find a man waiting to guide you in." Jenny slid away as silently as she had arrived, leaving Sneeth smouldering with rage.

Sneeth assembled the Doll Army, a toy of which he had soon tired. The musty livery, neglected for half a decade, had lost its gloss. Moth-eaten jackets with epaulets of lizard droppings ruined the requisite regularity of their uniforms. The soldiers' vacant eyes stared dully at naught. The lengthening shadows indicated the time to march. As promised, a man waited by the Hanging Gate.

Corporal Small guided the eerily silent soldiers through rarely used service corridors. Because many of the citizens had already fled, Captain Harry had opted for the smaller ballroom to create the sense of a crowd. Small herded the Doll Army into an adjacent room where they waited, shoulder to shabby shoulder, for orders.

Guests milled in ceaseless circles, taking care to see and be seen by those with influence. Like peacocks flaunting their magnificent plumage, the attendees paraded in silks and satins, displaying frothing fountains of lace and lavish ropes of pearls and jewels.

Xanderamm spotted Harry and gestured for him to follow. The ex-King headed for a study in search of writing materials. His guards paid too close attention for him to smuggle in his own. Harry entered the room as the young man rifled through the desk.

"What do you think you are doing, Sir?"

The young man pantomimed writing, then spread his hands wide.

Harry rounded the desk and slid open a drawer, revealing parchments and inks. "Help yourself." He watched intrigued as the young man wrote a single word, then tapped his chest. *Xanderamm.*

Meanwhile, Victor greeted and thanked the patrons like old friends as they arrived, making each one feel they were the guest of honour. Dancers whirled in an organised riot of colour, determined to outdo one another by stepping higher, twirling faster, and laughing louder.

The Doll Army encircled the room before the first panicked scream rent the air and the musicians stuttered into silence. Expressionless, the soldiers seized the dancers in a macabre choreography, separating the men from the women and children, and forcing them to opposite sides of the room. Cold clammy hands tight on hot sweaty necks ensured compliance.

Jenny sauntered to the centre of the room and beckoned a confused Victor to join her.

He shuffled towards her, fear shining in his eyes. "What are you doing? This isn't the plan?"

"The plan is whatever I say it is, old man. Do as you're told, or join your guests. It's all the same to me."

Brummagen folded his arms into his sleeves and looked at the floor.

Outraged at the host's complicity, and the manhandling of his wife and daughters, a merchant snatched at a Doll's sword. The vacant-eyed soldier lifted the man off his feet, arms flailing and face suffused with blood, and held him swinging by his neck. The animalistic grunts and gurgles of the choking man filled the chamber.

"He wanted your sword." Jenny smiled angelically. "Give it to him."

The Doll spitted the struggling man, twisting the blade as he withdrew his weapon. The man clasped both hands over the gaping wound, desperate to keep his entrails inside. A greasy mess slithered through his fingers and pooled on the floor below his twitching feet.

The abattoir stench overpowered the fragrance of hot-house flowers and exotic perfumes. The rank smell of fear rose from the captives, as evidence of their terror spilled down their legs, and stained their finery.

"Ladies and Gentlemen, thank you for coming tonight. The number of fresh widows or orphans we will create depends on your obedience. Kneel to welcome your new ruler, The Most High Lord Draqshet."

The lamps and candles guttered and failed as the Dolls forced their petrified dance partners to their knees, strangling stray whimpers. The ballroom doors slammed open and a black-cloaked figure rustled onto the darkened dance floor.

Harry's eyes widened as recognition of his former King soothed the niggling itch at the back of his brain. Thinner and without the superior attitude, but definitely King Xanderamm. Captain Field dropped to one knee, but Xanderamm hauled him up, shaking his head and frowning. The King seized the pen once more. *Cursed.* He tapped his throat.

"By whoever moved the Army of Dolls?" Harry asked.

Xanderamm nodded, then both men froze. The music and laughter from the ballroom stopped, replaced by an ominous silence. Harry cracked open the study door and listened. Naught. No speech making by self-important personages, no polite titters at failed jokes, no clatter of glasses or cutlery.

"Victor Strong!" Harry whirled around to Xanderamm.

"Victor Strong is Grand Vizier Brummagen. I thought he looked oddly familiar. He's behind this?"

Xanderamm shook his head, then see-sawed his hand.

"Someone more powerful is using Brummagen?" Harry asked.

The King nodded and shuddered theatrically.

"The city's remaining elite remain crowded into that room. Do you know what's going on?"

Xanderamm shook his head helplessly.

"Stay here. I must discover what's going on."

Xanderamm raised his eyebrows and shook his head. He held up both forefingers, pointing to Harry and himself, then brought them together.

The two men crept towards the ballroom, Harry shielding Xanderamm.

Sneeth watched as he clung to the ceiling. When the Master discovered Jenny had allowed Captain Harry and King Xanderamm to escape, he would punish her. Better yet, Draqshet might gift her to him. Sneeth slithered away, filled with gleeful anticipation.

The ballroom doors swung outwards and Harry only had time to shove Xanderamm into a deep alcove and huddle next to him before Jenny and The Dark Lord stepped out. The soldiers followed, each grasping a guest by the neck.

"We'll put them in the dungeons for now, My Lord," Jenny said. "They'll motivate the rest of the citizens to comply."

Draqshet paused mid-stride and sniffed the air. "I smell the pig."

"The whole place reeks of him, My Lord. Don't worry, I'll track him down."

Draqshet turned slowly to Jenny. "I'm not the one needing to worry. If you don't deliver him and the Captain, I'll set Sneeth to hunt you down."

~

Harry pulled Xanderamm after him and the pair crept back towards the ballroom. They covered their mouths and noses to mask the fetor of terror. Harry stooped to close the eyes of the abandoned corpse of the heroic husband as he passed. Xanderamm stared wild-eyed at the chaos. Despite his old paintings depicting him in valiant military poses, this was his first encounter with conflict deadlier than sharp words. Captain Harry tapped his arm.

"There's naught else we can do for him now. We will avenge his death by escaping and vanquishing our enemy."

Xanderamm nodded and swallowed the bile rising in his throat. They cautiously approached the balcony, staying low and looking for guards. Neither man saw patrols. Wasting no time, they jumped the balustrade and wound their way through huge potted plants until they reached the Palace wall.

Xanderamm crooked a finger at Harry and scuttled along the wall. He stooped before a massively overgrown bougainvillea and patted about until he found a cracked pot. He raised the rusted key in victory and pulled back the thick curtain of spiky foliage, revealing a half-sized iron-shod door. The lock was immovable until Harry pushed Xanderamm away and forced the key to turn. Harry dragged open the small door, wincing at the creaks and groans of ancient iron. He shoved Xanderamm through first, then pulled shut the door behind him. He fumbled for the key before locking the door from the inside.

Xanderamm ran practiced fingers along the wall and located a tinderbox. The sulphur sticks were still dry and the candle stubs shed enough light to see an arm's length ahead. Captain Harry raised an eyebrow. He'd heard rumours of hidden passageways which the King had used to reach secret assigna-tions, but dismissed them as mere hyperbole.

"How many exits to this tunnel?"

Xanderamm grinned and held up four fingers.

"Security was sloppy in the Palace, but we can't risk being caught at the city gates. They'll expect us to flee, therefore, we'll burrow as deep into the centre as we can."

The King led the way, twisting and turning through narrow stone corridors until they reached an iron door, with a key hidden in a cracked lintel above. Harry drew his sword and stepped in front of Xanderamm. He pushed the door, which swung on well-oiled hinges, and stepped into a garden room decorated with cushioned divans and exotic song birds hung in gilded cages.

"Does this place belong to one of the captive families?" Harry squinted into the gloom; the extensive and well-main-tained gardens obviously belonged to a person of taste and wealth.

Xanderamm shook his head.

"But a friend of yours?"

The King pursed his lips then rummaged in his pockets for coins. He dropped the coins onto Harry's palm and dragged the Captain to a chaise and made kissing noises before collapsing with laughter.

"A paid friend?" Harry's eyes grew wide and his jaw dropped. "We're in a brothel?"

CHAPTER ELEVEN

The crisp air pinked Dexter's cheeks as his steed bore him into the unknown. His leather jerkin and cloak of courage kept him warm as he charged through the day and into the night. He ate and slept in the saddle. More at ease atop his horse than lying on the ground, Dexter slowed to a canter while he dozed. He awoke on the third day to the unadulterated splendour of breaking dawn. Gold and rose fingers of blazing light peeled back the darkness, revealing a landscape ripe with produce and early risen workers trudging to the fields, armed with scythes and rakes.

Dexter spurred the horse to a flat-out gallop, determined to reach Salvation Valley before nightfall.

Netta caught the insistent rhythm of beating hooves. Not a signature of Bill Barry's horses, therefore an approaching stranger, and one not attempting stealth or concealment. She raced to a high vantage point, hoping to identify the visitor.

The young man clinging to the heavy horse was clearly exhausted, and his steed appeared to continue by sheer will-power. Both needed rest. Netta called for Theo. His enchantments prevented unwelcome visitors from finding their way into the Valley.

Theo squinted into the gloaming, then broke into a smile. "That's Dexter, the stable lad from Kingston, who looked after my boars. He wouldn't come without good reason. I'll let him in the front door."

Netta shuddered. She had never enjoyed travelling at the speed of thought, and recently, the mere thought churned her stomach. Her dragon-skin boots gave her the ability to travel twice mortal speed, and that was enough.

The High Lord Consort materialised on the road ahead of Dexter and waved both arms for him to stop. The rider whispered in the horse's ear and the pair slowed to a walk, coming to a halt beside Theo. Netta watched as the rider collapsed from his steed into Theo's arms. The horse skittered, but allowed Theo to take the reins. Netta couldn't see Theo transport the group to the homestead, but her far-hearing picked up the raised voice of Martha issuing orders, and the whicker of the destrier being coaxed to the stables by Theo and Bill Barry.

When Netta arrived at the homestead, Dexter was by the fire, cradling a steaming bowl of mutton stew and a hunk of rye bread. Annie was listening intently, a frown creasing her forehead.

"No, Milady. Nobody got hurt, and nobody saw naught. A great gash across the grass, naught else."

"Before you left, had anybody claimed responsibility?"

Dexter wiped his mouth with the back of his hand, then blushed. "Pardon me, Milady. No, only a steady stream of rumours from folk wi' nowt better to do. But Captain Harry, he said only someone, or something, with substantial power could reverse your curse and dare to challenge your authority. He said evil stalks the land. Looked fine to me as I rode through, but Captain Harry, he's clever, and not prone to talk rubbish like most, so I believe him. You're under threat and Harry said to put myself in your service."

"Thank you, Dexter. I also value Harry's opinions. Finish your meal and Martha will find you a bed." Annie raised her hand. "Don't worry, your wonderful horse is already being cared for. Rest, we will talk again tomorrow."

Roic twitched his tail and compulsively raked his talons through the dirt. Dew still sparkled on the short grass, but all the dragon's attention focussed on the potential threat, not the beauty of nature.

"We now know for certain there's a real problem," Netta said.

"I'm going. This entity wants my attention. The sooner I deal with it, the better we'll all feel."

"No, you're not racing off to face an unknown adversary. I forbid it," Theo said.

The group froze.

"You forbid it?" Annie stared at her husband. "Are you forgetting I am The Goddess Reborn? I have a responsibility to my people." *I am not my Mother. I do not walk away when circumstances become inconvenient.*

"Are you forgetting your total collapse when you over-exerted yourself? We have no idea of what this entity is capable. We're a team, remember? That means we work together." Theo folded his arms. "Yes, my love. I forbid you to put yourself in unnecessary danger, risking your very existence, and the welfare of all creation."

Netta laid a hand on Annie's arm. "Don't do this, please. Not yet, at least. Doubtless, this thing is powerful, but we need more information. Theo's right. You would be reckless to go storming in, knowing naught."

"I said naught of storming," Annie said. "Only that a quick resolution is preferable."

"If I wished to hurt Annie," André said, looking slowly around the group, "I'd target those she loves most. Try to provoke a response, make her emotional and therefore more prone to make careless errors."

"You mean this monster will come for us?" Netta shot a panicked glance towards the crèche. Gabrielle, her firstborn, dug enthusiastically in the dirt beside Martha, who managed to entertain the littlies, gently discipline them, and feed the community, while maintaining a serenity Netta envied.

"Maybe." André nodded towards the homestead. "But we're not necessarily easy targets. The Guardians, however... They couldn't protect themselves."

"Are you suggesting we can't leave to confront this entity, in case it targets the Guardians?" Theo asked. "We can't allow evil to stalk the land unchallenged."

André shook his head. "I'm suggesting you and Annie create the strongest barrier or glamour to hide the Guardians. Keep them out of sight, unattainable. You know best how to achieve that. Then we leave, drawing attention to ourselves."

"Distract the monster and make it come to us? I like the idea," Annie said. "We need an isolated location."

We need the armour of information. This entity has been gathering knowledge about us since before we suspected its existence. We must discover its weaknesses. Roic flexed his wings. *Consider, what if, like AnnieRah, this entity draws power from heat and light? If I were to blast it with my fire, I'd not only not kill it, but might strengthen it. We must first hear the tales from Pacer's ancestors, and any myths Vert can pry from the forests.*

"While we wait, Theo and I will build stronger protections

for the Guardians than those that ever warded the Great Temple."

～

Bill Barry murmured to Dexter's destrier, and the horse ceased stamping his hooves and rolling his eyes, instead, twitching his ears to better hear the boy's whispered words of reassurance. The tub of bran mash with chopped carrots and apples cooled while the horse assessed his surroundings. The two giant draft horses leaned out of their stalls to greet and nuzzle the lad, and the stallion relaxed further when Bill Barry led out a pair of younger horses and loosely tethered them while he groomed them and crooned nonsense. From where he worked, Bill Barry monitored the comings and goings at the homestead, hoping for an opportunity to see Annie.

When Annie left the house and headed for the hives, Bill Barry raced to intercept her. She was deep in thought when Bill Barry almost collided with her.

"I heard the news, Milady. Will you be away over winter?"

Annie startled. "What news would that be?"

"You and Lord Theo are going off to fight monsters. You're on your way to tell the bees, right? I've summat to tell 'em, too." Bill Barry grinned.

"Should I infer your young lady has accepted you?"

Bill Barry nodded and blushed.

"Congratulations," Annie said, then her smile faded.

"You don't look too pleased, Milady. Have I offended you?"

"No, I'm just thinking. Lord Theo and I will leave in a few days, along with Mistress Netta and Master André. We will place extra wards and protections around Salvation Valley. You should plan for your betrothed to join you, or you may find you cannot meet for a long time."

"The rumours are true, then?"

"Flashy rumours often have their roots buried in the muck of truth."

"I might be a father by the time you return, Milady."

"Indeed, you might. Accept my blessing, that you, your bride, and your babies will be healthy and content."

Bill Barry hung his head. "I'm dead scared, Milady. I'm an orphan, and the closest to a mother I've known is you. Begging your pardon, if that's presumptuous."

"I'm flattered, Bill Barry. Thank you. You'll make a wonderful father when the time comes."

"Do you think children inherit characteristics from their parents, or do they make their own? I mean, you're a fire-witch, but your mum wasn't, was she? I'd like my children to be good with animals like me, and clever and beautiful like their mother."

Annie halted. "My mother wasn't a fire witch," she whispered. "Bill Barry, you're a genius." Annie whirled about and raced away, leaving Bill Barry slack-jawed.

"A genius?" Bill Barry shook his head. "No idea what she means."

Annie pelted up the hill to Roic's glade. "I think I know what happened to Elanrah." She flopped in front of the dragon and lay panting. "Was my mother a fire-witch, like me?"

Roic slid open his great jewel eyes and regarded the Goddess sprawled before him. *Greetings, Lady Annie. I cannot claim any recollection of Elanrah using the fire-gift, but she loved to bask in the sun. She loathed cold weather. Why the sudden interest?*

"When Theo and I were ridding the dark North of its ice, I collapsed. Vert revived me by surrounding me with heat and light. I trapped Elanrah in a dark room and she disappeared, leaving only a fading ember. Do you see the connection? I killed my mother by depriving her of light. She told me her favourite place was the sun-drenched courtyard."

When Vert recovered, he trudged back to the spot where Theo had left him, and called for the Consort to transport him back to Salvation Valley. Theo and Vert arrived in Roic's sun dappled glade to find the group waiting anxiously. Vert immediately crawled under Roic's chin, taking comfort from the familiarity.

"The trees shared an ancient memory. I recognised the woman as the original Elanrah. Her terror overwhelmed me as darkness relentlessly pursued her. She ran, as far and as long as possible, but the evil hunted her until she collapsed. I experienced her panic as the monster gained on her. She had nowhere to run, no one to turn to. Her instinct to burrow deep and hide only strengthened the monster, who grew stronger and more fearsome in the darkness."

The group murmured impotent words of anger and disgust.

Vert swiped his eyes and huddled further back under Roic's chin. "Her despair was all-consuming, but he experienced naught, not even anticipation or victory. The trees couldn't tell me more, but I doubt she escaped."

When Roic announced Pacer's approach, Theo sped to meet her and guide her through the wards. Knowing she brought potentially disturbing information tempered their joyful greetings.

The ancestors wanted to meet with you all directly, Lady Annie, to prevent any misunderstandings. We ought not to waste further time.

The group formed a circle, with Pacer leading the ritual. She sang to her ancestors, calling for their attention. Although the language sounded unintelligible to the rest of the group, the emotions were apparent. Pacer offered respect and deference, but the threads of urgency and anxiety running through the fabric of her song stood out, creating an uncomfortable texture.

A golden mist grew around the group, thickening and solidifying. A tall brindle wolf emerged, glossy with vitality. She positioned herself beside Pacer, and turned her calm gaze on each participant. Her telepathic voice rang clearly.

I am Accalia, here at Pacer's request. If I understand correctly, you desire knowledge of an ancient evil, a darkness which once stalked the land in pursuit of the Creatrix, and whom you believe has awoken and is abroad once more. You identify the entity by its lack, its emptiness. Yes?

"I am AnnieRah, the Goddess Reborn. My companions and I sense something beyond the edges of reality, a creature of immense power. We will appreciate whatever you can tell us."

My story is fragmented, it dates from the beginning of creation. No doubt details are lost, conflated, or confused, but I will endeavour to be accurate. The creature styles himself, The Most High Lord Draqshet. We do not know his origins, but the threads of stories mention he lusted after Elanrah, who fled his attentions. Accalia looked deep into Annie's eyes. *My Lady, this is an unpleasant tale where your ancestress suffered unspeakable anguish. Are you sure you wish to be present?*

Annie nodded. "I thank you for your concern, Mistress Accalia, but I need to know what happened."

Draqshet assaulted Elanrah one fateful night, eventually driven away by the rising sun. He abandoned her, humiliated and dishonoured, in the desert. Screaming curses, the Creatrix expelled his seed

71

onto the burning sand. The shrivelled spawn tried to protect itself from the light by covering itself with its wings, but Elanrah blasted the abomination with her fury, the flames consumed the carcass. Or so she thought.

Netta reached out and gripped Annie's trembling fingers. Accalia watched the women comfort each other, and allowed them a moment to compose themselves.

The Creatrix fled to the most isolated place she knew, terrified the monster would follow her.

Throughout the day, the scorched spawn suffered in the heat, mewling for comfort or release, but it survived until nightfall, when its dread father claimed it. Legends say Draqshet wept tears which fell on his son and revived him. Other legends say the father opened his own veins to feed his son.

"What happened next?" Netta asked, squeezing Annie's hand.

Father and son disappeared for eons. Hints of their continued existence surfaced from time to time. Draqshet remained hidden. But his son, whom we believe goes by Sneeth, makes his presence known in service to his father. We are unclear whether Draqshet acknowledges the relationship. Sneeth only ever refers to himself as a servant. We believe he was recently active in a southern desert town. Villagers and townsfolk found corpses with their hearts ripped out.

"Elanrah recovered," Theo said. "She survived."

Her ordeal forever changed the Creatrix. Accalia gazed upon Theo. *She realised her vulnerability. Her response was to create a protector. She invited Creation to gift this boy with favourable characteristics and skills. Bears brought size and strength; beavers brought craftsmanship; cheetahs brought speed and agility; ants brought building skills; swans gave him loyalty and grace. All of creation bestowed upon him their best attributes.*

Elanrah doted on her creation, and blessed him with immortal-

ity. He reached manhood in one cycle of seasons, attaining perfection beyond the rest of creation, and again Elanrah grew fearful.

Theo leaned forward, a frown of concentration creasing his forehead.

The Goddess forbade the young God to go among the people any further. His popularity was growing among men, and his fame was spreading. She confined him to the complex of the Great Temple and banned all records of his name or image. She destroyed all statues and paintings of the young God, and his name faded from the world's memory.

Fearing Draqshet's jealousy, Elanrah hid her creation, and set wards around the Great Temple so only the pure of heart could find it. She allowed none of her servants to leave the complex, in case Draqshet scented their trail and followed it back.

"Stop." Theo held up his hand. "I am Elanrah's creation? She made me as her protector but then spent her time protecting me?"

Accalia inclined her head.

"And when we destroyed the Great Temple," Annie said, "we sent a signal to Draqshet. What have I done?" She buried her face in her hands.

CHAPTER TWELVE

Netta tucked the lovingly stitched quilt around Gabrielle and shuttered the lamp, leaving the barest sliver to shine over the sleeping child. She kissed Gabrielle's brow and brushed back a curl. How could a mother hurt a child, much less her own?

André raised his head as she entered the living area. "You look unwell. The story of Elanrah troubled you?"

Netta curled into a padded chair and drew her feet under her. "How could the Mother of All reject her own child? I would give my life to protect Gabrielle."

"Didn't you once tell Annie that Elanrah would make a better aunt than a mother? Not everyone is meant to be a parent. How lucky are we, not only to be deliriously in love with each other, but to have a gorgeous baby girl?"

Netta hugged herself. "Elanrah tried to kill her own child. That's not natural."

"I'm not saying what she did was right, but the circumstances were horrific. She was hunted and raped. You can hardly blame her for rejecting the baby." André spread his hands. "I don't know what a natural response should be, but I understand her revulsion and terror."

"She could have fostered the babe, if she couldn't bear to keep him." Tears welled in Netta's eyes.

André perched on the edge of her chair and wrapped his arms around his wife. "Shush. We can't change what has already happened, but we can make certain Draqshet doesn't live to hurt anyone else."

"What if we're too late? What if Draqshet has grown too powerful?"

"Netta, my beloved. Remember to whom you are wedded. I am Grand Master André, and I pledge upon my honour, no dark dwelling depravity shall get the best of me. I will defend you and Gabrielle, and every mother and child, with my dying breath."

"Blatherskyte." Netta lifted her tears-stained face and kissed her husband. "You distract the bastard with fancy words, while I shoot him with scale tipped arrows."

Annie filled every room with light, making the house a blazing beacon in the darkness of the forest.

"If I hadn't been selfish and impetuous," she said, "we wouldn't find ourselves in this dangerous situation. I thought I was doing the right thing, but I was wrong. Again."

"You can't blame yourself unless you blame me, too," Theo said. "I did naught to stop you, in fact, I encouraged you. Mayhap, if Elanrah had been honest with me, I could have supported her and she wouldn't have grown tired of Creation. There is no point, my love, in seeking to apportion blame."

"What does Draqshet want? Can we appease him?" Annie looked hopefully at her husband, but Theo shook his head.

"I doubt we can negotiate with a creature who relentlessly hunted a distraught woman almost to her death, then assaulted and abandoned her. I don't believe he has a better nature to which we could appeal. Other than to announce his presence and flaunt his power, why did he take the Doll Army?" Theo rolled his shoulders. "Why does he need them?"

"He wields enormous power," Annie said. "I can't imagine he needs the Doll Army for anything practical. He attracted our attention. The Dolls would terrify mortals. Are they mere puppets or has he given them agency?"

"Tomorrow we leave and mayhap find our answers. Dexter can return to Kingston, and I will seal the Valley. We will hunt down Draqshet and destroy him, and his vile spawn."

CHAPTER THIRTEEN

" I hope you treated these women well." Doubt coated Harry's tongue. "We're asking a lot."

Xanderamm frowned, suddenly unsure of his welcome. The act of buying a woman means I treated her as a commodity, not a person. I thought we were having fun, but I was the King. How else could they have responded? At least I paid them well. I wonder if...

Xanderamm scanned the garden room, trying to remember. He pulled aside a rug and dropped to his hands and knees to examine the flooring. The marble slabs looked undisturbed, no chips marked their edges. As far as he could tell, this emergency stash remained safely buried. Mayhap the others also remained undiscovered.

Harry watched the King scrabbling at the edges of the marble paver before silently passing him a short dagger. Nodding thanks, Xanderamm worked away at the edges until he could get his fingertips deep enough. Harry helped him drag the slab away. Together, they hauled the iron-bound chest out of the hole.

The padlock posed a problem. Xanderamm had lost the key years ago. Harry nudged him aside. "My party trick." He blushed as he inserted the slender tip of a dagger into the lock, closed his eyes, and jiggled the blade. The locks snicked open and Xanderamm clapped his hands in delight, then threw open the chest.

He pulled out the smallest bag and hefted the weight, before throwing it onto Harry's lap, pointing between himself and the Captain.

"This is our getaway fund?"

The King nodded, then pointed to the chest and house, back and forth.

"You wish to give a portion of this to the women?"

Xanderamm stood, frustrated at his inability to talk. He touched one of the gilded cages, then used both hands to signal a voluptuous woman.

Harry frowned. "The harlots are caged? Kept like pets?"

The King took a deep breath. He poured the contents of one bag across a divan. The egg sized jewels winked in the wavering candlelight. Stones of every imaginable colour, mixed with water clear diamonds, spilled over the cushions. Harry glanced at the chest and noted eleven more sacks.

"Tell me again, slowly," Harry said.

Xanderamm swirled his forefinger over the treasure and looked at Harry.

"All the treasure? Yes?"

Xanderamm nodded and repeated the double hand sign for a woman, then locked his thumbs together and fluttered his fingers like wings, swooping from the cage to the open arches.

"You wish to donate the treasure to the women, so they can escape from their cages? So they can be free?"

Xanderamm sighed with relief and sank onto a divan.

"If you hand over all these jewels, what's stopping the

women from betraying us? We lose our bargaining power. I recommend you show them samples, letting them know there is more, much more, once we've gone."

The King shrugged and threw Harry a salute.

"That means you agree? Then we must rebury the chest, keeping our bag, and samples for the ladies."

CHAPTER FOURTEEN

Jenny doubled the patrols on the city walls, then doubled them again. Offering rewards and incentives to the Dolls was a waste of effort. They followed orders, but lacked emotional motivation. She paced her newly appropriated chamber, oblivious to the rich rugs and colourful tapestries, while fear of The Dark Lord's fury filled her mind.

How could Xanderamm and Harry have escaped? She would blame Sneeth. Her task had been to ensure the smooth running of the event, making sure the bumbling Brummagen fulfilled his role. Expecting her to supervise Xanderamm at the same time was unreasonable. But the Master was unreasonable. And unpredictable. More, he was unforgiving. Jenny had pieced together fragments of information, enough to work out The Dark Lord was on a quest for revenge, over some real or imagined slight from eons ago.

The Dolls were implacable. When they encountered resistance, they continued like a juggernaut, regardless of injury to either party. They rounded up the City Guard, showing no mercy to, or recognition of, old comrades, and confined them to barracks. Attempts to escape or negotiate resulted in the use of terminal force. When the City Guards realised they couldn't kill the Dolls, their officers ordered the enlisted men to capitulate.

Those who hadn't witnessed the return of the Doll Army soon learned and took cover within their homes or businesses. Ordinary citizens locked themselves indoors, hiding under stairs or in cupboards. The Dolls ignored them. Darkness faded and dawn broke over a silent city.

Pigeons strutted about the marketplace, pecking and preening. A stray dog snuffled through scraps, but scampered away yelping when the freakish army marched past. The city held its breath, the inhabitants unsure of who was in charge and what this meant for them.

Brummagen wandered around the chambers he'd inhabited as Grand Vizier, noting the absence of the valuables taken to help fund AnnieRah's projects. Back in his old rooms, surrounded by the remains of his own possessions, he finally realised he was a prisoner. The Dolls standing guard inside and outside his doors didn't respond, except to put their hands on their sword hilts when he ordered them to stand aside. Defeated, he huddled in his study amongst his once beloved books and scrolls.

Consternation at seeing the two fugitives in her garden room rendered the woman momentarily speechless, but she quickly recovered. Hers was a trade where the shocking and unexpected were normal. Pasting a professional smile on her handsome face, she glided closer.

"Gentlemen, we rarely receive early morning callers. Mayhap I can offer you a light breakfast?"

Xanderamm stepped forward, arms open wide.

"Your majesty? Is it truly you?" The woman sank into a deep curtesy, skirts billowing about her.

"Madam, please," Harry took her arm and guided her to a cushioned bench. "We need your assistance."

"There is a generous bounty for information about the whereabouts of two dangerous outlaws. You must be the deadly Captain Harry Field," she said, offering her hand, "while this fine gentleman must be none other than the famous mute, Rex Strong. You may call me Lady Amora."

"You seem uninterested in the bounty, Lady Amora. Was the amount insufficient to tempt you?"

Lady Amora tapped her rouged lips with a painted fingernail. "Whoever delivers actionable information receives in return a lifetime supply of coin, guaranteed to cover all needs. Sir, I am a businesswoman and I doubt the veracity of offers couched in vague language. I do not know the character of those making the offer, but I wager they would measure any lifetime in mere hours, Mayhap only minutes."

"Are you saying you cannot be purchased, My Lady?"

"I run a House of Pleasure, Captain. Such a claim would be disingenuous. No, I strike a concrete bargain; particular services for an agreed price. No surprises for either party."

Harry passed a hand over his mouth to disguise a smile.

"Under the circumstances, I am prepared to make an exception. King Xanderamm was an exceptionally generous benefactor, gifting my girls ten times what other patrons offered. Fear of the Dolls has damaged my business, and we have seen no regular soldiers since the debacle of the Doll's reanimation. I will help you escape, and on Xanderamm's return to power, he will officially endorse my House."

Xanderamm rummaged behind the divan cushions and produced a heaped handful of sparkling stones, and poured them into Lady Amora's lap.

"The King has expressed his desire to set free each lady of this house and provide sufficient funds for her to live exactly how and where she pleases, answering to no man. The jewels you have are a sample, less than one hundredth of what the King will give you," Harry said.

Lady Amora held the jewels to the light, one by one. "These are magnificent. The sale of a single jewel could provide a lifetime of luxury for a sensible person. I would be a fool not to accept your offer, but I must tell you, I'd have happily helped gratis, to spite that foul Jenny woman who is parading around town like she owns us."

CHAPTER FIFTEEN

Dexter returned to Kingston at a more leisurely pace than he'd left. Knowing Captain Harry would appreciate a report, Dexter took time to observe the harvests and the busy markets, the well-dressed traders and the plump goodwives. He heard chanting and singing from both schools and fields. The kingdom appeared prosperous and peaceful. He sat up straight as he rode, confident Lady AnnieRah and High Lord Theo would resolve the issue with the Doll Army.

A farmer, with a wagon crammed with crates of live chickens, slowed as he got within hailing distance.

"You're wasting your time, lad." The farmer shook his head. "They've closed the town, you can't get neither in nor out. Maggot-brained officials. Must be summat going on, but they're not tellin' us little folk. A bunch of shabby soldiers searching for two runaways. Yer may as well turn about now and head home, lad."

Dexter considered the chicken farmer's words as he watched him disappear down the road. Kingston had no slaves, so what did he mean by runaways? And if someone had run away, why close the town to traders? Captain Harry would never lock the city gates, nor would he allow his soldiers to look shabby. Stone me! The only remotely shabby soldiers are the Dolls! Captain Harry wouldn't allow the reprobates to take charge, so either he's dead, or he's a runaway!

Sensing Dexter's agitation, the destrier pranced and fidgeted, searching for an enemy to rear up on and beat into the dirt. "Easy, boy, easy." Dexter patted the horse's neck and mumbled into his ears. He dismounted and led his mount off the road. He found two apples in the saddlebags, courtesy of Martha. "One each, my friend. Can't say fairer than that."

Dexter leaned against a tree and settled himself to watch. A trickle of wagons and carts grew to a steady stream, returning from the capital. Dexter glanced at the sun, and calculated the disgruntled traders had been denied access to the city shortly after dawn.

A girl leading a string of goats spied him and waved. "If you're one of them with a bounty on 'is 'ead, you ought to scarper. Nasty lookin' lot after you. Don't know what you've done, mister, but I shouldn't hang around. They'll be here soon."

"Don't you want to collect the bounty, lass? Compensation for leading your goats there and back on a fruitless errand?"

The girl laughed. "Don't reckon I could wrestle you to the ground and hold you there, unless you was willin', like. 'Sides, there's summat not right about them, whereas you, you're goodly looking."

Hours after Dexter's dawn departure, Netta rested her fists on her hips as she surveyed the caravan arrayed before the homestead. "This reminds me of old times."

"But this time," André said, "we'll not be parted."

Annie patted the boars, then Theo helped her into the carriage, where Pacer and Vert already waited. She squinted into the predawn skies, searching for Roic.

"He's scouting ahead," Vert said.

Netta mounted her stallion, brother to Andre's mount, and patted his sleekly muscled neck. "And this time, we have horses. If I'm going into battle, I prefer to be part of the cavalry, not a foot soldier." She checked her knives and slingshot before nudging her ride into a gentle trot.

"Dexter reported he saw naught amiss on his way in," Annie said. "I'd prefer to keep the people out of this if possible. We will deal directly with Draqshet, minimise potential conflict."

Theo placed a hand over hers. "Draqshet has proven himself to be ruthless and without conscience, my love. Be prepared for him to resort to whatever filthy tricks will benefit him."

"He will stoop to depths incomprehensible," Vert said. "Roic said the monster lacked emotions, but I disagree. Envious rage and hatred of all beauty fuels him. He focuses only on destruction. The power to shield such a mania must be immense, and I am afraid. We should all be afraid."

Pacer leaned her head against Vert's hip, a wordless offering of comfort.

Jenny breezed into Brummagen's apartments, wearing a sunny smile and fashionable silks. She glanced at his untouched breakfast. "You'll address the citizens, telling them to go about business as usual. The city will re-open its gates to traders and The

Most High Lord Draqshet expects the marketplace to operate at full capacity."

"I'm not an errand boy, or a vulgar mouthpiece." Brummagen said, fingers twisting convulsively. "You said you'd raise me up over all men. This isn't what I imagined."

Jenny shrugged. "Your lack of imagination is of no concern to me, nor your Master. Look at it this way." She led him by the hand to the tower window. "The city elite are festering in the dungeons while you're in your tower, far above them all." She gave him a two-handed shove, and he staggered backwards, bruising his hip on the window-ledge. "You could so easily fall from favour."

Brummagen blanched. "Shall I write a script, or have you already prepared one?"

Jenny handed him a small scroll. "Don't improvise. You're not in a popularity contest. The Dolls will collect you at midday."

The ex-vizier stared after her. She'd be crowing with glee if she'd captured Xanderamm. Her silence on the matter could only mean defeat. The Dark Lord was neither as omniscient nor omnipotent as she pretended.

Lady Amora, attended by two of her most alluring girls and a troupe of well-armed guards, studied Victor Strong from the perimeter of the marketplace. His guards hustled him onto a podium, and he delivered his speech in a monotone. Amora recognised him, even from a distance, as ex-Grand Vizier Brummagen. His status as a prisoner or collaborator was unclear, but he'd obviously betrayed his King.

She pursed her lips as she recalled his efforts years ago, to convince her the King's generosity entitled him to a girl of his choice. The sniveler constantly tried to get something for naught, attempting to impress everyone of his importance. And there he stood, a traitorous puppet.

Lady Amora's House of Pleasure was one of the last places scheduled for searching. Jenny decided an establishment in the centre of town, with frequent visitors and numerous staff, was not an ideal place to hide. Coupled with the untrustworthiness of harlots, and their known grasping for gold, no one would be foolish enough to seek sanctuary in a brothel.

Acting on Jenny's spiteful orders, the Dolls barged through the door, shoving aside women and security with equal violence. They overturned chests of linen, and trampled the contents, emptied and investigated containers of all sizes, ripped open closets and shredded female apparel.

One Doll entered the garden room, stared vacantly at the delicate furniture, then methodically smashed the contents of the room to smithereens, before tearing down the gauzy curtains, leaving shredded remnants on the floor.

Harry and Xanderamm crouched in the tunnel behind the locked and hidden door, subconsciously holding their breath, until certain the mindless vandals had moved on. By the time Lady Amora returned from the meeting, they'd tidied the mess into piles: splintered furniture frames, torn cushions and curtains, and smashed ornaments. They'd repotted the trashed plants as best they could.

"You were wise not to take refuge inside these past days. I was foolish to hope we would elude their attention forever." Lady Amora assessed the damage with a practiced eye. "I've called a physician to treat cuts and abrasions on my ladies and staff." She clenched her hands to disguise the trembling. "One of my girls sustained a broken leg. All of this violence was utterly unnecessary, they weren't resisting."

She stepped close to Harry and looked carefully at his face, running delicate fingers over his cheekbones. "Has anyone ever told you what pretty eyes you have, Captain?"

Harry jerked away and Lady Amora spluttered with laughter. "Don't panic, your virtue is safe with me. You're not my type." She winked. "Come, both of you. I have a plan."

Lady Amora led them up into the loft, past security staff and women who deliberately averted their eyes, and through a door hidden behind a wardrobe spilling its contents onto ruined silk rugs. "You'll spend the next day or two here while we transform you." She grinned at Xanderamm. "We can work miracles with cosmetics and costumes."

Harry and Xanderamm squeezed into the confines of the tiny room and shared a confused shrug.

"Victor Strong spoke on behalf of our new ruler. I recognised Victor as Grand Vizier Brummagen. Traitorous turd. He said the city will reopen its gates to traders, which is most convenient. I have two country girls, well trained in the art of love, but sadly lacking in the grace and delicacy required by the sophisticated patrons of my establishment. I'm sending them to work in a less aesthetically demanding house in a smaller town."

Xanderamm shrugged his incomprehension.

"Are you suggesting we dress up as women?" Harry asked.

"Certainly not," Lady Amora said. "You will become women. You will walk and talk as women do. You will be women. For a few days. The first thing must be hair removal. It's a stinky, time-consuming practice, but you'll be silky smooth for weeks. Then I'm going to darken your skin. The Dolls are searching for pale-skinned men, not olive-skinned girls."

"No, I'm not doing it. It's unnatural," Harry backed himself to the wall.

"Don't be silly. I'm sure you've endured all manner of unpleasant things during your military training. This is no different. Well, possibly more painful. You're not afraid of a little pain, are you, Captain?"

Dexter lurked along the roadside, picking up the gossip. The town was opening again for trade, The Doll Army having ascertained the fugitives were no longer in the city. Dexter's certainty did not falter; if Harry was one of the hunted pair, he would not have fled the city. The Captain possessed nerves of steel and would await the right moment. He wouldn't run like a frightened rabbit. But he would pass this way to reach Salvation Valley.

Roic flew high above the clouds, beyond mortal sight, and enjoyed watching the sun rise and set the sky alight. He inhaled, searching for a wisp of discontent or envy. Fragments of healthy ambition and rivulets of friendly rivalry feathered over his tongue. The land was fertile, and the communities thrived.

Forests and fields spread like a gorgeous tapestry beneath him. Towns and settlements adorned the bright ribbons of rivers and sequins of lakes. Kingston should soon be in view, the epicentre of embroidered roads and trade routes.

Roic shook his massive head and circled his target. The capital lay obscured under a colourless blanket of fog. Roic expected to encounter a miasma of anxiety and fear, but no scent of negative emotions drifted up to him. The roads into the capital were busy, thronged with carts and wagons, pedestrians and strings of livestock, and as they approached the city walls, they disappeared from his view.

Targeted magic, hiding a city from a select audience, screamed immense power and skill, unlike anything Roic had previously encountered. He ascended to where the air cooled and studied the scene. People passed obliviously, unaware of the shield, and Roic shuddered. Draqshet possessed more power than previously believed. He had anticipated a reconnoitre from above and successfully outmanoeuvred them.

Vert lay sickened to the depths of his soul, and it was this soured milk odour that Roic followed as a beacon. The Woodsman had cried and twitched all night under the shelter of Roic's chin, and his distress had lodged in the back of Roic's throat, choking him. Returning with news of Draqshet's superior skills and advanced planning would not ease Vert's pain.

Roic landed heavily, shaking the ground as a substitute for stamping the life force from Draqshet. The horses and boars skittered at the ends of their tethers, snorting their unease. Roic huffed smoke and lashed his tail. The six friends approached in a semi-circle.

"I fear you bring us bad tidings, my friend," Annie said. "Has Draqshet destroyed my capital and its inhabitants? Is the Doll Army marauding unchecked through the countryside?"

My Lady, I know not how to explain what I witnessed. The countryside is healthy, but Kingston remained hidden from my sight and scent. Draqshet anticipated our interest and blocked us. That alone scared me, but what makes it truly terrifying was people entering and leaving the city unaware of the ward. The

Dark Lord created fell magik targeted directly at us, or mayhap only me.

"I find interesting the fact he keeps the city unharmed," Netta said.

"He is using the city as bait," André said. "He hopes to lure us in."

"If you are correct," Annie said, "the implication is that his power is weakened over distance."

"Or he wants to be close to better savour our fear?" Theo looked around the group. "Harming Annie will not provide the satisfaction he craves. He needs to witness her suffering."

Annie frowned. "What if he needs to lure us, or me, close, because he can only operate under specific conditions?"

Pacer cocked her head. *What are you suggesting, My Lady? That his environment controls his strength or weakness? Like a sunflower following the path of the sun? Or birds who migrate with the seasons?*

"From what the trees shared with me, I believe he avoids sunlight." Vert took a deep breath and clasped his hands. "He hunted Elanrah across the world, but only during the hours of darkness. He hid from the sun, and he launched his attack in the depths of night, while she was weak." Vert choked back his tears. "That might also partially explain why he has shielded Kingston, to filter the light."

"But Roic said the people coming and going noticed naught," Netta said. "A permanently dark city would surely disquiet them?"

Theo held up a hand. "I have read texts where scholars claim the theoretical ability to split light. Don't ask, because I don't remember the details, but there is a possibility Draqshet is filtering only the part of light harmful to him. This may provide the key to his weakness. Do we know a scholar, a scientist?"

Netta and Annie grinned at each other. "Lady Xarah!"

Jenny quailed in the gloom of the Audience Chamber. Two nights and two days of relentless searching had failed to produce results, and The Most High Lord Draqshet's displeasure throbbed through the emptiness.

"No, My Lord. We haven't yet found them."

The Dark Lord's breathing rasped loudly as he arranged and rearranged the folds of his cloak. "I do not tolerate failure or ineptitude. You have one more day. Do not disappoint me."

Sneeth sniggered from a shadowy corner.

"Do not think I am unaware of the games you play, Sneeth. I trusted you above all others, but you lied. You knowingly allowed my prey to escape. You, too, will suffer my displeasure if you fail to return the men. Your punishment will be greater than hers. She demonstrated ineptitude, but your betrayal was deliberate."

CHAPTER SIXTEEN

Theo wrapped an arm around Annie to transport them both, as quick-as-thought, to Lady Xarah's mountain hideaway.

"Try not to fret, my love. Your shield covers a wide area. Our friends are safe."

"I don't believe we'll be truly safe until we vanquish Draqshet," Annie said. "But I feel better, now we are taking action. Lady Xarah is the most learned person I know."

"Close your eyes, it helps stop the dizziness," Theo said. "Now you can open them."

Lady Xarah's home was exactly as Annie remembered, and the tall woman gliding to meet them hadn't aged a day.

"I've consulted many texts overnight, and I think we can construct a weapon of intense light. Such a weapon will not kill The Dark Lord, but will, I believe, incapacitate him. Come into the library."

"Will this weapon of light hurt anyone else?" Annie asked.

"You must understand, Annie, this is experimental. I wouldn't recommend looking directly at the weapon when you unleash the energy, it could cause temporary blindness. Prolonged exposure could cause severe burns."

"Would heavy clothing protect us?" Theo asked.

"I cannot say with certainty, My Lord. But I would recommend covering your eyes. What do you know about Draqshet's physical characteristics?"

"We have no definite information," Annie said, "but we know he is always heavily robed and wears a deep hood. Even so, he waited until nighttime to rescue his newborn child. He wouldn't risk the desert sun," Annie said.

"Most dark dwelling creatures have limited vision," Lady Xarah said. "Some are completely blind, and yet others rely on different senses, heightened hearing or smell. You would do well to assume he possesses these gifts."

"I remember the first time I rode on your back, Lord Roic," Netta said, as she settled into a convenient depression at the base of the dragon's neck. "Either stay and risk being raped and sold into slavery by rogue D'Nasians, or go with you and risk being eaten. Terror froze my limbs, and Annie had to shove me up. You weren't as big back then."

We have both grown, Mistress Netta. You are stronger and more confident. Your far-sight and far-hearing may give us more information about what is happening under Draqshet's shield. Roic launched himself into the cloudless sky.

André, his hand clasped around the hilt of his sword, stared into the vastness long after his wife and their dragon friend disappeared from sight.

Netta marvelled at the autumnal colours spread below. She thrilled at the signs of a successful harvest, an assurance of a comfortable winter. The roads thronged with carts and wagons, laden with produce of every imaginable variety.

The festival scene disappeared under a shield of mist. Roic circled high over the capital, while Netta strained to see or hear. Kingston had disappeared, as though torn from the fabric of reality.

"Take us back to camp, Roic. We are wasting our time and peering into the void is making me sick and dizzy." As soon as they landed, Netta puked into the nearest bushes.

Are you unwell?

"Draqshet's foul magic churns my stomach."

You've encountered foul enchantments before and slain fell serpents without qualms.

Netta shrugged. "I'm older, with more to lose." She placed a hand on her belly and finger-drummed a response to the heartbeat only she could yet hear.

~

Annie checked the protective shield before lighting the campfire.

Netta shuddered. "When I looked, I felt I was peering into a bottomless pit. There was naught to fix my sights upon. But the people below remained unaffected. I think we need to see the city from ground level."

"Lady Xarah was confident she could make a weapon of light," Annie said. "She couldn't say it would kill Draqshet, but would at least render him helpless."

"He deserves to die, after what he did to Elanrah." Vert whispered.

"He will," Theo said. "We will find a way."

Roic huffed. *Did Lady Xarah say how long she needs to produce this weapon?*

Annie shook her head. "She promised to contact us when she has a prototype. A few days."

The Most High Lord Draqshet hunched atop the throne in the nearly empty Audience Chamber. The hastily bricked-up windows lacked beauty, but in the cloying darkness, nobody complained, because The Master took perverse delight in spoiling what was previously lovely.

Jenny and Sneeth knelt at Draqshet's feet, but as far apart as possible without incurring The Dark Lord's further displeasure, or straying beyond the glow of the single shaded candle allowed in his presence.

"Jenny, delicate little Jenny. You have disappointed me and I must devise a fitting punishment, one which will serve as a warning to others. Sneeth has yearned for this moment since he first saw you, but you will not become his reward, for he too shall feel the weight of my wrath." Draqshet gouged deep wounds in the gilded arms of the throne and revealed the wood beneath the gold.

Mesmerised, Jenny watched Draqshet shred the naked timber with his terrible talons, and her skin crawled.

"Do you still remember when I rescued you, Jenny?"

Mouth too dry to speak, Jenny nodded. Her earliest memory involved Draqshet scooping her into his arms. Before that, she recalled only cold and darkness.

"Almost dead, locked in a lightless chamber. Unloved and forgotten. I saved you from an ignominious death. I brought you back from the brink and gave you power over death. What do you think would happen if I recreated that miserable prison? Would you eventually wink out of existence, a blessing, or would you linger for eternity, cursed and unable to die?"

The words slithered from Draqshet's lips like vipers, crawling over Jenny's skin, boring holes in her veneer of control, and injecting the poison of fear deep into her core. Trembling with terror, Jenny focused all of her willpower on not collapsing. She drew strength from Sneeth's rapid breathing, and his disappointment at being denied a new toy.

Draqshet turned his attention to the winged creature.

"Not only have you disappointed me, but you coldly and deliberately betrayed me. You insulted me by assuming your intelligence surpassed mine. I tolerate no insult, but especially not from you. My son."

The darkness intensified, and the silence thickened, choking the kneeling supplicants.

"Father?" Sneeth forced out the word before it strangled him. His arms reached out in the darkness, but he snatched them back, huddling in to himself. "You speak true?"

"I am not the one guilty of lying," Draqshet rasped. "What does it profit me to claim such a miserable creature as my spawn? I tell you only so you may better appreciate the depths of my disappointment."

Jenny concentrated on the solitary candle, guttering in a pool of wax between herself and Sneeth. A fragile flicker of hope in the enveloping obscurity where Draqshet dwelt.

"Consider yourselves confined to your quarters until I decide how to deal with you."

The prisoners shuffled backwards from the throne, Jenny carrying the flame. Blank-faced Dolls lifted them to their feet and escorted them to their rooms.

Jenny paced back and forth, worrying at Draqshet's words, seeking to extract the marrow of hidden meaning like a street dog gnawing a dry bone. That Sneeth is his son is shocking, but why share the secret now? A message for me to step lightly? To warn me that The Most High Lord will not tolerate his son being ousted? In which case, Draqshet cannot mean to return me to eternal night? Or mayhap he wishes to see me with my hopes raised, the better to dash them? Jenny clenched and unclenched her fists, as frustration and fear warred within her breast. Does The Dark Lord mean to warn me I will fare far worse than his previously unacknowledged son? Jenny paused. Draqshet may be sending Sneeth a message which is naught to do with me. Perhaps the point was to humiliate the miserable creature before a witness? One expects mistreatments from a Master, but to be ill-treated by a parent? That's a deeper degree of abuse.

Sneeth huddled in the darkest corner of his apartment, wings wrapped around himself for comfort. Two words thundered in his head: my son. The Master was cruel, but always cruelty based on a sharp barb of truth, never a dull lie.

The scorched and scarred creature quivered under an onslaught of unfamiliar emotions. All his memories revolved around learning to please The Dark Lord, with nary the slightest hint of a paternal relationship or affection on either side. Draqshet deliberately inspired fear, but Sneeth experienced a surge of loathing, not only for his newly discovered Father, but for the woman who bore witness to his shame. The woman who had inspired his treachery. The woman he held responsible for this new humiliation.

Draqshet only ever appeared heavily robed. The only clues to his appearance were his vicious talons, glowing red eyes, and infrequent chitinous rustles when he rearranged his limbs.

Sneeth stood and unfurled his wings to examine himself. Not as tall as Father, but with the same deadly claws. Is that all we have in common?

What, or who, was my mother, other than a worthless strumpet, who abandoned me? No doubt as unworthy of Father's attention as Jenny has proven to be.

Jenny woke drenched in cold sweat and panting in terror. She scrambled backwards until she struck her skull against the wall, the sharp pain slamming her back into the present. Gasping for breath, she sought with blind fingers for the candle. The flame wavered before gathering strength, the sphere of pale light making the night blacker.

She'd been running, pursued by a merciless monster. The creature lurked in city squares, forcing her out into the fields, through tangled jungles and finally driving her towards the drifting dunes of the desert. Hunted to exhaustion, she'd collapsed on the shifting sands. Jenny jolted from her nightmare as the monster reached for her.

None of that was real, I was only dreaming. She shook out the damp sheets and climbed back into bed, relying on the fragile flame to deter further dreams. She clutched the linens with desperate fingers, eyes wide, but the nightmare returned, dragging her into murky somnolent depths.

The desert night imploded, folded in on itself, and pressed her into blessed oblivion. Dawn crept slowly over the dunes, fearful of what it might find. Fingers of light touched her, and she curled away, flinching from the memory. The harsh sunlight rekindled her horror and humiliation.

Fists bunched and knees bent, she screamed her revulsion,

forcing the abomination out and onto the sand where it lay, mewling and unaware of the crime of its existence.

Filled with fury, she bathed the vileness in fire, and fled the scene of her violation.

Jenny woke screaming.

Jenny and Sneeth cowered before the seat of power, awaiting The Master's judgement.

The Dark Lord smiled his grim satisfaction. The woman had rejected him and denied their son, but now she relived the memories. His gift to her. Had she accepted his suit, he would have worshipped at her feet, but now she knelt before him.

"I trust you slept well, Jenny?"

Sensing a trick, Jenny remained silent with her head bowed. Encouraged by Jenny's reticence, Sneeth raised his head.

"Father?"

The Most High Lord Draqshet stared at his spawn, talons gouging ever deeper into the throne, neither giving nor denying the creature permission to speak.

"What happened to my Mother?"

"She abandoned you, left you to perish in the desert. You repulsed her."

Sneeth swallowed his next question. He had not expected to receive the blame for his mother's perfidy.

Draqshet's words filled Jenny with terror and dread. Was her dream of the hunted woman real? Was the mewling scotched scrap Sneeth?

"What would you do, if by some miracle, you could meet your Mother?" Draqshet vomited the question and Jenny closed her eyes.

Sneeth squirmed. "I would punish her, but first I would ask

her why she wouldn't love me. It's a mother's duty to love her children."

"Jenny? Do you not agree all children deserve to receive love from their Mothers?" Draqshet leaned forward. "Should a woman who deliberately abandons a newborn infant receive discipline?"

"My Lord," Jenny licked her lips, "extenuating circumstances may apply."

"Are you suggesting an innocent infant deserved to die?" Draqshet's robes rustled as he shifted on the throne, and the darkness pulsated with eager anticipation.

"No, My Lord." Jenny clamped her lips to prevent the burgeoning scream escaping.

"Tell my son why you engulfed him in flames and left him to die. Explain to my boy how you refused to acknowledge his existence and didn't recognise him when you met."

"Father?" Sneeth rose to his feet.

Draqshet pointed to Jenny. "Ask your Mother why she tried to kill you."

CHAPTER SEVENTEEN

In the tiny hidden room, the girls tittered and whispered as they applied the rank paste. Xanderamm submitted gracefully, but Harry muttered and fumed.

"Do you know who we are?" He grabbed the nearest girl by the wrist. "Do you recognise me?"

"Of course we do. You're Rose and your friend is Jasmine, you've been here for almost a year, but you are failures." She pulled her arm away. "It isn't your fault, sisters, you can't help being ugly. Lady Amora says you might even develop a devoted following in a country town. She says there's a market for broad-shouldered women in certain places."

The girls dissolved into a fit of giggling, as they expressed mock sympathy for their sisters' misfortune to be neither pretty nor delicate.

"Why does this have to smell bad? I am reminded of a back alley full of cats?"

The girls doubled over, tears of laughter running down their naturally smooth cheeks.

"Not even the hardest soldier endures such indignity,"

Harry muttered, as the girls gathered themselves together and scraped away the mess. He rubbed his chin. "I hope this grows back."

"Less than a moon cycle, you'll be a bear again," said the prettiest girl. "Being beautiful isn't easy. Much easier being a rough unpolished man."

The cosmetologists, as they called themselves, handed a narrow band of cloth to each man and ordered them to strip.

"Protect your modesty," the girls said in unison, hands over mouths to stifle their giggles. "This walnut oil will make your skin darker, but it stains everything, so you must remain standing. One of the security guards will come by later. He will show you how to tuck your parts away, to hide unladylike bulges."

Harry's hands flew to cover his genitals. "I'll not have another man touch me. It's unnecessary."

"Some men can't keep their hands to themselves, and being ugly offers no protection, so it is very necessary you not risk discovery. A dress would disadvantage you in a fight. It's no different from a physician," the girl said dismissively. "But if you're worried you might enjoy it..." She shrugged. "You're too old for him."

Xanderamm waggled his eyebrows, and Harry sighed.

"Tonight, you will dine with Lady Amora. You must remember, you only speak when spoken to, you keep your eyes downcast, and you never contradict a man, regardless of what inane twaddle he spouts."

Harry knew visiting a House of Pleasure might prove educational, but this was not the teaching he expected.

The Captain held out his arms and turned on the spot. "How do I look?"

"Like a triple skin girl," said the most forward cosmetologist.

Harry examined his swarthy arms. "What's wrong with my skin?"

The girl poked him in the chest. "You're a girl who only appears attractive after a man has imbibed a skinful, or in your ugly case, three skins. But you'll pass. Probably. With a veil. From a distance."

"I don't know whether you mean to insult or comfort me," Harry said. "We've spent all day, but I'm still not pretty enough?"

"I told you, it's difficult being a woman. We don't know how long you must maintain your disguise, so tomorrow we'll teach you both to apply your own cosmetics and to help each other dress."

Captain Harry fought not to rub his elaborately painted eyes. After a day of applying, removing, and reapplying makeup, his eyes burned, and he ached for a hot bath and a soft bed. His skin itched and he couldn't breathe properly in the constrictive clothing. A forced march over rough terrain was infinitely preferable to learning how to walk in heels and not trip over long skirts. Just as he was looking forward to scrubbing his face clean and crawling into bed, the cosmetologists announced the ultimate test. Harry wanted to weep.

Lady Amora's loyal personal guards arrived to escort her guests to dinner, as befitted fine ladies. The gentlemen bowed and smiled before offering their arms. Xanderamm immediately placed the tips of his fingers on his escort's sleeve. Harry copied, assuming the King had more experience taking ladies into dinner. Eyes watering with pain, Harry limped behind Xanderamm, managing only the tiniest of steps. Harry's high-heeled embroidered slippers embraced his feet with a fierce passion, unwilling to release their oversized prize. His escort nodded encouragement.

"Well done, Captain," Lady Amora said. "You managed to not walk like a navvy as you entered the room."

"Why the stone do women wear these instruments of torture?" Harry asked. "I can barely stand upright. I wouldn't have made it without leaning on Danny." He nodded at his escort, who smiled back.

"Many men find helpless women attractive," Lady Amora said. "Men are not entirely to blame; women also contribute to the narrative."

Harry and Xanderamm stared blankly, baffled by her words.

"Perfect! Keep that expression, unless a man is telling you how marvellous he is, in which case, try to look thoroughly enraptured by his brilliance. Avoid speaking."

"Master? Father? May I speak with you?" Sneeth grovelled on the floor at Draqshet's feet. "About the woman."

The Dark Lord sighed. "You desire to tear her apart? To rend her limb from tender limb? To bury your snout in her pulsing innards?"

"No, My Lord. She is my mother. Although it means naught to her, I have yet to decide what the relationship means to me. But I would see her confined, for I trust her not."

"I have already confined Jenny to her quarters, and she is well-guarded."

"You ought to chain her in the dungeons, revoke all the powers with which you gifted her. No returning from the dead, shape-shifting, or rising into the sky without wings." Sneeth fought the urge to stand, not daring to challenge the Master more openly.

"I hear you tremble before me, but your words are demanding. Not what I expect from a servant begging a favour." Draqshet leaned forward, his robes rustling like dead leaves. "Are you opposing my authority?"

"No, Master." The creature bit back the words jostling to escape, animal instincts urging silence as a means of self-preservation.

Draqshet watched his son cower before him, paying close attention to the tensed shoulders and the barely discernible flickers of movement in the tightly furled wings. The Dark Lord smiled at his son's barely contained agitation.

"Very well," Draqshet rasped into the gloom. "Escort her to the dungeons, incarcerate her as you see fit, but inflict no permanent damage. I may have further use for her."

Sneeth backed out of his father's presence, suppressing his elation lest The Dark Lord change his mind. The creature hurried to Jenny's apartments and entered without knocking. He gestured to the Doll guards who dragged her out of the suite, along corridors, and down stairs, which grew meaner and narrower the further they descended. The dungeon Sneeth selected was tiny, barely more than an upright coffin. A blank-faced Doll buckled a thick leather belt around her waist, to which he chained iron handcuffs and a neck collar. He shackled her to the wall before Sneeth dropped a leather hood over her head.

"There's naught for you to see, nor do I wish to look upon your face, Mother. You will find a slim ledge around the wall to prevent you slumping and choking yourself to death. Unlike you, I am merciful."

"What do you mean to do with me?" Jenny asked, her words indistinct under the hood.

"I have not yet decided. The discovery of a mother, even one who loathes me, is novel, an unexpected gift. I am gone from being an orphan to possessing a surfeit of parents. Albeit, only one who cares for me."

Sneeth gently closed the dungeon door, locking his mother into a silent and sightless torment. His steely control frightened her far more than his expected ravings.

She waited until only the beating of her heart and the blood coursing through her veins filled her ears. Not even the rocks groaned this far below the surface. Jenny wriggled, testing the boundaries of her restraints. The rough walls were as close as a lover's kiss and skimmed her goose-bumped skin. The collar and cuffs weighed her down, forcing her to seek the spurious relief of the ledge which cut into her thighs, stopping the blood flow to her feet.

Gritting her teeth, she forced herself upright, then deliberately allowed her knees to bend and dropped her head forward. She cracked her forehead against the door, the chain too long to strangle her. The hood slid against the door as she rubbed her head. She couldn't raise her hands from her waist, but she persisted in dragging the hood incrementally further by putting her head on the door and wriggling, then repeating the action.

She lost track of the number of times the hood slipped back down, but she persisted; she had naught else to do. Her hair was damp with sweat, and her cheeks wet with tears of frustration, when she flipped the hood down and caught it with her fingertips. The bucket shaped hood was smooth all round, no eye or mouth holes. Mayhap Sneeth intended to starve her to death? Her busy fingers found the long ties designed to secure the hood around the neck. An oversight that the Doll hadn't fastened them, or Sneeth offering her... what?

Jenny smoothed and folded the hood into a cushion, using one tie to make sure it stayed as arranged. The other tie she fixed to the leather belt which held her handcuffs. If her fingers fumbled, she would lose her one luxury. By delicate manoeuvring, Jenny placed the cushion on the vicious ledge and eased herself onto her seat. She ran the links of chain between her fingers like a string of perverted prayer beads.

She worried at the first link, tracing the rough weld. Her earliest memory surfaced; a powerful figure whisking her from a similar dungeon, infinitely dark and lonely. She could not recall the reason for her incarceration. Or who was responsible.

The second link was equally rough, made purely for strength, no thought spared for aesthetics. She rotated the link, scarred and pitted with time. Who or what had she been before The Dark Lord rescued and remade her?

The third link slid into her hand, a now familiar shape. Was she condemned to relive her punishment over and over, a chain of events she could not control or influence? Would Draqshet rescue, brain-wash, and incarcerate her in an eternal cycle?

Her fingers caressed the fourth link as she considered the woman in the desert and the blackened holocaust from which she fled. The iron weight of guilt dragged her hands to her lap. The innocent child deserved protection, not immolation. Jenny felt the terror take hold of her, squeezing her heart, and she trembled, desperate to escape, to run, to get away. An explosion of white light filled the stone walled coffin, blinding her. The effulgence remained in her inner eye after the flame burnt out.

Dazzled, Jenny fumbled for the fifth link. Like the woman in the desert, she had spontaneously created an intense burst of fire. Any lingering doubts she entertained about the identity of the woman in the desert seared away. Sneeth, the foul abomination who made her skin crawl, was her son. She was his mother.

CHAPTER EIGHTEEN

Danny and Paulie, their escorts from the previous evening, roused Xanderamm and Harry before dawn and hustled them into make-up, wigs, and veils.

"Try these." Danny held out two pairs of jewelled sandals. "They're mine." The golden slippers were a perfect fit, although higher heeled to retain the perfect proportion. "Don't worry, you won't need to walk anywhere, and if you need to run... you'll be better hoofing it barefoot."

Paulie adjusted their wigs and gowns before shoving them towards the stairs. "Remove your shoes until you get down. Remember, once you're in the wagon, don't say a word, keep your heads down and do exactly as you're told."

"We'll be going through the gates as soon as they open. Hopefully, we won't attract attention in all the commotion," Danny said.

Lady Amora met the fugitives beside the wagon. She glanced at their footwear and nodded her approval. "Danny and Paulie will drive the wagon and guard you. Don't think less of them because they like to sashay around in heels. They are my two best men. In a fight, they'd make mincemeat of your best men, Harry." She smiled. "Good luck to you both, ladies."

The covered wagon lurched and rolled to the gates, joining the short queue to leave. Harry and Xanderamm stared at one another, engulfed by genuine helplessness.

"I'm used to being the protector, not the protected," Harry whispered. "I feel sick to my stomach."

Danny turned round and frowned at the pair, putting a finger to his lips. "Button it, girls."

The wagon creaked and groaned as Paulie guided it through the gate where the Dolls apprehended them for inspection.

"What goods are you carrying?" A rote question, spoken without inflection.

Paulie jerked his thumb backwards. "The ugliest whores you've ever seen. Been in training for nigh on a year, but no bugger wants 'em. Gonna trade these dogs for a couple of kittens from another house."

A Doll lifted the canvas side of the wagon and gave a cursory look. "Should have drowned them ugly pups at birth," he muttered, dropping the cover. "Pass."

As the morning wore on the wagon's fashionable and weatherproof leather cover created a muggy atmosphere.

"Hey, can we pull back these curtains? It's stifling in here."

"Sorry, girls," Danny said. "Gotta keep the goods out of sight, for your own safety. Orders from Lady Amora. We can stop for refreshments at a respectable tavern and hire a private dining room. Stay veiled until we're inside."

Physically discomfited, Harry fumed over the Doll's casual insult until they pulled into the tavern yard.. "Cheeky bastard," Harry muttered, as he gracelessly clambered from the wagon. "My arse is prettier than that Doll's pock-marked face ever was."

Sneeth prepared a scroll for Brummagen and slithered into his apartment unannounced. The ex-Grand Vizier darted from the window, heart in his mouth.

"How may I serve you?" Brummagen bowed deeply, keeping his eyes averted.

Sneeth passed the scroll. "You will address the citizens and make clear to them the consequences of non-compliance."

Brummagen skimmed the contents of the declaration and blanched. "You're going to murder a prisoner each day the fugitives remain free? But what if the citizens know naught?"

Sneeth exposed his jagged teeth in a caricature of a smile. "They know something, and it is in your interests to persuade them to talk." Sneeth shrugged, his wings half unfurled. "But if I am mistaken in my judgement, then you are no further use to me."

Sparkling mullioned windows and a freshly thatched roof suggested a level of comfort. The tavern was cleaner than most and attracted a more affluent and discerning clientele. More silk merchants than turnip farmers. The public rooms were almost always empty. Dexter shook his head at the peculiar preference for securing private rooms to dine, as opposed to mingling with other travellers and merchants. Gossiping was the best way to gather news and opinions about current events.

The fancy wagon drew his attention. The heavily armed guards looked useful; the kind of men you'd want on your side in a brawl. Dexter watched the exchange between one guard and the owner of the tavern, who bobbed and nodded, before scurrying back inside. The veiled ladies who emerged from the confines of the wagon appeared unexpectedly robust, more like farm hands than refined gentlewomen. However, their guards treated them with great respect and ushered them swiftly into the tavern.

Dexter squinted in both directions, but the road remained stubbornly empty of traffic. The traders heading for the reopened city had passed earlier, eager to secure an advantageous position. None of the citizens with whom he'd struck up conversations admitted to knowing anything about Captain Harry's whereabouts, although one ladies' maid had expressed her indignation that the coward had scarpered at the first sign of trouble, leaving the town to the mercy of The Dolls.

Knowing wealthy ladies would refuse to acknowledge him, and expecting short shrift from the guards, Dexter decided a quick chat with the tavern kitchen-hands might be worthwhile. If they chased him and threw things, he hoped they'd be edible. Martha's provisions were long gone, along with his coin.

"I'll groom the horses for a meal," he called to the wench chopping vegetables.

She looked him up and down, paring knife by her waist. "I've seen you lurking around, talking to people. What're you looking for?"

"My friend. I was expecting him to come this way, but I'm starting to think I've missed him."

"Stay away from them horses. They belong to Lady Amora, and her guards are very particular who touches their outfit. They'll have your guts for garters if you get too close. Tell you what, handsome. Chop that pile of wood and I'll make a packet of bread and cheese to see you on your way. I'll throw in some apples for the horse, too. Yours, is it?"

"He's not stolen property, if that's what you mean."

"A bit strange, an expensive beast like that, ridden by a man begging for his dinner."

Dexter shrugged. "Not everything is as it seems, mistress."

"None of my business. Chop the wood and you can wash up at the pump by the trough."

The wood was still green and the axe sharp. Dexter worked quickly and efficiently under the appreciative eye of the kitchen girl. He was dousing himself under the pump when the guards escorted the ladies back to the covered wagon.

One of the fine ladies stopped in her tracks and grabbed the other, pointing to Dexter. The kitchen girl giggled to herself. Doubtless, the woodchopper was a fine specimen, but well-bred ladies usually showed more restraint. The guards hustled the women into the wagon before one went to talk to the water-sodden beggar.

"Are you Dexter? You're wanted."

Dexter pulled his jerkin over his head, playing for time. His ride was tethered out of reach, and he didn't fancy his chances against these two. "I'm not Dexter, you've made a mistake."

"Nobody's who they say they are today, but the lady claims she knows you. It'd be rude not to come and say hello." The guard grabbed Dexter by the arm and propelled him to the rear of the wagon.

The veiled ladies peered expectantly at him, their gossamer swathed bosoms heaving with excitement.

Dexter stepped back, straight into the chiselled masonry-hard chest of the guard.

"Dexter! It's me. Harry."

Dexter's jaw dropped and his eyes grew wide as the familiar deep voice boomed out, and a hard hand shot forward to grip his shoulder.

"Harry? Is that you? Are you under an enchantment? We'll get you to Lady Annie, she'll save you."

"We're only in disguise, me and King Xanderamm. But we still need to reach Annie."

Dexter's knees buckled, a combination of shock, relief, and hunger. He grabbed the back of the wagon to support himself. "I worried I'd missed you, or you were dead."

"We're attracting too much attention." Harry glanced at the kitchen maid. "Follow us."

Dexter watched the wagon roll out of the tavern yard before collecting his bread and cheese.

"I hope you find your friend."

"I'm sure I'll catch up with him, somewhere down the road."

CHAPTER NINETEEN

Dexter cantered after the wagon until Danny flagged him down on a secluded stretch of road and pointed through the brambles towards the stationary vehicle. Dexter dismounted and led his ride through the partially denuded trees, and over the fallen leaves thick underfoot.

Harry and his friend still wore feminine disguises. The only concession allowed by the guards was the removal of veils. The Captain pressed a bag of coins into Dexter's hand.

"If we stay with the wagon, we must remain in costume; too many people have already seen us. But we'll travel faster by horse. Buy two mounts, and men's clothing. Not bothered about the clothes, but find quality rides."

"What about them?" Dexter jerked his chin at the guards.

"Don't worry about Danny and Paulie. They're more than capable. They've agreed to help us when we return."

As soon as Dexter headed towards the next town on his mission, Danny and Paulie showed Harry the wagon's secret compartments.

"I'd have never guessed," he said, running appreciative fingers over the daggers and swords.

Danny grinned. "Doesn't matter now, but you'd be shocked how much untaxed merchandise passed your men, vigilant as they were. This wagon is full of surprises; a few pretty faces, and a flash of flesh, didn't do any harm. Men." Danny pursed his lips and tossed his hair. "They're all so bloody predictable."

All four burst into laughter. Harry recovered first.

"I might not have the opportunity later to say meeting you was an honour. The courage you've shown on this mission is exemplary, and I'd be proud to count you as friends."

Paulie grabbed him and swung him in a full body hug. "Promise me one thing, Captain. No more heels. Frankly, you're an embarrassment."

"That's a deal."

Harry and Xanderamm made their weapon selections, marvelling at the workmanship. They risked kicking off their shoes and practicing barefoot. Danny and Paulie gave no quarter, and the fugitives were soon breathless and signalled capitulation.

"You only won because we're in skirts," Harry puffed.

Danny smirked. "We won because we're better."

"If ever you're looking for work..."

"Captain, we won't be looking for work. King Xanderamm has made us rich beyond our wildest dreams. Trust me, they can be wild," Danny said. "But if you ever you need a hand, we're here. You have our word."

Xanderamm doubled over, snorting with laughter, in a decidedly unladylike fashion.

"What?" Harry frowned. "What's so funny?"

At sunset, Dexter returned, leading a beautiful pair of saddled mares. He chucked the bundle of masculine attire to Harry.

"These ladies are sisters, grown up together, so they'll travel well together. The man I bought them from admired my horse, paid a lot of attention, asked a lot of questions." Dexter shrugged. "Not sure how far I could trust him, so I gave him some waffle about taking two town ladies on safari in D'Nasa. Told him we'd be hunting leopards. He recommended these gorgeous girls. Said they were good tempered, to which I can attest myself, and he claimed they have exceptional stamina."

Harry looked at Xanderamm. "Are you comfortable riding through the night? No need to go hard, but I'd feel better getting some distance covered."

Xanderamm nodded and reached for the bundle of clothes.

"We'll head back to town in the morning," Paulie said. "Sane people don't drive wagons through the night."

While Harry and Xanderamm wiped their faces and changed their clothes, Danny helped Dexter wrap the horse's hooves in heavy leather.

"Won't last forever, naught ever does." Danny winked at Dexter. "But they'll help you through the night a little quieter. Go easy."

CHAPTER TWENTY

"I wasn't expecting you back so soon." Lady Amora's heavy skirts skimmed the unswept cobblestoned stable-yard. "Did all go well?"

Danny jumped from the wagon. "We met someone the ladies knew, so after a fast change, they galloped off into the night, promising to return with help."

"Most of the servants and all the girls have gone," Lady Amora said. "You're free to take your share of the King's treasure and leave, while you still can. Take the wagon."

"What? Leave you unprotected?" Paulie looked around the stable yard, noting the empty stalls. "Surely you know us better than that?"

"I take it things have taken a turn for the worse? Or was it the lure of treasure?" Danny put his hand on Lady Amora's wrist. "We're not leaving without you. You supported us over the years, we'll support you."

"The Dolls are still searching for the fugitives," she said. "I haven't seen a real soldier since the night of the charity ball, and the town elite are still missing. Nobody knows for sure if they're dead or alive, but that awful man made another announcement after you left, threatening consequences if someone doesn't turn in the fugitives."

"What sort of consequences?" Danny asked, unloading cases.

"The little shit was mumbling, seemed scared to death. I missed half of what he said, but the gist was Sneeth would begin sacrificing people. The Dark Lord does not tolerate dissent."

"Nasty," Danny said. "But I assume he means to start with the elite? Which means they're still alive."

"Fortunate the girls got away when they did," Paulie picked up the luggage. "Can't imagine any of them resisting physical threats for too long."

Lady Amora led the way back into the house. "I feel so useless. What can I do?"

"Gather information," Danny said. "Captain Field and the King will return. We promised our help. We need to discover everything possible about this new Lord and his pissant puppets."

"How well guarded are the barracks, or are they relying on fear?" Paulie raised his eyebrows. "If we could free the soldiers, we could form a resistance movement."

"The Dolls easily overcame the soldiers," Lady Amora said.

"True, but that was in a fair fight," Paulie said. "When they thought the Dolls still retained part of what made them genuine people. We know they fight on after they're wounded, but I bet they'd not survive fire."

"I knew a sailor once. Claimed he could make a sticky fire that's impossible to extinguish." Danny drummed his fingers on the table. "I might still have the recipe tucked away with his love letters. He promised some old twaddle about his love for me burning forever. Until he met a younger, prettier lad with sea-blue eyes to drown in."

"Ouch. That must have hurt," Paulie said.

Danny shrugged. "I felt better after holding his head in a bucket of water. The pain eased when the bubbles stopped."

The gardens of the Pleasure House offered seclusion, and mature spreading trees offered shade. Lady Amora wore a heavy leather apron as she stirred the resinous concoction with a long wooden paddle. "Are you sure we need quick lime?"

"Chuck water on this and the lime makes it burn even fiercer, My Lady." Danny stood downwind as he emptied the sack into the cauldron. "Once it's afire, ain't no way to extinguish the flames. Perfectly safe until you light it, only don't get it on your clothes."

Lady Amora wiped a glaze of perspiration from her brow, and Paulie took the paddle from her.

"My turn," he said. "You must be a lot stronger than you look."

"I'm motivated, Paulie. I object to these... people... thinking they can take over and run amok in my town. I don't know them or what they want, but I refuse to stand by and see my friends suffer. And it's rather exciting, isn't it?"

Lady Amora and the guards ladled the mixture into fist-sized, cork stoppered, clay containers, and tied a length of fuse around the jar necks. They filled crate after straw-lined crate, ready for storage in the secret tunnels.

"We ought to test them before committing to a proper mission," Lady Amora said.

"Not here," Danny said. "Too dangerous. Out of the city, somewhere isolated, and preferably rocky."

"We could take a picnic to The Demon's Swimming Hole," Paulie said. "Hide the missiles under a bit of cold meat and pickles. I'd like to see if it's true, what they say about this stuff burning under water."

～

Lady Amora drove her carriage drawn by a matched pair of dappled grey ponies through the city gates, accompanied by two mounted and liveried guards. She decided they were safer with individual means of transportation if plans went awry.

The Demon's Swimming Hole received few visitors at this time of year, and they found no evidence of recent foot or wheel tracks. The group of conspirators continued over the sand and up onto the rocky plateau, from which cascaded the waterfall, to foam into the stony bowl below.

Danny and Paulie cleared a barn-sized area of debris, while Lady Amora unpacked the picnic. Paulie carried the crate of combustibles and Danny offered his arm to Lady Amora.

"We've set up some targets," Danny said. "Watch what we do first, then your turn."

Paulie hefted a clay container and swapped the stopper for the fuse. Danny struck a sulphur stick, lit the fuse, and Paulie flung the container. The pot smashed against the bundle of twigs, and the gelatinous mixture flowed over the makeshift target.

For a heartbeat, naught happened, and Lady Amora opened her mouth to express disappointment.

Then the fuse reached the mixture, and a ball of fire exploded. Intense white flames reduced the wood to ashes, then consumed the ashes, leaving only a blackened smudge on the rocks.

"Fuse was too long," Danny muttered as he sliced the next

cord in half. "Better if it explodes on impact. Don't want the Dolls to learn they can put out the blasted fuse." He pushed Paulie and Lady Amora back. "Too risky on a short fuse." He prepared the container, struck the sulphur stick, lit the fuse, and lobbed the jar in one fluid movement.

The clay pot shattered, splattering the resinous mixture, and the burning fluid crawled greedily over the target, consuming every particle. The conspirators cheered and whooped their approval.

"My turn," Lady Amora said. "How long?" She held out the fuse for Danny to shorten it, but he shook his head.

"First throw with a long fuse. Need to be sure you're accurate before we make you deadly," Danny said.

She shrugged. "That means I get two throws. Lucky me." Lady Amora's aim, like her taste in costumes, was impeccable.

Paulie pulled a half-dead branch from a tree and poured the contents of a jar over the leafy end. "Watch this," he said, setting fire to the dry end. He stood on the waterfall precipice, holding the smouldering branch over the sheer drop. He let the branch fall, and they watched it explode into fierce flames before it hit the water, where the conflagration continued to burn white hot, churning the foaming water to a bubbling froth. The branch sank slowly, but the white fire remained visible until it utterly consumed the entire branch.

"Well, Paulie," Lady Amora said, "I think you proved conclusively that sticky fire burns underwater." She led them back to the picnic. "Have you considered how we could utilise fuses of different lengths?" She looked at the guards as she handed round the food. "A short fuse, flung with accuracy, is instantaneously deadly, but what about leaving pots with longer fuses? In places we knew the Dolls would congregate? Do they eat and sleep? Do they bathe? We could take out dozens at a time if we plan properly."

~

Lady Xarah tied on her eye protectors and pressed the red crystal button. A mushroom of white light burst from the device, illuminating every nook and corner of her study, eliminating all shadows. She nodded her satisfaction and switched off her invention. The light faded slowly, like midsummer dusk reluctantly giving way to the nighttime. Dropping her eye protection in her pocket, she gathered a second, differently shaped prototype from her desk, left the house, and headed up the mountain.

The moonless night was the perfect opportunity to test her gadgets. She placed the device she'd tested in her study on a flat rock and pressed the button. The light exploded, filling the wide glade and invading the surrounding trees. The fountain of light flowed under and over obstacles, cascading down the mountain. Within a heartbeat, the valley was awash with light brighter than the midday sun, swarming in all directions, vanquishing shadows. The range was wide enough to drown an entire city in blazing light.

Pleased with her first success, Lady Zarah allowed the night to reclaim the forested valley. The second device was tubular, and she hoped would produce different results. She selected a newly dead tree with a girth five men would struggle to encompass. The beam of energy she released was as slender as a maiden's finger and slashed through the hardwood trunk like steel through curds. Startled by her achievement, Lady Xarah inspected the toppled tree. The cut felt as smooth as well polished furniture. She offered a silent promise to the tree not to waste its flesh, but to give it new life as building material or a carriage, an artefact both admirable and useful.

Lady Xarah turned her attention to a boulder. She aimed and fired; the blade of light shattered the rock to dust particles.

She selected another boulder and discovered if she swiped like a sword, she could shave away slivers of stone. This was a weapon Annie would appreciate.

Annie, Theo, please come immediately. I have something to show you. Lady Xarah hurried back down the mountain to find Annie and Theo waiting expectantly on her porch. After Lady Xarah collected two more pairs of eye protectors, Theo transported all three of them back to the mountaintop for a demonstration.

"This light bends around objects," Annie said, filled with awe. "Draqshet will have nowhere to hide."

"Depending on his sensitivity to light, I'm not sure how much damage the light will cause. I doubt it will affect his Army of Dolls. But you'll like this, My Lady," Xarah said. She pointed to the felled forest giant. "One pass with this weapon brought it down." She pointed to the pulverised boulders. "Light reduced a boulder to dust, but I discovered if you approach the target from the side, you can carve it like a festival roast."

Annie's eyes widened. "You smashed granite to powder? With light?"

Xarah showed Annie how to hold the device. "If you hold the button down, the light will continue cutting through whatever is in its path. Brief bursts are safer."

Annie pointed directly at a melon sized rock. "A direct hit will pulverise the stone?"

Lady Zarah nodded, and Annie fired. A ball of granite dust drifted on the breeze, the only evidence the rock had existed.

Annie pulled off her eye protectors. "How many of these weapons do you have?"

"These are the only two prototypes. I wanted to ensure they worked properly before making more." Lady Xarah looked at the stars as she made her calculations. "This is not a device I will entrust lightly. By dawn, without interruptions, I can manufacture one each for you two, André and Netta, and Vert. You will need to practise before engaging with an adversary. They give you an advantage, but will not make you invincible."

Theo wrapped an arm around each woman, transporting them as fast-as-thought back to Lady Xarah's study. Hair thin wires and exquisitely cut crystals jostled for space on the desk, alongside partially constructed models.

Annie put her hands behind her back and leaned closer. "I can discern the patterns, it's an elegant weaving of energy. I can help."

Lady Xarah hesitated. "You risk blowing us all to smithereens if you make an error. But you are famous for your clever fingers and attention to detail. Watch first."

Lady Xarah worked quickly and efficiently, but Annie easily anticipated how the components fitted together. Theo watched the women manipulate microscopic parts, memorising each detail. His fingers lacked the delicacy for such finessed work, but his mind grasped the mechanics.

Seeing his disappointment, Lady Xarah set him to work assembling eye protectors. "Construct as many as you can, the lenses are delicate, so I expect you'll break a few. Your followers will need protection, too."

By dawn, Xarah and Annie had completed five sun-bombs and seven individual light weapons. Theo had filled a sack with dozens of eye protectors.

"As skilled swordsmen, you and André may possess the skill to handle two weapons at a time," Lady Xarah said, "although one seems enough destructive power for any individual to wield."

CHAPTER TWENTY-ONE

Sneeth interrogated the Dolls and received the usual vacant stare and monotone responses. Blank-faced and empty-headed, the Dolls had recognised no leads and lacked the cognitive abilities to make deductions. The fugitives continued to elude capture, and the creature cringed. Lack of results had already stretched the Master's patience membrane thin.

On the third day after Brummagen's declaration, Sneeth had no choice but to show the citizens Draqshet would tolerate their intransigence no longer. He ignored the rank odours of death and defecation swilling through the dungeons as he made his selections. After a week of captivity and only intermittent food and water, the prisoners lacked the energy even to cower. He reminded himself mere mortals required daily care, or they expired.

"You two." Sneeth gestured to a pair of guards. "Henceforth, you are responsible for the welfare of the prisoners. You will provide fresh food and water each day. You will flush away their waste and remove any dead bodies. Do you understand?"

"Sir, yes Sir!" The guards stared unseeing into the mid-distance.

"Get to it, you addle-pated imbeciles. Now." Sneeth fumed his frustration. No wonder the Dolls couldn't locate the fugitives. He doubted they could find their own cocks with both hands. He returned to his study of the prisoners. Should he sacrifice a stronger one whose screams would be louder and last longer, or save those for later, and use the feeblest before they died and lost all potential value?

He settled on a young woman, and what he assumed was her child. The two clung together, as though proximity lent them strength. A concept far removed from his experience. The snot-nosed infant whimpered all the way to the battlements, jangling Sneeth's nerves. He shoved the victims into a cage where they crouched together, trembling. Sneeth nodded for a Doll to sound the bugle, summoning the town's inhabitants to attend. When a sufficiently sized audience had reluctantly assembled, Sneeth commanded the Dolls to swing the cage out on a beam where it swayed at the end of a creaking chain. Dispensing with Brummagen's irritating and reluctant services, Sneeth addressed the crowd directly.

"I gave you ample opportunity to deliver the fugitives. You failed to cooperate, forcing me to sacrifice this young widow and her helpless babe. Look at the misery you have caused. For what purpose? To protect a pair of dangerous criminals who care not for your safety or wellbeing? Unless you deliver the fugitives, you will be responsible for two more sacrificial deaths tomorrow."

The crowd muttered, but none stepped forward with information. But nor had they the courage to protest the wanton cruelty. They dispersed more quickly than they assembled, driven by helpless whimpers.

Sneeth watched jealously from the shadows as the crows

fluttered to the cage, thrusting beaks into still warm flesh and swooping away with their stolen prizes. Blood dripped from the cage onto the cobblestones, staining the pavement with guilt.

"If Lady Annie and Lord Theo left Salvation Valley the same day as you, we ought to have intercepted them by now." Harry scuffed dirt over their campfire.

"Unless Lord Theo performed his faster-than-thought magic," Dexter said. "But if they'd gone straight to the capital, we'd have heard about it from the traders. Unless they're also in disguise?"

"Sooner or later, they'll go to Kingston," Harry said. "I see naught to gain traipsing about the countryside. We're going back."

"The Dolls are still searching for the pair of you." Dexter jerked his chin at Xanderamm. "By now, there's likely a bounty on your heads."

"But they're not looking for you, Dex. You could get a message to Lady Amora."

Xanderamm grabbed Harry's arm, shaking his head. He pulled Harry down and sketched an outline of the city in the dirt, marking the palace, the barracks, and the marketplace.

"This is Kingston?" Dexter crouched next to him. "The gates are here, here, here, and here." Dexter marked the roads into the capital.

Xanderamm grinned and waggled his eyebrows. He stuck a finger deep into the dirt, making a distinct hole next to the wall. He repeated the action near the barracks, then mimed diving into the hole near the wall and surfacing from the one near the barracks.

"There's a tunnel under the wall?" Harry sat back on his haunches.

"How do you know?" Dexter asked.

Xanderamm clutched at his heart and fluttered his eyes, before rolling on the ground in silent laughter.

"I believe," Harry said, "our ex-King used the tunnels to leave the city on secret romantic trysts. No doubt there is a smattering of Royal bastards among the local peasants."

Dexter stared at Xanderamm. "I'd heard rumours, but I thought them a load of old codswallop."

"Are they as well built as the tunnel to Lady Amora's house?" Harry asked.

Xanderamm nodded, serious again.

The three men rode steadily throughout the day, each wrapped in their own concerns.

Dexter cast surreptitious glances at the ex-King. His reputation as an arrogant and selfish monarch didn't match the strange man riding alongside him, who paid close and respectful attention to all he saw and heard, and who frequently nodded approval or understanding at new developments and initiatives.

Xanderamm hoped the tunnels remained undiscovered and intact, and that the citizens were safe. His guts churned at the possibility of Draqshet wreaking his revenge upon them because he'd escaped. He wondered if Brummagen was still alive, and in what capacity he served The Dark Lord. Xanderamm glanced at Harry, asking himself how such a man had escaped his previous notice, then blushed with the realisation that he would have ridiculed Harry for the very qualities he now admired.

Harry pondered how to use the tunnels to their advantage. Getting in and out of the city unnoticed opened a range of enticing possibilities. Mayhap they could smuggle out citizens, or they could harass the Dolls using guerrilla tactics? Three men posed no threat to an army, but they could chip away until Annie and Theo arrived.

They camped beside a stream and prepared to bed down when the night sky blazed brighter than day.

Harry leapt to his feet, sword in hand, while Xanderamm and Dexter scrambled from their blankets, fumbling for weapons. Eyes streaming, they squinted in search of aggressors. Dexter stumbled towards the panicked horses, muttering soothing noises. He pulled their saddle blankets over their eyes, which helped calm them almost as much as his mumbled ministrations.

The light faded, receding like floodwaters. Harry and Xanderamm stood back to back, circling as they searched. Xanderamm jabbed an elbow backwards at Harry and pointed to a patch of light fading behind a low range of hills.

"The sun doesn't set in that direction," Harry said. "Whatever it is, it isn't natural. I must investigate."

Dexter saddled and soothed the horses while Harry and Xanderamm broke camp. They rode almost to the crest of the hill before dismounting and tethering their mounts. They crawled like desert lizards to the ridge and spied five distant figures in the depression before them.

Then the rock beside Xanderamm's head exploded.

CHAPTER TWENTY-TWO

"Something moved." Netta strained her far-sight in the gloaming. "I think I hit an animal. Theo, take me up there. I need to put it out of its misery if it's still alive."

"I'll come, too," Annie said. "Mayhap I can heal the poor beast if it's not too badly injured."

Theo embraced the women. "Close your eyes. You'll be less dizzy. We're here."

The trio stumbled on the uneven ground of the ridge as they tripped over a bloodied man and his companions.

"Who are you, and what is your business?" Theo asked, stepping in front of his friends.

"Lord Theo?"

"Dexter? I thought you were returning to Kingston?" Theo said.

"Explanations later," Annie said, "give me room." She knelt next to the bleeding man and pulled his hands from his face. "Keep your eyes closed. I need to remove the particles before I heal your injured flesh."

The man moaned, either in pain or in response to her

instructions, but he submitted to Annie's ministrations without flinching. She then turned to the victim's unidentified companion, who was blindly plucking shards from his cheek and shoulder.

"Hold still," Annie said. "This won't take long."

"Yes, My Lady."

"Harry? Is that Captain Harry?" Annie touched his cheek. "First things first. Let me fix you up, then we'll get everybody back to camp and you can tell us what you're doing out here."

With a flick of her wrist, Annie expelled the stinging shards of stone from Harry's torn flesh and a soothing wave of healing restored the perforated skin. She performed the same exercise on Dexter, who fidgeted under her ministrations, his attention distracted by whickers and snorts from over the ridge.

"My Lady, the horses? I'm not sure if they're physically hurt, but they're distressed and might harm themselves if I don't calm them."

Annie nodded. "Theo? Take Netta and these men to camp, then return for me and their horses?"

"As you wish, my love."

They disappeared in a whirl of dust, and Annie skipped down to greet the horses. Dexter's destrier, as aggressive as always, reached to bite her. The two mares stamped and twitched their distress, but exhibited better manners. Annie sent a gentle wash of soothing energy over all three, healing any scrapes and scratches.

"Impressive beasts," Theo said as he arrived by her side. He grabbed the three sets of reins, wrapped an arm around his wife, and transported the group to camp, where their guests were peering around, dazed and confused.

"I've never become used to moving as fast-as-thought," Netta said, guiding them towards the campfire, hands clasped over her belly, "and it still makes me queasy."

Theo tethered the guests' mounts next to their own, taking a moment to give them water and forage, before joining the group.

"I have fed and watered the horses, even your bad-tempered mount, Dexter." Theo patted his shoulder. "So, what are you doing out here? And who's the stranger?"

Harry stood to address the crowd. "Best get any awkwardness dealt with first. This young man, who is under my protection, is ex-King Xanderamm." He looked directly at Annie. "The one styling himself, The Most High Lord Draqshet, reversed your transformation, but imposed muteness on the man. Draqshet meant to use him as a puppet, but we escaped. My Lady, My Lord, Draqshet has captured the elite of Kingston and thrown them into the dungeons. He controls the Doll Army."

Xanderamm flinched slightly when Annie approached with her hand extended. She touched his throat and frowned. Doubtless, this was the man she had cursed, but no longer arrogant. His humility pulsed under her fingertips.

"May I?" Without waiting for an answer, she pushed a warm surge of power through Xanderamm. "That should fix those niggling pains and cramps you've experienced since resuming your natural form."

Xanderamm sank to his knees, massaged his throat and swallowed. "My Lady, I owe you thanks and apologies in equal measure."

"You're a changed man, in more ways than one, your Majesty. What say we start anew?"

Midnight passed without a plan yet formed. Xanderamm grew excited about the sun-bombs and lightning-sticks, while André,

Theo, and Harry disagreed who would traverse the secret tunnels and plant the ordinance. Annie asserted her right and duty to lead, but the rest of the group vehemently opposed her.

"Harry and Xanderamm possess the best knowledge of the Palace geography," Theo said, "but as André pointed out, we don't know what changes Draqshet has made. Going with false confidence is worse than going in blind."

"You're impulsive," Netta said. "Don't you think Draqshet knows that? If I was in his position, I'd try to entice you closer and capture you. He's been planning this forever. As your friend, I'm begging you to take the time to make a proper plan."

Vert poked at the dying embers of the campfire, coaxing forth the last remnants of light and warmth. "Draqshet has issued an incontrovertible challenge by reanimating the Army of Dolls, and by reversing Xanderamm's curse. He must believe he is powerful enough to succeed. My Lady, you are too important to risk, and on a personal note, I could not survive knowing you to be in the power of that vile monster. Grief would kill me."

"I'm only a stable lad, the least valuable or knowledgeable person here, but I have one outstanding advantage. My face is unknown, nobody is looking for me. I know the city inside out, and if I sneak through the tunnels, I can reach Danny and Paulie. They promised to help and they're resourceful." Dexter shrugged. "I'm the obvious choice."

"Assuming we're not about to dash off and liberate the city tonight," Xanderamm said, "I suggest we sleep on the idea. My head is spinning, and I wager I'm not alone."

Xanderamm woke early and lay observing the stars fade like misconceptions, as the sun's truth burned away the mists of misunderstandings. A far off glitter caught his attention, and he idly watched the glimmer gain shape as it rapidly closed on the camp. He scrabbled across the dew damp dirt and shook Harry with one hand, pointing wordlessly with the other.

"Your Majesty, you are about to meet Roic the Magnificent. He usually creates quite a whirlwind, so you ought to cover your head," Captain Harry said.

"The dragon is real? I had thought him merely part of AnnieRah's legend."

Roic circled, waking the slumbering campers with the clatter of his wings and swirling buffets of debris laden air. He skidded to a halt, huffed, and stretched out in the dawn light. Xanderamm reminded himself to keep his mouth closed, but struggled to take his own advice when the tallest wolf he'd ever seen loped out of the dawn shadows and placidly settled next to the dragon's snout.

"Mistress Pacer," Harry whispered. "Leader of her pack, and greatly respected by Annie and her friends."

"A wolf queen?"

"You could say that," Harry said.

Annie, Theo, and Vert ran to greet the newcomers, the woodsman immediately clambering under Roic's chin and finger-combing the smallest, most delicate scales back into place.

I circled the city until I was nigh dizzy, but found not one weakness. Yesterday, something changed. Roic snorted a brief flame. *I cannot say with certainty what happened, other than something caused fear and revulsion amongst the traders who left earlier than is their wont.*

Pacer growled. *I couldn't risk getting closer, but I agree with*

Roic. The traders, usually jubilant and ready to celebrate on their way home, appeared intimidated. They hunched over, their shoulders bunched; nobody called to anybody else. They were afraid. Shocked and grief stricken may be a more accurate description.

"The pattern isn't clear," Annie said, driving her knife into the dirt. "Is Draqshet terrorising people only for his perverted pleasure, or for a more sinister purpose?"

"I will accompany Dexter through the tunnels, to gather intelligence," Theo said. "The lad's right, he knows the town best, and if things go awry, I can whisk us away."

"I agree Dexter should go," Vert said, scrambling from under Roic's chin, "but with all due respect, My Lord, you are the wrong choice. While you have the skills to make a rapid retreat, you are too conspicuous." Vert offered a self-deprecating smile. "I am unknown and unremarkable, so there is less risk of alerting The Dark Lord to our presence."

Once everyone had agreed, with varying degrees of enthusiasm and reluctance, Xanderamm spent most of the day drilling Dexter and Vert on the layout of the tunnels and their entrances. Taking any kind of map, no matter how rough, was impossible.

"I'm the only one with any knowledge of these tunnels. Not even Brummagen knows of their existence. Under no circumstances can this knowledge fall into enemy hands," Xanderamm said. "We need every advantage we can get."

When night fell and darkness thickened, the pair said their farewells and Theo transported them, fast-as-thought, to an agreed spot beside the city walls. As soon as they located and opened the door, Theo disappeared.

A stench of age and neglect pervaded the tunnel and decades of undisturbed dust softened their foot falls. They found lantern and sulphur sticks where Xanderamm promised. Dexter lit and trimmed the lamp, revealing a passage of well-dressed stone receding into the distance. Because of his keen woodsman senses, Vert insisted upon taking the lead. The tunnel twisted and turned exactly as Xanderamm described, leading to an iron-clad, child-sized door. Dexter reached up, almost to the ceiling, fingers questing for the loose stone, behind which the key lay hidden. The aridity had kept the key rust-free, and it slid easily into the lock, in an embrace of long-lost lovers. The tiny click sounded loud in the silence and they froze, awaiting a response.

Dexter extinguished the lamp before they risked pushing open the door. Daggers in hands, they stepped outside and locked the door behind them. Vert sniffed the air and shuddered. He placed a hand on Dexter's arm, leaning close to whisper in his ear.

"Watch where you step, lad. There's been blood spilled here, I can smell death, carcasses." He inhaled again and looked at the swaying cages, silhouetted against the starry sky. He shoved Dexter. "That way, keep your eyes down. Move."

Dexter turned to look, but Vert clouted his ear.

"I said, eyes down, lad. We'll come back a different route. At least now we know what scared the traders."

The duo threaded their way through the abandoned streets, staying in the deepest shadows, before coming to a cautious halt opposite Lady Amora's famed House of Pleasure. The windows, which usually blazed a bright welcome, remained black, shuttered against the terrors stalking the streets, hoping to remain unnoticed.

"I'll go," Dexter said. "Lady Amora's guards will recognise me. Get around the back." He shot across the street and through the gates without waiting for a response.

The house crouched in silence: no music, no girlish giggles, or voices raised in sultry song. The building held its breath as Dexter waited for a response to his knock.

"We're closed. Case of the dripping pox. Go away."

"Danny? It's me, Dexter. I want to talk to you about those ugly puppies you wanted rid of."

The door cracked open a fraction, blocked by Danny's bulk. "Dexter?" The light went out, and a hand grabbed Dexter and yanked him inside. "Are you alone? Where's Rose and Jasmine?"

"They're well. They met up with some old friends."

Paulie opened the lamp, spilling golden light into the reception area. "You'd better come through. We've got some interesting news," he said. "We've decided we're not taking this lying down. We're gonna fight."

"Sounds like I'm in the right place," Dexter said.

Before dawn, Pacer nudged Annie awake. *You have all the personnel you need, and all the information I could provide, My Lady. My continued presence is unnecessary and I confess, the proximity of the city oppresses my spirit. With your permission, today I travel back to my pack, where I belong.*

"Mistress Pacer, you will always have a place here." Annie tapped her chest. "But I respect your need to return. Take with you my gratitude for all you have done."

Pacer thumped her tail and bounded into the predawn darkness. By the time the camp was breakfasting, she was ghosting through heavily wooded mountains. As she ran, she composed a song, alerting her people of her impending return.

CHAPTER TWENTY-THREE

"I planted you in her belly, you whom she so vehemently rejected, but she never realised I'd also infected her with a malaise. I left a seed of discontent in her heart, preventing her from truly experiencing the supposed joys of life." Draqshet's cackle echoed through the Audience Chamber. "My seed filled her with dark desires, but she could never assuage them. Desires which led to her eventual ruin."

Sneeth raised his head, sensing the Master wanted to gloat. "I'm not sure I understand."

"She healed her bites and scratches without a second thought, but it was already too late. I had polluted her soul. As slowly as a mountain grows, her all-encompassing love for her magnificent creation withered. The world collapsed into chaos around her, and she cared not."

"You captured her, made her your pet." Sneeth encouraged The Master.

"I was poised to take my rightful place until that weaver-girl, Annie, took the responsibility upon herself to rebalance and rejuvenate the world." Draqshet's simmering rage flowed from the throne, scalding Sneeth with its intensity. "The chit outwitted me. But I vowed no mere upstart female would bamboozle you."

Sneeth's taloned hands crept to cover his mutilated genitals. Draqshet had torn away all outward signs of his manhood eons ago, long before AnnieRah stepped onto the world stage. This was the first lie Sneeth heard slither from his father's lips, disturbing him more than being neutered had.

"Yesterday's sacrifices brought no intelligence?"

"Not yet, Master." Sneeth held his breath, anticipating dire punishment.

"I ought to rend you limb from limb, or flay you alive." Draqshet flicked splinters from the arm of the throne. "But watching you writhe under your Mother's rejection and revulsion is vastly more satisfying. Yes," Draqshet hissed. "Living with the knowledge you are not only unloved, but despised, shall be your eternal punishment."

Sneeth laid his ear against the door of his Mother's dungeon, and listened for her breath, her heartbeat. For five days he had resisted the urge to visit, to exult at her diminishment. Had he prolonged her agony too far? Had he denied himself the pleasure of her distress too long, thus allowing her to escape into death?

He hauled open the door to reveal his prize. Jenny slumped against the wall in her heavy restraints, all her remaining strength concentrated on gripping the chain between her handcuffs. Her cracked lips moved soundlessly, but she didn't acknowledge his presence. He reached out tentatively and caressed her cheek with the back of his finger, astounded by the combination of her physical fragility and iron-willed persistence.

Sneeth gestured for the guards to release his prisoner. He noticed her face turn to the raised lamp they carried. He snatched the lamp and moved it back and forth, up and down. Like a flower following the sun, she tracked the light. The creature shuttered the lamp and watched her droop. He shooed the guards out of his way and scooped her into his scarred embrace.

He hesitated at the top of the dungeon stairs. He felt the chill seeping through her and debated which was most important for her recovery: light or heat. *I'm not saving her life, I only want to question her before she dies.* Sneeth chose the quickest route to her previous apartments, high in a tower, filled with light and housing a massive fireplace. He beat his wings to speed his way up the winding stairs, calling for palace servants to bring extra lamps and candles, and wood for a fire.

The servants carried out their tasks efficiently and without making eye-contact, except one elderly lady who approached the bed where Jenny lay like a marble effigy.

The serving woman tutted to herself and shook her head. "Poor child's chilled bone deep. She needs soup, hot soup. And hot bricks on her feet. I'll fetch some."

Sneeth opened his mouth to speak, but realised he had naught useful to say. He stared open-mouthed as the woman bustled away, paying no attention to his fearsome reputation, his terrible countenance, nor his exalted status. Snapping his jaws shut, he returned his attention to Jenny. Her bloodless skin remained cold, but her chest rose and fell and her heart beat, weak but steady.

The hugely ornate bed screeched on the tiles, and his sinews stretched, as he pulled the massive structure closer to the fire.

The old woman returned with a tray of hot soup, and two younger women bearing hot bricks and clean dry clothes. The young women put half the heated bricks under the bedcovers by Jenny's feet and placed the rest on the hearth to keep warm. They scurried out, returning with a train of servants bringing hot water.

"Help me sit her up," the old servant said, as she prepared to spoon feed Jenny. "Good, now support her, that's right." The woman dribbled the thin liquid into Jenny's mouth, wiping away the spills with her apron. Flabbergasted at being ordered about by a mere mortal, Sneeth silently followed her instructions. Jenny reflexively swallowed tiny amounts of soup, satisfying the old woman.

"You must leave," the woman said. "We need to bathe and dress the poor girl, and the bedclothes need changing." She looked directly at him. "If you wait outside, I'll call you when she's decent. Now, out you go."

Sneeth bared his teeth and sniffed the air, but tasted no fear emanating from the woman. Bewildered, he allowed her to push him into the stairwell, where he listened to the muffled sounds of housekeeping and lowered voices.

When the old servant opened the door, a gaggle of girls fled with arms filled with soiled bedding and clothes fit only for burning. Jenny sat propped up on pillows, but still moon pale and kitten weak. Sneeth sought permission before entering and seated himself on the low stool beside the bed, to which the woman pointed.

"If you want to make yourself useful, keep checking on the bricks. Put the cooling ones on the hearth and replace them with hot ones. Make sure they're well wrapped, so she doesn't burn herself." The woman nodded at him. "I'll be back soon with more soup and spiced wine."

Sneeth listened to the woman's footsteps as she slowly

descended the twisting stairs. He heard her catch her breath with the unusual exertion, but noted she'd breathed calmly in his presence. Strange. Worthy of later investigation.

Jenny's fingers twitched, compulsively fidgeting for what wasn't there. Her eyelids fluttered as she slept. Not wanting to earn a reprimand, Sneeth frequently checked the bricks and was midway through changing them when the strange woman returned. She smiled her approval when she saw how carefully he wrapped the flannel around each one before tucking it next to Jenny.

"What do they call you?" Sneeth asked.

"That depends on which they you mean." She tucked a piece of linen around Jenny's neck. "My name is Vera, Milord." She began dribbling spoonfuls of soup into Jenny's mouth, showing all the tenderness of a mother to a newborn.

Sneeth crawled onto the bed next to Jenny and wrapped a supportive arm around her.

"Thank you, Milord. She's not yet got the strength to sit unaided, but it'll come. Poor girl needs some love, that's all."

"You do not fear me, as others do," Sneeth said, filled with curiosity. "Why?"

Vera continued spooning and wiping while she considered her answer, then she dabbed Jenny's chin clean with a damp cloth and returned the bowl and spoon to the tray.

"That you dragged this girl to the dungeons is common knowledge," Vera said, straightening the bedcovers. "And that you chose a particularly cruel and nasty cell to keep her in. Although she'd estranged the entire town with her silly affectations, within and without the palace, she didn't deserve the living death to which you condemned her, Milord. But you had a change of heart."

"You know not the crimes this unworthy woman has committed. But you haven't answered why you do not fear me."

"You want the poor girl alive. I'm helping her get well. At least for now, I'm worth more to you alive than dead," Vera said. "Would you feel better if I quaked? Do you need my fear as a boost for your self-esteem?"

"You tread dangerously, Mistress Vera. You should show more respect."

Vera shrugged. "I apologise, Milord. I assumed you are too intelligent for a mere outward display to satisfy you."

Sneeth's jaw dropped, then he burst out laughing, unfurling his wings and shaking them, before loosely furling them. "I am searching my memories, Mistress Vera, but from the beginning of time, I cannot recall being addressed with such casual familiarity. I am undecided whether you most amuse or annoy me."

"Neither was my intention, Milord."

"You cannot mean that." Sneeth leaned forward. "Those who annoy me do not last, but I richly reward those who amuse me."

Vera folded her arms. "I've loyally served three anointed kings, now I serve the one styling himself The Most High Lord." She snorted her derision. "My remaining years are few, and likely filled with pain. Death would be a blessing. Rewards hold no interest for me, knowing I'll not survive to enjoy them."

"Do you not have family? Someone to inherit your good fortune?"

"Many years ago, I birthed a son, like you."

"Like me? How could a son of yours resemble me?"

"He, too, was a misshapen monster. People feared him because he was ugly, but he was soft-hearted and died of misery while only a boy." Vera wiped her eyes with her fresh apron. "That's why I don't fear you, Milord. I don't believe a person's outside necessarily matches their inside."

Sneeth stared as tears trickled down Vera's wrinkled cheeks.

"If he was so hideous, why did you keep him?"

"He was my son. I loved him."

CHAPTER TWENTY-FOUR

Danny led the way into the kitchen where Lady Amora stood, gripping a carving knife in a white-knuckled fist.

"This man claims to be a friend." She gestured with the gleaming blade to Vert. "He let himself in the back door."

"Vert's with me," Dexter said.

Lady Amora smiled, but her eyes remained cold as she looked Dexter up and down. "That's most reassuring. And you are?"

"This is Dexter, the friend who rescued the puppies." Danny looked meaningfully at Lady Amora.

"I see. What can we do for you?" She returned the knife to the block and waved Vert to a chair.

"We need your help," Dexter said. "AnnieRah possesses weapons, the likes of which you have never seen, but we need help to move our people into the city without attracting attention. We need up-to-date information, what's changed since the coup, that sort of thing."

"You're not the only one with new weapons," Lady Amora

nodded at the guards. "We've been making and testing something I think you'll find useful."

"I had an old recipe for sticky fire," Danny said. "We made a batch and the results are incredible. We could target the Dolls. Wounds from blades or spears don't slow them down, but I reckon an inextinguishable fire will stop them."

"Is this the fire famous for burning fiercely underwater?" Vert leaned his elbows on the table. "I've heard of it, but never seen it. Everyone believed the recipe lost, or deliberately hidden from the eyes of men, such is the substance's destructive powers."

"Can't say ought about the history, but I dropped a lit branch into a pool and the fire burned brighter than the sun," Paulie said. "We've got jars of the mixture ready to go, and we've been experimenting with fuse lengths. Lady Amora had the idea to hide the jars in places the Dolls congregate, light long fuses, and be far away when trouble erupts."

"I can get you maps of the city, even the palace," Lady Amora said. "We plan to get maps ourselves, to help identify targets and escape routes." She looked at Vert and Dexter. "I assume you know about the King's love tunnels?"

"We've heard, yes," Vert said. "A word of warning, though. Make no marks on any map, My Lady. Such documents falling into the enemy's hands would impede the cause, and your punishment would be severe. We saw the caged remains of bodies swinging in the marketplace."

Danny clenched his fists. "Bastards deliberately invited families, including children, to that charity ball. Those women and children had committed no crime. This is Draqshet's way of persuading the citizens to betray the fugitives. He's convinced they're still hiding in the city."

"Draqshet summoned everyone to watch," Lady Amora whispered, hand over her heart. "Brummagen, the traitorous turd, issued a declaration the day Danny and Paulie went out of town. The murders started yesterday. A woman and child both days." She stifled a sob. "They leave them exposed to the mercy of the crows. I've seen naught so cruel or sickening in my entire life."

"Seems to me," Paulie said, "the quicker we formulate a plan, the better."

～

Lady Amora stuffed two satchels with mattress ticking, pulled from the cold bed of her most popular girl. "This should stop the jars clanking together," she said, as she arranged the sticky-fire devices to her satisfaction. "The Dolls patrol all night, and although they're neither observant nor motivated, you don't want to risk getting caught."

Dexter and Vert hitched the satchels over their shoulders and checked the street for any signs of the Dolls.

"One last question before we go," Vert said. "When you went on your picnic, did you notice anything strange when leaving or returning to the city? Mayhap, a persistent mist?"

Lady Amora, Danny, and Paulie looked at him blankly.

"We know The Dark Lord has erected a shield over the city," Vert said. "We want to know whether it is visible from the ground."

"We noticed naught, and I've heard no rumours of such," Paulie said.

"That's what we expected," Vert said. "Our theory is Draqshet fashioned the enchantment only for us."

"I know naught of magik or enchantments," Lady Amora said, "but what you suggest implies significant power and finesse. And a disturbing depth of knowledge about you as individuals."

"Indeed, My Lady. Draqshet has been plotting and preparing for eons."

~

Jenny listened attentively to Vera and Sneeth. Had she been well, she would have roared laughing at their interactions, but in her weakened state she had strength only to eavesdrop. That Vera thought she, Jenny, needed love was a ludicrous assertion, and far beyond acceptable for a servant to think, far less dare to say.

The overwhelming sense of security from being supported by Sneeth, as Vera spoon fed her, came as a shock. It must be a trick. Jenny wriggled her toes and found the hot bricks, meticulously flannel-wrapped by Sneeth. Her son and enemy.

The stool next to the bed creaked.

"Mother? Can you hear me?"

Jenny kept her eyes closed and lay as still as a corpse. She fought the urge to scream as her son bent closer, then stroked her cheek with a single finger.

"You breathe differently when you sleep, Mother. I know you're awake. Would you like a sip of spiced wine? Vera left some tucked in the hearth."

Sneeth's leathery wings brushed the bed, his talons tapped on the tiles. The footstool's feet scraped as he returned, then a tiny pop as he pulled the stopper, and a clink as the wine bottle clumsily kissed the cup, followed by the splash of wine, and the heady scent of fermented summers.

"Try this. Vera said it'll help you feel stronger."

Jenny slitted her eyes at Sneeth, as he proffered a cup balanced on his outstretched palm. His curling talons wouldn't permit him to hold the drink any other way. She manoeuvred herself to a sitting position.

"Quite a performance you and Vera gave." Jenny accepted the drink and sniffed it before risking a taste. "We loathe and despise one another, so I confess I'm not sure where you're going with this charade. But it's much nicer than the dungeons, so I'll go along with your performance." She tipped the wine in salute and swallowed the entire contents in a single gulp.

Sneeth looked at her like a mistreated puppy. "Does it offend you when I call you Mother?"

Jenny carefully placed the empty cup beside her. "Draqshet claims you as his son, and has sent me visions, leading me to believe I birthed you."

"He chooses the cruelest of truths, but he does not lie. He says the worst punishment he could inflict is knowing my mother finds me abhorrent and unlovable." Sneeth's wings slumped in defeat. "You must have had feelings for my father, once."

"Of course I had feelings for him. If the visions he showed me were true, he terrified me. I fled his attentions, but he hunted me, almost to death, then he raped me." Jenny lifted her head and glared at Sneeth. "Do you really expect me to show devotion to the resulting abomination? You expect me to think fondly of a monster created from pain and humiliation?"

Sneeth shifted back on the stool. "Rape?"

"He hasn't told you, has he?" Jenny cocked her head. "I was the victim, violated and left for dead, once he'd satisfied his lust."

"But you tried to kill me. You blasted me with your fire and abandoned me."

"I'm not about to apologise, if that's what you expect. With hindsight, you were not to blame for your father's actions, but I was scared. Scared and furious. I never meant for you to suffer, I only wanted you not to exist. Can you understand?"

"Vera had a son like me, a misshapen monster, but she still loved him."

"Doubtless, the father was the love of her life. Two incomparable scenarios."

Jenny's heart raced as Sneeth leaned in, only to clumsily pick up her wine cup.

He jiggled the bottle. "It's still warm. Would you like more?"

She nodded, and he passed her a refill.

"Does the manner of my conception matter so much? Or is it because you find me displeasing to look upon? The latter is partly your fault."

Jenny refused to turn away. The ugly spawn can't help how he looks. "Your conception coloured your entire existence. You proudly committed evil acts in Draqshet's name, as did I, but he recreated me, reformed me. I have no memory of my existence prior to being rescued from the icy depths of darkness. Are you going to return me to a living death in the standing chamber?"

"You explain your behaviour, excuse what you have done, and abdicate all responsibility by blaming the influence of Draqshet." Sneeth stood to pace the room, wings furling and unfurling. "You had a choice. You could have refused to follow his commands. And I've witnessed your delight in the degradation of your victims. A part of you revelled in wickedness."

Jenny shrugged. "The choice to comply or die isn't much of a choice. I am not a good person. Perhaps I never was. Mayhap I was evil before I met your father. I don't know. Mayhap, you wouldn't have been such a snivelling suck-worm without his guiding hand."

"That's either a courageous or foolish way to speak to a monster who holds your life in his misshapen hands, Mother."

"Knowing what I now know, what makes you think I harbour any desire to continue living?"

"The Dark Lord punishes us both by sharing that which was unknown for eons." Sneeth dropped to his knees beside the bed. "We are both experiencing unprecedented pain. Vera said you needed love, but she failed to mention, I also have the same need. I would that circumstances were otherwise. The need feels weak, contemptible, yet it rages within my breast like a storm."

This is the trick? "Are you suggesting we join forces against your father? That familial love will lend us strength to defeat him?" Jenny's laughter rippled around the room, bright and malicious.

Dexter led Vert through back alleys, down snickets, and past houses shuttered and dark. The swish of an owl's wings and the panicked shrieks of a shrew accompanied them as they travelled unnoticed through the almost deserted night. A fox paused mid-step to watch them pass before continuing his dainty-footed marauding.

"Seems the Dolls only patrol the principal streets," Dexter said. "I reckon whoever's giving them orders ain't local. All the street urchins know these rat-runs."

Vert touched a finger to his lips and pointed to a pair of silhouettes lurking at the end of the pathway. He melted into the overgrown hedges, pulling Dexter after him. Shrouded by frost-rimed foliage, they watched the soldiers stamping their feet, either combatting the cold or counting time, before moving on. Swords clanking noisily, the Dolls continued their patrol, making no attempt at discretion.

The fox trotted past, head held high, a plump chicken limp between his neat jaws.

"If Mr Fox thinks the way is clear, we're safe enough," Vert said.

They swam through deep pools of shadow, pausing every few steps to listen. The silence soon filled with the pattering of tiny feet and the curtailed screeches of careless creatures, unceremoniously added to the owl's menu.

More than half a decade's growth of tangled ivy disguised the door to the secret tunnel, and only with their combined weight could they shove it open. Dexter slipped through first, leaving Vert to rearrange the foliage before pushing the door shut behind him. Candles and sulphur sticks survived intact in the metal box, their light making the darkness blacker. A short flight of steps led to a dry passageway, and more stairs leading upwards.

Vert extinguished the candle before opening the door to where Theo waited beside the city walls, ready to whisk them back to camp.

CHAPTER TWENTY-FIVE

"If my men return as planned on the quarter day for their wages," Harry said, "they'll walk right into Draqshet's gaping maw."

"Are they still working in the communities, or are they en route to Kingston by now?" Netta passed around bowls of porridge.

Harry stirred his breakfast. "Most will be travelling by now. That's hundreds of men, riding to their doom. Even with Theo's help, we can't possibly reach them all."

"We don't need to reach them all," Theo said. "If we catch the ones closest to Kingston, we can turn them back and they can intercept and relay the message to others."

"I can estimate with reasonable accuracy each team's position," Harry said, a smile of relief spreading across his face. "I'll sketch a map and we can plot the most useful route."

∽

Vera cast Sneeth a look as she left Jenny's chamber. "She's still weak, Milord. Treat her gently."

Vera addressed him as a mere mortal, a man like any other, and his reaction confused him. Her indifference outraged him, and filled him with an urge to strike her down, to instil fear if not genuine respect. Draqshet had trained him to treat servants with cruelty, but an unexpected and surprisingly strong response was the secret thrill of being recognised as a person, not a monster. He discovered he looked forward to their inter-actions.

"You're letting all the heat out." Jenny pulled the bedcovers close.

"You're sitting up. Are you feeling better?" Sneeth sidled to the edge of the bed and settled on the waiting stool.

Jenny paused, the spoonful of fruit-filled porridge suspended in midair as she looked at him, her eyes creasing with suspicion.

"You think I wish to trick you, Mother? To lull you into trusting me, before I slam you back into the pitchy darkness?" Sneeth followed a line of stitching on the elaborately embroi-dered counterpane with a black talon. "Previously, that would likely have been true, yes. I need your trust, but I have no idea how to gain such a valuable commodity. What must I do?"

"Mother! How unnatural that sounds, spilling from your lips. Are you certain you wish to remind me how Draqshet forced me to spawn an abomination?" Jenny licked clean her spoon before pointing it at Sneeth. "I've accepted the idea I likely gave birth to you, but that does not make me your mother. I have no desire to claim you as my son. That Draqshet should try to force the issue baffles me. I thought The Dark Lord was cleverer than this."

"My father is not aware that I have removed you from the dungeons. At least, I have not supplied the information. Your continued revulsion would no doubt please him. He told me he could conjure no greater punishment than your response."

"What do you want from me? Realistically, you must understand we're never going to share a familial fondness. And while your father is still all powerful, why would I further displease him?"

"Are you not curious about your past, before my father rescued you?"

Jenny sighed. "No. I must have committed terrible crimes for someone to incarcerate me in eternal darkness. Obviously, I was not a pleasant or popular person. I cannot imagine Draqshet recruiting a woman of impeccable virtue into his service, but dwelling on my past serves no purpose. I cannot change what happened, but I may still have a future."

"You employ faulty logic, Mo—Milady. Draqshet limits your knowledge of your past to what he wants you to know. Do you think he furnished you with the unmitigated tale? Or did he inform you only enough for his own purposes?"

"I'm saying this upfront, so there can be no misunderstandings. Your father brought me back to life, therefore I owe him all that I am. Doubtless, he has purposes to which I am not privy. Equally doubtless, he is using you as his pawn, and you will report back to him everything I say. My loyalty to The Dark Lord remains unchanged."

Sneeth suppressed a smile. *Your loyalty remains unchanged, because it is only to yourself and your own interests.* "My father said he planted a seed of darkness within you. A seed which grew over time. You were not altogether responsible for your crimes. We were both pawns."

"Don't tell me: without Draqshet's influence, we'd be delightful and loveable creatures." Jenny's laughter shimmered like a taunting desert mirage. "We should run away and live idyllic lives, filled with sunshine and rainbows."

His breath caught as his skeletal chest tightened. Jenny was right. An accident of birth didn't make family. She would never trust him, and he was weak and foolish to entertain the idea that she could ever feel a smallest sliver of affection for him. He stood and bowed.

"I will leave you to rest, Milady. Ring if you need anything. The servants will bring whatever you desire."

He moved as quietly as he could, minimising the scratching of his talons on the floor. No need to feed her disgust any further. Sneeth slipped out and closed the door quietly behind him. He leaned on the wall to steady himself. His desire to rend her limb from limb bubbled and seethed in his belly, warring with his self-pity. Pawns. Draqshet used him and Jenny with equal disregard. Being Draqshet's son brought no advantage; being Jenny's son brought only loathing.

Sneeth slithered down the stairs, habitually staying in the shadows. Vera's words from yesterday echoed in his head. He was my son. She spoke them with such love and reverence, announcing the sacred bond, fully expecting the listener to understand the nuances.

Jenny shoved back the covers and wobbled her way to the window. She leaned out as far as she dared, but saw naught of use. One mistake would bring certain death on the unforgiving cobbles below. No balconies, no protuberances of any kind to aid a descent. Sheer stone walls, without so much as a finger-hold.

She gripped the windowsill as she contemplated her choices: bluff her way past the servants, or fashion a rope and attempt to clamber down. Neither filled her with optimism. The servants would detain her and report to Draqshet if she tried to walk out, and he would confine her to the lowest dungeon again. She flexed her arms, but although she had recovered much of her strength, she dared not trust her life to knotted bedsheets. Death by splatter was distinctly unappealing. She huffed. With her luck, she'd not die, but sustain injuries preventing movement. Draqshet would enjoy keeping her alive but in constant agony, visited by her simpering spawn. A fate worse than death.

Jenny dragged herself to the fireside chair, already exhausted by the minimal exercise. Sneeth and Vera had been unexpectedly kind, and she mistrusted both. Five years wasn't much, but she'd packed a lot of experience into half a decade and she'd never met anyone who didn't act from self-interest. Sneeth and Vera must have something to gain by helping her. As an elderly servant, Vera would likely to be open to bribery, providing a more comfortable old age, but Sneeth? He presented a different scenario. His needs were basic and his existence was relatively comfortable, as long as he continued obeying Draqshet's bidding.

Jenny held her translucent fingers to the fire as she contemplated her son's possible motivations. The first and most obvious was that he was trying to hoodwink her, with the cruel intention of delivering her to his father and thus worming his way back into The Dark Lord's questionable favour. Second and less likely, Sneeth planned a coup and something in her past could help him. She shook her head. An enormous risk, especially for a creature trained over eons to unquestioning obedience. The third and final reason. Could the idea of a mother's love so bewitch Sneeth he'd risk his father's displeasure? The creature had survived an eternity with neither a known parent nor any semblance of affection. No, he wouldn't gamble his existence for a prize as ephemeral as love.

The only reasonable explanation was Sneeth must be an

agent for Draqshet. The Dark Lord, nor his misbegotten son, would not allow love to weaken them, and neither would she.

Jenny rang the bell, summoning Vera.

Sneeth pointed to a couple clinging together. "Bring them," he ordered the guard, before heading to the city walls. His belief the sacrifices would swiftly reveal the whereabouts of the fugitives had faded. The reluctant crowds swirled below the cages, and the quick corvids massed, greedily anticipating their daily feast. Brummagen stood supported either side by Dolls, his eyes shut and his knees trembling. Dispirited, Sneeth allowed him to look away this time. The howling wind chilled Sneeth's furled wings to the temperature of the stony battlements, and the cold sank deep into his bones.

The woman's shrieks jarred Sneeth's nerves, and he ordered the guards to slit her and her husband's throats before stuffing their corpses into the cramped cages. The crows descended enthusiastically, screaming their carnivorous gratitude before shredding the tender flesh.

Sneeth sidled up to Brummagen. "I'm beginning to think I'm making the wrong sacrifice. The citizens know naught, whereas you must know something. You served by Xanderamm's side for years. You must know all his secrets. Where do you think he'd hide? Think on it, my friend, and think well. If you can't answer to my satisfaction tomorrow, I'll find another way to gain satiety. I'll have you stuffed into the cage for the crows to gorge upon."

Vera tapped and entered without waiting for a response. She carried a bowl and placed it on a table near Jenny.

"What strangeness have you brought me?" Jenny inhaled appreciatively.

"Oranges, Milady. From the hothouses. My son used to call them globes of liquid sunshine." Vera selected a fruit and expertly peeled it, throwing the bright rind onto the fire, and filling the room with a warm and exotic citrus scent. She passed the fruit and a napkin to Jenny with a smile. "The juiciest ones can be messy."

Jenny sniffed at a segment. "This is unusual, and therefore expensive." She popped the fruit into her mouth and bit through the membrane, releasing a taste explosion onto her tongue. "Does The Most High Lord Draqshet know you're raiding his hothouses for rare fruits?"

Vera shrugged. "Milord has no interest in fruit. He cares naught for anything sun-kissed."

"He must pay you well to spy for him. I can double the amount if you help me."

"Double or quadruple, Milady, it's still nowt," Vera snorted. "Not everything is for sale."

"You spy for free? I can make you rich."

"I'm not for sale, not to you, nor the one styling himself Lord." Vera folded her arms. "You ought to be more careful with your words, and to whom you say them, Milady. Eat, build up your strength. I'd heard you're a clever girl. Listen with your heart."

"What's that supposed to mean?"

"You cannot buy anything of true and lasting value with coin. You have a potential ally, drowning in an ocean of unfamiliar emotions. He needs your help, as much as you need his."

"You overstep the mark, madam."

"Yes, Milady. Shall I arrange for another servant? One who knows her place and won't speak? One owned by Draqshet?"

Jenny glared at Vera, who stared back impassively. The orange peel sizzled in the flames, delivering wave after wave of intoxicating scent, stinging Jenny's eyes and forcing her to blink back tears.

"A gloriously sweet fruit, but a drop of oil from the skin, or juice from the flesh, can play havoc with your eyes, Milady. The trick is to choose the parts you want, without paying a hefty price."

CHAPTER TWENTY-SIX

"Walk with me." Annie jerked her chin at Xanderamm. "I wish to speak with you while Theo and Harry are busy redirecting the soldiers."

"My Lady." Xanderamm formally offered his arm.

Annie placed her fingertips on the back of his proffered hand and briefly closed her eyes. "I wasn't expecting that. You truly have no desire for the population to recognise you as the rightful King." She led him past the tethered horses and began a wide circuit of the camp.

Xanderamm blushed and studied the frosty ground as they walked. "I'm not sure what you just did, My Lady, but no. I have no desire to be King. The kingdom fares well under Harry's guidance."

"I apologise, that was rude of me," Annie said. "I can read what is in a person's heart if I touch them. It was necessary to know your intentions."

"No need to apologise, My Lady. I didn't exactly impress you with my integrity when we last met. For what it's worth, I am ashamed of who I once was."

Annie turned to face him. "Mayhap neither of us were our best that day. I was hasty, and I beg your forgiveness. I'd consider it a favour if you called me Annie."

"Very well, Annie. I accept your apology for being hasty, if you accept my apology for being... a swine." Xanderamm smiled. "In truth, I owe you thanks. You forced me to reassess how I lived, my values. I shudder to think of the consequences had I continued as I was."

"This conversation isn't proceeding quite as I expected. You are naught as I remember."

"I will take that as a compliment. Do you know much about me? My upbringing, I mean."

Annie shook her head. "I was an orphaned weaver. I had no opportunity to associate with the aristocracy."

"My older brother was destined to rule. He was the heir, while I was most definitely the spare. Our father trained him in kingly duties whilst I ran amok, amusing myself as I pleased, with nobody to say me nay."

"What happened?"

"A foolish hunting accident. His horse stumbled on a rabbit hole and threw him. My brother landed on his short sword. He died instantly, so they said. The blade went straight into his heart, and I went straight onto the throne. My father died within a moon cycle, without sharing one word with me. He couldn't bear the loss of his eldest and most beloved son."

"I had no idea. That's tragic."

"Tragic or not, it was no excuse. I had no expectations or ambition for kingship, but more importantly, I lacked interest in learning to rule. I was lazy and arrogant, finding it easier to hand over responsibilities than take time to master them myself. Like a farmer expecting to harvest the fruits of the land without the nuisance of tilling the soil."

"How do you see your future? Once this is over."

Xanderamm shrugged. "I'm still getting used to not having to worry about becoming bacon. I have treasure, although technically that may belong to the crown."

"You're not a fool. Instead of surrounding yourself with mercenary leeches, you could put together a team of good men and women. You could become a ruler of whom your father would have been proud. Captain Harry and Dexter are honourable men. You have an existing army dedicated to improving the lot of the ordinary people. You've already made the start."

"But, you're the Protector of the Kingdom. From what I've witnessed, the Kingdom is more prosperous than ever chronicled. Why would you allow me to reassume the throne?"

"I never sat on the throne, nor do I want to rule a kingdom. I have other, wider, responsibilities. You've changed, matured. Why should you not rule?"

CHAPTER TWENTY-SEVEN

Brummagen bumbled about his apartment, tears blurring his vision. Terror tightened its grip, and shook him in an anti-lullaby, as he envisioned being squeezed into a blood-encrusted cage by blank-faced Dolls, and hung out for the carnivorous crows to peck and plunder. The birds first plucked the eyes, so he believed, deliberately blinding their victims. Bile rose to Brummagen's throat, burning and acrid, as he imagined wickedly sharp beaks stabbing into his orbital sockets and bursting the viscous balls of black fluid.

He leaned out of the window and vomited a thin trail of vileness down the outer wall of his eyrie. Thin stings of spittle hung from his chin, staining the once sumptuous tunic covering his heaving chest and quivering belly. He wiped his mouth with his embroidered sleeve, careless of the result.

The muscles in his thighs trembled, as though he had raced cross-country for his life, and lost. Leaning helplessly against the wall, he rescanned his apartment, searching for a non-existent escape route, or a flash of inspiration. If he had the slightest inkling where Xanderamm had holed up, he'd betray him in less than a heartbeat to avoid his own suffering or discomfort.

Brummagen slid down the wall and covered his eyes with his hands. He recalled nights when the randy little shite disappeared, rumoured to be rogering the local gentlewomen while their husbands were abroad on the King's business. He'd wheedled and coaxed, simpered and fawned, to no avail. Xanderamm kept his under-the-covers missions covert. Teams of servants, paid handsomely for their loyalty, searched the royal apartments and surrounding corridors for hidden doors and secret passageways, but Brummagen's gold coins, like the licentious King, had vanished with nary a trace.

The ex-Vizier's shoulders slumped further as he realised that if he couldn't then buy the information with gold, he had no chance now of trading goodwill or fealty. The citizens recognised him as a traitor. He anticipated their cheers when Sneeth announced his substitution for an elite couple. Would Sneeth show mercy and slit his throat before caging him? Would the monster allow him to wear a blindfold to protect his eyes? Brummagen shuddered. If Sneeth learned of his fear, he'd likely order a Doll to slice off his eyelids. Brummagen stifled a scream.

Quivering on the floor, a heap of terrified jelly served no purpose. Brummagen forced himself to re-examine his options. Two exits, one through the window leading to certain death, or the Doll guarded door. Empty of emotions, the Dolls were beyond purchase, threats, or flattery. Even if he possessed the physical capacity, wounds which would kill mortal men had no impact upon these unnatural abominations.

He crawled to the window on hands and knees and peered over the sill. A determinedly nonathletic youth grown into a physically weak and inept adult, Brummagen knew the climb was far beyond his capabilities. Knotted sheets were an option, but only for someone possessing greater upper body strength than him. Either he'd lose his grip and fall, or the Dolls would haul him back.

Knowledge represents power. Brummagen built his career on accruing and trading information, or using secrets as a weapons. Think, man, think! That the tunnels existed was beyond dispute. They were generations old, therefore, if they led to homes of the elite, it was not the nouveau riche, but the long-established families. How many such homes existed?

Brummagen stumbled to his desk and rummaged around for writing materials. He laid out a large parchment, holding it flat with assorted pen and quill holders, ink-pots, sticks of wax and a sandbox. Fear-numbed fingers refused to grip the pen, so he tied it in place with a ribbon. He sketched a large rectangle to represent the Palace with lines radiating out for the major roads. He marked the older houses, scribbling family names next to them. Those with especially beautiful wives or daughters received an asterisk. If the tunnels were as ancient as believed, it was the fabled beauties from generations past who would have originally attracted Royal attention. He frowned as he strained to recall family portraits hanging proudly in private rooms. Pictures of beautiful women had not interested him, while a moderately pretty flesh and blood girl was in the vicinity. Yet another foolish vice he might not live long enough to regret.

He whirled around his bookshelves, searching for records of family histories, always a deep mine of information if you knew where to dig. In his excitement, his tied on pen knocked over an ink-pot, ruining his map. He choked back a sob, fearful of attracting the attention of the Doll guards.

Sneeth dithered; desire to speak again with his mother warred with his duty to find the fugitives as demanded by his father.

He shook out his wings; the tips tracing patterns on the painted ceiling, his tail extended to its full measure. What advantage would gaining his mother's affection bring? He twitched his tail, deliberately suppressing his fury with the obstinate woman. Naught in his experience gave him guidance on how to behave towards her, or how to deal with her undisguised revulsion of his person. Knives sliced his innards whenever he recalled her expression. Confounded by her contempt, he decided to deal first with Brummagen.

The Dolls opened the doors to Brummagen's apartment as soon as they heard Sneeth approach. He appreciated their mindless deference, reassuring him of his rightful status and power. He slithered into the room where Brummagen sprawled across his desk amidst a mess of ink and writing materials. The man wept onto the ruined parchment before him, smearing his scribbles.

"I have naught," Brummagen whispered. "All night I ransacked by mind for clues, but I have naught. Only a theory about the love tunnels rumoured to run under the Palace."

"You think to buy your miserable life with this worthless scrawl?" Sneeth poked a talon at the ruined map, stabbing through an asterisk. "What does this represent?"

Brummagen licked his lips and swallowed. "Sire, I am sure the tunnels exist, but despite extensive searching whilst I was Grand Vizier, I never found them."

Sneeth bared his jagged teeth. "You are telling me naught I wish to hear, old man."

"The love tunnels are ancient, as old as the Palace. Logic dictates the tunnels would lead to the greatest beauties of bygone days." Brummagen looked hopefully at Sneeth. "With time, I can complete my research. We can seek the tunnels at the opposite ends from where I've searched." Brummagen rose unsteadily to his feet and tottered to his shelves of family histories. "I can discover where the most desirable women lived. That's where you'll find your fugitives."

"I see." Sneeth tapped his talons on the map. "The information I need is all on your shelves?"

Brummagen nodded rapidly, wringing his hands. "All I need is time to research."

Sneeth advanced slowly as Brummagen backed away. "Then I have no need for you. Any semi-literate scribe can do the job." Sneeth turned to call the guards; whether a genuine mistake or a moment of mercy, even he wasn't certain.

Brummagen launched himself out of the window before the guards crossed the threshold, and Sneeth did naught to stop him. He could have swooped and prevented him from crashing to the unforgiving cobblestones, but Brummagen's death was inevitable.

Sneeth leaned from the window and gazed at the broken remains of the vainglorious man. "Collect all the pieces you can," he told the Dolls. "Put them in the cage for the crows, as promised. No need for them to miss a promised feast."

With nary a flicker of emotion, the Dolls turned to carry out his orders. Sneeth perched on the sill, as the Dolls herded concerned and horrified citizens away from the fractured bones and meaty fragments that had been Brummagen, and shovelled the entrails into buckets. Sneeth swivelled to examine the shelves to which Brummagen had pointed with such hope and pride. He rolled up the ink-wet map and pushed it into the fire. The dying flames leapt joyfully to consume the offering, dancing and whirling in the grate until only ashes remained. Sneeth scooped the warm ashes and rubbed them between his calloused palms, crushing them to the finest dust, before offering them to the wind, which whipped them away, scattering them in a grey benediction over the city.

CHAPTER TWENTY-EIGHT

Jenny studied her reflection in the polished metal mirror. Her colour had returned, pinking her lips and cheeks, but the shadows under her eyes were a new and unwelcome development. She hid the mirror under a cushion, refusing to acknowledge her fear, but the writhing ball of maggots in her gut continued to celebrate this unprecedented festival of fear.

In the dungeon, she had resigned herself to flickering out of existence like an untended lamp. She'd slip away, unmissed, unloved. Unmourned. But here she was, still breathing, with new opportunities beckoning. The fear of dying squirmed in her belly, and she sighed, wishing it was only a physical object she could regurgitate. She closed her eyes and concentrated on squeezing the terror into a tight ball. Mayhap she could crush it into oblivion, like a nuisance insect.

The rap on her door startled her, and she called out without thinking.

The door cracked open, and Sneeth's talons curled around the edge, announcing his presence. He leaned through the gap, but didn't enter.

"May I come in, My Lady?"

Hmm, not calling me Mother, today. "What do you want?"

"To keep you company for a while. I have interesting news. Information which could benefit us."

I can't afford for the monster to know more than me. Jenny nodded her agreement, reluctant to speak.

Sneeth established himself on the footstool, his wings trailing on the ground. "Can I get you anything? Do you require more hot bricks? Or a warm drink?"

Jenny shook her head, eyes narrowed.

Her son sniffed the air, a predator searching for prey. "You ate all the oranges? If it isn't impertinent to say, you look much improved, Milady."

"Thank you." Jenny stared into the fire as she waited for Sneeth to continue.

"Yesterday, I realised Brummagen was the person most likely to know where the fugitives have fled." Sneeth flicked a glance at Jenny, but she steadfastly refused to look at him. "I gave him overnight to come up with a solution, otherwise I promised he'd hang in a cage like the other sacrifices and feed the birds."

A faint smile flittered over Jenny's face, but she resolutely kept her gaze on the flames.

"Are you not interested in his idea?"

Jenny turned towards him, staring over his shoulder. "You'll tell me what you want me to know. That is why you're here?"

"Brummagen had a theory about the legendary love tunnels. He believed they led to the homes of the beauties of bygone days, and that's where Xanderamm and Field sought refuge."

Jenny frowned. "I cannot understand how that is helpful. The tunnels are ancient, the women are long dead."

"Because they're ancient, we can eliminate newer homes,"

Sneeth said. "Brummagen had drawn a rough map, marking the oldest houses within the city."

Jenny sat up straighter.

"The idiot spilled ink over his masterpiece, but recreating a copy should be child's play."

"Can we salvage anything from the original?"

"I burned it, and scattered the ashes," Sneeth said. "There is no evidence of its existence."

"Are you as addle-pated as you are repulsive? That map could have been our key to regaining favour with Draqshet."

"My Lady, perhaps I have no desire for Draqshet's favour. Perhaps I crave my freedom."

Jenny sank back into her pillows. "Without Brummagen's knowledge, we can't recreate the map. We certainly don't know which women were most desirable generations ago."

"Identifying the oldest houses is not beyond our capabilities. Even dim-witted monsters can recognise old from new, and the city archives contain maps dating back to the city's origins. Furthermore, my repulsive status doesn't prevent me from studying Brummagen's family histories, which he was kind enough to show me, before diving to his demise."

Jenny stared, blank-faced as a Doll, at her son. The tremor in his voice sliced her heart, but she could not, would not, apologise for her insults.

Sneeth rose to his feet, gathering his shredded dignity. "I will keep you informed, My Lady. In the meantime, I wish you a speedy recovery. Send a message if you wish to converse. Or if you need anything." He bowed stiffly and left without a further word, closing the door quietly behind him.

Sneeth heard Vera puffing before she rounded the curve of the stairwell and noted she clutched her side as she climbed. He nodded an acknowledgment as they crossed paths and she smiled a response but spared no breath for idle speech. Sneeth turned to offer assistance, but thought better of it. After all, she was merely a servant, and perfectly capable of mustering a couple of girls. Nevertheless, he felt a warmth spread through his breast whenever he met her.

Vera leaned heavily against the wall at the top of the stairs, waiting for her heart to stop galloping like a runaway horse. She rubbed her eyes and blinked, hoping the frame of darkness around her vision would disappear, or diminish, then took a steadying breath before knocking on Jenny's door.

"You look brighter, Milady, if I may say so." Vera plumped the pillows and tweaked the bedclothes. "I saw your visitor leave. From his expression, I think you were unkind to him."

"I don't know why he insists on visiting, not when he knows he is unwelcome." Jenny plucked petulantly at the embroidery on her sleeve. "Entertain me, Vera. Tell me the Palace gossip."

Vera perched on the edge of the bed, ignoring Jenny's raised eyebrows. "There was a proper kerfuffle earlier. That odd little man, Brummagen, landed on the cobbles below his apartments."

"Suicide?"

"Nobody knows for sure, but everybody has an opinion, dressed as an indisputable truth. Some say he jumped, over-come by remorse for his role in allowing Draqshet to take control of the city. Others say Sneeth himself tossed him out of the tower. Punishment for failing to discover where his former master has gone to ground."

"And you? What's your opinion?"

"I wouldn't presume to have an opinion on such weighty matters, Milady."

"Do you know when they will hold his funeral?"

"Funeral! His remains scattered over a wide area. The Dolls salvaged all the meat they could and stuffed it into a sacrificial cage. There won't be no funeral, Milady. Probably for the best."

Vera shrugged. "I can't imagine anyone volunteering to speak the words of passing for him. He was a singularly unloved man."

Jenny clapped her hands. "So you do have an opinion."

"No, Milady. I merely made an observation." Vera winced as she spoke, her hand involuntarily reaching for her side.

"You're in pain. Why don't you see an apothecary, take a potion to ease the discomfort?"

"I already have, Milady. The highest dose I dare take without snuffing myself."

"You should stay home, rest." Jenny openly assessed Vera. "You are without fear. How do you face death without trepidation?"

Vera sighed. "When I cross to the Summer Fields, I will meet with my loved ones. What is there to fear? Death is only a portal, from limitless pain to unending joy. But I'm not ready yet. I still have work to complete."

Jenny lowered her voice. "Is there anyone to speak the words of passing for you?"

"Are you offering, Milady? That'd be a rare sight. A fine young lady speaking for an old serving woman." Vera spluttered a laugh.

"I think I am." Jenny blinked. "You're the first person not to judge me and knowing my... misdemeanours... still show kindness. It would be my honour to speak the words for you. If it's allowed, and you don't have something already arranged, of course."

Vera reached forward and patted Jenny's hand. "Mayhap I'll hold you to that, Milady, but not just yet. We need to move you to safety, first."

"Why are you here?"

"I came to see what you needed, Milady."

∽

The Doll patrols were fewer, but wise citizens stayed indoors after dusk. Vera stuck to the unlit back alleyways, frequently stopping to listen. The wind howled a dismal dirge down the shadow-filled snickets, catching at her cloak with chilly fingers, but the cunning fox and the owl hunted their respective patches with equanimity, lending her the confidence to continue.

The night predators had grown used to the darker shadow, recent experience teaching them it presented no threat, despite the rank odour of despair it trailed.

The close-shuttered house shed no light onto the street, not even the gardens, but Vera negotiated the path with ease. As she approached the entrance, a waft of warm air spilled down the steps.

"Quickly, my friend." A hand reached out and guided her inside, then pulled her into a hug. "Are you certain nobody followed you?"

"I took precautions, Lady Amora, but even if I attracted unwelcome attention, there is no law against old friends gossiping over tea and cakes. At least, not yet."

Lady Amora led Vera into the warmth of the kitchen, where Danny relieved her of her cloak and Paulie pulled a chair for her.

"Is it true Sneeth tossed the treacherous turd from the tower?" Lady Amora leaned forward.

"I wasn't there, so I can't say with conviction, but I doubt Sneeth would waste a resource. He believed Brummagen knew more than he realised after being close to Xanderamm for so many years and threatened him with the cage unless he divulged useful information."

"We're safe then," Lady Amora said. "Brummagen knew naught of the passages."

"He knew of their existence," Vera said. "Silly man spent a sack of coin trying to find them, back in the day. Of course, he never came close, but fear sharpens a man's mind and Palace scuttlebutt says he produced a theory."

Danny poured the tea and Paulie served the cakes while Vera explained that the maids who'd cleaned Brummagen's room had complained about all the spilled ink around the edges of his desk. One of the brighter footmen suggested the old man had used a large sheet to create a map. Spilling the ink may have infuriated Sneeth, who threw him out of the window in an evil fit of temper.

"The speculation of a lowly footman is unlikely to shed light," Danny said, pinching together his crumbs to make a last sweet morsel.

"I wouldn't lend much credence to such either, but Sneeth went back to Brummagen's rooms and pored over the old family histories books. One of the maids said he was like a cat at a mouse hole. He knew something was there, but couldn't reach it." Vera frowned. "He carried a stack of books to his rooms and ordered the footmen to fetch the old maps of the city from the archives. He's clever, he'll eventually work out where the tunnels lead."

Lady Amora shivered, despite the comfort of the roaring fire and heavy curtains. "I cannot comprehend your affection for the evil creature."

"I don't believe he is evil. He was misguided and mistreated by the foulness, now claiming to be his father, who carefully crafted Sneeth's behaviour and attitudes. He doesn't know better, and his misshapen body colours how people respond to him."

"With all respect," Danny said, "your attitude towards the creature seems coloured by your son's unfortunate experience."

Vera nodded. "If I had not showered my son with love and

affection, he too could have become a monster, exactly as people expected."

"But Sneeth is a monster, whether by education or election," Lady Amora said.

"I've seen him show tenderness and restraint," Vera said. "He is not beyond redemption."

"And that woman, Jenny? I suppose she's just misunderstood, too? A victim of unfortunate circumstances?" Lady Amora tapped a knife on the edge of her plate. "You see goodness in everybody, my friend, and I am grateful you saw it in me... but that jumped up little trollop is corrupt to her core."

"Redeemable or not, by your own admission, Sneeth is still searching for the fugitives. I can't see a positive outcome, not if he's as clever as you believe," Paulie said. "Why don't you take one of our sticky-fire bombs? Incinerate him while he sleeps. If he sleeps."

In the sanctuary of his room, Sneeth rocked back and forth on his haunches, his wings covering his head and shoulders. Shame blazed through him: he had frozen with fear when he learned Vera associated with people who had access to sticky fire. His mind raced to recall the fragments of legend about this weapon. Draqshet had taken pains to nurture his fear of infernos, but sticky-fire elevated the threat to a different dimension.

The tears streamed uncontrolled down his hollow cheeks. Hunched in the damp shadows, he'd heard Vera defend him and refuse the weapon. The lumps choking him sat heavy and rough in his chest. No matter how much he spluttered and hacked, he couldn't cough them up. He leaned back against the wall, willing the nausea and dizziness to pass. Such weakness was unacceptable.

Using his wings for balance, he fought to his feet and stood swaying in the cool night air. The pain in his chest grew, expanding like a carcass rotting in the sun, restricting his breathing. He clasped his hands behind his skull and concentrated on breathing evenly.

Flames roared inside his head and his thoughts flittered above the bonfire like floating ash. The crackling conflagration crowded out rational thought. Protect Jenny. The potential threat to his mother was the only idea he could firmly grasp. Sneeth staggered along the corridors and up the stairs, clinging to the walls for support. The Dolls standing guard at strategic points, had no orders pertaining to him, therefore, they ignored him.

His skin puckered in the frigid air, the stone flags on the floor adding naught to his comfort, as he collapsed in a shivering heap outside Jenny's door. Sneeth pressed his ear to the wood and listened. He gasped and half rose, when a log popped on her fire before realising what he'd heard. He closed his eyes, pushing away the usual night sounds of the Palace groaning as the ancient stones and beams cooled and settled.

Jenny shifted in her sleep, the rustle of bed linens clearly audible to Sneeth. Her breathing was slow and regular, and Sneeth exhaled in relief. Wrapping his wings around himself as protection from the cold, he stretched himself before her door and waited for dawn.

CHAPTER TWENTY-NINE

A confused but grudgingly compliant crowd swirled and eddied in the dark courtyard; a susurration of whispers rose and collapsed back into itself, no citizen daring to attract attention. Dolls loomed atop the walls, their spears and arrows glinting in the trembling torch light. The soldier's stolid silence crushed the citizens' complaints or questions before they uttered them.

Friends and families shuffled closer for comfort, shoulder to shoulder, swaying together with shared trepidatious breaths. Ill-prepared individuals sought familiar faces, groups to invade or cling to, a facade of fake fortitude.

Groans of wood and iron echoed off the high walls, further cowing the herd into submission, as the Dolls hauled barricades across the entrances, trapping the populace. Blank-faced soldiers, their arms and legs conspicuously bound in protective cloths, poled a shrieking, clanking wheeled platform into the arena. Searing air crackled around the device, which rumbled like a resting dragon. Those closest drew back from the scorching heat, whilst Dolls dragged waist high wooden trestles around the contraption, and those citizens careless or too slow to get out of the way, they ruthlessly trampled under hobnailed boots.

Blaring trumpets crudely announced the dignitaries' arrival, and all heads swivelled towards the balcony. A bulky silhouette, darker than the night, glided forward, resting wicked talons on the balustrade. The deep hood hid eyes avid for the planned entertainment. Lurking behind The Most High Lord Draqshet was Sneeth, and the detested Jenny, the woman most of the crowd held responsible for their troubles.

The Dark Lord's words rasped like sandpaper inside everyone's head, the eerie sensation compounded by his unnerving stillness.

"Citizens of Kingston, I have been most generous, allowing you to continue trading and living as you have been accustomed. All I asked is that you surrender the traitors, fugitives gone to ground in your town, who, as I speak, must be cowering in one of your homes." The heavily robed figure leaned forward, his eyes burning like coals deep within his cowl.

The crowd shuffled uncomfortably, but remained silent.

"Understand, I care naught if this town thrives or crumbles to dusty ruins. Your brief lives mean naught to me, whereas I shall endure for eternity. As a demonstration, tonight you will witness the extinction of your elite. They are useless to me, therefore I have no reason to keep them alive." Draqshet withdrew into the darkest shadows while the Dolls carried out their orders.

"Strikes me as petty and childish, for someone so powerful," Danny whispered into Lady Amora's ear.

Together with Paulie, they had clambered onto a stonework buttress to avoid the crush near the barricades. The trio wore capacious cloaks, and sensible boots suitable for running or kicking.

A ripple of distress spread from those closest to the iron contraption as the Dolls paraded the prisoners. Filthy and emaciated, they clung together, their sunken eyes too filled with despair to recognise the impending danger towards which they shambled.

Without warning, two Dolls grabbed each prisoner, seizing arms and legs, and flung them onto the sizzling contraption. The victims first wailed and writhed in agony on the giant griddle, too weak to stand. Clothes and hair exploded into flames, creating man-sized torches. Skin burst open on limbs, revealing bubbling flesh and heat-cracked bones. The newly dead danced as their sinews shrank and their limbs contorted. The stench of scorched meat and singed hair filled the courtyard, and greasy black smoke stung eyes and flooded lungs.

The crowd surged towards the exits, animal instinct propelling them from peril. Panic spread as the crowd fought to clear the barricades and Dolls barred their way with drawn blades and low held spears.

Sticky-fire bombs crashed onto the balcony, too close together to count. The blaze lit the courtyard. Draqshet's terror-filled scream burst eardrums as he fled to safety, leaving his forced entourage to fend for themselves. Flaming Dolls spread the inferno as they continued tossing prisoners onto the grill, oblivious to the fire dripping onto them from above.

Not waiting to see the results of their actions, Lady Amora led her companions towards an undistinguished door set into the palace wall. They slipped through into the relative calm of a servants' passageway.

"Is this one of them famous love tunnels?" Danny asked, groping in his pockets for sulphur sticks.

"No, merely a disused servants' corridor leading to the stores. It's a maze, but we should come out behind the market."

Sneeth leapt after his father and hauled on the balcony door handle, to no avail. Draqshet had left them to burn. A high-pitched needle of sound pierced his brain, and he whirled around, the conflagration creeping inexorably towards Jenny and her flowing silk gown. Deprived of her gifts, she could not escape. Cursing himself for a fool, Sneeth leapt over the cracking flames and wrapped his wings around his mother. Choking on oily smoke, he staggered to the balustrade. He should drop Jenny and launch himself into the night air, away from the deadly flames.

He leapt to the ground, wings firmly wrapped around his mother. Sticky fire dripped onto his leathery limbs, eating through flesh and bone, transporting him to a new world of excruciating pain before he passed out.

He stared at the stone floor, mere handspans from his face as it swam in and out of focus. Muffled voices sounded nearby. A groan escaped his blistered lips.

"I'll bring you water, you'll have to suck through a straw." Vera's skirts rustled next to him. Her footsteps faded and returned. "I'm too old for this," she muttered, as she slid a wide bowl underneath him with a slippered foot.

Sneeth glimpsed his reflection. Bandages as he expected, but the charred remains of his face, with revealed patches of bone, shocked him and he couldn't suppress a shriek.

Vera sank to the floor and repositioned the bowl before holding a straw to his ruined mouth.

He turned away, as far as his bindings allowed. "No." The word caught in his smoke scorched throat.

"Don't start that foolishness," Vera said. "If you're concerned you've ruined your pretty looks, don't worry. I'm the only one as looks you in the face." She gently touched his bound hand. "I've not words to express how proud I am of what you did, but my heart is full to bursting. You were a proper hero, saving that girl."

"Has my father visited?"

"No, not yet."

"And Jenny?"

"She didn't stay long, but she wanted to thank you. Other than a nasty cough and a bit of singed hair, she's unhurt."

"I don't want her to see me. She won't come again, but if she does, send her away. Tell her I said to stay away."

Vera waggled the straw. "Drink. Then I'll change your dressings. Can't promise it won't hurt, because it will, but I've some cream to help ease the pain a bit."

"You ought to have left me to die. It's what your friends wanted," Sneeth croaked.

Vera hesitated, then offered the straw again. "Don't sell yourself short, Milord. It's what the entire town wanted. But a popular choice isn't necessarily the right choice."

"You're making a habit of treading dangerously."

"Indeed, Milord. What do you propose doing about it? May I respectfully suggest you get your strength back so you can resume your reign of terror? With that in mind, drink."

Sneeth sipped the bitter tasting water while Vera patiently held the straw. His vision blurred, and he felt himself relax.

"You've drugged me." The slurred words dripped from his mouth and he watched them pool in the dish before he slipped into blessed unconsciousness.

"There's no virtue in keeping company with pain," Vera said. "Besides, it slows your recovery." She clambered gracelessly to her feet, panting with the exertion. Tears welled in her eyes as she looked at the ruins of Sneeth.

His wings were mere tattered rags, the leathery membranes burnt to the bone. His exposed spine gleamed dully. She'd cleaned as much roasted flesh as she dared, but sections of his tail looked beyond repair. Under the bandages, his ears were melted, fused to his skull. The pain alone should have killed him, but demons must be different from mere mortals. Leaping from the sticky-fire into the regular flames below had saved him. She shuddered to think what damage the sticky-fire could have wrought upon him had he stayed.

Vera waited until Sneeth was completely unconscious and removed from further pain before she began her ministrations. She dampened his dressings with warm water before gently peeling them away, to reveal angry red flesh, which she covered with fresh aloe slices. She sang softly as she worked, words she'd crooned long ago to her own son.

"Hush my son
close your eyes.
The sun and the moon
all the stars in the skies
are watching over you tonight.
Lay your head
down to rest
safe in the knowledge
you're loved best."

Sneeth drifted in the darkness of his drugged dreams. He screamed soundlessly as sheets of white-hot fire swept over him and he wept for an incalculable but nameless loss. Featherlight fingers dabbed fluids onto his blistered lips and he lapped and sucked with the fierce instinct of a newborn, before sinking into a somnolent stillness.

There it was again, the voice dragging him into consciousness. He fluttered his eyes, forcing himself to focus. A paroxysm of pain engulfed him in a vicious embrace, and he stared glassy-eyed at the floor. Vera? Who else cared enough?

"Water," he croaked, the single word grating his throat. "Please." The extra effort was like swallowing knives, but his desire to show gratitude outweighed the discomfort.

Vera huffed and chuffed into position, and held a straw for him, careful to keep his reflection out of sight. "Go slowly," she said. "You don't want to fetch it all up again. I'll just bide awhile until you're ready to try again." She arranged her skirts as a cushion and leaned back against the bed.

"Your singing... woke me..."

"Sorry, Milord. Always did sound like a strangled cat."

"No, it was... comforting."

Sneeth twitched his wings, but they lay immobile.

"Try not to move, Milord. You've sustained enormous injuries, they'll take time to heal."

"My wings?"

Vera sniffed. "Only time will tell, Milord. Heat from the fire shattered the bones, but the physicians believe they'll knit well enough."

"Strong enough... to fly?"

"It's not the bones as is the problem, Milord. It's the skin between them."

Sneeth took a deep, agonising breath. "Tell me."

"They saved your life, yours and Jenny's. Using them as a shield saved you both."

"At what cost?"

"The membrane has burned away, Milord. No one can say if

it'll grow back. We must hope for the best. I've seen men with wooden legs," Vera said. "I was thinking, if the skin doesn't grow back... I could fashion wings from waxed silk or linen."

Sneeth's silence filled the room, crashing in waves up the walls, and drowning Vera's forced enthusiasm like a litter of unwanted kittens.

"I cannot live... crippled."

CHAPTER THIRTY

The fox and owl noticed her unsteady steps and registered her distress, but paid her the compliment of ignoring her. She presented no threat to them. The two shadowy silhouettes sidling down the snicket in her wake paid her a great deal of attention.

Vera entered the blinded house of pleasure, and Vert shrugged at Dexter.

"She must be a friend," Dexter said.

"That is my assumption, too. However, I am in no rush to enter a trap. I would hear her conversation before we join the party."

Vert and Dexter crept around the side of the almost deserted house to the kitchen window, where slivers of warm light escaped the hastily pulled curtains. Fragments of low-voiced conversation seeped into the garden, where the pair of listeners gathered them into a patchwork.

"... warned... sticky-fire... Sneeth knows... friends... crippled..." from the old woman.

"... the map now... who else..." Lady Amora said.

"... opportunity like this... him die..." Danny's voice rose in frustration.

Vert tapped the pre-arranged signal on the kitchen window and an unknown hand shuttered the lamps before Lady Amora opened the door. Vert and Dexter slipped into the dim warmth of the kitchen, their night adjusted eyes easily picking out the stranger, Danny, and Paulie. Lady Amora readjusted the curtains and slid open the lamps before greeting her guests and introducing everyone.

"You launched an attack on the Palace? Without waiting for backup?" Dexter's voice rose an octave. "You could have got yourselves killed."

"We didn't have a choice," Danny said, folding his arms. "The entire town was summoned to attend, or face the consequences."

"Draqshet lost patience, only sacrificing two victims at a time. Wasn't getting the results he expected." Paulie shuddered. "He had built a giant... griddle. A massive iron box with fires inside. The Dolls tossed the prisoners on top, cooked them alive, without so much as blinking. We couldn't just stand there and do nowt. We couldn't save anyone, but we showed 'em we're not gonna take this lying down."

"You revealed your secret weapon to The Dark Lord. You threw away the element of surprise. He'll be planning a counterattack, or at least a defence," Vert said.

"He's not shown himself since," Vera said. "Mayhap you're right, or mayhap he's hiding. I don't know as anyone has challenged him afore."

Vert placed himself opposite Vera. "You occupy a unique position, Milady. An easily compromised position."

Vera smiled. "A polite way to ask if you can trust me? If I wasn't trustworthy, I'd tell you otherwise, so there's naught I can say that'll convince you."

"If I heard correctly," Vert said, "Sneeth knows your friends are responsible. How long before he attempts reprisals?"

"His recovery is uncertain, Milord. The physicians have never afore treated such a one. They argue amongst themselves and what they suggest is pure guesswork. I treated his burns initially with aloe, now I'm using honey."

"How is he progressing?" Lady Amora asked.

"Not well. I had to tell him the extent of his injuries. Seems he's lost the will to live."

"Nobody will mourn his passing," Danny said.

"I will," Vera said. "Just like I mourn the passing of Draqshet's other victims. All so unnecessary."

"My friend," Lady Amora said, "you cannot truly think he is a victim? After the atrocities he has committed?"

"In his father's name, at his father's bidding," Vera said. "He knew no better. He wants approval, like the rest of us."

"Disregarding his motivation," Vert said, "when do you think he'll come looking? He must want revenge."

"I wish I could give a definitive answer. For now, I'm keeping him drugged and asleep to speed his healing."

"The quickest route to regain Draqshet's approval will be to hunt down those responsible for the fire," Dexter said. "Sneeth knows where you live, he doesn't need to come in person. He can send his minions."

"Dexter's right," Vert said. "You all need to leave the city, including you, Vera."

"I can't abandon him. Not while he's vulnerable."

"What better time is there to leave?" Paulie threw his hands in the air.

"I'm a foolish old woman, with little time remaining," Vera said. "But I won't risk my friends. I don't believe he will, but if he turns on me, I don't want to have any information to give."

She shrugged. "I cannot guess how long I'd last if tortured. Make your plans when I'm gone."

Vera closed the door behind her, tears streaking her withered cheeks at the thought of never again seeing her friends.

~

Roic and Annie waited on the edge of the camp for Theo to return with Vert and Dexter.

Try to relax. Theo or Vert would have sent a message if they were in danger.

Annie stared into the night. "I should have gone, this is my responsibility, Roic."

We all agreed you are too important to put yourself at risk. Roic huffed.

The two friends watched the stars milling overhead. They had naught useful to say. A smile creased Annie's face. "Theo says they're on their way back."

Vert and Dexter stumbled on the rough ground when Theo released them from their faster-than-thought trip. The spies told their story as quickly as they could to an increasingly agitated audience.

Annie looked with disbelief at Vert and Dexter. "The misbegotten monster not only potentially knows how to find the tunnels, but also knows the resistance has sticky-fire?" She threw her hands in the air. "And this crazed servant woman has a son fixation? While he's injured and in her power, she's protecting him?"

Vert shrugged helplessly.

Theo frowned and folded his arms. "Are you certain the woman is not working for Draqshet?"

"I cannot be certain, with so much at risk, but she feels genuine. I'll not deny addle-pated, but her motivation is not evil. However, regardless of her intentions, she presents a risk." Vert shook his head. "I understand the desire to fight back, but Lady Amora and her men should not have revealed the sticky-fire."

"At least the monster, Sneeth, is out of action," Dexter said. "What I don't understand is why he's delayed searching for the tunnels if Brummagen furnished him the information."

I say we don't delay. Roic twitched his tail. *I can't see details, but I know where the town is. I will incinerate every building. Draqshet won't survive.*

"No, I can't allow you to do that, my friend," Annie said. "I can't be responsible for needless deaths. The remaining citizens deserve our protection."

"This is strange and unexpected," Theo said. "I suggest we allow ourselves time to digest the news. Xanderamm and Harry should join us at breakfast, they have knowledge of the town, which will be useful."

The moist sweetness of honey drew Sneeth towards consciousness. He swam through the frigid darkness, striving towards the light, towards the voices.

Two voices, and two pairs of hands ministering to his wounds, both with butterfly gentle fingers. Vera and Jenny. Sneeth fought back a scream. That Jenny, she who loathed and despised him, she who found his existence unbearable, should witness the humiliation of his maimed body was almost more than he could bear.

"I think he's awake," Vera said. "Talk to him."

Sneeth listened to slippered feet shuffling and felt the draft of a door opening and closing. He sensed the warmth of a nearby body, as a predator feels the heated presence of nearby prey.

"Vera made this for you." Jenny slid a steaming bowl of broth under his face and held the straw.

Sneeth turned as far away as his injuries allowed. He had an inexhaustible list of questions for this woman, but he couldn't summon a single word. If he attempted to speak, all his misery and humiliation would spill out of his ruined mouth, flooding over the floor in an incontinent mess, from which he'd never recover.

Jenny jiggled the straw. "Vera warned me you'd be difficult. She said to call the footmen if I need help. They'll turn you over and hold you in place while I spoon feed you. Sneeth? I know you're listening. Please, eat. Not for me, but for yourself. You must regain your strength."

Sneeth eased himself back. Being manhandled by footmen was an experience he'd prefer to avoid. The meat rich fluid was enticing, and he gripped the straw between his teeth. He sucked, slowly at first, but with increasing enthusiasm, like an inebriate with a fresh jug.

"I need to say thank you," Jenny said. "You risked your life, you almost died, to save me. I know you could have spread your wings and escaped unhurt. Why? Why save me? You don't even like me? And I've hardly endeared myself to you."

Sneeth guzzled the final dregs from the bowl and dropped the straw. "You.. wouldn't... understand."

"Draqshet locked the door when he fled, trapping us in the inferno. He must have expected you to fly away, leaving me to my fate. Saving me isn't likely to get you back in his favour."

Sneeth shrugged, sending currents of agony racing around his torso. He ground his teeth and swallowed the groan.

"I knew you regretted saving me."

"Help me... sit up," Sneeth gasped.

"I can't do that, I'll need help. The surgeons spread and splinted your wings. I'll call the footmen."

"No. No footmen." Sneeth closed his eyes against the pain, taking only shallow breaths. "Put cushions... lie... where I can... see... your face."

Jenny dragged cushions down beside her and lay on her side so they could see one another.

"Tell me... what happened?"

"Vera found us," Jenny said. "She organised a team of servants to haul us inside. I was unconscious but apparently uninjured, so she packed me off to bed with a mild sedative. But you? She thought you were dead at first. She didn't believe anyone could survive such severe injuries. But she wouldn't give up. She called in a team of carpenters to modify your bed, ordered them to cut the hole for your face and make you as comfortable as possible with the padded leather edging. Then she made them build extensions so you could stretch your wings while they heal."

"My room?"

"Yes, Vera thought you'd be more comfortable in your own room."

Sneeth twisted his head towards Jenny. "You didn't flinch."

"Before the fire, Vera told me to look with my heart. I didn't understand what she meant."

Sneeth blinked and waited for her to continue.

"Nobody has ever been kind to me without an ulterior motive. I don't understand why you rescued me, but I am grateful. You had naught to gain, but much to lose."

"You're my Mother."

Jenny reached to stroke his cheek. "My Son."

Sneeth's tears ran unchecked as Jenny caressed his ravaged face.

CHAPTER THIRTY-ONE

A fitful breeze conducted a successful campaign against the modest warmth of the campfire, and the group huddled before Roic, their shoulders hunched and brows creased.

"I confess, I am at a loss," Xanderamm said. "Vera may well have been in my service, but I do not remember her. Only the youngest and prettiest maids would have attracted my attention back then, but I can't recall their names, either." He blushed. "But Lady Jenny made an impression. The lady forced an acquaintance with Brummagen and we had to leave town because of her machinations. She and the foul creature, Sneeth, followed us to Kingston. Jenny is a skilled manipulator, and wrapped Brummagen around her little finger in no time, the poor fool."

"Why would the creature withhold information from Draqshet?" Theo asked.

Xanderamm shook his head. "That makes no sense. Sneeth and Jenny are bitter rivals. I'd expect him to be scrambling to tell The Dark Lord all he knows, to prove his superiority and loyalty."

"I can't comment on Draqshet's minions," Harry said, "but I know Vera. Not well, but she's served in the Palace for decades. A good, hardworking woman. Always ready to help others. Although the evidence is strongly against her, I cannot accept she is an agent for Draqshet."

We can theorise endlessly about motivations, but it does us no service. Sneeth's injuries incapacitate him, and Jenny is out of favour. Draqshet has disappeared for now, but we can be sure he'll return. The sticky-fire is no longer a surprise weapon, Sneeth will offer his intelligence and Draqshet will seek out Lady Amora and her men. It is safe to assume they are dead, and their stores of sticky-fire are in enemy hands. The Dark Lord will not hesitate to use it against us.

"You paint a bleak picture," Theo said.

"Always prepare for the worst during conflict," Harry said. "But I'm hoping Lady Amora and her companions escaped. Fine men, and a brave woman."

"We are assuming Draqshet was uninjured. He's either fled," Xanderamm said, "which seems unlikely, or he's taken up residence in one of the sublevels situated below the dungeons." He looked around the group. "They're difficult to access, but, as far as I know, there's only one entrance. He's trapped himself."

"I didn't know there were levels below the dungeons," Harry said. "The builders must have quarried them out of solid rock."

"I can make a map." Xanderamm frowned. "But I'll need time, it's been a while."

"If we can ambush him deep underground," Annie said, "we can eliminate him without risking the citizens. Blast him with light and seal his tomb. I'll wear my dragon skin suit to protect me from getting burned."

Theo snorted. "First, we draw up a plan, then we decide

who is best suited to lead the assault, my love. Using dragon skin armour is an excellent idea, but I cannot risk your safety. I'll go."

Annie glared at Theo. "We can discuss this later. In private. Meanwhile, Xanderamm needs writing materials."

~

"It's a trap." Paulie hauled on the wagon's reins.

"Or an opportunity," Danny said.

Slightly askew, the gates hung open. The fire had utterly consumed most of the Dolls; the conflagration leaving only memories. Without direct orders, the surviving Dolls took no action. Although an irate group of traders had forced open the gates, there was little traffic. Since the fire, people stayed indoors, only venturing out for necessities. Those passing through the gates were families leaving in wagons and carts piled high with their possessions.

"If anyone is watching, we're only attracting attention dithering about," Lady Amora said. "Let's go."

Paulie flicked the reins, and the horses ambled forward, the wagon creaking and swaying through the shadowed passage and out into the pale wintry sunshine, unchallenged by the lackadaisical lone Doll.

"I hope Vera is safe," Lady Amora said. "I don't trust that abomination, nor that upstart little trollop. Vera's always been an excellent judge of character, but she's blinded by grief for her son."

CHAPTER THIRTY-TWO

Sneeth listened to the pitter-patter of his Mother's dainty feet as she moved around his apartment, gathering cushions and quilts to make herself comfortable on the floor beside his bed. He studied her as she arranged herself. He noticed a change, a softening, but mistrusted his judgment. Am I seeing a tenderness because I need to see it? Is she demonstrating conspicuous compassion because she is still in thrall to Father, and will report back all I tell her?

"There are things you must know, Mother. Information which will change your way of thinking. But first, how familiar are you with the Goddess myths? The Great Mother?"

"Very little, my son. Probably less than most." Jenny shrugged. "Does it matter?"

"Yes, very much."

"Truly, I know only she created the world and all creation. Didn't she get bored and a long-lost daughter take over her responsibilities? But it's a children's story, naught else. Neither she nor the Goddess Reborn are real, are they?"

"My Father recently shared a story about the Great Mother."

"He doesn't seem the type to tell stories," Jenny said.

"Which is why I think it's important. It's an unpleasant tale, but you deserve to hear it." Sneeth took a deep breath. "Draqshet fell in lust with a beautiful woman and relentlessly hunted her. He planted me in her, and as we know, she rejected me, and Draqshet took me into his sole care."

"I don't want to hear this again," Jenny said.

"This is something you don't know. Please, just listen. He boasted to me how he'd also planted a dark seed within the woman, a seed of which she knew naught. It grew rapidly, spreading tendrils throughout her being, changing her, making her dissatisfied with everything, unable to ever again be content. She began searching, not knowing for what. But the quest consumed her, led her to neglect her duties. The world began, gradually but inexorably, to change."

Jenny waved a hand. "Wait. Are you trying to make me believe I was the Goddess? I was the Great Mother? Balderdash!"

"Is it? You have no memories because The Dark Lord stole them from you. You've been in his service for five years, roughly since the Goddess Reborn assumed her duties. He said your jailer walled you up in the darkness. Without light and heat, you faded away. Sound familiar?"

"That's a lie. I'm nobody; besides, I've seen her statues. I look naught like the Great Mother. Sneeth, I've accepted you as my son. I'm grateful to you for saving me, but please, don't endeavour to make me something I'm not. Being any mother presents a challenge, but the Great Mother?" Jenny snorted. "If you'd suggested Vera for the role, I might believe you. But not me. I'm not the maternal type."

"Neither of us truly knows who we are. The Dark Lord

thoroughly moulded and manipulated us. He kept us in the dark, figuratively and literally. I thought, together, we might find our way to the light."

"I think Vera's been putting something extra in your broth."

"Perhaps you're right. But if she has, I enjoy being this way, thinking new and daring thoughts. Will you do something for me? Take the history books from the table and burn them. Not a trace must remain."

Jenny examined the books. "These are antique, quite valuable to the right collector."

"Priceless," Sneeth said, "to the wrong person."

"The kitchens have a couple of gigantic fireplaces, but the furnace is probably bigger. I'll get some footmen to carry them down."

"No. They mustn't leave this room. I want you to burn them in the hearth here, page by page, if necessary. Vera can help, but nobody else must know."

Jenny leafed through the books, but found naught of interest. She had no curiosity about family trees and obviously embellished recounts of valour or courageous commercial dealings of long-dead characters. When Vera arrived with new dressings, Jenny had almost finished the task. Fine ash filled the hearth, which Vera raked and put in buckets for the maids to carry away.

The two women worked efficiently, peeling away the old bandages, washing the wounds, and applying fresh honey and new dressings.

"Tell me true," Sneeth said. "Is the skin growing back? Whenever I try to move my wings, I fail."

"The wounds no longer look angry," Jenny said, "but I see no fresh growth. You must be patient."

"I'll send for the physicians," Vera said. "The bones look

repaired, and removing the splints may help you regain movement."

"How is my father?"

"I cannot say, Milord. After the conflagration, he disappeared into the bowels of the Palace with a handful of Dolls. The general consensus is that he is licking his wounds and plotting an extravagant revenge."

Jenny winked. "Have a care, Vera. You're coming dangerously close to expressing an opinion."

Sneeth was drowsing when his apartment door burst open, halfway between midnight and dawn. He tensed at the clatter of booted feet: the Dolls had arrived, doubtless at his father's behest. He held his breath when he heard the rustle of heavy fabric sweeping the floor.

Draqshet inhaled theatrically. "You have been burning unusual fuel. Why?"

Sneeth remained silent. What did The Dark Lord already know and what was he trying to discover? A flood of icy air washed over his exposed back as Draqshet approached, and Sneeth's ravaged skin pimpled with goosebumps. Whatever his father wanted, Sneeth was certain he wasn't visiting to deliver sympathy or paternal concern.

Draqshet drew a cruel talon across the mangled wings, snagging bandages and raw flesh with equal disregard. "You disappoint me. I did not expect you to befriend the woman who spawned and abandoned you," Draqshet rasped. "I did not expect you to risk your life, and my displeasure, for a worthless female." He turned to the Dolls. "Bring in the women."

Sneeth forced himself into stillness. *They're safer if I feign disinterest. I'm the one he wants to punish.*

The air exploded from Vera's chest as a Doll threw her to the ground.

"Bastard!" Shuffling and moaning followed. "You'll be all right, Vera. Keep breathing."

Sneeth squeezed shut his eyes, willing Jenny to hold her tongue.

"How sweet. The harlot has developed a heart. After all these years. Such a pity you can't see them, mother and crone clinging together."

"I am glad to see you healthy, Father. And I am grateful you found time to visit," Sneeth said. "I worried about you, but as you can see, I'm immobile." Stop rambling, you fool.

Draqshet stabbed a talon into the meat of Sneeth's shoulder. "Your wings are beyond repair."

Sneeth swallowed the scream which filled his head with white light, momentarily blinding him. The women's whimpers crawled over the floor like crippled kittens, persistent but useless.

"I'd like you to sit up, so I can see your expression," Draqshet whispered into his ear. Without further warning, The Dark Lord sank his talons into Sneeth's shoulders and tore away the ruined wings, casting them across the room to slide bloodily down the wall.

Sneeth's shriek cracked stones in the walls, and roof tiles slithered off to crash on the cobbles below. Great gouts of blood painted the room with bright scarlet pain.

Draqshet turned to the guards and flicked a wrist. "Cauterise the wounds."

Two Dolls stepped forward and thrust their flaming torches into the bleeding flesh, and a sickening stench of scorched meat filled the apartment. They hauled Sneeth to his feet and propped him carelessly in a chair. His ragged breathing reassured the women he was still alive.

"Why did you burn books? What secrets are you hiding?" Draqshet loomed over Sneeth.

"Naught. They were worthless, stories for children."

"You lie. I see you care more for these filthy women than for yourself. Very well." Draqshet seized Vera by her hair and raised her to her tiptoes. "What was in the books, woman?"

"I didn't see."

"Nor shall you ever see again," Draqshet hissed and dropped her.

Vera's hands flew to her bloody eyes, and her wail of pain and fear trembled the torch flames.

"They know naught," Sneeth gasped.

"Tell me what I want to know."

"They were children's stories about the Great Mother," Jenny said. "Rubbish fit only for the fire."

Draqshet peered at her, searching the depths of her bruised soul. "Your son finally told you who you really were, then? How does it feel to know you're responsible for so much suffering? That those who once worshipped you now despise you for all the chaos and perversions your sordid quest for fulfilment brought?"

"You are wholly responsible for the devastation," Jenny said. "You planned it all."

"Indeed, you and your spawn are helpless. Tend to his injuries. His weakness sickens me. I will return after he recovers." Draqshet left the apartment in a billowing swirl of robes, darker than any nightmare.

Sneeth edged forward, breathing in short bursts, gripping the padded chair arms. "We don't have long. We must leave immediately."

"You're in no state to travel," Jenny said. "You need to rest."

"Although my father despises weakness, he won't pass up an

opportunity to gloat or torture. Mother, you must find a wagon, one with space for me to lie down."

"Sneeth is right. Draqshet won't rest until he discovers what we know. For the sake of our friends, we must escape," Vera said. "Jenny? I need you to take me to the hothouses; there are medicinal plants I must collect."

"The less toing and froing we do, the better," Jenny said. "We'll go together to the carriage-house, I'll harness the horses and Sneeth can stay out of sight in the back, while we get your plants."

Sneeth nodded his approval.

"Shuffle forward," Jenny said. "I need to bandage your wounds before we move."

Bare bone gleamed among the blistered flesh, but at least the cauterised wound wasn't bleeding. Jenny slathered the remaining honey over the ragged mess and wrapped linen strips tightly around his torso. She rummaged through a wardrobe and selected a loose tunic and a long cloak.

"Raise your arms." She dropped the tunic over his head, and arranged the folds as loosely as possible, then handed Sneeth a pile of clean sheets. "An imperfect disguise, but better than naught. Can you manage these? We'll need fresh dressings. I'll lead. Vera? Hold on to my belt. Sneeth will follow and make sure you don't fall."

Jenny pulled open the door and listened. Her pulse pounded in her ears, but she heard naught to cause alarm. "Keep your right shoulder to the wall for balance. We'll stop on every landing, although it's too early for the servants to be working yet."

Sneeth was panting and dizzy with pain before they reached the bottom of the stairs. "I can't keep up, you must go on without me."

"I'm not leaving without you," Jenny said, tears brimming.

"There're canvas stretchers behind the apothecary door," Vera said. She fumbled for her keys. "The master key, the plainest one, opens every door." She held out the bunch for Jenny.

"You two can't carry me," Sneeth said, as Jenny darted away. "I'm too heavy, even without my wings."

"Never tell a mother what she can't do for her child, because she'll always prove you wrong," Vera said. "If that girl had to carry you on her back, she'd do it, and you'd hear no complaint."

The co-conspirators froze as a rhythmic squeaking approached. Sneeth gripped Vera's hand, ready to haul her away.

"Look what I found," Jenny said, as she got closer. "A wheeled chair with handles behind. Never seen such an ingenious contraption before. I brought what I hope are painkillers, too."

Sneeth fumbled his way to the chair. "I can't sit on this. My tail."

Jenny reached under her voluminous skirts and withdrew a short blade. She slashed the leather back of the chair. "You can now."

Sneeth gripped the chair arms as Vera and Jenny pushed the creaky contraption along the corridors, Jenny whispering instructions and warnings to Vera. Sweating with anxiety and exertion, they reached the carriage house and stables. Before The Dark Lord's coup, the guards had meticulously maintained the carts and wagons that lined the far wall. A thick layer of dust now overlaid the neglected vehicles.

Sneeth pointed. "That one. Plain enough not to attract attention, big enough to sleep in."

"We must harness four horses," Jenny said. "That's a heavy wagon. The guards used it to move supplies."

"Yes, we did." A familiar voice issued from the darkest corner of the yard. A figure emerged brandishing a glittering sword, moonlight dancing along its freshly sharpened edge.

"Corporal Small. What are you doing here?" Jenny stepped forward, smiling brightly.

"Methinks a better question ought to be what business do you and your friends have here, Milady?" Small waved his sword. "Does The Most High Lord know of your predawn escapade? I think not." A sly smile slithered across his narrow face. "I'm certain he'll reward whoever apprehends you."

"Are you threatening me, Corporal Small? Surely you know better than to try to intimidate your betters." Jenny moved closer to the traitorous soldier.

"Rumour has it, mistress, you've fallen out of favour. You ain't nobody's better, not now."

Jenny lunged, lightning fast, opening Small from crotch to sternum with her wicked blade. He clutched wildly at his greasy intestines as they spilled onto the cobblestones. She stopped his scream by driving her dagger up through his throat.

Eyes bulging, Small gurgled a foamy fountain of blood down his tunic.

"I might be out of favour," Jenny said, stooping to wipe her blade on Small's uniform, "but I'll always be better than you, you miserable sack of maggot meat." She stepped back and aimed a vicious kick between his legs. Small curled into a foetal position as he bled out.

"What just happened?" Vera whispered to Sneeth.

"My mother eliminated an enemy," Sneeth said. "We dare not risk the hothouses. Come, Vera, climb aboard." He lurched to his feet and guided her into the back of the wagon. He leaned his forehead against the vehicle, waiting for the world to stop spinning or at least slow to a manageable speed.

Jenny dragged Small's corpse into the darkest corner, and

tossed forkfuls of horse manure over it, then scattered generous armfuls of straw over the trails of blood and innards.

"Hurry, Mother. Get the horses. I can help with the harnessing."

Jenny brought a team of horses from the stables, and a mazy tangle of straps and buckles. Sneeth sighed in dismay, but Jenny smiled and shook them into order.

"I know what I'm doing," she said.

The horses skittered at the sight of Sneeth, but Jenny soothed them into submission with soft hands and softer whispers.

"I'd like you to teach me how to do that," Sneeth said.

"They don't like the scent of blood, it makes them nervous," Jenny said as she checked buckles and tightened girths. "When you're stronger, I'll teach you to drive."

She ducked under Sneeth's shoulder and supported him to the back of the wagon, where he joined Vera. Jenny clambered through to the front seat and cracked the reins. "Hoi!" The horses strained and took up the slack, then the wagon rolled on its massive iron-bound wheels.

Jenny guided the wagon through moon-washed streets and drove unchallenged through the shadowy gate. The road unspooled before her, a bright ribbon of pale gravel. She drove towards the dawn. Towards the light.

Sneeth woke mid morning, face down in the back of the wagon. The cessation of motion had disturbed him, and now Vera's hand lay over his mouth. He covered her hand with his own, squeezing gently to indicate he understood she meant him to remain silent.

Jenny laughed and flirted with someone beside the vehicle.

Sneeth's bandages prevented him from hearing the stranger's responses, but his mother sounded relaxed. Sneeth caught the clink of coins and more laughter before the wagon lurched into motion again.

"I have a basket of food," she called over her shoulder. "Stay where you are for now." The wagon swayed and groaned, and the horses chuffed quietly as they clopped along. Jenny eventually found a suitable spot and guided the horses through light scrub to a chuckling stream.

"We can breakfast here, but we ought to travel far from Kingston before nightfall. I bought bread, cheese, tomatoes, and a jug of milk. Sorry, Sneeth. No meat."

Sneeth sighed. "With the odour of my own roasting flesh lingering behind my throat, I'm content to pass on meat for a while."

CHAPTER THIRTY-THREE

Wind-blown leaves and debris littered the Audience
Chamber, swept in through the carelessly bricked
and boarded up windows. Mice droppings accumu-
lated in corners and under the throne, their pungent odour
an unequivocal announcement of a new order. The Dark Lord
shivered with perverse pleasure at the disrepair and increasing
shabbiness of the once magnificent hall.

Draqshet seethed inwardly at his son's sedition. Clearly, the
woman Jenny wielded inexplicable power. He had underesti-
mated her, but her influence would end with her death, and his
renegade son would be brought to heel.

A Doll approached the throne and bowed mechanically.
"Most High Lord, they are not there."

Draqshet glared at the Doll. "Not there? Where are they?
One wounded almost to death and a blind old woman. Look
for them, you mindless dolt. Find them."

"Where should I look, My Lord?"

Draqshet descended carefully from the throne and lurched

towards the Doll who stared blankly. Draqshet entwined his fingers together inside his sleeves and took a deep breath.

"Fetch Corporal Small. He's usually lurking around the stables. Is that within your meagre capabilities? Do not return without him."

The Dark Lord remounted the throne. Frustration thrummed through his every fibre. Soon, he would dispense with the remaining Dolls. Once he had lured interfering Annie into his clutches, he would need nobody else. Not the disastrously inept Dolls, not his traitorous son, and not the upstart female. He would make Annie watch as they died. If she turned away, or closed her eyes, he'd pin her head and cut away her eyelids. He would not tolerate defiance. She would bear him sons, almost as powerful as himself, and together they would create a dynasty to rule the world.

A dragging sound interrupted his delusional fantasy. The doltish Doll hauled an untidy bundle to the foot of the throne. The stench of horse shit rose into the air, swirling veils like an exotic dancer.

"Corporal Small, My Lord."

The corpse leaked a trail of intestines.

"He's dead," Draqshet said. "You've brought me a dead man."

"Yes, My Lord. I found him gutted under a pile of manure. You said not to return without him, My Lord."

Draqshet slithered down from the throne, his fetid, laboured breaths filling the chamber. He placed his claw-like hands on either side of the Doll's head and wrenched it off in a single effortless move. The Dark Lord's roar of frustration rattled the rafters, and drifts of dust snowed down, decorating the recently deceased, like icing sugar on a festival log.

CHAPTER THIRTY-FOUR

Sneeth thrashed on the wagon floor, pounding with feet and fists and tail. Blind Vera shuffled out of range to dodge his flailing limbs.

"Hold tight," Jenny yelled over her shoulder. She yanked on the reins and drove the team off the road, towards the limited shelter of a brake of naked trees. The wagon jounced and shook, and Vera clung to the sides with all her remaining strength.

"Stay away from her!" Sneeth snarled like a wild beast, talons ready to shred his invisible opponents. "She isn't your creature." Tears streamed down his face and blood seeped through his linen wraps, the wounds torn afresh by his abandoned ravings. He reached out, then sagged, like a marionette with its strings slashed, and lapsed into unconsciousness.

Jenny brought the agitated horses to a grateful halt. She swiftly wrapped the reins around the footrest and clambered into the rear of the wagon.

"Are you all right?" She touched Vera's arm.

"I'm fine, My Lady, but he's been running a fever since breakfast. The heat's pouring off him, and he's hallucinating."

Jenny whipped off her apron and placed it in Vera's hands. "Fan him with this. It's the best I can do for now. I'm taking the horses' water bucket to those trees. If there're trees, it stands to reason there must be water."

Vera nodded, inwardly cursing her blindness, while Sneeth moaned and twitched, lost in his nightmares. Vera couldn't see his jerks and spasms, she could only feel the erratic rocking of the wagon.

Jenny returned with the bucket of water and unceremoniously sloshed most of it over her son. Puddles marbled with dark blood pooled on the wagon floor, soaking the feet of both women. Sneeth muttered incoherently, but stopped twitching.

"He needs fresh dressings," Vera said, "but there's no honey." She leaned forward and sniffed. "I'm sure his wounds have become infected. Is it too dark to see? You need to look for aloe plants. Not too close to the river."

"It's not fully dark yet," Jenny said. "You mean those great spiky plants? I won't be long." She leapt from the wagon and the night swallowed her.

"Can you hear me, Sneeth? Your mother and I are here... hold on... follow my voice back from wherever you are." Vera sang to the wounded creature, in the desperate hope of calling him back from whichever nightmare he currently inhabited.

"Hush my son
close your eyes.
The sun and the moon
all the stars in the skies
are watching over you tonight.
Lay your head
down to rest
safe in the knowledge

you're loved best."

She sang the words over and over, until her throat grew too dry, and choked tight with unshed tears. Somewhere, Sneeth heard the familiar song and grabbed hold, following the delicate thread of affection back home.

Back to a world of pain.

Annie jerked awake and elbowed Theo. "Did you hear that?"

Theo sat up and rubbed his eyes. "I dreamed I heard animal howls of anguish. Go back to sleep."

"I heard the same thing, Theo. We weren't dreaming the same dream." Annie swung her legs out of bed and pulled on her boots. "Never have I heard such distress. I'm going to find out what creature is creating the commotion. There! Again. Did you hear that?"

"Neither man nor woman, nor any animal I know could produce that sound. Mayhap Roic recognises the source."

Annie and Theo wrapped themselves in dark cloaks and crept to the edge of the camp where Roic slept.

The dragon was awake and waiting for them. *We are sensing the physical and emotional pain of an entity I cannot identify, and the lack of knowledge makes me nervous. I suggest I fly closer to this being, try to sense who, or what, it is.*

"I must come with you," Annie said. "The wretchedness is curdling my stomach. Mayhap there is something I can do to ease the creature's pain."

Theo placed an arm on Annie's shoulder. "I can't stop you

going, but I don't like it. Promise me, my love, if this thing presents any hint of a threat, you will retreat?"

If anyone threatens the Lady Annie, I will not hesitate to incinerate them. Roic extended a foreleg for Annie to use as a ladder. *You are the Goddess Reborn, but I am your sworn protector, and brook no argument on this subject.*

Roic launched himself into the starry skies, the cold air making Annie shiver in a way potential dangers did not. Tiny lights glowed far below in secluded houses, but the land was mostly dark, with only lakes and rivers reflecting the stars.

Annie clung on with wind-numbed fingers, her eyes tearing from the rushing air. The clamour of agony and confusion grew more intense as they closed on their target. Roic turned in lazy circles, drawing the unexpected scents deep into his throat.

Spirit and body have become separated, held together by the most slender of threads. Two women tether this creature to life, and one of whom is barely hanging on herself. This entity confuses me, Lady Annie. I sense great age combined with only a newborn self-awareness.

"Take me down, Roic. I must see for myself. Further speculation is merely time-wasting. I must relieve this creature of its misery, one way or the other."

Roic landed with less drama and more elegance than usual, in an effort not to alarm the already distressed party more than necessary.

Annie slid to the ground and checked her blades before striding towards the bulky mass where the distraught women and their mutilated companion huddled. She lit a small fireball which hovered before her and called out a greeting. "Hallo. Whoever you are, I am here to offer aid. I feel your suffering. May I approach?"

The supple figure of a young woman separated from the

mass. "We welcome any succour, but can defend ourselves if you prove false."

Annie stepped closer. "I, too, can defend myself. My dragon companion will annihilate you all, if he so much as suspects you intend harm. Now the pleasantries are out of the way, show me the way to your companion."

The young woman hesitated, and a flicker of fear danced over her features. "You must be AnnieRah, the Reborn Goddess. Which means the dragon can only be Roic the Magnificent."

Annie nodded. "And you are?"

"Begging for your mercy. Not for myself, but for my companions." The girl dropped to her knees and bowed her head.

The suffering creature is Sneeth. He is drifting dangerously in an ocean of anguish. Roic's voice boomed inside Annie's skull and her hand automatically sought the hilt of her short sword. She halted mid-step and seized the girl's bare wrist in a fierce grip.

Annie staggered under the onslaught of unrestrained information and emotions she received from Jenny. She dropped the wrist and wiped her hand on her cloak.

"Get to your feet, Jenny. You are not as expected, but I will decide your fate under less urgent circumstances. Sneeth is slipping away."

Annie's wrath glowed within her like a storm lantern, as she stood over the ruined creature who lay with his head cradled in the lap of an elderly woman.

"Please," she said to the old woman. "Move away."

Jenny rushed to assist the older woman, guiding her to sit upon a fallen trunk, and Annie realised the woman was blind.

Annie crouched beside the misshapen monster and held his hand. She flinched as a tsunami of emotions engulfed her.

Again, this creature defied her expectations. She closed her eyes and poured a soothing wash of energy over Sneeth, cooling and diminishing his torment. Again and again, she sluiced his agony until the creature ceased his silent screams into the universe, and Annie's innards stopped churning.

She opened her eyes to find Jenny kneeling opposite her, tears silently streaming down her cheeks onto Sneeth's bandaged torso.

"What happened to him? All the stories speak of a winged creature. He didn't lose his wings in the fire?"

"He destroyed his wings in the fire when he saved me, sacrificing himself. Draqshet tore away the remains in a fit of anger, exposing Sneeth's spine, ribs, and shoulder blades. The infected wounds have caused his delirium." Jenny wiped her eyes. "What will you do with us?"

"There is a war in my heart. You deserve to die for your crimes, but what I have discovered from your touch tells a different tale."

Jenny cocked her head. "I heard children's stories about you reading people by touching them, but I didn't believe. Touch Vera. She is pure and good." She tugged Annie. "Vera saved us both."

Annie knelt before the old woman, who was listening intently. "Mistress Vera, I am AnnieRah. May I hold your hand?"

Vera held out both gnarled hands to Annie. "Don't be hard on them, My Lady. Unfortunate circumstances shaped them, and they know no better way to survive, but they are learning to love. They are redeemable."

A feeling of tremendous wellbeing suffused Annie, a sensation which reminded her of drinking Lady Zarah's liquid sunshine all those years ago.

"Your blindness is a recent affliction?"

Vera nodded. "It matters not, I have very little time left before I join my friends and ancestors over the Rainbow bridge."

"Do you not desire to have your sight returned?"

"I have only one desire, My Lady. To see Sneeth healed, body and heart and mind."

"Then you must have your sight returned to witness such a miracle, mistress." Annie ran her fingertips over Vera's eyelids.

"You have restored the sight of my youth, My Lady." She kissed Annie's hands.

Annie returned her attention to the resting Sneeth.

"I have soothed his pain, for now, but his injuries are beyond severe. I can help him, but complete healing will take time and his cooperation." She shook her head slowly. "I cannot promise his absolute restoration. Much depends on his desire to attain wellness."

"When can you begin the process?" Jenny laced her fingers together to stop them from trembling.

"Today, but not here. I must get him to camp where I have a friend skilled in the use of medicinal plants and rituals."

"How can we help?" Jenny asked.

"Help me carry him to Roic. In the morning, continue on this road. Keep going until we find you."

CHAPTER THIRTY-FIVE

Roic flew steadily as Annie cradled the monster in her arms. She pushed gently on the doors to his mind and they swung open. The darkness spread to infinity, unrelieved by starlight or any other beacon. Only the throbbing pain of discovery offered a sense of direction. The monster's misery and despair pulsed a broken-hearted tattoo.

Annie cast a golden thread towards the dread drumbeat, like a hopeful fishing line into unknown waters. The piteous cries of a lost child drew Annie closer.

"Sneeth, I'm here. Hold on. Jenny and Vera sent me to rescue you. Take hold of the line. You need to come with me, Sneeth. Back to the physical world."

The cries grew quieter, less desperate.

"You're not alone. Tie the golden cord around your wrist. Come with me."

Annie felt the faintest shiver on the cord as Sneeth secured a knot.

"I'm bringing you home."

Theo stared at the mangled and bloodied body oozing fluids onto the camp-bed, his disgust and confusion undisguised.

"This is the abomination? Why did you bring it here? Why not kill it and end this pointless charade?"

"This is no farce. Sneeth and his companions confounded me," Annie said. "I expected to encounter unequivocal depravity, and I planned to incinerate them. But when I touched them... they are not the epitome of evil. Don't mistake me, Sneeth and Jenny have committed many wicked and deliberately cruel acts, but they were not fully responsible."

Theo stepped back and folded his arms. "How can a mature creature not be responsible for its own actions?"

"Consider your own experience. Although you didn't actively contribute to the chaos Elanrah wrought, you did naught to prevent the destruction, because she schooled you to believe there was no other option."

"Elanrah kept me secluded and lied to me in a misguided effort to protect me. It's hardly the same thing." Theo frowned.

"My point is, when you hear only one source of information, only one person's values, you accept their version of the truth, because you have naught to compare." Annie shrugged. "All living creatures seek to belong. Sneeth was no different, but he received a twisted education, a perversion of the truth."

"You think you can save him?"

"He seeks redemption," Annie said. "Redemption or extinction."

Netta shuddered and turned away from the unconscious creature, refusing to enter the roughly constructed bivouac. "You should have killed the vile monster when you found it."

"I held his hand, Netta. His emotional pain almost over-whelmed me." Annie pleaded with her oldest friend. "Why are you so against giving him a chance to redeem himself?"

"His foul exterior reveals his inner evil. This despicable crea-ture must be wicked; one look suffices to understand that." Netta curled her lip. "I don't know how you can bear to touch him."

"Once you get to know him—"

"I won't be getting to know that... that abomination," Netta said. "You've made a mistake and I'm not the only one to say so." Netta stomped away, leaving Annie open mouthed.

Xanderamm strolled over to the shelter he and Harry had hastily erected and bowed to Annie.

"I suppose you heard that," Annie said. "Are you going to tell me I'm making a terrible mistake, too?"

The ex-king leaned on the doorway and peered into the gloomy interior at the unconscious body. "Yes, I heard what Netta said. A commonplace assumption, but no. I hold a different opinion."

"I'd welcome a fresh perspective," Annie said.

Xanderamm cleared his throat. "As a royal child, then King, I learned I was special, above all others, more important. People cringed and fawned in my presence." He offered a half smile. "Then you came along and I learned I was naught but a preening popinjay, a worthless fool, neither loved nor respected."

Annie opened her mouth, but Xanderamm raised his hand.

"Wearing a beastly form, I saw the world in a new light. I learned to keep a low profile, lest I become someone's dinner. But I also learned to watch and listen. Brummagen was a learned scholar, an astute man, but often concluded poor deals, where less clever, but more attractive, men fared much better"

Annie half shrugged. "So?"

"Beautiful people receive better treatment than the rest of us. It isn't fair, but it's true."

"I see your point. I hadn't given it much thought before, but I agree."

"No reason why you would give it much thought. It's a system designed to benefit you, and others like you. You and Netta, for example, are the two most beautiful women in the kingdom. You don't need to work to convince an audience of your good intentions. People find themselves naturally drawn to you both, they want to like you, they automatically think the best of you, simply because you're attractive."

"How does this apply to Sneeth?"

"Sneeth is the most grotesque person I've ever laid eyes on. Not even the travelling circuses had anyone so hideous on display. Looking as he does, I daresay he learned certain behaviours in order to survive. When people scream in terror at the mere sight of you, I suppose being terrible comes naturally. Imagine having to convince everybody you ever met that you were harmless, especially when you're equipped with wicked fangs and talons."

"Only you call Sneeth a person, not a thing."

"When Lady Amora smuggled me and Harry out of town dressed as women, we automatically adopted different ways of moving, and different expressions. We didn't plan to act differently, but we automatically conformed to expectations. Don't tell him I told you, but Harry took offence when a soldier called him ugly." Xanderamm laughed, then became solemn again. "Draqshet offered Sneeth one role. What else could he do?"

"What are you suggesting? If I heal Sneeth, you think he'll return to his previous behaviour?"

"You have the power not only to heal him, but to change his anatomy. Why don't you ask him?"

~

Annie picked up the jar of Vert's salve, turning it over and over. She'd eliminated the infection overnight and numbed the pain of Sneeth's physical wounds, a simple enchantment, but still he muttered and twitched in his sleep.

She closed her eyes and plunged into the darkness, following the golden cord.

"Why am I here? Why have you not killed me?" Sneeth's voice was weak, but clear. "Are you here to gloat over my weakness?"

"Do you know me?" Annie asked.

"Only the Goddess Reborn would have the power or courage to encounter me openly. They say you are merciful. Save the women, they are not responsible."

"And you? What do you ask for yourself?"

"Lord Draqshet would advise me to tell you naught which you could use against me." Sneeth paused. "I am exhausted, My Lady. I cannot play games. I find I have no stomach for subterfuge. A quick death, but not by fire, would prove your leniency."

"I, too, have no desire to play foolish games, Lord Sneeth. Nor do I desire your demise. You are not what I expected, therefore I have revised my plans. I can, and will, heal you."

"Why? News of my death would please many. I am not even sure I wish to continue."

"I have a proposition. Rather than continue, I am offering you the opportunity for change."

"You said no games, My Lady."

"Allow me to explain," Annie said. "I believe you wish for a new life."

"My old life is closed to me, I cannot return."

"I'm not making myself clear. Do you enjoy instilling fear in people? Imagine your life if people responded kindly?"

"I am grotesque, the stuff of nightmares," Sneeth said. "Even you cannot make the entire world look kindly upon me."

"But when I heal you, I can change your appearance. This is your opportunity to become a new person, Sneeth."

"Who would I become? What would I do?"

"Who do you want to be? You could start over, you could do what makes you happy."

"I would trade Master Draqshet for Mistress AnnieRah? I would enter your service?"

"No. Absolutely not. There are no conditions attached to my offer. I can restore your age-old form, or you can design a new one."

"Wake me. I would have this discussion in the physical world, My Lady."

"Very well. Follow the golden cord. I must warn you, though. Your physical body is in ruins. You will feel no pain, because I have numbed your nerves, but your movements remain restricted, and you are extremely weak."

Sneeth bit back a moan as he regained consciousness. Annie had told the truth. He felt no pain, but he lacked the strength to turn himself or sit unaided.

"May I?" Annie asked.

Sneeth nodded, and Annie manoeuvred him into a sitting position, putting his hands on his lap. He looked down at the fresh bandages and sniffed.

"That's Vert's herbal salve," Annie said. "Pungent but powerful."

"Can you make me look less charred?"

223

Annie nodded. "I will give you plump, blemish-free skin. What else?"

Sneeth ran his talons over his scalp and he fought back tears. "I once saw a boy-child with the most beautiful chestnut ringlets. They bounced with his every movement, brushing his shoulders like a mother's loving touch. I was more jealous of those joyous curls than anything I've seen, before or since."

Annie smiled. "A crown of chestnut ringlets you shall have. May I suggest less jagged teeth?"

"Draqshet ripped away my wings. He tore them away." Sneeth looked straight at Annie. "My wings made me special. Set me apart from everyone else. Can you understand that?"

"I shall create magnificent new wings for you, a gorgeous feathered pair."

"No, no wings. Draqshet knew I defined myself through my wings, and tearing them away was a punishment. I don't want them back. I want to be ordinary. Take my tail and talons, too."

"Are you sure? Take time to consider."

"I desire to walk through a marketplace without garnering a second glance, to be unremarkable."

CHAPTER THIRTY-SIX

Xanderamm stuck his head through the open doorway. "Thought you might like some company."

Sneeth looked at the young man, unsure how to respond. What would a reasonable and ordinary person do? "Come in."

Xanderamm stepped inside and looked around with frank curiosity. "We didn't have time to set you up for guests. Do you mind if I perch here?" He patted the edge of the grass-stuffed pallet and made himself comfortable. "It's customary to bring fruit and flowers to a sick patient," he said, digging into his pockets. "Best I could do. I'm Xanderamm, by the way." He handed Sneeth a slightly bruised pear.

"Why are you here?" Sneeth asked.

Xanderamm shrugged. "Couldn't help but notice your lack of visitors. Thought you might expire from boredom or loneliness. If I'm interrupting, say the word and I'll go. No hard feelings."

"You know who and what I am? But you seek me out? Why?"

"Rumour has it that Lady AnnieRah is going to reform you, re-make your body and make you beautiful. She's good, but I'm not sure she's that talented." Xanderamm winked. "That was a joke. You're supposed to laugh."

Sneeth bared his fangs in a semblance of a smile.

"On second thoughts," Xanderamm said, "don't smile until after your transformation."

"I have asked Lady AnnieRah to make me look unremarkable," Sneeth said.

"That's unexpected. Most people would want to be attractive. I'd like to be a handspan taller. Especially if AnnieRah was serious about reinstating me as king. People often assume height and authority go together. How will you live, once we defeat Draqshet?"

Sneeth frowned. "Having choices is overwhelming. How do people choose?"

"Many people follow family traditions, but that's not an option in your case. What do you enjoy? What talents do you have? Besides scaring the stones out of folk?"

"I'm not sure enjoyment has ever been a consideration, but I usually prefer to be alone. I'm an exceptional hunter. I can track anything, anywhere."

"Is being alone a genuine preference, or was that your only option?"

Sneeth opened his mouth to speak, then snapped it shut.

"When I was a child," Xanderamm said, "I won every game and challenge. I grew up thinking I ought to win by the right of innate superiority. Only recently have I had to exert myself. Fencing practice with Captain Harry has been quite an education. Not only have I learned how woeful are my sword skills, but I've learned how exhilarating a genuine improvement feels."

"You are saying my years of experience are an unreliable indicator, because of limited circumstances?" Sneeth nodded slowly. "A servant woman befriended me recently. She took outrageous liberties... but somehow... she became a friend. Vera rescued me and tended my wounds after the fire. She saved my life. I enjoyed her company."

"You have many new experiences ahead of you. Some you'll enjoy, others not so much. But one of the most rewarding experiences you'll ever have is making loyal friends."

Netta ran down the slope from her lookout post. "The women are coming. I'll go to meet them, they're already anxious," she said.

"Bring their wagon next to Sneeth's bivouac. They'll want to be close to him," Annie said.

Netta nodded and ran towards the road. For all she cared, these women could load the fire damaged freak into their wagon and disappear. She'd even soil her hands to help them.

The driver slowed to a halt when she saw the stunning young silver-haired woman waving at them.

"You must be Jenny and Vera. I'm Netta. Annie sent me."

"Climb aboard," Jenny said. "How is my Sneeth?"

"Annie has rid him of his infection and he's resting," Netta said, paying close attention to the women's responses. My Sneeth? Why is she claiming him? "You look familiar? Have we met before? I used to be a seamstress, mayhap you once purchased something from me?"

Jenny smiled and shook her head. "I don't think so. I'm certain I'd remember you if we'd met before." She clicked the horses into motion.

Jenny had delicate pampered hands, Netta noted, yet she drove the wagon expertly, with one silk-slippered foot casually resting on the footboard. Vera kept her arms wrapped around her midriff, flinching at each jolt. Netta cocked her head and listened. The older woman's heart beat an irregular rhythm and her lungs laboured to pump air. She was dying, but her eyes shone with determination. And fierce love.

Netta sighed. This pair made her skin crawl, yet they had convinced Annie of their integrity. Annie's unerringly accurate gift of touch proved invaluable, but Netta felt distinctly uneasy around these unexpected guests. She heaved a sigh of relief when they drew alongside Sneeth's accommodation and she leapt down, glad to put space between herself and the strangers.

"I'll have someone see to your horses," Netta said. "Go in."

The women gripped hands as they stepped through the doorway. Netta raised her eyebrows. A fine lady and a rundown servant? Intimacy and familiarity could develop over time, but Netta recognised the rarity of such imbalanced relationships. She shrugged to herself and went in search of Dexter.

Dexter, Harry, and Xanderamm were lurking nearby like naughty schoolboys. She sent Dexter to look after the beasts and turned to Harry and Xanderamm.

"Did you recognise either of them?"

Xanderamm nodded. "Jenny's no ordinary woman."

"There are no ordinary women," Netta said.

"Jenny's a demon, disguising herself as a woman. She's killed men without so much as blinking," Xanderamm said. "She's Draqshet's pet."

"I recognise Vera," Harry said, "but I can't fathom how she's mixed up in this. According to Dexter and Vert, she's friends with Lady Amora. This makes little sense."

"Bringing that monster into our camp makes even less sense." Netta folded her arms.

"Netta!" André's voice boomed across the open space as he hurried towards her. He nodded to Harry and Xanderamm. "I need a private word with my lovely wife. Excuse us, gentlemen."

He gripped Netta by the arm and propelled her towards the tree line.

"Ouch! Slow down." Netta wriggled out of André's grasp. "You're hurting me."

"Apologies, My Lady. But you are hurting everyone else, especially Annie. You can't go around spreading dissent. Annie is your best friend and our leader. She deserves our trust. If you don't trust her, then we'll go back to Salvation Valley together."

"Of course I trust her. But I don't trust these strangers. They've befuddled Annie."

"So you don't trust her judgement, her gift of touch?"

Netta glared at André. "Sneeth and Jenny are both demons. They're using wicked trickery."

"I'm not doubting for a single heartbeat they are demons, but Annie's gift is reliable. I believe in goodness. I believe a demon having a change of heart is more likely than Annie being fooled or enchanted. Don't you think Roic would have sensed the odour of foul magic?"

"That monster—"

"That monster received wounds, almost unto death," André said. "Roic scented his distress. That was genuine. My Lady, choose right now. Either stand with Annie, or stand down."

Vert followed Netta as she stormed away from camp.

"Why are you following me?" Netta whirled around, fists clenched, eyes brimming with unshed tears. "Have you forgotten I can hear you from miles away?"

Vert held up a hand to placate his furious friend. "I have forgotten nothing, but I suspect you may have lapsed. You haven't told André, have you?"

"I don't know what you mean." Netta's cheeks flushed a dull red.

"My hearing is second only to yours, and the new heartbeat you carry is loud and clear. Not to mention your inexplicable queasiness. Soon enough, someone else will notice how often you hold a protective hand over your belly."

"Promise you won't tell him?"

"I have no desire to interfere between a husband and wife," Vert said.

"If André knew, he'd want to send me home. He'd launch into Grand Master role and be overprotective. He'd treat me like a child, when I have a part to play."

"Deceiving him is not the answer."

"I haven't lied."

"You have deliberately withheld the truth from your devoted husband and your loyal friends. One touch from Annie in an unguarded moment, and she'll know."

"I'm protecting Annie from herself. She's gullible, only seeing goodness where evil lurks below. That... that abomination has her fooled." Netta choked back tears. "If something bad happens to Annie, we'll all suffer. My Gabrielle, my unborn, everyone. Don't you see? I must stop Annie from making a mistake."

CHAPTER THIRTY-SEVEN

"Does she possess the power to recreate you? Is such a transformation safe?" Jenny clutched Sneeth's taloned hand as she knelt beside his pallet.

"I entertain no doubt of her power, Mother. Annie has transformed many men into goats, and Xanderamm became a pig, just by her uttering the word. It's my choice, Mother. She will restore me to my natural form, or I can choose a new shape."

"You cannot be certain of her intentions, Son."

"Mother, she's had me totally at her mercy. If she wished me ill, she could have annihilated me the night we met. She says I contain a kernel of goodness. If my outside is more... pleasing... people will more readily accept me."

"She's right," Vera said. "I recognised the good within you, but few see past the tail and talons. Give yourself a chance. Life can be harsh, you owe it to yourself to take every advantage."

"But will I still recognise you?" Jenny sobbed.

"I rather hope not," Sneeth said. "But I will recognise you, Mother."

Annie stood for a moment at the entrance, realised she was eavesdropping, then coughed. "May I come in?"

"Enter, meet my Mother and my friend, Vera." Sneeth was pleased to invite Annie in, and to show off having both a mother and a friend.

Annie shook hands with the women again, double checking her previous readings. "I'm pleased to make your acquaintances under friendlier circumstances," she said. "Sneeth has told you his news?"

"Indeed," Jenny said. "He is excited, but I confess I feel a mother's nervousness."

"The transformation is an enormous undertaking," Annie said. "But Sneeth has committed himself, as have I."

"Why? What's in it for you?" Jenny eyed Annie suspiciously. "What do you gain?"

Annie hesitated while she mentally reviewed all she knew about Jenny. "I'm not looking for gain, simply to help someone."

Jenny slitted her eyes, searching for a catch. "Sneeth helped me, but it didn't turn out too well for him, did it?"

"He gained his mother's affection."

"Whose affection will you gather from this splendid display of power and altruistic charity?" Jenny asked.

Annie heaved a sigh. "If you must insist upon probing into matters which are not your business, know this. Healing your son brings me only loss, not gain. My friends believe me to be dangerously misguided, or delusional. They are turning from me. I am risking much for naught but the certain knowledge I am helping someone in need." Annie shook her head. "You wouldn't understand."

She turned and ducked out the door.

Vera chased after her. "My Lady, please wait." Vera steadied herself on Annie's arm. "Don't take notice of what the girl says. She doesn't know any better."

Annie patted Vera's hand. "I know. Truth be told, I know her better than she yet knows herself. I will return at sunset, when you and Jenny will retire to your wagon. The transformation will be unpleasant to watch, and I cannot allow your distressed cries or whimpers to distract me."

Vera watched Annie trudge back to the main camp, shoulders slumped and head bowed. She didn't pretend to understand Annie's motivation; she was simply grateful.

Annie paced the camp perimeter, unwilling to face her friends' confusion and contempt. What she'd said to Vera was true. She knew Jenny better than the girl knew herself. The poor woman was coming to terms with the knowledge she had spawned Sneeth, a product of rape. She was processing the idea that Draqshet had wiped her memories and remade her as his tool. Jenny had only the vaguest idea that her lack of responsibility had wrought worldwide chaos. She failed to realise that in her search for love, she had birthed and abandoned countless generations of girl babies. She did not yet know it was Annie who had confined her to the dark chamber from which Draqshet had rescued her. Jenny had yet to understand that she was Annie's great-beyond-counting grandmother. Her newly beloved Sneeth was Annie's great-beyond-counting uncle.

Eventually, Jenny must be told the whole truth, not only the selected convenient parts. But not all at once. Annie dare not risk the Great Mother of Us All having another breakdown.

True to her word, Annie returned to Sneeth's shelter at sunset and shooed Jenny and Vera to their wagon. "Ladies, rest while you can. Sneeth will need you when he recovers. I will summon you the instant he is fit to receive visitors."

Vera nodded and smiled as she climbed painfully into the back of the wagon, but Annie sensed a conflicted swirl of anxiety and jealousy with Jenny.

Sneeth smiled, closed-lipped, when she entered. "Xanderamm visited," he said. "He tells me there are rumours around the camp you're planning to remake me with a beautiful form. You won't do that, will you? My dearest wish is to look ordinary, to pass unnoticed."

"I give you my word, I will make you as unremarkable as possible," Annie said. "Now, please lie back, make yourself comfortable. I'm going to induce a light trance state but you will undoubtably experience pain. Don't run from it, stay with me, I won't have energy spare to chase after you if you go inside yourself. Grip the golden cord as tightly as you can. Ready?"

Annie secured the golden psychic tether, ensuring Sneeth couldn't drift far, regardless of his discomfort. The less he struggled, the faster and easier the procedure would be. She erected a golden net of protection around the shelter to keep out those whose curiosity might overcome their decency.

Before Annie completed the transformation to her satisfaction, she was a trembling, sweaty mess. Sneeth whimpered and twitched, but he impressed Annie that not once during the traumatic transformation had he tried to pull away. She sent another sedative wash of energy over him to mitigate the pain as his teeth and bones reconstructed, muscles and sinews learned their new configurations, flesh filled aching vacancies, and luxurious auburn curls sprang forth. Every cell of his anatomy transformed.

Sleep beckoned Annie, but first she must inform Jenny and

Vera of the successful outcome. The cool night air dried her damp skin, and she shivered. A well-sheltered light glowed within the wagon.

"Ladies?" Annie whispered. "Sneeth sleeps, but you are welcome to watch over him while he rests. If he wakes before I return, do not allow him to stand unaided. He must relearn how to walk."

The women tumbled from the wagon, mumbling their thanks. Vera hung back, allowing Jenny first look at her reformed son. Exhausted, Annie left them to their medley of tears and laughter. Tomorrow, she would speak with Jenny.

Annie woke later than usual and assessed the mood of the camp before rising. Curiosity curled like a rampant vine, clinging to every surface, but couldn't camouflage the fear and trepidation crawling and creeping like an infestation of locusts.

Xanderamm and Harry had made it their business to dress Sneeth in normal attire. They stepped aside to allow Annie to view her creation.

"How do I look?" Sneeth tottered uncertainly towards her. "Xanderamm insisted trousers were necessary."

Annie stifled a smile. "Xanderamm and Harry had no right disturbing your rest, but yes, you look fine. You're wearing what every other man is wearing."

Sneeth extended his arms to steady himself. "Clothes feel peculiar against my skin. Slithery, but not unpleasant."

"Your skin is new, and sensitive, like a newborn's. Those sensations will quickly fade. Are you experiencing any pain or discomfort?"

Sneeth writhed, his eyebrows drawn together in concentration. "No, Annie, no pain, thank you. Itchy. My back is itchy. But I feel lighter, like I could float away."

"May I see your back?" Annie asked.

Sneeth wobbled around and lifted his shirt. Xanderamm and Harry dashed to his sides to support him.

Annie smiled. Sneeth was already making friends. She ran her fingertips over the smooth flesh; neither scars nor inflammation marred its perfection. She washed his back with a splash of cool energy.

"You look hale and hearty," she said.

"You'll likely experience more itchiness over the following days as your body adjusts, but it doesn't last," Xanderamm said, flashing a quick smile at Annie.

Xanderamm and Harry pulled the shirt back into place and helped Sneeth turn around.

"My Lady," Sneeth sunk to one knee, "I cannot offer adequate thanks. Not only for my new body; which, to my eyes, is beautiful; but for trusting me and giving me a second chance. I vow to dedicate my new life to your service."

Annie held up her hands. "No, please. I didn't remake you as a retainer. Dedicate your life to doing good for others in whatever ways you are able. You have demonstrated great physical courage, rescuing your mother and bearing the pain of transformation. Take that courage and use it to call out oppression and prejudice. Make your name synonymous with fairness."

Xanderamm and Harry helped Sneeth to his unsteady feet.

"My understanding is that Sneeth is learning to be ordinary," Xanderamm said. "Ordinary people eat breakfast. Let's teach you some common table manners, my friend."

With his new friends supporting him, Sneeth staggered into the morning sunshine.

"Vera? Jenny? Come, break your fast with us," Harry called

to the women. "I make a blistering porridge. Best of all, Dexter washes the dishes afterwards."

~

Annie wandered behind Sneeth's impromptu support group, trying to be unobtrusive. The only person who didn't walk past to gawk at her guests was Netta. André hovered and gestured for Annie to join him on the edge of the camp.

Netta's husband looked thoroughly dejected, not at all his usual self-important persona.

"I assume from your expression that you spoke to her." Annie said.

"I may have been too overbearing," Grand Master André said. "I told her if she couldn't stand beside you, we would return to Salvation Valley. This morning I cannot find her, or her horse."

"Did she pack her belongings? She could have simply gone for a ride to clear her head." Annie looked about, as though she expected Netta to reappear.

"Her bow and slingshot are missing, as are her throwing knives," André said. "She could be hunting, but she normally hunts afoot."

Annie closed her eyes and took several deep breaths. "I will ask Vert to track her, to make sure she is, in fact, heading home."

"Where else would she go?" André looked panicked.

"Where, indeed? Go with Harry and count the weapons of light. Try not to attract too much attention."

"You don't think..?"

"Netta possesses strong opinions, and she mistakenly believes Draqshet is sheltering in the bowels of the Palace. Her bravery is not in question, only her commonsense. This may be her way of protecting me."

~

Harry stared open-mouthed at Grand Master André. "Surely not."

"I hope I am wrong. I hope she's only furious with me and has set off home. But I would not be surprised if she has assumed a mission for herself."

Harry shook his head. "Look." He pointed at the fresh drag marks. "Somebody has already been here."

Harry and André dragged the crate from under the pile of rocks. Captain Harry counted twice and sat back on his haunches. "Two blades of light and a sun-bomb are missing."

CHAPTER THIRTY-EIGHT

Netta rode easily, not rushing or drawing attention to herself. She planned to reach the capital around breakfast, chat with the stallholders to pick up the latest gossip, then make her way into the almost deserted Palace.

Are you listening, little one? Mamma's going to annihilate Draqshet before the monster has a chance to threaten you or your sister, Gabrielle. Annie will thank me once she returns to her senses, and she'll banish that abomination. All will return to normal, and I'll have my best friend back.

The unguarded city gates hung open, and the shadowy entrance gaped like a hungry mouth. Netta shivered and pulled her cloak close. She trotted her horse up and down, searching the wall for any sign of soldiers. Naught. Not even a lewd comment hollered from on high. Netta wheeled her mount around and guided the beast through the gates. Two stray dogs stopped scrapping over a remnant she didn't dare to identify, but otherwise the marketplace was empty and eerily quiet. Pennants and flags flapped listlessly above abandoned stalls, and the ubiquitous crows strutted and boasted loudly in their glossy black livery.

Netta dismounted, certain she could run faster in her dragon-skin boots than her iron-shod horse could gallop over the neglected cobbles. She led her mount to the stables and dumped a pile of feed on the ground for him. His crunching echoed across the yard, but nobody came to ask her business, or offer assistance. She surreptitiously drew a short blade, keeping it close to her hip, as she surveyed the eerie space.

She squinted at the unswept ground. Using her advanced tracking skills, she read clues that a slipper-shod woman had recently harnessed four horses and driven a wide-wheeled heavy cart through the gates. A wheeled chair lay toppled on its side. Sneeth and his companions? The slashed chair back suggested someone had attacked them. A recent patch of blood stained the cobbles black, the streak clearly showing where the assailant had dragged the victim into a dark corner. Netta shuddered and turned away.

Horses whickered nearby. Netta cursed when she found the empty feed and water bins in each stable. Sneeth must have slaughtered the last stable lad. Mayhap he had been the brave and desperate attacker. After she'd killed Draqshet, she was going back for his monstrous son. Naught Annie could say would stop her.

Netta pumped water into the trough and tipped more feed onto the floor. One by one, she opened the stable doors and the hungry horses trotted out. If they're still there when I get back, I'll chase them off to fend for themselves.

She closed her eyes in an effort to remember. Harry had drawn rough maps of the city. The barracks were next to the stables. However unlikely, she needed to know if any loyal city guards survived.

The barracks had no ground-floor windows and only one

door. Netta hesitated to shout, but rapped on the door with the hilt of her sword. She pressed her ear against the wood. Naught moved or breathed. *How long have they been without food? Do barracks have kitchens, or must soldiers go to the mess hall?*

The massive padlock showed no signs of tampering, no doubt the citizens too terrified to attempt a rescue. Netta pulled her dragon-scale knife from her boot and cut through the tempered steel chain like a fruitcake. She dropped the chain and the attached lock to the ground and pushed the door. A rat scampered over her foot and she yelped, her nerves stung too tight to hold back her surprise.

The door opened less than a handspan before jamming. Netta's questing fingers found furniture stacked behind the entry. Tears blinded her as she realised not only had the soldiers given up on being rescued, but they had died in fear of predators. She pulled the door shut, the only respect she could offer to the inhabitants of the mass tomb.

Netta carefully returned the knife to her boot and reassessed her plan. No chance of picking up a tasty breakfast and juicy gossip in the marketplace. Only the noisy murder of crows and scavenging dogs betrayed any signs of life.

Naught standing between me and The Most High Lord.

CHAPTER THIRTY-NINE

Roic inhaled the rancid scent of panic rolling in heavy waves off Annie and lumbered to his feet. *Annie, come. We'll fly towards the capital and intercept her.* Roic's voice cut through the clamour in Annie's head.

He launched himself into the air as soon as Annie seated herself. He flew closer to the ground than usual, not wasting valuable time to gain height.

Annie sent out call after frantic mind-call to Netta. "She's not answering, Roic. I can't imagine her being peevish enough to not acknowledge me. Maybe she's had an accident, fallen off her horse. She could be lying unconscious and helpless."

Vert tracked her out of camp and said she left well before dawn. The worst scenario is that she's already reached the town, and Draqshet's shield is blocking contact.

Roic felt Annie tense as she considered her friend's situation. They both knew Netta's skill with bow and arrows, or a slingshot, were beyond compare, but she was no match for the pure evil of Draqshet, or even an assault by Dolls.

Roic scoured the road and the surroundings, searching for

sight or scent, but the unusually quiet highway offered no clues. He circled and soared above where he knew the city to be, but the gaping vortex pulled at him, like a millstream tugging a twig. Disoriented, Roic slipped into a headfirst dive.

"Pull up! Pull up!" Annie hauled helplessly on Roic's scales. "Roic! Close your eyes, turn away. Stop looking into the shield."

Roic dipped lower, and one wing scraped the foul enchantment. The dragon screeched in agony at the acid-like burn, and desperately beat his wings in a futile effort to escape the noxious whirlpool. His violent movements unseated Annie, and she fell, flailing the air, until Roic seized her in his claws, like an eagle hunting a salmon.

He flapped a clumsy, lopsided retreat, desperate to escape the unexpected threat, before checking Annie, who lay limp in his grip. Roic selected an empty pasture, flew as low as he dared, and dropped Annie onto what he hoped was relatively soft ground, before wheeling around and landing himself.

Roic nosed at Annie, turning her over to examine her for injuries. Her sword arm lay fleshless, burned to the bone as far as her elbow. The dragon-skin suit hadn't protected her from the acidic effects of the shield. Roic sniffed carefully, but found no evidence of the foul enchantment clinging to either Annie or himself.

Annie, I'm here. Grip the golden cord. Don't drift away.

Roic curled his tongue under Annie and lifted her into his mouth. Gripping her with his claws would mean another dropped landing, and more potential injuries. He alerted Vert and Theo as he flew back to camp. *Annie is badly injured and unresponsive.*

Theo raced to take his unconscious wife into his arms. "What in the name of creation happened? Is she hurt elsewhere?" Faster-than-thought, he carried Annie to their tent and laid her on the bed.

Vert peeled away the remnants of Annie's sleeve and examined the damage while Roic relayed the memory of his dizzy fall and their contact with Draqshet's shield directly into their minds. No excuses, no filters. Roic lumbered away to tend his wing. He could regrow his wing, but Annie, as far as he knew, couldn't regenerate.

"Theo? Get inside her head, talk to her, don't let her stray. She's trying to escape the pain." Vert rummaged in his collection of salves and potions. "I can't do much with this degree of damage. I can dampen the pain, but not remove it." He slathered a paste over her arm and wrapped the skeletal limb in a linen bandage.

Theo held Annie's uninjured hand as he stroked her hair. Tears streamed silently down his cheeks.

"Keep talking to her," Vert said. "I'll be back shortly." He stuffed an empty vial into his jerkin and jogged to where Roic crouched.

Roic turned his head away. *I'm supposed to be Annie's protector, but I very nearly got her killed.* A huge tear rolled down his snout. *She's going to lose her arm, her sword arm, because I didn't do my job.*

"I don't know how you are to blame for failing to protect her against an unknowable danger," Vert said. "My only concern is finding a way to regrow her arm."

Roic thrummed with frustration. *I would give my very wings to help.*

Vert pulled the vial from his jerkin. "That won't be necessary, my friend. All I ask is a sample of your blood."

Roic extended his neck, meekly exposing the delicate scales under his throat. *Will this work?*

"Ask in a few days," Vert said. "This is purely experimental.

Hope married to guesswork."

Vert dribbled Roic's glittering blood over the remains of Annie's arm. The priceless ruby-red fluid disappeared, absorbed into the bones, like the memory of a dream at daybreak.

"Is it working?" Theo nudged Vert.

Vert stood back. "See for yourself."

Theo glanced at Vert, then bent over to examine Annie's arm. "I've seen naught like it," he whispered.

Vert slapped Theo's hand as he reached to touch the miracle. "You don't want to risk an infection." They stared, mesmerised, as threads of vein and sinew crawled over bones, stitching scraps of muscle into place; movement as slow but inexorable as stars traversing the sky.

Annie fled from the pain into the deepest recesses of her mind. She found a loom, the warp threads tightly strung, and a waiting shuttle. She made herself comfortable on the stool, but her arm hung limply at her side. Annie leaned forward, resting her forehead head on the side of the loom. The blood red threads called to her, begging her to weave them into a new fabric. The throbbing ache in her arm threatened to over-whelm her mind, but her fingers automatically threaded the shuttle back and forth, defying the agony. She passed the shuttle to and fro, tamping the layers between each pass, until her fingers bled, staining the fabric with a living pattern. Hands and feet danced the familiar steps with shuttle and trea-dle, and the tapestry grew. The longer she wove, the further the torment receded. The pattern blurred before her eyes.

Strong arms wrapped around her as she collapsed from exhaustion.

~

Sneeth dangled his legs over the back of the wagon and studied the camp. Netta's disappearance had sparked a flurry of activity, making his exclusion more apparent. The intimacy of anxiety drew the group closer together, making more obvious his otherness. A lull in activity marked Roic's dramatic departure with Annie, as people stared into the sky, then drifted away, when they realised they were in for a long wait.

A burst of packing up camp and weapon preparation followed, as everyone sought to distract themselves but appear useful. Vera and Jenny took themselves for a short walk. Waiting for Roic and Annie to return with Netta set their already shredded nerves on edge and they couldn't sit still.

Jenny's jubilant victory cry rang out over the camp. "Look who I found driving past!" Lady Amora's stony expression clashed against Jenny's enthusiasm as she waved like royalty from the front seat of the cart. Harry and Xanderamm rushed to greet Lady Amora, and Dexter showed Danny and Paulie where to tie up the horses and cart.

Sneeth winced at his mother's insensitivity. Jenny placed her hand on Lady Amora's shoulder to steady herself as the cart trundled into camp, utterly oblivious to the fact Lady Amora held her responsible for the collapse of her city. He flinched again when he realised his mother knew naught of Lady Amora's pyrotechnic adventures.

When the women clambered down from the cart, Jenny grabbed Vera's hand and pulled her along with Lady Amora, chattering like they were best friends.

Lady Amora stopped mid-stride and rounded on Jenny.

"Madam, you are a traitor and an embarrassment to your sex. I have no idea how you inveigled your way into this group, but you will never hear welcome from my lips. I am here on urgent business. Leave me, or I will call my men to deal with you." She gave Jenny no opportunity to respond before whirling around and striding away, drawing Harry and Xanderamm in her wake.

Annie fought her way back to consciousness. She fluttered open her eyes, disorientated to discover herself back in camp, with Theo stroking her hand, and Vert peering anxiously at her. She struggled to sit up, and Theo leapt to help.

Annie sipped the water Vert offered, taking the opportunity to collect her thoughts. She remembered slipping from the panicked dragon... then naught. She raised a hand to explore her skull.

"I think I must have bumped my head when I fell," she said, fingers searching for lumps and bruises. "What? Why do you both smell so worried?"

Vert retrieved the empty cup. "You don't remember what happened?"

"Netta!" Annie's hands flew to her face. "She's trapped in the capital. Roic and I were too late." She swung her feet to the ground. "There's no time to lose. We must find her before Draqshet does."

"My love," Theo said, "you and Roic had a terrible accident. Vert restored your arm, but I doubt it will yet have full strength. A side-effect seems to be your new ability to scent emotions."

Annie glanced from Theo to Vert and back, then extended both arms for comparison. "I remember, now. The shield

247

consumed the flesh on my arm. How am I whole again? What about Roic? Is he recovered? Was it an illusion?"

Jenny's victory cry interrupted them, and all three turned to stare as Lady Amora guided her magnificent cart into camp.

"Lady Amora has brought her sticky-fire," Annie said. "We must launch our rescue immediately."

Theo took charge, inviting to the meeting only those he imagined having direct involvement, but he still faced a crowd. Lord Roic the Magnificent avoided eye-contact; Grand Master André couldn't keep his fingers from his sword hilt; Vert constantly looked at Annie, who kept her head down. Xanderamm and Harry flanked Sneeth like a pair of hired mercenaries. Lady Amora still seethed, evidenced by the furiously burning spots on each cheek.

"Mistress Netta is in grave danger," Theo said. "We need to bring her out of Kingston without attracting Draqshet's attention."

Sneeth spoke quietly. "I fear you are already too late."

"It's in your interests to say that," Lady Amora said. "I still can't comprehend why this monster is here."

"Sneeth is here because I have read his heart and I trust him." Annie looked around the group, ensuring she made eye-contact with everyone. "My beloved Netta is missing because she could not accept my judgement. Her reckless actions have endangered the rest of us. If anyone feels they cannot trust me, or Sneeth, now is the time to pack up and leave. No recriminations."

Lady Amora gazed coolly at Annie, then momentarily shifted her attention to Sneeth and his new friends. "I apologise without reserve for any offence my words may have caused.

Lady Annie, although the Goddess Reborn, is a stranger to me. However, I have reason to trust Captain Harry and King Xanderamm. Therefore, I pledge my services to Lady Annie."

Annie nodded her acceptance. "Good. Now, Sneeth, please explain why you believe we are too late."

"Draqshet is only active under cover of darkness, but when you crashed into his shield, it would have been like a fly falling into a spider's web. He would have read the traces you left behind, he'd know exactly your injuries, although I doubt he will anticipate your miraculous recovery, My Lady."

"But he doesn't know about Netta," André said.

"The residents have almost deserted the city, as Lady Amora can confirm," Sneeth said.

Lady Amora nodded. "There are a few families remaining on the outskirts, I believe."

"Draqshet will have sensed each individual," Sneeth said. "He will assess Netta as a threat, merely because she dares enter the city. He will have sniffed her out by now, mapped each step she has taken, and assumed she comes as your emissary. If she remains outside, she may survive until dusk. If she has ventured into the gloom of the Palace, she may already be dead." Sneeth locked eyes with André. "I am truly sorry. The only reason he will keep her alive is to use her as bait. To lure Annie or Theo."

André looked towards the sinking sun, tears blurring his eyes. "Our best hope is that Draqshet holds Netta hostage. Can we launch a rescue at dawn? What are The Dark Lord's habits? What can we turn to our advantage?"

"I have never seen him challenged," Sneeth said. "His only weakness is his aversion to light and fire. He only allows a single candle in the Audience Chamber."

"I vote we burn the entire city to the ground," Lady Amora said.

"Not while there is the slightest chance my wife is still alive," André said.

"Where and when does he sleep? That surely is when he'll be most vulnerable," Vert said. "Is he guarded? By Dolls or enchantments?"

"After the fire," Sneeth bowed slightly to Lady Amora, "he hid below the dungeons, according to Mistress Vera. But his favourite place is the Audience Chamber. Sitting on the throne feeds his ego."

"There are secret tunnels leading close to the chamber," Xanderamm said. "I propose Theo transports a group of us to the city wall. We can use a secret tunnel into the city, dodge around to the Palace tunnels and launch an attack."

"I will lead this brave expedition," André said. "The rescue of my wife is my responsibility."

Balderdash. You are too close. You cannot go.

"I hear you, Roic, and I agree. André will not be a member of the rescue party. If the rescue goes badly, I would not want Gabrielle an orphan," Annie said. "Lord Roic, I do not ask lightly, but there are members of our group who lack the gift of mind-talking. For my plan to work, I need you to confer this gift."

Roic huffed his agreement. *Intimate communication should foster greater trust. Group them between my forelegs.*

Annie herded the latest mind-talking recruits before Roic. "Sit as relaxed as possible, even better if you lie down."

"The dragon is going to turn us into mind-readers?" Xanderamm waggled his eyebrows suggestively. "A new career, Sneeth?"

"This isn't a game, Your Majesty. There are rules, etiquette, if you will. Don't make me regret this." Annie glared at Xanderamm.

"Sorry, Annie. My way of coping."

Annie addressed the four. "Breathe in, hold... now out. Deep breathe in... and out...in..."

Roic blew gently over the four as they inhaled. *My advice to you is to say naught yet.* Roic's words sounded loudly inside their heads. *If we have time, Annie and I will go through exercises to teach you to control your gift, before you alienate all your friends. Nod if you heard me.*

All four nodded, eyes wide with wonder.

"Xanderamm's suggestion is wise," Annie said. "A small crew operating with familiarity in what has become a hostile environment. I suggest Xanderamm, Captain Harry, and Sneeth, because you all have recent knowledge of the Palace. Theo will transport you. Any objections?"

"What about me?" Lady Amora asked. "I brought the sticky-fire."

"A valuable weapon, for which we are grateful. However, your person is of greater use here than in the first attack," Annie said, deliberately shielding her thoughts. *Lady Amora is brave, but too impulsive.*

CHAPTER FORTY

Netta searched the stables for a lantern. The thought of entering the lightless Palace raised goosebumps on her arms. But it won't be dark for long. I'll bring light like he's never seen. She found a shallow alcove where the stable master kept the records, and on the corner of the tiny desk sat a shuttered lamp. Netta shook it and shrugged at the meagre slosh. Not enough oil, but she'd find more once inside the Palace.

Lamp in one hand, sulphur stick in the other, she followed the faint tracks of the wheeled chair to a narrow door where she stopped to listen. Mice and rats squeaked and rustled up and down the yawning corridor, exactly what she expected to hear near a stable yard. She knelt and lit the lamp, sliding the shutter until only a needle thin sliver of light escaped. No point showing myself as a target.

She paused every few steps, but her far-hearing betrayed no signs of life. Too late, she realised her mistake. Dolls exhibit exactly the same life-signs as a table. As she stepped through an open doorway, she caught a flash of movement before the Doll smashed her unconscious with the butt of his spear.

CHAPTER FORTY-ONE

With a hand below each armpit, the Dolls dragged their trussed prisoner into the murky Audience Chamber and dumped her on the ground. A war drum pounded a deadly rhythm in her head, too big for her skull to contain. The throbbing expanded, invading her neck and shoulders. She forced open her eyes and squinted against the booming cacophony at the filth in which she lay. A bundle of military clothing lay beside her, the roiling stench threatening to choke her. The collection of shabby rags came into awful focus: a decapitated Doll. Rats feasted on the soft belly, dragging out the greasy innards while maggots infested the gaping neck. Blood seeped into the marble tiles, creating a permanent memory. From an unseemly distance, the pale face stared with vacant eyes at Netta's dawning comprehension.

She retched and tried to scramble away, only then discovering the Dolls had secured her ankles, wrists, and elbows behind her back. As she fought to escape, a rope tightened around her neck, her vision narrowed to a pinprick.

"Cut the noose." An icy voice sliced through her confusion. "She's more valuable to me alive than dead, at least for now."

She winced at the hiss of a blade withdrawn from a scabbard, then the snick of slashed rope beside her ear. Netta gasped, and rolled away from the rotting corpse, before sucking air deep into her lungs. A burning flash of pain flooded her shoulders; now the Dolls had eased the pressure, she concentrated on the pulsating sensation, a distraction from the putrefying remains.

"You have removed her weapons?"

A clatter of blades shivered across the floor, then the Dolls tossed her broken bow and snapped arrows on top. Her slingshot and bag of pebbles landed with a thwack alongside.

"So, little girl. You brought rabbit hunting equipment to kill me? You are remarkably brave or incredibly foolish. Either way, prepare to meet your doom, stone-slinger."

Netta glanced at her pile of confiscated weapons and hung her head to hide her involuntary smile. The doltish Dolls had failed to recognise the threat of her light weapons and lacked the initiative to explore their potential.

"Not even the most devoted Reborn follower would dare come so ill-equipped. Strip her and search for hidden weapons. Then dress her in one of Jenny's gowns. Go. The sight of weak mortal flesh sickens me."

The Dolls hoisted Netta and carried her face down, along corridors and up stairs. The carpets grew thicker and more luxurious the closer they got to Jenny's room, and the tramp of the Dolls' booted feet were muted in unappreciated luxury.

Enormous windows framed a gloriously starry sky; no city lights offered competition. The large enough to walk into fireplace contained cold ashes, and the air was redolent with citrus. The Dolls dropped Netta onto her knees beside a bed piled high with pillows and cushions in luxurious fabrics. Under different circumstances, Netta would have enjoyed the exquisite work-manship.

The blank-faced Dolls stepped back, one holding his spear, the other gripping his sword. "Strip."

"You must untie me first." Netta lurched to her feet and turned her back to present the restraints.

Sword Doll stepped forward and sliced the ropes holding her elbows, then wrists and ankles. Netta stumbled against the bed, rubbing her arms to regain circulation. Her fingers tingled with vicious pins and needles. She stamped her feet to bring back the feeling to her toes.

"You fellas are clever with knots," she said. "I need a minute to get my fingers working again." She made a virtuoso performance of massaging her extremities and wincing as the blood flowed back.

The Dolls looked on, expressionless, unmoving.

"Would you get me a gown? You know how us women take forever to choose, always complaining we have naught to wear." Netta nodded at the massive wardrobe across the room.

The Dolls hesitated but found naught in their orders telling them not to assist. If it meant returning the wench to Draqshet faster, then the Most High Lord would be pleased. They existed only to please The Dark Lord. They swivelled to the wardrobe, confident the tiny woman, dispossessed of weapons, presented no hint of a threat.

Netta reached inside her bodice and withdrew two light blades. The bright beams cut through the Dolls, instantly cauterising the slabs of meat, the butchered sections thudding to the floor. Netta circled the slabs of dead Doll, checking for the slightest twitch. She nudged the chunks apart with the toe of her boot. Blushing at her previous carelessness, she flicked the beams a second time and decapitated the bodies.

Shivering with fear and cold, she selected a fur-lined cloak from the wardrobe. She'd find her way back to the Audience Chamber in the pitchy dark. A lantern presented too great a risk. Soon Draqshet would send more Dolls to find her. She would track them back to their depraved master and blast him and his unnatural minions into oblivion.

Draqshet gripped the arm of the throne, crumbling to dust the remaining wood and plaster. He lurched to his feet, searching for a victim, knowing the Palace and environs were empty. He kicked the mouldering Doll remains as he traversed the length of the hall.

Fury bubbled and seethed in his gut. Betrayal by Sneeth and Jenny burned acidic in his belly; citizens had fled the capital, depriving him of entertainment; and yet another chit of a girl had fooled him. The Dolls were impervious to seduction, yet the rabbit-hunter trollop had overcome his armed guards. Or, they had killed her, and didn't dare to face his wrath. That option presented a pleasing outcome. He would slaughter them for their incompetence.

He listened intently, but only mice and rats moved in the darkness. He adjusted his hood and raised his head to sniff out any intruders. The odour of the hussy lingered, redolent with fecundity. Draqshet fell to his knees, snuffling the carpets for clues. An odour within her natural scent announced her gravid state.

Draqshet's robes billowed behind him as he navigated the corridors and stairs to Jenny's room. The stink of Sneeth filled his nostrils. Once the boy knew he had a mother, he changed, fawning for her attention, when he ought to have destroyed her. Draqshet stoked his anger, wallowing in the certain knowledge

Sneeth dared to keep secrets from him, and sided with the upstart rebels.

The Dark Lord gouged his talons through the painted and gilded plasterwork on the corridor walls, snapping the laths as he passed. He would find this foolish rabbit-hunter, gouge her flesh and snap her bones. Her screams would bring her colleagues racing to her defence.

Halfway down the corridor, Netta heard Draqshet's destructive approach and fumbled for the light-bomb. Her eyes grew wide. She must have dropped it somewhere on the plushly carpeted corridors when the Dolls carried her here. Hacking at him with a light-sword might work, but unless she immediately incapacitated him, he would certainly fight back with foul magic. Netta scurried backed to the room and peered out of the window. Too high to jump, and naught to hold going down. She looked up at the fanciful architecture. Giving herself no time to think, she leapt onto the windowsill, grabbed hold of the gable and flipped herself up. She pressed herself to the grave-cold stonework. The fur-lined cloak fluttered to the ground like a wounded bird.

Draqshet burst into the room, an explosion of evil. The door shivered from the impact as the crystal doorknob impaled the wall. The Dark Lord roared his rage at the sight of his dismembered guards. In a tornado of temper, he whirled through the room, shredding and smashing, shrieking his outrage. Then he bent to examine the remains more carefully, noting the lack of blood. He stood, sniffing for clues. Only extreme heat, or fire, cauterises wounds. He swivelled, searching the ruined room for a place the rabbit-hunter could hide. Draqshet dragged out the contents of the wardrobe, rattled a poker up the chimney, and knelt to look under the bed. Nothing. He peered out the window, and the fluttering cloak snared his attention. He snuffled the window sill, confirming his prey had crossed the threshold.

His sigh of disappointment gusted noisily into the night. Her survival appeared unlikely, but if she was, by a strange chance, only injured, he could still enjoy himself. He could still punish her defiance.

The Dark Lord lowered himself to the cobblestones and inhaled deeply. Jenny's scent, overlaid with the faintest dusting of the stone-slinger, but no broken body or cooling corpse. Not a single drop of blood. A distraction he'd been foolish enough to follow. He picked up the heavy cloak, held it close to his face, then ripped the furred garment to shreds, rending and tearing mere cloth and fur in place of flesh. Breathless with exertion and frustration, he hobbled back to the sanctuary of the Audience Chamber, to preside over rats and mice, beetles and maggots.

CHAPTER FORTY-TWO

"We won't get a second chance, we must get it right the first time," Captain Harry said. "Check once more you can access pockets and weapons smoothly. Double check all straps and buckles, then check your neighbour's equipment. Anything frayed or weak gets replaced."

"I have a request," Sneeth said. "I have a transformed body with a fresh outlook. You've all been unbelievably generous. There is one other new thing I desire, to complete my transformation before I encounter my father. I would like a new name, not the one he gave to me."

"Are you asking for suggestions?" Xanderamm asked.

"I have chosen Seth, but my choice counts for naught if you don't use it."

"Seth is a good, powerful name." Theo clapped him on the shoulder. "Pleased to have you on my team, Seth."

Harry nodded his approval. "An upstanding name, trustworthy. Not the name of a snivelling sneak."

"Sexy," Xanderamm said. "The ladies will swoon at your feet."

Seth's jaw dropped in astonishment. "I don't—"

Harry laughed and shook his head. "Seth doesn't need you to lead him astray, your Majesty. Let him be."

"I do not expect to carry this name for long. When Draqshet realises who I am, or rather who I was, he will target me. But, I think I will die content if I die with honour," Seth said.

"Codswallop. None of us are going to die, and you're going to return covered in glory," Xanderamm said. "Probably blood and other unspeakable bodily fluids, but definitely glory. And then I will teach you about ladies."

Netta crawled over the roof on her belly, looking for a skylight or maintenance hatch. Who builds a Palace without a means to maintain the roof? She propped herself up against a cold chimney stack as she considered other methods of getting back inside. The chimneys were cold. Not cool, but grave-cold. Netta clambered up to look inside. No glimmer of light, not the faintest waft of heat.

The palace roof sprouted a veritable garden of chimneys to choose from. Netta spun in a slow circle, trying to identify the kitchen chimney, which she expected to be widest, and the kitchens an unlikely place for Draqshet to frequent. Not to mention the possibility of rearming herself with weapons she understood.

She chose the likeliest looking stack, based on width and the heavy accumulation of soot. Netta sat on the ledge and swung her legs across. She took a steadying breath, braced her feet against the opposite inner wall, and lowered herself inside with her back firmly pressed against the brickwork. *This is for you, little one.* She shuffled her feet down and lowered herself, a finger-width at a time. Her knees trembled and her thighs quivered, but she crept ever lower. Deprived of light, she soon lost track of time, her world reduced to burning muscles, soot, and rough brick.

~

Draqshet prowled the silent and empty Palace. His Dolls were either dead or too broken to be of further use. An attack must be coming. He smiled. At least they wouldn't come from the skies. He had damaged the Reborn and her overgrown pet lizard too severely for them to try that trick again. The effort of maintaining the shield had proven worthwhile. He doubted the Reborn would recover soon, if at all.

He paused in his patrol. Why bother with the ruined beyond repair Reborn, when this silver-haired creature was almost within his grasp? She was at least as beautiful, and possessed of wild courage. Although mortal, she would make a worthy, albeit temporary, mate.

This time around, he would restrain himself and not deliberately disfigure his offspring. Unless they defied or otherwise offended him.

Unidentified sounds vibrated through the Palace walls. Were his adversaries finally making their way through the fabled secret tunnels? They were breathing as heavily as a wounded Uronk. One wounded Uronk. One person. Draqshet put his ear to the wall. Laboured breathing, and two rapid heartbeats. With wicked talons, he searched for tremors. Which way was the creature travelling?

The Dark Lord reached out with all his predatory senses. His conscious mind blanked as pure animal instinct took over. No footsteps, only shuffle-shuffle-slide. He slithered from chamber to chamber, corridor to corridor, hunting the sounds, not in the walls, but in the maze of chimneys. He tracked the intruder descending from floor to floor, the bellowing lungs and hammering double heartbeats betraying their location.

He waited, patient as a snake, in the kitchen shadows, as soot snowed over the dead hearth. Draqshet inhaled the kitchen odours of decaying meat and rotting vegetables, sifting and sorting the one which didn't belong. The rabbit-hunter. The clever little creature thought to ambush him.

The Dark Lord glided to the yawning fireplace and surveyed the soft bed of cold ashes, and the spits and knives and other potential weapons his prospective consort might use against him. Better to immobilise her before she attacked him. He leaned his head against the stonework, listening to and smelling her progress. The creature was nigh exhausted after her unusual exertions, close to collapse. He crouched on the hearth, and as soon as he saw her boot shuffle down the wall, he struck, as swift and deadly as a viper. He grabbed her ankle and yanked her from her precarious position, cracking her head on the iron grate as she landed. Draqshet pulled his prey from the ashes and shook her.

The rabbit-hunter swung loosely by her ankles, rag-doll arms flopping over her head, grazed knuckles brushing the floor. Twin cylinders rolled across the slate tiles. Draqshet nudged them warily with his toe. He dismissed the strange crystal embellished objects as some feminine frippery, naught with which he was familiar, nor saw a use for. Nevertheless, he scooped them up and slipped them inside his robes.

His prize moaned and struggled weakly before passing out

again, and The Dark Lord smiled grimly within the depths of his hood. She wouldn't escape a second time. Not with her life. He lifted and shook her again, but naught else came loose. He slung her over his shoulder and lurched back to the gloomy Audience Chamber.

CHAPTER FORTY-THREE

Theo released his team into the shadows of the city wall. The river of stars flowing overhead glittered and winked in the frosty night air, eager witnesses to the unfolding drama. Xanderamm immediately turned to the hidden door. Harry found and lit the lamp.

"This tunnel brings us out near the marketplace," Xanderamm said. "There's a service door nearby, leading into the Palace kitchens."

"If, as I fear, Draqshet has captured Netta," Seth said, "he'll either have her locked in the deepest dungeons, or he'll be gloating over her in the Audience Chamber."

"We can follow service corridors to the Audience Chamber," Xanderamm said, "but there's only one way to access the dungeons."

"Which do you think most likely?" Harry asked.

"Clearly, the dungeons offer more security," Seth said, "but Draqshet does not fear you. He will most likely try to lure you into his presence by using Netta as bait."

"The faster we move, the quicker we rescue Mistress Netta," Harry said. "Let's get going."

Seth put a finger to his lips. "The quieter we move, the closer we can get to The Dark Lord before he hears and intercepts us."

Xanderamm jerked his head, and the team followed. Harry extinguished the light before opening the door into the marketplace. Only the glittering stars witnessed their emergence from the tunnel.

Seth paced up and down like a hunting hound, scenting the air. "She was here." He took a few steps, sniffing as he went. Dawning comprehension of Netta's pregnancy wormed into his consciousness, twinned with the equally strong realisation his comrades were unaware. He instinctively wrapped the knowledge in secrecy. No point adding further stress to an already horrific situation. "This way, towards the stables." Seth's confidence grew with every step. Netta had moved around, but the freshest scent followed the path he'd taken the night he escaped.

He raised a hand as he stepped through a doorway, bringing the group to a halt. "Dolls were here." Seth dropped to the ground, rechecking for Netta's scent. "Netta came this way, but I think they carried her from this point onwards. There's a faint whiff of blood, but I don't think from a serious injury."

The group moved carefully, conscious they were in enemy territory, and most likely under observation. When they transitioned to carpeted corridors, walking silently became easier.

Stop. Theo's voice echoed inside their heads. He stooped and picked up a palm-sized object. *Either the Dolls discarded this, not knowing what it is, or Netta dropped it.* He slid the sun-bomb inside his jerkin. *Nice to know we're on the right track.*

Xanderamm tapped Seth on the shoulder. *Can you tell if the young lady is still alive?*

Seth shook his head. *She was alive when she passed this way. I cannot say whether she still lives. If she is in the chamber, I should soon be able to hear her heartbeat.*

Harry smiled grimly. *That will give us an advantage.*

Not really. Draqshet has the same abilities I do, only sharper. He'll already know where we are and how many.

Xanderamm squared his shoulders. *Then we must distract him.*

The corridor stretched before them, unavoidable and terrifying.

"If the bastard already knows we're here, what're we waiting for?" Xanderamm sped forward, threw open the door, and marched down the centre of the chamber. Theo, Harry, and Seth fanned out behind him, presenting a diffuse target.

"Hey, Lord Ugly? You're sitting in my chair." Xanderamm stood, hands on hips, before the dais. "You and I need a chat about royal etiquette."

Draqshet stared at the four men, discombobulated by their attitudes. Beside him, on a spindly gilt chair, sat Netta, gagged and blindfolded, her ankles and wrists bound to the chair legs and arms. Hanks of blood-matted hair hung over her massively swollen and bruised face.

"Your rescuers have arrived, my dear." Draqshet stoked Netta's arm with a clawed hand. "Not an army as befits your beauty, but a paltry quartet. Shall we play with them, or dispose of them mercifully? The decision is my wedding gift to you, my dear." The words slithered from his lips like crippled insects.

"Don't you recognise me?" Seth moved sideways, drawing Draqshet's attention. "Am I not worthy of a prodigal's welcome?"

Draqshet swivelled towards the familiar voice and Theo slid the sun-bomb from his jerkin and hurled it towards the ruined throne.

Light, brighter than the sun, immediately flooded the

chamber, burning away the shadows, pouring into every nook and corner. Faster-than-thought, Theo grabbed Netta and her chair and deposited them outside the city walls. He lit the fuses on his sticky-fire bombs, and returned to the throne room, before The Dark Lord had a chance to open his mouth to protest.

Light burned The Dark Lord like acid. He collapsed, writhing and screaming, unable to escape. Theo tossed the sticky-fire bombs onto Draqshet's steaming robes and grabbed his friends, pulling them faster-than-thought to the far end of the chamber.

The fire roared and crackled as it fed, drowning its victim's pleas for mercy. The black shape rose and fell in a macabre dance. Flames reached for the rafters, consuming the age old tapestries and paintings hanging on the stone walls. Even the dust combusted and whirled through the air like demented fire-flies. The wood and gilt chairs exploded, like dozens of expensive firecrackers, cracking the bricks and setting alight the rough boards over the ancient stained glass windows which shattered under the intense heat.

Theo extended his arms and walked the length of the chamber, drawing the burning debris into a single pile. Seth, Harry, and Xanderamm watched in awe as, with mere gestures, Theo pulled up the marble floor like a rug and smothered the remains of the inferno.

"Sorry about the mosaic," he said. "Only way to save the building."

Wrist to forehead, Xanderamm sighed theatrically. "You leave me no option but to redecorate. I can't deny a fresh look was overdue."

A smouldering rafter cracked and collapsed, bringing down chunks of the ceiling. Seth leapt forward and shoved Xanderamm to safety. The cascade of architectural rubble crushed Seth to the ground, a section of carved marble pinning him in place.

Theo lifted the marble as though it were a mummer's painted prop, while Xanderamm and Harry pulled Seth free.

"He's not breathing," Xanderamm said, wide-eyed with panic.

Harry pounded on Seth's chest, while Theo pinched his nose and breathed into his mouth.

"Don't you dare save my life, then die." Xanderamm's voice cracked. "I promised you'd return covered in glory, not a shroud."

CHAPTER FORTY-FOUR

Harry released Netta from her restraints, and Theo transported the group back to camp in a faster-than-thought clumsy huddle. Annie and Vert stood ready to tend the injured. Netta collapsed in a sobbing heap, unable to look anyone in the eye.

Annie pulled Netta to her feet and wrapped her in a fierce embrace. "I thought I'd lost you." The women rocked together and Annie used the contact to assess Netta's injuries. She ran her fingers over Netta's head, removing the bruises and swelling, and healing the hairline fracture.

Annie jerked back, eyes filled with shock. "Do you have something to tell me?"

Netta shook her head.

"You need a bath," Annie said, "then one of Vert's potions to help you sleep without dreaming. We'll talk when you're feeling better." Netta's rash actions angered Annie, but her secret astounded her more. She turned from her friend to study the hero.

Seth lay like a serene, funerary effigy, utterly still. Annie picked up his cooling hand and closed her eyes. Images from the rescue filled her inner vision: the marketplace, dusty corridors, the overturned wheeled chair, the decaying remains of the dead Doll, and Netta. Netta tied to a chair and displayed as a trophy. The icy emptiness of Draqshet, a void which should have overflowed with fatherly love and pride, provided a bitter flavour. The pictures whirled in a kaleidoscope of horror, but Seth's terror of Draqshet and the coming use of fire overlaid all else. His expectation of drawing Draqshet's ire had not come to fruition, and Seth was floating in a void, unsure of where he belonged, not yet strong enough to inhabit his new identity with confidence.

"He isn't dead," Annie said. "He's undecided. Physically, I have healed him. His ribs have knit, and his heart and lungs are working."

"What can we do?" Xanderamm asked.

"He's tasted friendship and belonging for the first time. He's overwhelmed and can't accept either that they will last or he deserves them. You are closest to him. Talk to him. It doesn't matter about what, only that you get his attention and tether him. I'm going to fetch his mother, and Vera."

Seth hovered, proud but confused. In his new persona, not only had he helped rescue a woman from Draqshet's despicable clutches, but he'd sacrificed himself to save a friend. Being remembered as a hero appealed to his ego, while fading into comfortable obscurity did not.

Voices disturbed his contemplations. He combed through the clamour, identifying individuals. His mother cried as she stroked his curls, and his belly clenched. For eons he'd secretly fantasied about having a mother who wanted to take care of him, dress and feed him, but he'd learned to hide the childish and shameful desire for love and affection. Seth sighed into the void as he recalled multiple instances of Jenny brazenly manipulating audiences for her own benefit. She could play the passive grieving mother to perfection for all eternity, but would she welcome the active role of a loving parent with infinite enthusiasm?

Vera's fingers entwined with his own, and he felt her fragility growing. She fought the pain colonising her body, while knowing she would lose the battle. Her overwhelming concern was for him. She neither asked nor expected anything in return. She loved him unconditionally. The rising lump in his throat choked him, and he turned, psychic arms outstretched to embrace her spirit.

Xanderamm paced beside Seth's pallet, too agitated to stay still. The King alternately pleaded and cursed, begging Seth to return so he could reward him, and threatening dire and eternal consequences if Seth abandoned him.

Seth's desire to return grew, as did his worry that he was unworthy. He sensed a presence moving through the void, following the golden cord, tugging impatiently at the connection. AnnieRah.

She faced him, arms folded, and face creased into a frown. "Are you worthy? Probably not. Nobody ever is." Annie leaned in. "The trick is to become worthy, to earn the love which you have received. Uncle Seth, if you think you can up and leave, you are seriously mistaken. People here are desperately waiting for good news, and you will not disappoint them."

"Are you suggesting I can become truly worthy?"

"Allow me to share a secret: genuine love comes without conditions. Receiving this priceless gift feeds and nurtures a soul. You become a better person by accepting love because you want to be worthy. Does that make sense?"

"No, it's an inversion of cause and effect. But I trust you, and I want to believe you."

"Good. Now, are you coming back, or do I have to drag you?" Annie shook the golden cord.

"I'm coming. Thank you. I have much to learn."

"If you've been listening to Xanderamm, you'll know he's got a whole curriculum planned." Annie laughed. "He can't decide whether he wants to hug you or strangle you. But he'll make a loyal friend."

Seth gasped and opened his eyes to a sea of concerned faces. Everyone started talking at once, offering thanks and praise.

Annie held up her hands. "That's enough. You've witnessed Seth's return to the living. Now he needs time to recover. You can visit him tomorrow. Go, shoo!" She flapped her hands, smiling as she did so.

"The young lady suffered quite an ordeal," Seth said. "How is she?"

"Physically, she's fine. Mentally and emotionally? We must wait. She has to come to terms with the consequences of her actions."

"For what it's worth," Seth said, "she acted to protect you. Will you pass on to her my wishes for her speedy recovery?"

Annie nodded. "You hold her no ill-will?"

Seth took Annie's hand. "The lady likes me not. She has no reason, but she loves you and believed her actions would save you from making a mistake. Truly, if her actions had not resulted in pain and injury? If she had killed Draqshet without hurting herself? Would you be angry? I think your anger stems from fear; fear of losing a beloved companion."

Annie released Seth's hand. "She put our friends at risk."

"Your friends came here with you to challenge and destroy

The Dark Lord. That put them at risk, long before Mistress Netta acted without permission."

~

Netta struggled out of bed, woozy from the deep dreamless sleep, her leg and arm muscles still burning from climbing down the chimney. She reached for the golden cord connecting her to Annie, but her friend's anger throbbed, a dark red fog of fury buffering Netta, blocking mind-talking between them. If Annie was avoiding her, then she'd start her apologies with Roic.

The dragon slumbered on the outskirts of the camp, the winter sun sparkling on his metallic scales. His lopsided silhouette brought a fresh batch of scalding tears cascading down Netta's cheeks. Knowing Roic was actively regenerating didn't make his mutilated wing any easier to witness.

"Roic, can you hear me?" Netta stood before her friend, not daring to embrace or even touch him.

I hear you, Mistress Netta, and I am pleased to see you. Are you recovered? Roic lazily slid open a great, jewelled eye.

Netta stumbled to her knees between Roic's forelegs. "I came to apologise, but I don't have the words to express my sorrow or shame. This," she waved her hands towards Roic's outstretched wings, "I didn't plan for this to happen."

Roic allowed the sobs to flow and develop into hiccups before he spoke. *You allowed fear and hate to govern your actions. Rather than believe the evidence of Annie's gift of touch, you followed your prejudices. You must look deep into your heart and examine your reasons, I cannot offer absolution.*

"Are you sending me away?"

Never. We are each responsible for our own actions. I am disap-

pointed in myself that, as Annie's protector, I endangered her. She disappointed herself; as the Mother of All, she failed to protect you.

"Is it true? Your blood healed her?"

Hmmm, it may have helped speed the process. Roic inhaled and drew Netta's scent deep into his lungs. *When do you intend to tell your husband your good news?*

CHAPTER FORTY-FIVE

Annie's suggestion that the camp pack up and move immediately to the capital met with unanimous approval. Agendas ranged from repairs and renovations to burials, reestablishing trade to catching and rehoming lost or abandoned animals, reemploying staff to recalling the soldiers. Cleaning and disinfecting the city of Draqshet's evil presence would take long months and many hands.

Lady Amora and her guards declined the invitation to return to the capital, insisting they had plans to travel the world, seeking adventure in far-flung locations. "We'll return to regale you with our experiences, but not for many years. Good luck to you all."

They waved like excited children on holiday until they were out of sight, the magnificent wagon swaying and groaning as it bore them towards the coast.

Dexter insisted on riding ahead of the caravan. "The Dark Lord is dead. Long live the King!" He cried at every village and hamlet, announcing the good news and starting the recruitment process. By the time the group entered the capital, they had a sprawling entourage, encompassing every trade and class of citizen.

Seth hesitated when he entered the Palace. Should he return to Sneeth's tower rooms, or find different accommodation?

Xanderamm jabbed him with an elbow. "So many changes, eh? I can't face my old apartments with all the gaudy ostentation I once believed sophisticated. Help me search for somewhere new? Preferably with an adjoining apartment for you?"

"I'll happily help you find suitable rooms, but I don't think I should move in next door. There exist protocols about who stays closest to the King," Seth said.

Xanderamm shrugged. "I'm sure, and I will retain those which are useful and sensible; others I will discard. However, the Defender of the King must remain by my side."

Seth frowned. "Defender of the King?"

"Oops, I need a secretary, too. My first royal appointment will be to confirm you as my official Defender. You risked your life to save mine. As the King, it behooves me to recognise and reward that action." Xanderamm cocked his head. "Unless you have a better prospect, Lord Seth?"

"As you know, I have no prospects whatsoever. But, I must caution you. Giving me a place of honour may be political suicide, my friend. Your citizens may well revolt when they learn my history."

Xanderamm shoved Seth towards a broad staircase. "This way. Your response only serves to confirm the correctness of my decision. Again, you place my well-being above your own. Hurry, before another snags the rooms I want."

"You're the King, you tell them to move out," Seth said.

"I could, and most would expect that. Especially those who only know me from before. I have no problem imposing my will when I think it matters, but for a set of rooms? There are hundreds from which I can choose, each needing redecoration and refurnishing. If someone reaches the prize before me, so be it. I expect I can survive a minor disappointment. But that's no excuse for lollygagging, my friend." Xanderamm increased his pace, forcing Seth to jog beside him.

"May I accept the position, but not the title, your Majesty?"

"No, the title confers authority. You cannot do the job properly without the requisite clout. People need to understand you have my authorisation."

"But my history may undermine your authority."

"Seth? Have you ever considered how similar we are?"

"A monster and a monarch? Yes, identical, in every significant way." Seth shook his head. "Your majesty, we are naught alike, we have naught in common."

"Codswallop! We had insular childhoods, each groomed to a particular way of thinking. Neither of us had interested parents; we've committed heinous acts, because of our twisted training and warped self-image. Most importantly, we've changed."

"You didn't murder people, nor take pleasure in hurting them."

"No, what I did was worse." Xanderamm seized Seth's arm as they jogged down a wide and sumptuously appointed corridor. "I ignored my people's suffering, because taking action was too much trouble. I allowed those outside my circle to starve while I feasted. I turned my face from the news of women and children being abused and killed while my wastrel friends feted and pampered me."

"You had nobody to guide you, your majesty. Sycophants surrounded you."

"I chose the sycophants and deliberately ignored or laughed at those who could have advised me. AnnieRah cursed me, but in reality, she blessed me. She forced me to reassess my values, whereas you reached conclusions by yourself. You are a better man than I, my friend."

"I don't think—"

"Good, because I don't want to hear your opinion." Xanderamm slowed to a halt and pointed to doors either side of the corridor. "Unless you want to tell me how fabulous our new apartments are?"

CHAPTER FORTY-SIX

Only a fragment remained of the evil psyche. A spark from the demonic form of The Dark Lord as he combusted entered a fleeing rat. The mutant rodent hid in the darkest corners, filled with a gnawing hatred of everything. The miserable creature ripped out the throats of any other rats it encountered, and terrorised the Palace cats employed to control the ubiquitous vermin. Consumed with a lust only to kill and destroy, the rat slaughtered creature after hapless creature, taking no time to feed, and remaining unsatiated.

The creature's reign of terror continued unchecked until people moved back into the Palace and established a new hierarchy. Refusing the intimidation of a broom, the creature leapt and attacked a maid, biting a chunk from her cheek before seeking sanctuary in the shadows.

News of the girl's nightmares reached Annie, who took Vert with her to interview the young woman. The girl lay on her pallet in an attic bedroom, her wounded cheek weeping.

"Are you certain it was a rat?" Vert asked.

"Yes, Milord. I've seen 'undreds in me time, but this one was different. Skinny and uncommon vicious, it was. I dropped me candle and the little monster took off, quicker'n lightning."

"Did you set anything alight?" Annie asked.

"Naught of value, only rubbish already piled up for carting away. I didn't mean to, it was an accident."

"You're not in trouble, I'm only trying to get a picture of what happened. I heard you're having nightmares?"

The girl closed her eyes and trembled. "Yes, Milady. I ain't afeard of no rats, leastways, I never have been afore." She opened her eyes and looked directly at Annie. "I dream the rat is biting me, swallowing my soul. Like I'm falling down a well and I know there's nobody coming to help me." Tears started from her eyes.

Annie reached forward and stroked the girl's cheek. "There, all gone."

"Thank you, Milady," the girl said, tentatively touching her healed cheek. "I didn't mean to be no bother."

"You are no bother, child. You have every right to have your injuries treated. Vert will give you a potion to help you sleep peacefully. Now that I have removed the poison, your night-mares should also cease. I'll return in a few days to check."

Annie and Vert left the girl peacefully drifting to sleep, rehearsing in her dreams how she would tell her friends the Goddess Reborn and a fine but spindly gentleman took an interest in her.

"A normal rat bite should not make anyone lose a sense of themselves," Vert said, as they negotiated the stairs.

"I knew exactly what she meant," Annie said. "When I touched Draqshet's shield, I felt myself hurtling into a never-ending well of emptiness. I prefer not to believe it, but could a part of The Dark Lord have escaped the fire?"

"I cannot imagine Draqshet choosing to migrate his self

into a lowly rodent," Vert said, "but if he was desperate enough, if it was his only choice..? Seth will sniff him out, if he's still lurking in the Palace."

~

Seth listened to Annie's theory and shuddered. "Draqshet always knew everything that happened," he said. "Oft times, I fantasied he could become a beetle or spider, a creature that crawls unnoticed. But I cannot imagine him remaining in such a fragile and unimpressive body for long."

"Well then, you'd better hunt him down," Xanderamm said, "and we'll squash him into oblivion this time."

"There's no reason for you to come," Annie said. "You'll be safer if you stay here in your rooms."

"My dearest Lady, there is every reason for me to come. This monster invaded my kingdom, and he slaughtered my citizens with impunity. Like you, I have a duty." Xanderamm raised himself to his fullest height. "A worthy king leads by example. Besides, I need to see his annihilation with mine own eyes."

"Very well, Your Majesty. From what the maid says, he still has an aversion to light or fire. We'll fetch the sun-bombs and light blades. Any other advantage you can envisage, Seth?"

Seth shook his head. "Naught I can think of. But if he had the ability to cast himself into the body of another, I suggest shielding the search area, to prevent his escape. I know not how to keep him from projecting into one of us, though."

"I can prevent that," Annie said. "I will cast prophylactic shields around each of us."

"A shield of fire?" Seth blanched at the thought.

"No, a golden shield which repels evil. You won't feel it, like you don't feel light," Annie reassured him.

Annie cast a protection over Vert first, then Xanderamm

who danced about like a child in a new festival suit, lunging with his bright sword at imaginary enemies.

"Hmm, leading by example, are you?" Annie asked.

"Yes, I'm demonstrating my faith in your shield." He winked at Seth. "Making it easier for my valiant Defender to follow."

"I'm ready," Seth said, standing with feet apart, arms extended, and eyes firmly shut.

"You can look now," Annie said. "Are you well? Not hurting?"

Seth cracked open his eyes, then blinked. "I feel I'm standing in sunlight, not unpleasant." He shrugged, as though settling a new cloak. "If it isn't impertinent to mention, the sensation is akin to being embraced, in friendship."

Vert stifled a grin. "We'll go ahead Annie, make sure the Palace servants are safely away, while you collect the weapons."

By the time Annie caught up, Xanderamm had cleared the Audience Chamber floor of servants, and set guards at the perimeter. Annie gathered the group and cast a protective shield over the area. She handed out eye protectors, and double checked everyone tied them securely, before arming her party with the weapons of light.

"Remember, this isn't any rodent we're hunting," Annie said. "This is Draqshet, or a fragment of him, inhabiting a rat. Seth? Will you lead, or shall I?"

"Easier if I go first. Hopefully, I can pick up his fresh scent," Seth said.

Sun-bombs in one hand, light-blades in the other, Annie, Xanderamm, and Vert followed. Seth moved cautiously, sniffing the air, then dropping to all fours to examine the rubble covered floor. His eyes watered from the sting of charred materials, which persisted, strong enough for them all to smell. The three instinctively formed an outwards facing circle around Seth, their eyes darting from cracked and pitted floor, to shadowy corners piled with broken masonry.

Seth moved away from the obvious pyre, eyes closed in concentration as he filtered the scents of regular rats and the hate-fuelled rodent who desired only to slaughter every living creature it encountered. He crept closer to the stone dais where the crumbled remnants of the throne remained.

Xanderamm jumped and blasted an errant leaf, blown by wintry gusts through the fire-shattered window. "Sorry." He held up both hands in apology.

Vert launched his sun-bomb under the throne as the King cringed his embarrassment. "There!" He pointed to an emaciated rodent caught in the light blast. Dazzled, the creature ran in frantic circles, a high-pitched scream torn from its throat.

Annie aimed her weapon, and the creature launched itself at her face. Before she could defend herself, Seth seized the creature and snapped its neck. He tore off its head and threw the pieces to the ground.

"Incinerate him!"

Annie threw a ball of fire, and engulfed the tiny corpse fragments in white-hot flames. "Did we kill him, or did he escape?"

"He recognised me." Seth sank to the floor. "I felt his shock, before he died. He's gone."

Xanderamm crouched beside his trembling friend. "We couldn't have done this without you. You defeated evil. You're truly free."

CHAPTER FORTY-SEVEN

Although they lived in the Palace, the group maintained a camping mentality, and convened in the kitchen for meals.

Netta sat as far from the fireplace as she could, pushing food around her plate, but not eating. Bruise-coloured circles under her eyes and newly hollowed cheeks confirmed her air of unhappiness. Master André brought her choice tidbits at which she smiled wanly, then ignored. She scanned the room like a hunted animal, avoiding eye-contact, constantly on high alert.

The conversation revolved around the ultimate defeat of Draqshet, and how the maid's response to the rat bite had alerted Annie to the danger.

"Had the girl's nightmares not woken her screaming every night, we might never have known," Vert said.

"I understood exactly what she meant when she described the sensation of falling down a well," Annie said. "When I touched Draqshet's shield, a heartbeat stretched to a century, I feared being condemned to fall forever. And the cold..." Annie shuddered. "Every scintilla of heat fled my body, and my blood froze in my veins."

Netta raised her head. "That's how I feel since Draqshet touched me. He dragged me out of that chimney." She nodded towards the fireplace, "and I cracked my head, but it was his touch that rendered me incapable. I was drowning in a river of ice, my life-force being sucked from me, as he pulled me into a whirlpool of emptiness."

André took her trembling hand. "He's dead and gone. He can't touch you now, nor ever again."

"But the void remains, pulling at me. Whenever I close my eyes, I'm dizzied by the swirling emptiness. I relive the experience of being tossed over his shoulder like a sack of wheat. I'd give anything to forget, to lose those memories." Tears cascaded down Netta's cheeks.

"I'm so sorry, Netta, but I can't remove those memories." Annie glanced at Theo.

"Annie's right," Theo said. "There's no way to remove or change your memories without destroying your mind."

Seth half raised a hand. "I can."

"You can remove memories? That's impossible," Theo said.

"Remove isn't the correct word," Seth said. "But, I can help the young lady alter how she responds to the memories, render them harmless."

Annie leaned forward. "That's an enormous claim. Have you done this before?"

"Draqshet wiped clean my mother's mind, remade her to his purpose. I'm not proposing anything as brutally extreme for Mistress Netta. But I can relieve her distress."

"He's not doing anything to me." Netta gripped her dagger. "I'll not have that monster come near me."

Seth raised both hands, palms out. "Without your cooperation, I cannot help you, mistress. I will leave you and your friends to finish your meal in peace. Mayhap your appetite will improve without my presence."

Annie caught a whiff of combined disappointment and humiliation as Seth passed her, and her suppressed anger bubbled to the surface. A flush of flames ran over her skin, briefly illuminating the darkening kitchen.

Theo raised his eyebrows. "Don't say something you'll later regret, my love."

"Seth was part of your rescue team. He risked his life to save you. He almost died saving Xanderamm." Annie fought to keep the flames tamped down.

"You forgot to mention how he saved Jenny from an inferno and how his father ripped away his wings. But he survived all that, too. Doesn't it strike you as the tiniest bit peculiar?" Netta glared at Annie.

Annie inhaled the wave of scent rolling off her best friend and screwed up her face, trying not to gag. Netta's bitterness stank of rotting potatoes. "I find strange," Annie said, "your inexplicable distrust, not only of Seth, but me. I have touched him, read his heart. I trust him."

"Netta, do you trust me?" Vert asked.

"Of course." Netta frowned in confusion. "I have no reason to mistrust you. Why do you ask?"

"Because I trust Seth. So much so, I plan to ask him if he will help me manage the memories shared to me by the trees. I am haunted by what happened to that defenceless woman. My memories disturb my sleep, and I cannot look at Jenny without a surge of anger on her behalf."

"You trust that monster enough to let him meddle inside your head? Are you already addle pated?" Netta stared wide-eyed at Vert.

"Firstly, the monster is a man. His name is Seth." Vert tapped the table with his knife as he counted each point. "Secondly, I trust Annie's gift of touch. If she says his heart is good, then I believe her. Thirdly, I have seen Seth in action. He acts instinctively, putting the safety of others first. Fourthly, I saw his injuries when Annie brought him in to camp. If he wanted to engage our sympathy, he didn't need to resort to such extremes. Fifthly, he saved Annie from being bitten by the rogue rat."

"The rat couldn't have touched Annie through the shield," Netta said. "Mayhap he killed the rat to claim the essence of The Dark Lord for himself."

"Enough!" Annie exploded into a column of fire. "I will hear no more of your nonsense. Based on the stench of rot rolling of you, if anyone has the essence of The Dark Lord within them, it is you!"

"You cannot mean that," Netta whispered.

Annie gripped Netta's wrist and pulled her to her feet. "No, the rot started before Draqshet touched you. Hear me well. I will tolerate neither mistrust nor the sowing of dissent." Annie released Netta and stormed out of the kitchen.

Seth huddled in a corner of his room, a blanket wrapped around his shaking shoulders. He startled at the gentle tap on his door and pulled the blanket closer.

"Seth? It's me, Vert. May I come in?"

Seth pulled the blanket over his head and rocked back and forth. *If I ignore him, he'll go away.* The door creaked open and light footsteps approached his corner, followed by the sounds of his ally sliding down the wall beside him.

Vert stretched out his legs and rotated his ankles. "Do you find the floor more comfortable than a chair, my friend?"

"Comfortable? How can I be comfortable when people

believe me to be the epitome of evil?" Seth pushed back his blanket hood. "I don't mean for you to pity me. I have committed heinous acts, but... foolishly, I hoped for forgiveness if I could redeem myself. What must I do?"

"I have an idea, although it is selfish," Vert said, clasping his twiggy fingers in his lap. "I am here seeking your help. The trees shared their memories, directly into my mind, of Draqshet hunting the Goddess. The wolves continued the tale of rape and the consequent trauma of your birth. Those images haunt me; I am sick to my soul whenever I see Jenny."

"You're asking me to help you manage those memories? I cannot remove them, only make them less disturbing."

"But you can do as you say? Throughout the three king-doms, I never heard such a claim."

"Draqshet and I travelled the world, far beyond the three kingdoms. We saw many strange things which the locals held commonplace. Changing perceptions of a memory isn't magic, but the process requires trust. Do you wish to start tonight?"

"I would start as soon as possible. I look forward to a restful night's sleep."

"We should set up in your room," Seth said. "You will be tired immediately after the session."

CHAPTER FORTY-EIGHT

J enny sat on the edge of her bed and held the spoon, trickling in the thin soup which was all Vera could now swallow. She wiped Vera's chin free of dribbles before offering more.

"You shouldn't be here," Vera gasped. "You ought to dine with the others, make friends."

"Twaddle," Jenny said. "Besides, I prefer being with you."

"You gain naught, staying with me."

"That's not strictly true." Jenny smiled. "I gain peace. I can't remember looking after anything or anyone before, but it's oddly rewarding."

Vera coughed, and Jenny wiped away the flecks of blood with a fresh linen cloth.

"I won't let you die, Vera. I won't."

"Stopping the cycle isn't your job, child. Never was. Everyone dies, it's part of living."

Jenny flew out of the room, galvanised by Vera's words. She raced down the stairwell, skirts gathered knee high, shouting for help as she ran.

Annie heard the commotion as she strode unfamiliar corridors to work off her fury. She almost collided with the distraught Jenny in a doorway.

"Come quickly, it's Vera. She's dying." Jenny seized Annie's arm. "Please?"

Annie hurried in Jenny's wake. "This corridor leads to your quarters."

"Yes, I made Vera stay with me." Jenny flicked a glance over her shoulder. "Vera is my friend, I couldn't allow her to sleep with the servants in a chilly attic."

Annie followed Jenny into her sumptuously appointed rooms. She raised an eyebrow at the truckle bed Jenny kicked underneath, but said naught. There in Jenny's high bed lay Vera, alabaster pale and barely breathing. Annie took her hand, feeling the fragile golden cord unravelling.

"Thank you for coming, Milady," Vera said without opening her eyes. "There's naught for you to do. Not for me, anyway. But Seth and Jenny still need your support."

Annie perched on the edge of the bed, trying to avoid disturbing the frail woman. "I can rid you of this disease, make you whole again."

Vera shook her head. "My time is nearly come, my son beckons to me. Our reunion will be wonderful." She squeezed Annie's hand. "Family is so important."

"What would you have me do, Mistress Vera?"

Vera crooked a finger, gesturing Annie closer. "Support your great-mother and great-uncle. I've done all I can."

"How do you know..?"

Vera opened her eyes and beamed fondly at Annie. "An adept servant pays attention, and I was the best."

Jenny tugged Annie's sleeve. "Can you save her?"

Annie shook her head. "Mistress Vera doesn't need saving. But she will experience no more pain." Annie closed her eyes to concentrate. "I've summoned Seth. He would want to be here."

Seth and Vert were arranging comfortable chairs before the fire when Seth froze, then his face contorted in a paroxysm of grief.

"Are you in pain?" Vert asked.

Seth shook his head. "Vera," he said, stumbling out the door.

Vert followed Seth to Jenny's apartment, helping his tear-blinded friend negotiate the stairs and corridors. Annie met them at the door, placing a finger to her lips.

"Mistress Vera is sleeping."

"Can't you help her?" Seth sobbed.

"She is in no pain. Mistress Vera refused further aid. She is looking forward to the next stage, to reuniting with her son in the Summer Fields. Her golden cord is fraying, she will drift quietly in her sleep."

Seth straightened his shoulders. "We must honour her wishes. She deserves our respect." He looked at Annie. "Does she know we're here?"

"I'm sure she feels your presence, but don't expect her to respond. Let her go gently, if you love her."

Seth nodded and found the small stool he'd sat on when he was Sneeth attending his mother. He took Vera's vein-roped hand in his newly soft one and kissed her calloused fingers. Then he laid his head on the coverlet and waited.

Dawn crept stealthily through the window, pale fingers reaching to caress Vera's cooling cheeks. Seth woke, his warm supple digits still entwined with Vera's cooling hand. His hunter's hearing confirmed what he instinctively knew: no heartbeat, no pulse. Vera's golden cord had frayed and snapped during the night, her slight smile telling Seth she passed happily over to the Summer Fields and into the waiting arms of her son.

Seth adjusted the bedclothes and folded Vera's hands over the coverlet. Rivulets of tears ran down his face, dripping unnoticed from his chin. He didn't recognise the sensation in his chest, an expanding bladder, pushing ever outwards, an unexpected leaden weight, but he guessed grief. He fought to breathe normally, while listening to his own sobs clutching for air.

Jenny sidled next to him and wrapped her arms around his shoulders. "Vera died as she wished. We'll both miss her, but we should rejoice she is finally pain free and reunited with her beloved son."

"I have seen much death," Seth said, "but never experienced grief. How do mortals cope?"

"I don't know, but I believe following rituals to farewell friends helps ease the pain. I promised Vera I would stand and say the words of passing for her." Jenny shook her head. "Vera found the idea of a fine lady saying the words for a serving woman amusing."

Jenny excavated the palace wardrobes for the most luxurious gown and cape for Vera to wear as she officially entered the Summer Fields. She also packed a bundle of more practical day dresses to place at Vera's feet, and dressed Vera's hair with particular care, slipping in extra combs and pins.

Seth chose a wide open space outside the city walls to build the funeral pyre. Xanderamm and Harry, Theo and Vert, André and Dexter volunteered to help. Seth turned them all away. Making his throat and tongue cooperate to produce intelligible sounds defeated him. Layer upon layer of crisscrossed logs grew, interspersed with winter dry bracken, a tower to reach the very skies. By brutal physical labour, he hoped to numb the pain of immeasurable loss.

As the sun blazed a glorious farewell sunset, the procession filed out of the city, bearing the shrouded corpse. Torches flared and bobbed as the party solemnly stepped to their destination.

Theo and Seth crossed arms underneath Vera's remains, lifting her as ritual demanded to face the rising sun, and arranging her gently atop the pyre, surrounded by the small gifts and afterlife care packages her friends and colleagues offered as they circled the funereal structure. Annie directed balls of flame deep into the pyre, while Jenny spoke the words of passing.

"Honoured Ancestors
dry our tears
and welcome our friend Vera
to the Summer Fields,
where exists only light and joy.
We ask you to wrap her in love
as she loved us.
Honoured Ancestors
help us keep safe
our treasured memories of Vera,
a unique jewel.
Honoured Ancestors
grant our friend Vera
everlasting youth and vitality,
peace and eternal gladness."

Seth winced at the intensity of the conflagration, and the mourners instinctively widened the space between themselves and the pyre. As the night progressed, and the structure gradually collapsed on itself, the bereaved retired to seek comfort within their own homes. Seth and Jenny kept vigil until the ashes reduced to dust and drifted away on the morning breeze.

"Come," Jenny said, linking her arm through Seth's. "It's time to go. Vera has gone."

Seth stumbled, as graceless as a calf, grief putting his newly formed limbs beyond his control. Jenny tucked herself under his shoulder and guided him towards the city walls where Xanderamm and Harry waited. They dashed forward, easing Seth from Jenny, who appeared far too small and frail to support him.

"We'll get him to bed," Xanderamm said, flicking a nod to a waiting servant. "This woman will help you to your rooms, Lady Jenny. Get some rest."

Jenny gratefully leaned on the woman, leaving Xanderamm and Harry to carry Seth to his apartment. Between them, they manoeuvred him into his bed.

"Vert said we must give you this." Xanderamm offered Seth a tiny cup. "He said it would help you sleep."

Seth shook his head and turned away.

"Oh, no. No, no, no. I'm not telling Vert you refused his sleeping draught. I command you to drink the potion."

Seth shrugged and held out his hand. He didn't have the energy to resist his friends, especially when he knew they had only his best interests at heart. He tossed back the contents of the cup in one swallow and closed his eyes. "Thank you."

"We'll stay," Harry said. "You won't be alone."

CHAPTER FORTY-NINE

J enny faltered when she saw Annie waiting outside her apartment, then readjusted her smile, squared her aching shoulders, and dismissed the servant.

"Lady Annie, what an unexpected pleasure." She beckoned for Annie to enter her apartment.

"We need to talk. The timing seems insensitive, but there's never an appropriate time," Annie said. "I can come back after you've rested, if you prefer?"

Jenny leaned on the back of a chair and slipped off her shoes. She wriggled her cramped toes deep into the silky pile of the rug and sighed. "I am exhausted, but I doubt I could sleep." She cocked her head. "Somehow, I don't think we will ever find the perfect moment. Let us at least be comfortable." She plopped into a fireside chair and gestured for Annie to do the same.

"Now that I'm here, all I rehearsed has fled. I wanted to inform you of your history, the years Draqshet hid from you."

Jenny sighed and knitted her fingers in her lap. "Whoever I was, and whoever I offended, we can safely assume they imprisoned me because I committed at least one egregious act, but Draqshet saw something in me which would serve his purpose. Does it occur to you, Lady Annie, that I may prefer to live in ignorance, rather than suffer the guilt of my actions?"

"Your desire to hear matches my desire to tell. However, you deserve the truth." Annie flicked a ball of fire into the dying embers and added a small log to reignite the flames.

"A handy skill." Jenny nodded at the hearth.

"One I inherited from you."

"Me? What ancestry do you and I share?"

"Seth told you Draqshet planted a dark seed of discontent in you?"

"Indeed, he implied I had been the Great Goddess, the All Mother." Jenny produced a bright brittle laugh. "Mayhap all sons wish for their mothers to be more than they actually are, to fulfil some fantastical ideal."

"All Seth told you was true. But Draqshet's seed poisoned you, making you careless of creation. He made certain you could never achieve the happiness you sought."

"Where is your proof of these ridiculous assertions?"

"You participated in the mortal world, seeking sensations which only left you empty and bereft." Annie held up her hand. "You birthed girl child after girl child, abandoning the mother and shifting your essence into the new potential."

"This is an ugly story, and you offer no evidence."

"I was the last girl child, orphaned like the others. I inherited your talents with textiles. Roic discovered me, and recognised my scent, your scent, after countless generations."

Jenny slitted her eyes. "I don't believe you."

"The world was collapsing into chaos without your guidance. I tried to return you to the Great Temple, but you resisted. You gave me no choice. I didn't understand what I was doing. When I came to release you, you'd gone." Annie flung herself to her knees before Jenny. "I didn't know you would fade away without light. Forgive me, please."

Jenny sat back in her chair, recoiling as far as possible from Annie. "You incarcerated me? You almost killed me? What do you expect from me now?"

Annie sat back on her haunches and wiped her eyes. "You are my many times great mother and Seth is my many times great uncle. I expect naught, but I would like us to be a family."

"You are mistaken, Lady Annie. You claim to have inherited certain skills from me, but I cannot create fire, nor can I so much as thread a needle. I've had an unpleasant day and a difficult night. I should like to sleep now."

Annie nodded, unwilling to antagonise Jenny by arguing. She left with a promise to return the following day.

Once alone, Jenny propped her feet on the grate. The images Draqshet had shared clearly showed a woman hurling fire at the newborn, which meant that at some stage, she had enjoyed the gift of fire. And before her son had released her from the standing coffin dungeon, she'd created a brief flare. If she'd created fire whilst incarcerated, she could surely do so again.

Jenny glanced around the room at the rugs and curtains, wooden furniture and fabric hangings. The ability to create fire needs balancing with the skill to control it, too. Her arms and legs ached from standing by Vera's pyre all night, and her head throbbed from the many tears she had shed. She would sleep before experimenting with pyrotechnics; outdoors rather than in her combustible fuel-rich quarters.

Seth woke late afternoon as the sun spread its final benediction over the fields and cities. Whispered voices from the room next door reminded him he was not alone. He listened idly to Xanderamm and Harry discussing renovation plans for the city and the Palace.

Enthusiasm for improving the servants' attic rooms, and the rest of the Palace, filled The King with excitement. Not until Annie and Vert described the sleeping space of the rat-bitten maid had Xanderamm given any thought to the comfort of the Palace servants. Seth listened as Harry described how a system of pipes and grates could carry heated air into the chilly rooms, and how they should start now, before winter arrived.

Seth nodded to himself. He needed a project to keep himself occupied, to distract him from the terrible reality of losing Vera, his first friend. He slid out of bed and pulled on a robe, then padded next door to his friends.

"You're up," Xanderamm said, coming to embrace him. "How are you feeling?"

"Physically, I'm fine. Vert is a gifted herbalist. Do you know where he is? We have unfinished business."

"Last I heard," Harry said, "he was pottering about the hothouses. Lots of rare and interesting plants in need of some love and attention."

"Love and attention," Seth said. "They solve the world's problems, don't they?"

Condensation fogged the hothouse windows, but Seth heard Vert crooning to the neglected plants. Seth slipped inside, and the tropically humid air caught in his throat.

"I was hoping we could continue your memory manipulation," Seth said.

"Are you up to the work?" Vert wiped dirt encrusted fingers on a cloth tucked into his belt.

"Helping you also helps me. It's what I believe Vera would have wanted."

Vert tidied up, stacking pots back on shelves, making sure his cuttings had water, and sweeping the dirt and debris into neat piles before shovelling it into sacks.

Back in Vert's room, Seth noticed the chairs were how he'd arranged them. "You expected me to return?"

"You're a man of your word," Vert said. "But I didn't think you'd be back so quickly."

Seth drew the curtains, extinguished all but one candle, and placed the fire-guard before the hearth, restricting the amount of light in the room. "I want you to remember the scene the trees shared, and why you were so affected. Take your time."

"I know men preying on women is not uncommon... but... she was utterly defenceless... nobody came to help her." Vert entwined his trembling fingers.

"Do you believe she should have been protected? By whom?"

"Women alone aren't safe."

"You are not responsible for what happened."

"I know, but... we're all ultimately responsible... monsters go unchallenged every day," Vert said.

"Do you think it's your job to stop them?" Seth asked.

Vert nodded.

"Do you think that's completely true and reasonable, or mayhap only partially?"

"Completely."

"I want you to keep your eyes focused on this flame," Seth said. "Wherever the flame goes, that's where you look. Move only your eyes, not your head." He held the candle before Vert, ensuring he had his attention, before moving the candle side to side, up and down, or diagonally.

Seth returned to the question of responsibility, while

distracting Vert with the moving flame. By the time the candle had burned halfway down, Vert admitted, reluctantly, maybe he wasn't totally responsible for challenging every monster.

"Where do you go in your head to feel relaxed?" Seth asked.

Vert smiled slowly. "There's a secluded valley, with a clear, rippling stream... I stretch out on a flat rock and bask like a lizard. The trees rustle and gossip... it's very peaceful. Only birds and squirrels break the silence."

"I want you to take your memory and fold it tightly. Imagine putting it into a strongbox, like the one Harry uses for the soldier's wages. Lock the box and secure it with the heaviest padlock. Now bury that box in the deepest hole you can dig. Cover the whole thing with rocks. Don't dig it up or try to look until I tell you."

Vert nodded. "Is that it?"

"For now, yes. Tell me, my friend, are you responsible for all the monsters?"

"Only some of them."

"Do you feel responsible for Draqshet's actions?"

"I know I'm not, but the thought of what he did nauseates me"

"What he did was indefensible," Seth said.

"But I was not responsible," Vert said, sitting up straighter. "Thank you, I think you've helped."

"We need more sessions," Seth said, "but you made excellent progress today."

CHAPTER FIFTY

J enny tossed and turned, then threw off the covers. Dawn caressed the city rooftops, whispering the inhabitants awake. She had slept only intermittently, disturbed by dreams of blazing conflagrations. The possibility of being a fire-witch sent her pulse racing. She needed to answer the question herself, before sanctimonious Annie returned as promised.

Dressed in a sensible tunic, trousers, and a heavy cloak, she made her way to the stables.

"My Lady Jenny, how can I help you?" Dexter ducked out of a stall, curry comb in hand.

"I require a well-tempered horse, one not easily startled," Jenny said, "but not an old plodder. I don't have all day."

"I'll saddle Presto for you, a sensible girl, but lively. She runs like the wind." Dexter pointed to a grey mare who pricked her ears at the sound of her name. "Are you going far?"

"I'm not sure. Mayhap you can advise me? I need an open space, away from prying eyes. I'm going to... make a fire."

"You're not planning on playing with that sticky-fire, are you? Lady Amora and her men tested out their concoction at

The Demon's Swimming Hole, but I reckon you'd find what you need closer to home. There's a river bend, with a wide gravelly beach, a short ride from here." Dexter gave detailed directions as he saddled Presto.

Jenny leapt into the saddle, scorning the aid of the mounting block, and muttered distracted thanks. That's why Lady Amora was so standoffish. She caused the fire in which my son nearly died. Does he know? Her thoughts raced faster than the horse. Lady Amora knew Vera, Vera befriended my son. Vera was the link. Jenny laid low over Presto's neck, urging the beast to greater speed.

She found the beach exactly where Dexter described, and perfect for her needs. She tethered Presto on a patch of short winter grass and walked the rest of the way. The river gurgled smoothly, with strings of miniature whirlpools suggesting greater activity below the surface.

Jenny found a hunk of bone-white driftwood, smoothed by water and wind. She placed the branch two strides from the water's edge before warily stepping back. Imitating Annie, she flicked her fingers at the log, which remained stubbornly unaffected. Not the barest flicker of flame or tiniest tendril of smoke. Naught.

Closing her eyes, she imagined herself back in the coffin dungeon. She allowed the fear and anger to flood through her body, and stamped her foot in frustration. She opened her eyes as a tiny blue flame winked out near her toe. Jenny jumped back, but no other flames burst into existence. She knelt and examined the scorched pebbles. Her questing fingertips found a dying hint of heat.

Disappointingly lacking in drama, but undeniably real.

Jenny rubbed her fingertips together, smearing the soot. Cultivating the gift of fire captured her imagination, but what price a gift if only fuelled by negative emotions? She stood and stretched, searching her heart for strong, positive feelings.

She concentrated on Seth, pushing away any self-imposed barriers. Accepting that his affection for her was genuine twisted her gut. She had accepted Draqshet's fiat that she was unlovable and had acted accordingly. For as long as memory served, she ensured nobody had the smallest reason to love, or even like her. At least this way, nobody could ever disappoint her.

But her son changed everything. He chose to love her, in spite of her actions. He unlocked powerful emotions within her she couldn't name. A heat began in her belly, bubbling and sizzling out to her fingers and toes. Like a chestnut nestled in embers, Jenny felt a shell burst inside her chest and she collapsed to her knees in tears. Only as she raised her hands to wipe her eyes, did she realise she was aflame. She held out her hands, turning them and admiring the fire flowing harmlessly over her skin, skittering across her clothes without leaving a mark.

She took a deep breath and pulled the flames deep into her core. She exhaled slowly, but the comforting warmth stayed within her, nourishing and cleansing her essence. Jenny stretched out on the gritty beach as the internal flame burned away the canker of bitterness and mistrust.

Annie had told her the truth, and to Annie she would return, to learn how to control the gift.

When Jenny rode into the stable yard, she spotted Annie questioning Dexter. They spun around at the sound of Presto's hooves clopping on the cobbles, and Annie rushed to greet her.

"You had to test the veracity of my words," she said. "I felt a disturbance, a tremor in life's tapestry."

"I didn't believe you, I needed to see for myself." Jenny dismounted and handed the reins to Dexter. "Thank you. Presto behaved perfectly."

Annie took Jenny's arm and guided her inside. "I don't need to ask if you produced fire, you're lit from within. You're glowing like a new bride."

"Can you teach me to control the gift, Lady Annie?" Jenny sighed as they approached the staircase leading to her quarters. "I was too nervous to experiment any further."

Annie nodded. "It would be my pleasure, Lady Jenny."

Jenny paused at her door, her hand clutching her chest. "I don't feel well. I'm choking." She leaned against the wall, gasping for breath. "Help me, please."

Two burning spots inflamed her alabaster pale cheeks, and she slid down the wall. Annie scooped her up, shouldered the door aside, and deposited Jenny in a fireside armchair.

Jenny hunched over, fumbling her fingers at her chest. "Here. It hurts here."

Annie leaned close and inhaled. She recognised the scent.

"Lean back." She pushed Jenny back into the chair. "Look at me. Do you trust me?"

Jenny fluttered open her eyes. "Yes."

"You will feel distress for a few heartbeats, but the pain is temporary. Keep looking at me." Annie plunged her hand into Jenny's chest and closed her fingers around a spiky lump of evil, the seed of discontent. Hair-fine tendrils retreated from Jenny's flesh, seeking access to Annie, whose lips curled in disgust as she pulled the seed free, closing and healing the wound in a single movement.

"Do you desire to view the cause of your distress, before I incinerate the evil thing?"

Jenny shook her head. "Is that what Draqshet planted within me?"

"Yes, Mother."

"Then, yes. I would see it. I want to look upon the cause of my misery." She looked into Annie's eyes. "I want to see it burn."

Annie knelt by Jenny's chair and opened her palm. The glistening bean sized lump was already shrivelling, the fine tendrils withering and disintegrating. She tipped the seed onto the blade of her dragon-scale knife, and scraped her palm along the edge of the blade, sacrificing a layer of skin to guarantee the collection of all the root filaments.

Jenny slipped her hand over Annie's, gripping the knife together. Having naught else to say, Annie unleashed a holocaust of flames; their hands remained fast until the flames consumed even the ashes, and the blade shone mirror bright.

"How do you feel?" Annie asked.

Jenny stared at the dragon-scale blade. "I'm not sure. Tired, but filled with... hope." She turned to Annie. "You called me Mother."

"That was presumptuous. I apologise."

"No. You surprised me, but a pleasant surprise. What comes next?"

"A journey of restoration, if you're willing. I believe you ought to reclaim your memories. You and I can mind walk together."

"This will not be a fun excursion, I presume."

"Not for either of us," Annie said. "You can, of course, remain as Jenny, we will still love you. Or you can learn how to re-become Elanrah. The choice is yours, Mother."

CHAPTER FIFTY-ONE

Seth popped a whole boiled egg into his mouth and swallowed, before looking around guiltily. Fortunately, the servants had left, and he was alone in his apartment. Xanderamm and Harry had both called out such behaviour as uncouth. Acceptance by polite society meant he must learn to cut his food into bite-sized pieces and chew slowly before silently swallowing. No gulping like a fish gobbling fly larvae.

Xanderamm had been insistent about bestowing the new title and set of responsibilities upon him. Where the King picked up his gossip remained a mystery, but he gleefully regaled Seth with his latest snippets.

"I have it on good authority, you are a shapeshifter." Xanderamm had doubled over laughing. "Apparently, you entered Draqshet's service to discover his weaknesses, then you set him afire."

"Where did you hear such arrant nonsense?" Seth asked.

"I have my sources," the King had said. "I also heard, from someone who knows everything worth knowing, that Sneeth died in the fire. Seth, so he informs me, is a djinn, kept in a bottle by one of Lady Amora's guards, a retired sailor, and finally released on the night of the great fire."

Seth had shaken his head while Xanderamm revealed his favourite truth.

"There are those who swear AnnieRah created you to be my defender. That the Reborn Goddess has made known her divine will only works in our favour."

"People believe this?" Seth had been incredulous.

"Most definitely. Rumours are easier to believe than truth, and they work to your advantage. My advice is to neither confirm nor deny, only smile enigmatically."

Seth shook his head as he sliced an egg. If the King wanted to encourage childish rumours, he would go along. His most pressing problem as Defender of the King was his utter lack of experience with mortal weapons.

Seth found Grand Master André with Captain Harry in the armoury, discussing potential armour suppliers for the next intake of recruits. The array of weapons mounted on the walls astounded Seth. Swords, daggers, and knives of every imaginable shape and size were displayed, alongside bows and arrows, axes and maces, whips and nets, and ugly items which defied Seth's powers of identification.

"I've been expecting you, Lord Defender. Captain Harry tells me although you are preternaturally fast, you have no weapons training. Are you ready to begin?"

"If you are happy to accept me as a student, yes. Will Mistress Netta not object? I have no desire to cause friction. Captain Harry could teach me."

André pulled himself up to his full height. "Captain Field is a career soldier, with battle experience. He is a more than adequate swordsman. However, I am Grand Master André. My skills are incomparable. The King's Defender being schooled by a lesser man is an insult. A girl's prejudices must never dictate Matters of State."

Seth bowed deeply to hide his smile, while Harry made his excuses and left.

"You are aware it was I who taught Lady Annie to fence?"

"I heard you called them dancing lessons," Seth said. "You taught her to be deadly while maintaining grace."

"And I shall endeavour to give you the same gift." André led Seth to a long whitewashed room with windows set high in the walls, where he had set up two strange contraptions, and a range of connected beams and ropes. "You are starting with an advantage over Lady Annie. You have speed and a predator's sensibilities. I suspect once shown the basic dance steps, you will quickly learn to improvise."

"I hope not to disappoint you, Master André."

"First, I will test your balance. Your form is still new, so I expect you are still learning control." André nudged one of the strange contraptions with his toe. A wooden circle, an arm-span wide and pierced with a sphere, wobbled and spun. Grand Master André leapt lightly aboard, feet shoulder width apart, knees bent. The board steadied beneath him. He nodded at the companion contraption. "Hop on. For your safety, you start without a blade."

Seth toed the other board, feeling its mass, then leapt astride the sphere, holding steady as a trader's stare. "Like this?" He grinned at André.

"Always look into your opponent's eyes. They will try to trick you, but their eyes give them away each time." André allowed his balance board to wobble and spin, then he lunged at Seth with a short dagger.

Seth leapt straight into the air, kicked André's knife from his hand, and landed back on the board with nary a quiver. André lurched from his board, clutching his wrist and staring wide-eyed at Seth.

"Do I pass the balance test, Master André?"

"I think we can move on, I usually start with defensive positions, but I suspect they are unnecessary." André bowed. "I meant no insult, Lord Defender."

"None taken, Master André. I appreciate your thoroughness." Seth jumped from the board and returned the bow.

"I will demonstrate the movements and you will copy. We'll put them together, like a dance, and practice until they are second nature. I usually start on the floor and move to the beams and ropes, but..."

Seth shrugged. "If we skip a step and it doesn't work, we can always return. Let's try the beams. I want to earn the right to call myself Lord Defender as quickly as possible."

André mounted a mid-height beam and gestured for Seth to join him. Seth leapt up beside him and mirrored his stance. The Grand Master took his pupil through a series of exercises of increasing complexity and difficulty, Seth followed flawlessly. The pair danced from mid to high beams, then to ropes without a single misstep.

"You are uniquely gifted, Seth. You possess the grace and balance of a cat, with the speed of a striking cobra. We will break for refreshments, then repeat the dance routine with weapons." André smiled. "For my safety, we will practise with blunt edged blades."

André led Seth into an adjoining room, furnished with two chairs and a table. "I often eat here, I find it saves time."

The men ate quickly, eager to return to practise, although Seth was mindful to cut his fruit and cheese into smaller pieces, as other men did.

"If it's not impertinent to ask, how is Mistress Netta faring?

Is she yet sleeping better?" Seth asked.

"I wish I could say she has improved, but she often wakes during the night, crying and trembling." André raised his hand. "Vert is trying to convince her to come to you, but she refuses."

"I am sorry she suffers," Seth said. "She would not have to come alone to a memory adjustment session. I am happy for you to accompany her."

"I will talk to her again. Mayhap, if I accompany her, she will feel more comfortable." André sighed. "Netta's attitude is out of character."

"Your wife perceives me as a threat, but I cannot fault a woman for protecting her children."

"Baby Gabrielle is the centre of her universe, but that is no excuse for unreasonable behaviour. You have proven your worth and passed Annie's touch test. Netta must accept she made a mistake." André shook his head.

Netta hasn't told him? Don't interfere. Seth assiduously shielded his thoughts and helped André clear away the remains of the meal before they returned to the fencing studio and donned protective padding.

André selected two long-bladed blunt practice swords and passed one to Seth. "These exercises allow you to become accustomed to the weight and feel of the weapons, but not to skewer me."

He showed Seth how to grip the hilt, before tying on a face guard. By the end of the afternoon, both were elated to discover Seth's innate ability allowed him to wield two swords at once, with equal facility.

André leaned both hands on the pommel of his practice blade. "I can't remember when I last worked that hard. And I can say in full truth, you are my most receptive student. Tomorrow, if you agree, we will see how you fare with a spear, and a bow."

CHAPTER FIFTY-TWO

As agreed, Jenny skipped breakfast to make her mind-walk easier. Although she was expecting her, Jenny jumped when Annie tapped on the door.

"Are you still certain you want to do this?" Annie laid her fingers on Jenny's arm, assessing her response.

Jenny flicked a glance at Annie's hand, but didn't pull away. "Truth be told, I'm terrified of what I'll learn, but that's no excuse to avoid my duty."

"We'll take our time, and we can stop if you get too overwhelmed."

Jenny nodded. "We can sit by the fire, but the bed offers more comfort."

Annie kicked off her boots and stretched, then turned to rearrange the pillows. She reached inside her tunic and retrieved a vial of dark green liquid. "Vert prepared this for us. He doesn't think we need more, or any elaborate rituals, because we're experienced." Annie pulled the stopper, dabbed a drop on her finger and smeared the drop under her tongue. "Now you." She passed the vial to Jenny, who sniffed the vial and wrinkled her nose, but copied Annie.

The Library of Memories was exactly as Annie remembered, and as she strode up the broad steps, she felt Jenny grasp her hand.

"Is this the place?" Jenny asked.

"All my memories are here," Annie said, "but lots of yours, too."

Jenny pulled Annie's hand. "I'm scared."

"You're safe, I promise. At least step inside. If it's too much, we'll leave. Annie pushed open the doors and pulled Jenny into a sunny space, piled floor to ceiling with boxes and bundles of books and documents in every conceivable format. Jumbled in amongst the dusty tomes were knick-knacks and trinkets, worthless pebbles and dried flowers which also contained treasure troves of memories.

"The courtyard is there, isn't it? I know this place. Parts of it, at least." Jenny wove her way towards an open door, drawing Annie after her. "This is delightful." Jenny wandered around the pool, admiring the fish and the flowers, before turning to the tapestry cushioned chairs. She ran her fingers over the stitching. "Is this my work?"

Annie nodded. "Do you remember making them?"

"No, but they feel familiar; my fingers recognise them." She knelt down and pulled out an intricately embroidered footstool. "I knew it was there. Let's sit and see what else comes back to me."

Jenny closed her eyes and Annie watched as the tension eased from her shoulders, micro muscles around her eyes and mouth relaxed as the always summer sun caressed her cheeks.

"I used to spend hours here," Jenny said, a smile forming.

"Were you alone?"

"Yes, I think so." Jenny turned her head towards the arcade

and winced. "No, there are other women here, but they avoid me. What have I done to make them so afraid?" Her smooth brow creased. "These are the abandoned mothers, aren't they?"

"They're not here now, you're starting to remember," Annie said. "Do you remember I visited you?"

Jenny closed her eyes again. "You came with Roic, and I was awful. I threatened him, but you stood up to me. Told me my behaviour was unbecoming." Jenny opened her eyes to look at Annie. "I must commend your courage."

"I can't take complete credit; mostly my courage was Lady Xarah's brew. It was like liquid sunshine and I felt invincible."

"Can we leave now? Seeing myself behave so disgracefully is difficult."

"I hoped you would recover some useful memories, remind yourself who you used to be."

"I suspect we've dislodged a barrier. When they break through, they may come in a torrent, not a harmless, wobbly kneed calf, but a stampede of enraged, sharp-horned bulls. I sense great misery and darkness, and I don't want you to witness my shame."

Annie raised Jenny to her feet and guided her out of the courtyard and through the library. "You have naught to be ashamed of, Mother. You were not responsible for your actions."

"Nevertheless, I prefer to keep private my degradations."

CHAPTER FIFTY-THREE

Netta tip-toed from her and André's apartment before dawn kissed the rooftops. She hadn't said a word the previous evening when her husband had enthused over the creature's skill and grace. Fury that André should help the monster bubbled from a lava lake of fear deep in her abdomen.

She couldn't breathe or think within the confines of the Palace, knowing the monster calmly walked the corridors, making allies of the Palace inhabitants. Netta wrapped herself in a heavy cloak and headed for the stables. A day's hunting in the mountains should help clear her head. Mayhap she only needed a fresh perspective.

Netta selected, saddled, and rode Presto through the gates without conscious decision. She pointed her mount at the purple shadowed mountains and gave the horse her head. Hamlets and homesteads passed in a blur as she lay along Presto's neck, encouraging her with soft words to ever greater speed.

Only when they reached the narrow mountain trails did

Presto slow, first to a canter, then a sedate walk. Netta rode with her sling at the ready, reins looped loosely around the saddle's pommel, hoping for a few plump pigeons, scanning the tree branches, not the track. Neither she nor Presto saw the snake until it was too late.

Startled by the warning hiss under her hooves, Presto reared in panic, front hooves thrashing the air. Netta slipped from the saddle, crashed to the ground, and hit her head on a boulder. More panicked than the horse, the snake struck, fangs sinking into flesh above the exposed ankle, before heading for freedom. Presto's flashing hooves decapitated the fleeing serpent, but the poison already coursed through Netta's bloodstream.

Presto huffed and whickered, but Netta lay unresponsive to even the most ardent nuzzles. When Netta refused to move, Presto cantered back to the security of the Palace stables.

Dexter dashed out when he heard her clopping through the entrance, ready to give a dressing down to whichever fool had taken a horse without permission. He stared for a moment at Presto, before leading her into her stall. He whipped off her saddle and tack, then raced to find Captain Harry.

Harry listened to Dexter, then ran a mental check on who he had and hadn't seen that morning. None of the servants would dare take a horse, so that narrowed the field.

"Who rode her last?"

"Lady Jenny took her out yesterday, she enjoyed the ride, but she isn't a regular rider," Dexter said. "She usually takes a carriage."

Harry slapped his desk. "I hope I'm wrong. Off you go, feed and water the poor beast. I'll be down there shortly." He waved Dexter out without further explanation and went in search of André.

He found André and Seth practicing archery in a walled courtyard. Their laughter led him to them.

"Master André? Where is Netta?" He shouted over their gleeful cheering as they shot targets straight in the bullseye.

"I can't say for certain," André said, flushing. "She left before I woke. Something she's done a bit recently. Takes herself off exploring. I can tell her you're looking for her when she returns."

Harry shook his head. "I think she's had an accident. A horse just returned without a rider. I'll organise search parties."

"No need," Seth said. "I can track her. If we three go, we can surely get her back without fuss or embarrassment."

Dexter examined Presto as she munched her oats and chopped carrots. She was filthy from her wild ride, with black mud spattered up her legs and belly. Dexter lifted each hoof, methodically checking for stuck stones or loose nails. When he ran his hand down her front leg, he noticed lighter coloured splatters of a different shape. Curious, he led Presto out of her stall for a better look at the rusty stains, confirming they only appeared on her front legs and chest.

Whoever was missing, they'd met with misfortune and doubtless Captain Harry would take a search team to rescue them. Dexter saddled four sturdy horses in anticipation.

When Harry, André, and Seth arrived in the courtyard, Dexter rushed to give them his news.

"There's blood splatter on Presto, but it's not hers. She's not got even a scratch."

Seth pushed forward and bent closer. He flared his nostrils, tasting the evidence. He shook his head. "Not Netta's blood. Her scent is on the horse, but the blood belongs to a serpent. I can't tell which species from such a minuscule sample." He looked at André. "We should ask Vert to bring his medicine pouch, just in case it has bitten her."

Dexter raced to fetch Vert from the hothouses, while the Harry led out the horses.

Seth pulled André into an empty stall. "If Netta has received a snake bite, not only might her life be in danger, but that of the babe she carries."

André's jaw dropped. "Netta is with child? How do you know?"

"The scent is unmistakable," Seth said, "but it's early days. She might not be aware."

"Then we must hurry. Mount up."

"I'll stay afoot," Seth said. "Easier to follow the track. Besides, I can outrun the horses."

Vert wasted no time asking questions. He mounted the smallest of the two remaining horses and nodded to Seth.

"I assume you're leading?"

Seth loped ahead, eyes scanning side to side as he followed the obvious tracks towards the mountains. He led them past villages and hamlets without pause, and turned onto a narrow track neither André nor Harry would have noticed. Vert wordlessly pointed to a hoof-scuffed stone to reassure them.

The track grew steeper the higher they travelled; and pines replaced the deciduous trees. Seth occasionally dipped to the ground, confirming the scent, but didn't slow his pace. The winter sun prepared to slide behind the mountain, and the lengthening shadows warned the men to expect a temperature drop.

Seth picked up the rank scent of bear moments before he heard the snuffling. Netta lay awkwardly amongst a pile of boulders, a discarded silver-haired doll, with limbs folded in unnatural positions. The massive bear shoved his snout at her, unsure whether she was food. Netta's head lolled as the bear batted her with an outsized paw.

The horses shied and whinnied, turning in panicked circles to escape the monstrous beast. Seth's roar shook the trees as he charged forward, arms raised, to challenge the mountain king. The bear rose on his hind legs, twice the height of a man, and shortsightedly sought his opponent, claws ready to shred any creature foolish enough to come close. The ground trembled when the bear thudded to all fours, head swaying belligerently, as it defended its found meal.

Impossibly fast, Seth leapt over the bear, jabbing its nose with his dagger. Surprised and enraged by his audacious attack, the bear lumbered to face him, snarling in defiance. Seth unleashed a bloodcurdling scream and launched himself over the bear, this time slicing the beast's ear and stabbing it in the rump. Confused by the noise and unexpected pain, the bear fled. The free meal proved too expensive. Seth roared his victory, provoking the retreating bear to greater speed.

Vert threw his reins to Harry and slid from his prancing horse. He knelt next to Netta, the swollen snake bite immediately obvious. Her shallow breathing reassured him she was at least alive, although corpse pale. The bloody gash on her head worried him most. He explored the wound and sighed with relief to find no bone fragments.

Harry took charge of the three agitated equines, soothing them with whispered nonsense. He led them upwind of the bear to ease their nerves. André stood over Vert, hand gripping his sword hilt.

"Find four goodly length sticks to splint her leg and arm," Vert said, pointing to a brake of trees. "Be wary of snakes."

"How can I help?" Seth asked, fighting to disguise the abrupt tremors in his legs.

"Support her while I straighten her arm. If she wakes, stop

her thrashing around. I'm worried she's unconscious, but it's the kindest way to move her." Vert tenderly straightened her limbs, checking for breaks, then rummaged in his pouch. He handed a tiny clay jar and a roll of bandage to Seth. "Smear this on her forehead, to stop infection, then wrap the bandage tightly."

"Will she survive?" Seth whispered, glancing over his shoulder at André.

"After you fought a bear to save her? I should hope so." Vert looked thoughtfully at Seth. "How good is your sense of smell? Has the venom travelled far?"

"Very little entered the wound. Most is on her skin and trousers." Seth bent over her leg and closed his eyes, pulling the scent of venom over the root of his tongue. "No more than halfway up her calf."

Vert blinked. "Knocking herself unconscious likely saved her life."

André cradled his wife while Vert, assisted by Seth, splinted Netta's broken arm and wounded leg.

"Is she..?" André choked on the words.

Seth patted his shoulder. "The poison hasn't travelled far. They'll be fine."

"I'd like her strapped to a stretcher," Vert said, determined to ignore the exchange, "but this trail is too steep and narrow. André, you'll have to hold her sitting before you."

Harry and Seth lifted Netta, and André pulled her close and wrapped his cloak around her. She remained unconscious throughout the process.

The group rode through the chilly dusk as fast as they dared. They arrived to discover Dexter had dismissed the other stablehands, to prevent the spread of gossip, and was waiting with a stretcher. Seth slipped away in the ensuing hullabaloo, certain when Netta awoke, he'd be the last person she'd want to see hovering.

Seth thanked the smiling servants who had hauled boiling water to fill his bath, an unaccustomed luxury he thoroughly enjoyed, and locked the door after them. Neither the gratitude nor the hot soak would have occurred to Sneeth. He sank chin deep in the scalding water and deliberately relaxed his muscles, starting with his toes and moving up. Seth slipped down, fully submerging himself, and held his breath. He surfaced, gasping and congratulating himself for the increased time he could remain underwater. He liberally soaped his body and hair, eager to rid himself of the stink of fear.

He saw again the glinting dagger length claws, and the thumb long teeth capable of crushing his skull. Why? Why challenge the king of the forest? Why risk his life? Seth couldn't explain his actions. He hadn't made a conscious choice. He'd acted instinctively. The same instinct that provoked him to risk his life to save Jenny. Irrational logic-defying acts.

Seth soaked in the cooling water, studying the whirls of his pruning fingertips, trying to make sense of the afternoon. He hadn't overcome his fear; only when he had vanquished his ursine foe did fear sneak up on him. Harry was a battle-hardened warrior. Mayhap he could explain Seth's confusion.

Annie rushed to Netta's side as soon as she heard the rescue party return. She quickly healed the broken bones and eliminated the venom, but Netta remained stubbornly unresponsive.

"This is the second time she's cracked her head recently," Vert said.

"And it's the second time she's taken off on her own. She

ought to know better." Annie's voice softened. "Has she shown any sign of consciousness?"

Vert shook his head. "Seth's challenge to the bear was loud enough to wake the dead, but she didn't flinch. Nary a flicker on the ride home, either. I can't help but wonder if she's damaged inside, where physical medicine can't reach."

"André, talk to her. Your voice might help guide her back. She's still angry with me," Annie said.

"She hasn't spoken a word to me since I told her I gave fencing lessons to Seth."

Annie closed her eyes and took a deep breath. "What was that about a bear? I healed a snake bite, not a bear attack."

André nodded for Vert to tell the story, while he stroked his wife's hand and whispered in her ear.

Vert described Seth bravely attacking the bear, his admiration clear. "Without Seth's selfless heroism, Mistress Netta would be dead."

CHAPTER FIFTY-FOUR

Xanderamm crossed the corridor and rapped on the Lord Defender's door. "I know you're there. Open up. I have breakfast, and a voracious appetite for gossip."

The footmen lined up behind him did their best to hide their smiles, but the King's enthusiasm was infectious.

Seth slid the bolt and stepped aside as Xanderamm led a host of food-laden footmen to the table.

"My Lord Defender, you can be such a grumpy bear in the morning, I'm here to cheer you with honey cakes and mead. We have honey glazed ham, too." Xanderamm leaned confidentially close to a footman, "We do have glazed ham?"

The footman smirked and pointed. "Yes, Your Majesty."

"Excellent. I couldn't bear to disappoint my friend." Xanderamm shooed out the servers, with orders to wait outside, and turned to Seth. "I have it on the highest authority you shape-shifted into a gigantic hairy ursine and fought an epic mountain shaking battle to save the fair Mistress Netta. Now, tell me the mundane truth."

"There's naught to tell, Your Majesty."

"Ah, modesty. Because you can't bear to hear praise?" Xanderamm laughed and waggled his knife at Seth. "It's no use, I will have your story."

"Very well. Mistress Netta went for an early morning ride and her horse threw her, then returned to the stables without her. I was part of the search team and I chased off a curious bear. I believe Mistress Netta is recovering in her rooms."

"No transformation? No epic battle? How very disappointing. And a little deceitful. Grand Master André could not praise you highly enough for your bravery. He said his wife would be dead, if not for your selfless actions."

"Is Mistress Netta recovered?"

"Annie healed her physical injuries, but she is still unconscious. She is under constant watch."

"Speaking of recovery, how is Lord Roic? Is he not joining us in the city?"

"Lord Roic likes not the city. Annie tells me he has returned to Salvation Valley and is being pampered and feted by the children."

"The children do not fear him?"

"In their innocence, they see only the wonder of him," Xanderamm said. "Nobody has yet taught them to fear."

"They are lucky," Seth said.

"Come, I came to celebrate with you. Tell me how it feels to be a hero."

"I'm not a hero, I acted on pure instinct. Had I hesitated to consider, I'm sure I'd have run away."

"But you didn't. You heroically defended a helpless woman. Not even Grand Master André had your courage."

"But I was quivering afterwards. I hid the tremors by helping Vert, but I felt bone-melting terror, not courage."

Xanderamm snorted. "If there was naught to be afeared,

then courage wouldn't exist. Acting in defiance of fear makes you a hero, not an absence of fear."

Annie glanced across at André. He looked like he hadn't moved from his wife's bedside all night. "Has she made any sign? A twitch? A blink?"

André continued to stroke Netta's fingers. "Naught. I'm not sure she hears me. Mayhap, she has travelled too far to return." A tear slid down his cheek.

"I refuse to believe that. Years ago, you taught me the importance of choosing to believe the best, unless faced with irrefutable evidence to the contrary. While she breathes, there is hope."

Annie picked up Netta's free hand and closed her eyes, reaching for the golden cord which had connected them for so many years. Annie gently tugged, only to discover the cord held no tension. She followed the loose line into the void until she reached the end. Not frayed or worn, but a deliberate and clean cut. Had Netta severed the bond, or was someone else involved? Annie cast about, seeking a connection, or the slenderest glimmer of golden thread, but Netta had left no clues.

Annie shouted her friend's name into a void so vast not even an echo returned. Confused and disoriented, Annie returned to her friend's bedside and her grieving husband.

"Did you find her? What did she say?"

Annie shook her head. "Netta has travelled beyond my ability to locate her. Our thread has been deliberately severed."

"We need a hunter," André said, "with unparalleled tracking abilities. We need Seth."

Seth sighed with relief when Xanderamm and his army of footmen finally retreated, carrying the breakfast remains with them. He perused his scant wardrobe for the least ostentatious clothing, planning to take a lesson from Xanderamm and wander the marketplace, gleaning gossip. The King's love of hyperbole eluded Seth's understanding, but he was curious to know what people were really saying. He wrapped himself in a long dark cloak, protection against the wintry weather and overly zealous observers.

As he pulled open his apartment door, Annie stumbled over the threshold, hand raised to knock.

"I'm glad I caught you. I need to beg a favour," Annie described Netta's peculiar absence and her own fear caused by the severed cord. "André thinks you're our best bet to pursue her and bring her back. Will you help?"

"You're asking me to hunt down a woman who hates or fears me? Are you certain that's a good idea? Have you considered such a pursuit may drive her further away?"

Annie folded her arms and frowned. "You're worried you'd be repeating Draqshet's behaviour? This is a completely unique situation. You'd not be hunting her as prey; you'd be saving her, at her husband's request."

"Annie, you and I know that, but what would Mistress Netta think?"

Seth allowed Annie to drag him to André and Netta's apartment. Annie barged through the door and presented her trophy to André.

"He didn't want to come; he thinks his presence will chase Netta ever deeper into the darkness." She frowned as she looked from André to Netta and back again. "No improvement?"

André shook his head. "I keep thinking she's stopped breathing, but she still mists the mirror." He tapped a palm sized metal disc. "I leave it on her pillow now, close to hand." He turned to Seth. "Thank you for coming. I understand your reluctance, but you're my only hope."

Seth edged closer to the foot of the bed. "Are you not worried I'll scare her away? It's no secret she loathes me."

"I cannot discount the possibility," André said, "but I must not miss an opportunity to find her, because I am afraid. If we don't try, we will never see her again."

"Get me close to her," Annie said. "I'll convince her to return. You can stay out of sight."

"Mistress Netta has convinced herself I am the same as Draqshet. She also believes you are somehow in thrall to me. We run a monumental risk of losing her completely," Seth said. "Could Lord Roic not track her?"

"Your skills are far superior," Annie said. "Besides, she thinks you've enchanted him, too."

"If we attempt a rescue, we must not fail. This situation is more urgent than mere life or death. If Netta loses herself in the void, she will never cross to the Summer Fields. We will lose her for eternity."

"If she chooses not to return," André said, "I will spend eternity searching the void for her. What use to me are the Summer Fields without my beloved?"

"My friend, you know not what you say. Do not tempt fate with careless words. Annie and I will find her." Seth placed his hand on André's shoulder. "I give you my pledge."

"Do you mind if we invite Vert?" Annie asked. "Someone needs to monitor us, to drag us back if we go astray. I can't ask you to divide your attention between us and your wife."

"I would welcome Vert," André said. "If Netta becomes physically distressed, he will know better than I what to do."

"He'll be busy in the hothouses," Seth said. "I'll fetch him. Does your wife have a favourite flower?"

"She likes freesia, why? You can't take them into the void with you."

"We need every advantage we can muster. While I'm gone, I want you to fill the apartment with all the things Netta enjoyed, no matter how trivial. A familiar scent or sound may be enough for her to catch hold of. Whatever else you do, keep talking to her."

By the time Seth returned with Vert and a fragrant bouquet, Annie and André had collected a range of items they hoped would snag Netta's attention. Seth nodded his approval at the preparations.

Vert acknowledged André and settled himself and his medical pouch next to Netta. He checked and double checked the golden cords tying him to Annie and Seth. "I have powerful connections with you, but if I feel either of you weaken, I'll pull you straight out. Make sure you don't lose your connection to one another. Good luck."

Annie led Seth into the void, as far as Netta's severed cord. He held the golden thread close to his face, pulling the scents deeply into him.

"I don't know if it is good news or bad, but Mistress Netta is alone. She cut the thread herself."

"Alone? You mean she's lost the babe?"

"No, the babe fares well. I meant only no outside entity is with her."

"Can you track her?"

Seth revolved slowly in the pitchy dark, testing for the most delicate trace of scent or faintest glimmer of light. He moved in expanding circles, covering his tracks repeatedly.

"Mistress Netta dithered," Seth said. "She meandered back and forth, undecided. This way."

"How are you doing this? Without physical footprints or snapped twigs?"

"Motes all creatures shed when they move. For me, they glint like mica in a shaft of sunlight. I can scent her confusion and doubt, too."

"Can you tell how close we are?" Annie whispered.

"Not close enough. When she is close enough for you to talk to her, I expect to see a glimmer, a beacon betraying her position. Hush, now. I must concentrate."

Annie followed Seth as he cautiously traced Netta's invisible track. Time expanded and contracted, crawling and racing, until Annie lost all perception and only a permanent now existed.

"Annie? Wake up, stay with me."

"How many days have we travelled?"

"We left shortly after breakfast, and it is not yet midday. Sing songs or tell stories to yourself. Don't lose yourself in the vastness."

"I've been here previously, but never for so prolonged a period."

"Draqshet often banished me to the void until he discovered I came here of my own volition to retreat from the world. This was my peaceful place."

"You must know it well."

"I would not presume to say, but I am acutely aware of the dangers. The absolute lack seduces a tormented soul, no pain, no stress, not even time. That is when a person's essence may become untethered, condemned to roam for eternity, unknowing and uncaring of who they once were."

"Are you suggesting Netta is choosing that cruel fate?"

"I cannot say, but the lady is deeply unhappy. Call to her. We may be close enough for her to hear us."

The darkness swallowed Netta's name as it threatened to swallow her essence.

"Try again. She heard you. She's drifting closer."

"Netta, it's me, Annie. I want to talk to you. I miss you. We all miss you. Netta? Speak to me."

"Leave me alone, I'm at peace." Netta's voice was weak and distant. "You don't need me, not now. You have a new family."

Seth gave Annie a gentle nudge toward Netta's voice. "She's fading, becoming part of the void already. Get close enough to cast your nets over her," he whispered in her ear. "We're going to have to bring her back by force."

"Netta? Talk to me, please. Take my hand." Annie moved blindly in the direction Seth pushed her. "Why did you sever your cord?"

"I don't need the cord anymore. It held me back. I'm free now."

Annie homed in on Netta's thready voice. She felt Seth's presence at her back, a hunting dog poised to retrieve.

"I want you to come back with me, your husband is waiting for you," Annie said. "Whatever is upsetting you, we can talk about it."

"There's no point talking, nobody listens. I told you, I'm free now."

"Go!" Seth launched himself forward, whipping Annie's net from her too slow hands and wrapping it around Netta. Netta's piteous scream cut Annie's heart, but she helped Seth by wrapping her golden cord around the writhing bundle which was her almost lost friend.

"Hold her tightly. I'll drag us home," Seth said. "No matter what she says, don't release her."

CHAPTER FIFTY-FIVE

Netta stopped thrashing but refused to open her eyes. She decided not to waste energy fighting a battle she couldn't win. An overpowering floral scent flooded the room. Freesia. Have they brought flowers for my funeral? Who is singing? Netta listened intently to the voices coming from the adjoining room. Songs sung at our wedding.

The aroma of cinnamon caught her unaware, and her stomach growled in anticipation.

She squirmed in embarrassment, toes unexpectedly touching hot bricks. She sighed her satisfaction. After the frigid void, the heat was more than welcome.

Whispered conversations swirled above her and she clenched the bedclothes tightly in concentration, slowly noticing the luxuriant silky fur under her fingers. Someone had gone to a great deal of trouble to welcome her back. Not the usual treatment of a prisoner.

She listened to footsteps, one set light, the other more deliberate, then inner doors opening and closing.

"I know you're awake and listening," Annie said. "That was Vert and Seth leaving. They thought you'd want some privacy."

"I didn't realise prisoners received such respectful treatment," Netta said. "I suppose the genuine test will be whether you release me from your net."

"You're not a prisoner," André said. "This was the safest way to bring you home."

Netta opened her eyes. "I'm still a captive while I'm tied up."

"Very well," Annie said. "Consider yourself a captive. You can purchase your freedom in increments by answering my questions."

"If I choose not to answer, what will happen to me?"

"Absolutely naught," Annie said, perching on the edge of the bed. "Apple tart?" She held out the plate of pasties, tempting her sweet-toothed friend.

Netta maintained her stoic silence, but her stomach growled its displeasure as she watched Annie bite into a fragrant, fruit-filled treat.

"You must talk to us," André said. "If you don't tell us what's wrong, how can we help?"

Netta shook her head.

"Do you have any recollections of what happened to you after you left yesterday?" Annie dabbed the errant pastry flakes with a licked finger.

"I remember saddling a horse. I thought a change of scene might do me good." Netta frowned. "I fell, the horse shied, and I wasn't holding the reins. I must have passed out. When I woke, I thought I was dead. But... I didn't mind. Naught mattered... I slashed my cord... it was too heavy... and now I'm here."

André and Annie exchanged glances.

"You didn't mind being dead?" Annie gripped Netta's hand.

"How can you say such a thing? What about your unborn child?"

Netta shrugged and stared into the distance.

André frowned. "I hear your words, but I confess I do not understand what you are saying, my love. You matter so very much. You are everything to me. Do you no longer love me?"

"More than anything," Netta said, twisting the fur between her fingers. "I thought, mayhap, you no longer loved me. I thought I had disappointed you." Scalding tears spilled down her cheeks.

"This," said Annie, throwing her arms into the air, "is utter twaddle. André, tell her what happened."

André collected Netta's hands between his own. "When a horse returned riderless to the stables, we discovered you were the only one unaccounted for. Dexter found blood on the horse's chest and legs, but Seth said it wasn't your blood, but a serpent's."

"The snake must have startled the horse," Netta said.

"Most likely, and then the horse trampled the serpent, hence the blood. Seth tracked you. You were lying beside the road, crumpled like a broken toy."

"I ought to thank him." Netta kept her eyes cast down, but the odour of her insincerity suffused the room like acrid smoke.

"You've not heard the best part," Annie said, nodding at André.

"A bear, the most massive bear I've ever seen, was pawing at you. The horses all panicked and reared up, trying to escape. But Seth didn't hesitate. He roared loud enough to shake the very mountains, and he attacked the bear. I couldn't see everything because my horse was prancing in circles, but he leapt on its back and sliced its ear."

"Seth attacked a bear? To save me?"

"Twice as tall as a man, it towered over him, slashing with

its sword length claws. But he won. The bear fled, blood gushing down its face, slashed and throughly humiliated."

"Was Seth injured?"

"The man's speed is incredible, but his courage? Incomparable. Had Seth not risked his life for you, I'd be a widower today."

Netta sank deeper into her pillows and closed her eyes. "He should have left me."

"That's a wicked thing to say." Annie stood. "How can you think such a thing?"

"Jenny is really Elanrah, isn't she?" Netta asked.

"Why does that matter?" Annie spluttered.

"And Sneeth, now Seth, is her son. Making him your goodness knows how many times great uncle. You have the family you always craved. You don't need me. And I've uttered unforgivable words."

"Netta, I will always need you. I love you." Annie flung her arms around her friend and the two women sobbed together.

Exhausted by her ordeal, Netta cried herself to sleep.

"There remains much to be done here," André said, "but I must take Netta back to Salvation Valley. She needs rest, and we both miss Gabrielle."

Annie nodded. "When will you leave?"

"I shall ask Theo if he will transport us back tomorrow morning. A road trip will be too arduous, considering Netta's health and the threat of snowstorms."

CHAPTER FIFTY-SIX

J enny winced. She shuddered at the thought of sharing more of Annie's memories, but she needed more information. Who was she? What positive memories could she unearth? Theo knew her from before Draqshet.

She witnessed Theo's return from transporting André and Netta. As she watched him in the stables, grooming his giant hogs, a sliver of memory shivered loose: Theo had completed his beautifully crafted carriage and was begging to take her for a drive.

"We must stay within the confines of the Grand Temple," she'd warned him.

"You won't get the full benefit of the speed I can accomplish, Ellie. I can think us from start to finish as fast-as-thought."

"Where's the fun in that? I like to admire the landscape."

Jenny blinked, and the memory gave way to the present. Theo smiled and waved when he noticed her.

"My Lady Jenny, would you care to accompany me on a drive?"

"You used to call me Ellie, if my memory serves."

Theo raised an eyebrow. "Indeed, I did, but Annie said you remembered naught from before."

"Watching you just then reminded me of a day long past when you also offered to take me for a drive."

Theo laughed. "You were singularly unimpressed, you wanted to admire the scenery."

Jenny moved to the finely carved vehicle, fingertips stroking the smooth wood and buttery leather. She frowned slightly and turned to Theo. "It's different from how I remember, bigger."

"This is a different carriage, my lady. I needed to build bigger when I gained friends and family. Are your memories returning?"

"That's why I'm here. To ask for your help. I hoped you'd be willing to share a few stories, to remind me of who I am."

"I'm delighted to reminisce with you, but I fear you will not find what you are seeking."

"Because I was a terrible person?"

"No, but who we were before is not who we became. We've changed. I look the same, but—"

"Oh, no, you look different. Physically, you're unchanged, but you have a confidence, an assurance I don't recognise."

"You look utterly different. Draqshet moulded you so you'd be unrecognisable. I suppose he dared not risk people hailing you as the Great Mother for fear you would remember yourself and challenge him."

"Not knowing myself is so confusing. I'm adrift."

"You are overthinking. I believe we are in a constant state of discovery. Do you think Seth knew he was heroic before he faced a bear? You have the opportunity to become whosoever you desire."

"So, my previous actions count for naught?"

"Not exactly. Whenever I build a new carriage, I review the

previous designs. I keep features I enjoyed or found useful, I discard those that didn't work. I adapt and innovate."

"Each iteration improves upon the last, or serves a new purpose," Jenny agreed.

Theo grinned. "Would you care to accompany me on a drive now? We'll go slow, I promise."

"This all feels so familiar," Jenny said, as she helped Theo harness the hogs. "When Seth, Vera, and I escaped the Palace, I drove the wagon, but I can't recall doing so in the previous five years."

"We worked together to design the hog's harness. I argued for a much fancier finish, but your sleeker, more lightweight design was more efficient."

Jenny paused, her forehead wrinkled. "You wanted armoured faceplates for the pigs! I convinced you shoulder high hogs didn't need face armour to look impressive." Jenny laughed, silvery ripples splashing the stables with simple joy.

"I tried it once, while you were away. Fearsome faceplates with spiked helmets and pauldrons. The hogs not only looked completely ridiculous, but they kept accidentally jabbing each other, which made them bad tempered. I destroyed the evidence. In my defence, I was young and foolish."

Theo helped Jenny into the carriage and offered her the reins. "Would you like to drive?"

"Why don't you drive, show off your skills." Jenny stroked the leather bumpers. "This is quite a development from your first rattletrap cart."

Theo drove sedately through the stable yard gates and trotted out of the city.

"Away from the mountains, please. No more snakes or bears," Jenny said. "Show me the farms and villages."

The light dusting of snow did naught to disguise the prosperity of the region. The buildings were in good repair and the harvests were neatly stacked in sturdy barns. Livestock carried sufficient weight to survive the winter, and the people they passed smiled and waved their greetings.

"Did we used to do this?"

"You tried to keep me a secret. You pretended I didn't exist."

Jenny remained silent as they rolled through the next village. "I can't remember; why were you a secret? Was I not proud of you? I should have been."

Theo slowed the hogs to a walk. "I don't know what triggered the idea, but you feared Draqshet would find me. The wolves say although you created me to be your protector, you reversed our roles and hid me away from the world. That's why you built the Grand Temple, with the wards and glamours to shield it from those not pure of heart."

"I'm sorry. You must have been lonely and frustrated."

"I knew no different." Theo shrugged, then grinned. "Do you remember the time I got roaring drunk?"

"I don't think so."

"I'd perfected the fermentation of rice drinks, and shared the knowledge with men, but then you confined me to the temple and I was experimenting with other types of grain. A warm fermented ale brews quickly, as I discovered to my detriment. The brew must have gone straight to my head, because I really cannot remember doing what I did, only your face when you returned."

"Had you done anything deliberately dreadful?"

"Naught I couldn't fix. I decorated every wall I could find with a painted riot of animals and plants, but to say they lacked artistic merit would be an understatement. Diverting a river down the central thoroughfare wasn't my best idea, either. Miraculously, the fish all survived, but my project ruined the mosaic pavements."

Jenny giggled. "Doesn't sound too terrible. You didn't harm anyone?"

"Not if you ignore the headache when I sobered up." Theo blinked. "That was the most intense headache I've known."

"Sounds like you punished yourself," Jenny said.

"You didn't say that when you saw the damage. You temporarily stripped me of my powers and made me repair the damage with my own hands. You refused to speak to me or acknowledge me until I completed the repairs. I was rather proud of the finished mosaics. I'm much better at crafts than art."

Jenny closed her eyes. "The mosaics you made? Down the central thoroughfare? Was it a river full of fish?"

"You remember? My creative efforts didn't impress you, but you allowed them to remain."

Jenny's hand flew to her mouth, and her eyes grew wide. "I rebuked you for your impudence, but secretly, your audacity thrilled me. I have a faint memory of walking your fake river by torchlight, marvelling at the fantastical fish, while I pretended to despise you, all the while terrified you would leave and fall prey to The Dark Lord."

"I must confess, I witnessed your torchlit promenades more than once. But I thought you were searching for faults, not admiring my craftsmanship. I am glad your memories are returning, without my perceptions colouring them."

"You are generous, Lord Theo." Jenny sighed. "The world would have been different had I possessed courage. I owed you honesty."

"There is naught for you to gain, mourning what ifs. You were afraid, and with reason. I believe you did the best you could, all while battling an unseen and unsuspected enemy, the seed of discontent growing within you."

"I cannot begin to express the satisfaction I experienced

when Annie allowed me to participate in the seed's destruction. A sensation akin to slaying The Dark Lord."

"You finally vanquished your violator. Come, I think we should return, before Harry sends out another rescue party."

Jenny nodded. "I discovered more than I hoped today. Learning to forgive myself is difficult, but if I was a carriage, I could redesign myself, discard the less useful or attractive attributes, and enhance others."

"No one's described themselves as a carriage before." Theo laughed and briefly hugged Jenny with his free arm.

"The idea I can recreate myself, with my past informing but not defining me, is liberating. I'm not wrapped up in discovering who I was, but you've helped me see I can become so much more."

"This time, you're not alone. Always remember, you have friends and family."

Jenny looked sideways at Theo. "I suppose friends and family are the equivalent of padded bumpers? To make the journey more comfortable?"

CHAPTER FIFTY-SEVEN

André darted back and forth, arranging and rearranging parcels and boxes in the carriage. Netta chuckled as her husband fussed over every detail, and Gabrielle tottered in his wake, her cheeks glowing pink with her father's infectious excitement. Netta rocked baby Meritt, who blew tiny milky bubbles, oblivious to the commotion.

"We'll be on the road a matter of days, not weeks, and we will pass countless taverns and hostels." Netta pointed to several of the packages. "Ditch those."

"But—"

"No buts, husband." Netta sidled up to André. "Even if we take only half these supplies, there'll still be more than enough for a month."

"I want to make certain you have all you need, my love."

"You, Gabrielle, and Merrit. What more could I possibly need?" She reached up on tiptoe and pecked André's cheek. "And Martha's freshly baked honey cakes. They won't last far beyond the first bend."

"Are you certain you're ready for this?" André held her at

arm's length. "We don't have to go. Annie and Xanderamm will understand if we send our excuses."

Netta jiggled Meritt until he chuckled and grabbed the air. "I've slain enchanted serpents and ridden a dragon. Do you think I cannot face a man I have wronged? Not only do I owe Seth an apology for my unforgivable behaviour, but I owe him my everlasting gratitude for saving my life. Neither I nor baby Meritt would be here without Seth."

"Can I safely assume the arrow tips you've been polishing for Seth are a gift, not execution equipment?"

"Roic gave his permission," Netta said. "Annie wasn't the only one to believe Seth an honourable man." She flapped a hand. "I know, I know. I was the only one who held out against Annie's divine judgment."

André performed a dramatic shrug. "Lady Amora took some convincing, and she's renowned as an excellent judge of character."

"But Lady Amora didn't race off on a secret mission and endanger everyone else. I have so many apologies to make." Netta's shoulders slumped. "Tell me true. Will they forgive me?"

"Roic forgave you, and Annie and I love you too much to bear grudges. Seth only ever expressed concern for your welfare. Of all of us, he most easily understood your actions."

"Hearing that only makes me feel worse." Tears pooled in Netta's eyes. "To have only experienced fear and loathing from others, and to exist with no hope of affection, is too terrible to contemplate."

André scooped Gabrielle into his arms and folded the entire family into a hug. "We can't change the horrors of the past, but we can ensure the future is better."

André guided the lurching carriage through the river shallows and onto the road. Gabrielle gabbled delighted nonsense at each unfamiliar sight and fresh sensation, while Meritt sat placidly in Netta's lap.

Netta pointed to a barely visible glittering speck drifting amongst the fluffy cumulus clouds. "Roic is seeing us safely on our way. Wave to Roic." She waggled Meritt's chubby fist, and Gabrielle waved both hands in every direction.

"Sit beside me, Gabrielle." Netta expertly wrangled her daughter onto the seat between herself and Andre. "Look what Martha made for us." She single-handedly unwrapped a greased paper packet and the sweet scent of honey cakes drifted like a magic spell.

Gabrielle shot out a hand. "Me!"

"Use your manners."

"Me, peese?" She flicked a glance at Netta before putting her outstretched hand in her lap. "Cake, peese?"

"Give one to Dada, first."

Gabrielle selected the fattest, gooiest cake and passed it to André in both hands. "No crumbs, Dada."

Andre winked and popped the entire cake into his mouth.

Netta stifled a giggle. "Not a good example to your daughter, Dada."

Andre moaned his pleasure around a mouthful of cake and rolled his eyes. "Mmmmm!"

"Mumeeee! Don't let Dada have more. He's silly. This is how you eat cakes." Gabrielle took a dainty bite and chewed slowly, careful not to spill crumbs. "Shall I show you again?"

~

Andre drove with flair, quickly enough to cover ground and put on a show, but carefully enough not to exhaust the matched horses. Bill Barry would never forgive him if the horses suffered.

They rolled through greening countryside, swollen and redolent with growth. Farms and cottages, windmills and granaries, schools and hospitals, all in good repair, declared the health of the kingdom. Labourers and merchants, herdsmen and children, all waved and smiled as the carriage sped past.

André refused to allow his young family to camp under the glistening stars and insisted upon hiring rooms each night. Gabrielle and Meritt attracted compliments as only very young children can.

"Aren't you a beauty?" The serving maid slipped an extra portion of fruit syllabub into Gabrielle's dish and winked.

"Yes, I am. I take after my mother," Gabrielle said. "But my brother looks like a boiled potato. Dada says he'll grow out of it." She plunged her spoon into her dessert, oblivious to the stifled laughter of the maid, and horrified looks exchanged by her embarrassed parents.

Netta closed her eyes as André drove through the main gates.

André placed a hand on her arm. "Are you alright? We can turn around and go straight home, if you'd prefer."

"The last time I remember coming through this gate, Draqshet had control of the city." She opened her eyes. "But Annie and Xanderamm have restored life and hope. The market is busier than ever. Even the scavenging dogs look well-fed and friendly."

"I heard Dexter has kennels for the strays. He feeds and shelters them, gets them used to people." André pointed. "See that? They're wearing collars with their names on. He runs an adoption scheme and a training school."

Netta blinked. "What a novel strategy. Why hasn't anyone thought of such a program before?"

"Dexter has an affinity with four-footed beasts and he's part of the new culture. Since AnnieRah reorganised the army into units with agency, the common people are motivated to take action about other issues. If you see a problem, find a solution. Harry has funded all manner of odd projects. Some failed, but most flourished."

"How do you know all this?"

André raised his chin and struck an exaggerated pose. "You forget, I am Grand Master André. I have sources, Mistress Netta."

Smiling servants bustled to unload the carriage and carry their luggage to a spacious apartment. The mingled scents of fresh paint, waxed floors, and fresh flowers bore testament to the exuberant energy permeating the Palace. A sense of satisfaction from those living and working there imbued the air like spring sunshine after a fierce winter.

Gabrielle galloped from room to room, stroking the tapestried brocades and sumptuous velvets, her eyes lit with excitement. "Pretty, pretty, pretty," she cried. "Soft and pretty."

"Our daughter appreciates life's little luxuries," André said, his arms wrapped around his sleeping son.

A tap on the door stopped Netta's reply. She grabbed Gabrielle and turned to André.

"May I enter?" Well-modulated tones of a cultured voice offered no clue to their visitor's identity.

"Come in," Netta called.

A tall man, with luxuriant auburn curls spilling onto his broad shoulders, stepped inside and bowed deeply. "I hope my timing is not inconvenient?"

"Seth!" Andre surged forward and embraced their visitor with one arm, before turning to Netta. "We're glad to meet you in private."

Netta curtsied, and Gabrielle performed an awkward bob.

"I am pleased to see you fully recovered from your ordeal, Mistress Netta. If it's not impertinent to say, you have a beautiful family."

Netta opened, then closed her mouth. A rising flush heated her cheeks. "I had a speech prepared, Lord Seth, but I discover I am bereft of words."

A mischievous smile twitched the corners of Seth's lips. "You never had much to say to me in the past." He held up a hand. "I apologise, that was rude and utterly unnecessary. Can we start again?"

Netta sucked in a deep breath and blew it out. "Lord Seth, I would like naught better than a fresh beginning, but I owe you an apology first. I behaved in an appalling manner, but you responded with kindness to my deliberate cruelty, and I am ashamed. If not for your outstanding courage, neither I nor Meritt would have survived my stupidity. Words are inadequate to express my gratitude. I beg your forgiveness."

"Meritt? An unusual name?"

"The name means second chance," Netta said. "My son is a constant reminder you gave me chance after chance. You offered friendship when I offered only enmity. Can you forgive me?"

"There is naught to forgive. Do you think I, of all people, would blame any mother for protecting her child against a perceived threat? I would be honoured if you allowed me to count you as a friend."

"I brought you a gift," Netta said. "As Defender of the King, you ought to have the deadliest weapons. I fashioned arrow heads from Roic's scales. They're sharp enough to slice stone."

Andre rummaged in a crate for the dragon skin wrapped packet, and passed it to Netta.

"With Roic's blessing. He said you have an honourable core." Netta handed the gift to Seth. "A measure of my trust."

CHAPTER FIFTY-EIGHT

Harry held the gilt-edged hand-written card between
finger and thumb. He could not ignore King
Xanderamm's invitation to breakfast. Although
couched in the most casual terms, it was nevertheless a
royal command.

Guests arrived promptly, none wanting to be either first or
last. Xanderamm burst out of the banquet hall doors, startling
the liveried guards, who were still adjusting to his unceremo-
nious style.

"Come in, welcome, help yourselves." Xanderamm herded
his guests towards the buffet and set an example by loading his
plate. "Only fruit juice or milk this morning. We need clear
heads for all the planning."

Xanderamm seated himself at a round table set for nine.
"Find a space, make yourselves comfortable, don't stand on
ceremony." He unfolded a sheet of parchment and held it in
place with goblets and cutlery, much to the wide-eyed horror of
the footmen.

Annie stretched her neck to see. "Quite a list, Your

Majesty."

"Now that the renovations are complete," Xanderamm leaned into Harry beside him. "They are complete, aren't they?"

Harry nodded.

"Good, yes, now the Palace is in tip-top order, it's time to establish a Royal Court. Annie, I want you to reconfirm me as King, a public coronation. We'll invite the usual suspects, and the royals from neighbouring kingdoms. Get them to bring their daughters."

"You plan to take a wife?" Theo asked with a smile.

"Let's not be hasty, My Most High Lord Consort. As King, I have a duty to provide heirs, and to make alliances. There's no rush, but I ought to start looking. In the meantime, I have a project I hope you'll develop, Vert."

Vert raised his eyebrows. "Me? What do you propose, Your Majesty?"

"I notice you spend a lot of time in the hothouses with the healing herbs. Most of the hospitals have herbalists, but rely on local fauna. I want you to build suitable structures at all the hospitals, and train people to use them? I envisage tremendous benefits from greater access to medicinal plants."

Vert's hands shook. "I am honoured."

"Will you continue the building and development works, Your Majesty?" Captain Harry asked.

"One of the items on my list," said Xanderamm. "The Dark Lord's influence severely damaged trade, so I thought we could host a convention, showcasing our skills and goods. We could conduct tours to show interested parties around our new schools and hospitals. I'd like to set up some sort of exchange."

Harry frowned. "I'm not sure what you mean, Your Majesty."

"Over the past five years, you've developed a new system, and the results are spectacular. We can sell our know-how and expertise, generate income, and continue funding your programs. Eventually, Vert might find time to set up teaching hospitals."

"It's an interesting idea," André said. "An expanded marketplace, trading services. A unique way to further your influence."

"I will create a court which welcomes and nurtures new ideas and rewards people on merit. Which brings me to the King's Defender. I want Seth's position recognised at my coronation."

"I would prefer to remain incognito, Your Majesty. I only want to venture down a street, or traverse the marketplace unremarked." Seth shuffled back in his chair.

"That was before you proved yourself a hero, worthy of our respect and affection," Netta said. "You cannot deny us the opportunity to celebrate having you in our lives."

"Accept the honour with grace, Son. You've earned it many times over." Jenny beamed delightedly around the table. "If I may, I have an announcement." She looked to Xanderamm, who waved a hand for her to continue.

"Seth's transformation fills me with pride, but I have struggled to work out who I am supposed to be, after being freed from The Dark Lord's influence. I have Lord Theo to thank for showing me that my experiences do not define who I can become. From this day forth, I wish to you to call me Ellie. I plan to travel, teaching textile crafts to any who wish to learn."

"We could use your skills in the exchange," Xanderamm said.

"Thank you, Your Majesty. I may accept your offer in the future, but for now, I need to make reparations for my neglect, and to learn who I shall become."

"You will stay for the coronation? And Seth's official recognition?"

"I wouldn't miss it for worlds."

CHAPTER FIFTY-NINE

Xanderamm's smile shone brighter than the refurbished Palace as he paced the corridors. He had kept his promise and installed a heating system in the servants' quarters. Tradesmen and apprentices had worked throughout the winter, rebuilding and remodelling, painting and glazing, creating furniture and hanging tapestries, planting and manicuring magnificent gardens.

Guests from every known kingdom, and of differing status, inhabited the guest rooms. Royalty and nobility, artists and inventors, philosophers and merchants, rubbed shoulders and clashed egos, much to the King's entertainment. Those with the temerity to complain, he removed, along with their inflated egos, to rooms less convenient and usually smaller. The King mentally deleted their names from any future lists of honours, and their daughters from his list of potential brides. He shuddered at the thought of demanding or entitled in-laws.

Few of his guests yet recognised him, and he wandered amongst them, listening and learning. He would later regale Seth with specious facts he'd harvested from unwary gossips. He made a point of denying naught, while some he encouraged with a confidential wink and a smile.

The King barged into the small ballroom where Netta and Ellie were teaching Seth to dance. Netta had roped in André to help demonstrate. Meritt rested in a nest of cushions and Gabrielle gambolled alongside, fascinated by the tall man who skipped with her whenever he had the opportunity. Because Seth learned quickly, the lessons were really only social gatherings. Seth had absorbed the teaching like one born to dance.

"The ladies won't be interested in me once they've seen you dance," Xanderamm said. "Mayhap you'll take a wife?"

"You could make me a grandmother." Ellie clapped her hands. "Annie would be an auntie."

Seth blushed. "Forgive me, but I have no intention of taking a wife."

"Seriously, why not?" Netta asked. "You're quite the catch. A hero, a friend of the King, a rumoured shapeshifter and a superb dancer. Not to mention your connection to the Goddess Reborn."

"I have no desire for a wife. I would not make a good husband. My duties to my King take up the entirety of my time."

Xanderamm squinted at Seth. "Dance lesson's over, my friends. I need to discuss matters of state with my Lord Defender. Seth, come walk with me in the gardens."

The King led the way to a secluded walled garden with low-growing plants, where none could sneak up on them. "No one can overhear us here. Tell me true, have you ever known a woman? Is that why you are reluctant to consider taking a wife?"

"Considering my history, that is a reasonable conclusion. If I am to keep my origins shrouded in mystery, then I cannot entertain the idea of marriage, or any relationship."

"I see your point. Very well, I shall tease you no more on the subject. But, I do not abandon hope. Netta was correct in her assessment. You will attract admirers. If the ladies are willing, I see no reason why you shouldn't broaden your education."

Seth shook his head. "That would be disrespectful and dishonest."

"You know you're meant to defend my person, not my morality?" Xanderamm sighed. "Some ladies are open to a relationship which doesn't lead to marriage."

"If I meet such wanton women, I shall make a point of sending them in your direction, Your Majesty."

"Under the circumstances, perhaps not. Getting married, choosing a wife, is a serious business. I need a woman sensible, open-minded, and not enamoured with the foolish fripperies of being a queen. Of course, I should be pleased if she possesses personal charms and I fall madly in love."

"Why didn't you marry before? Not lack of opportunity, surely?"

"I shudder to consider the disaster I would have made of marriage previously. I would have selected an extraordinarily pretty parasite and made her thoroughly miserable." Xanderamm glanced at Seth. "My priorities have changed, my friend."

Seth paced his moonlit apartment. Keeping secret his origins wasn't his only reason to avoid women. If he found a girl to love, to marry, what kind of monsters would he sire? Would a pregnancy endanger a wife? How dared he even contemplate such things? No, to walk unremarked through the marketplace should remain his highest ambition.

~

The private rehearsal of the coronation ceremony ran smoothly, except for Xanderamm's explosive fits of laughter.

Annie placed her hands on her hips and scowled. "Your Majesty, this is no laughing matter. Representatives of the known world will be watching you."

"I know, and that's why. When I get nervous, I laugh. Not exactly regal, is it? Can't we have a private ceremony?"

"No. The whole point is to have your coronation witnessed. If people don't see you being crowned for themselves, they will believe you a fraud. Vert can give you a potion to calm your nerves, but I think you can manage without. Imagine your father's pride if he could see you now."

"Do you believe I can do it?" Xanderamm turned serious eyes upon her.

"Of course you can. You've already done so much, this is naught. You are the King, not some callow youth. Remember, the audience wants to support you."

Xanderamm nodded. "Thank you."

Annie smiled. "You'll be fine. This is only stage fright. When the actual performance begins, you'll be magnificent. Now, I must speak to Seth."

She found him lurking on the periphery, alert for any threats, but trying to stay unnoticed. "Netta tells me you're going to make me an auntie. Who is the lucky lady?"

"Mistress Netta's imagination runs away with her," Seth said. "I have no lady, nor will I have. I cannot be a husband or father."

"Cannot? Or do not wish to be?"

"You know my history, what I was."

Annie steered Seth behind an ornate pillar. "You told me you wanted to be ordinary; unremarkable was the word you used. I remade you as you asked. You are now as other men. There is no physical reason you cannot have a wife and children, if you so desire."

Seth stared over Annie's shoulder. "I wouldn't endanger a wife? Or breed monsters?"

"No, you present no danger. And as Netta pointed out, you have a lot going for you." Annie couldn't hide her grin.

CHAPTER SIXTY

Brocades and silks shone, and jewels sparkled exactly as they ought under the early spring sunlight. Green grass glowed and the flower beds flourished. Musicians played with verve and their enthusiasm infected an audience seeking thrills and entertainment. Guests filled the Audience Chamber to overflowing and an excited hum of conversation filled the air, like bees buzzing over meadows.

A change in music alerted the attendees the ceremony was about to begin and the guests turned their attention to the three thrones on the low dais. The buzz of conversation gave way to respectful silence. Clad in their dragon-skin attire of bronze, gold, and silver, AnnieRah and Lord Theo claimed the outer thrones. Xanderamm, accompanied by Seth, paraded the centre aisle. Seth stood at attention while Xanderamm mounted the dais and claimed his throne. The Reborn Goddess and The Most High Lord Consort placed the crown on Xanderamm's head. AnnieRah blessed him and his house as the witnesses roared their approval.

Annie winked at Xanderamm. "I told you," she whispered.

Conscious of the unfamiliar weight on his head, King Xanderamm rose to address his subjects. He promised a new era of royal accountability, words most of the audience filtered out. He gestured to a page, and the lad proudly strode to his designated spot, carrying a glossy pelt.

"Approach, My Lord Seth," the King bellowed. "BearSlayer, and King's Defender."

Seth mounted all but the top step and dropped to one knee.

"I hereby declare, Seth BearSlayer to represent the King's authority." Xanderamm took the gigantic bearskin from the page and draped it around Seth's shoulders. "You will forthwith accord him every right and privilege due his rank."

The elated crowd showed their appreciation, stamping and clapping their approval until the rafters shook. Two young ladies secretly enjoyed the drama of being carried out when they fainted, overcome with an excess of emotion.

King Xanderamm's next official act was the promotion of Captain Harry Field to the rank of General. Harry beamed with pride as Xanderamm hung the medal around his neck and pinned the insignia to his collar, and once again the witnesses shook the Audience Chamber with their approval.

Eschewing the usual formal banquet, King Xanderamm led his guests into the ballroom, with a buffet organised next door. He ignored what he considered outdated protocols and mingled, chatted and laughed with his guests, enjoying his celebration, and watching the ladies flock around Seth and Harry, both of whom appeared nonplussed.

Satisfied he had spoken at least one word to each guest, he nodded to the orchestra's conductor before presenting himself to a pleasant-faced young woman. When he offered his hand to dance, she flushed as deep a pink as her gown.

Looking for more..?
Turn the page.

https://pagancatpublishing.com/

Learn more about Sam Woodgarth

If you enjoyed this book, please leave a review on Amazon and/or Goodreads. I appreciate this more than you know.

The Isle of The Immortals
November 2023
Sign up for my newsletter for regular updates.